SPIRIT WINGS

THE ACADEMY
BOOK ONE

BY
SANDY SOLIS

ILLUSTRATIONS BY SANDY SOLIS

SPIRIT WINGS PRODUCTIONS LLC
2011

This is a work of fiction. Names, characters, places and incidents are either a work of writer's imagination or are used fictionally. All resemblance to actual persons, living or dead, is coincidental or prophetic in nature.

ISBN-13: **9798730232402**

Oct. 2011

ALL RIGHTS RESERVED. No parts of this book may be reproduced or transmitted by any means except as expressly permitted from the publisher. Requests for permission should be addressed to:

Spirit Wings Productions LLC
10342 E 550 Rd
Colcord, OK 74338
Biblerock@sstelco.com
www.SpiritWingsOnline.com

Cover and interior images by Sandy Solis

Unless otherwise indicated, Scripture quotations are from The Holy Bible, English Standard Version® (ESV®), copyright © 2001 by Crossway, a publishing ministry of Good News Publishers. Used by permission. All rights reserved.

Library of Congress Cataloging- TX 8-003-969

Pronouns referring to God are capitalized
in the text for the sake of clarity.

> Give ear, O my people, to my teaching;
> incline your ears to the words of my mouth!
> I will open my mouth in a parable;
> I will utter dark sayings from of old,
> things that we have heard and known,
> that our fathers have told us.
> We will not hide them from their children,
> but tell to the coming generation
> the glorious deeds of the Lord, and his might,
> and the wonders that he has done.
> **Psalm 78:1-4**

To: Weston & Connor

Sandy Solis
2024

Acknowledgments:

Thanks to Brianne the "Grammar Queen"

Thanks to Sharon for her wisdom

Thanks to Kathryn the "Great"

Thanks to Tim for sharpening the edge

Thanks to Ron for the "spit polish"

Thanks to Rick Joyner for his book THE FINAL QUEST, for inspirational images and revelation

NOTE FROM THE AUTHOR:
YOU MAY WANT TO CHECK OUT THE SPECIAL FEATURE IN THE BACK OF THE BOOK. IT IS CALLED "TYPES AND SHADOWS". SOME WILL WANT TO SEE IT AFTER THEY READ THE ENTIRE BOOK, WHILE OTHERS MAY WISH TO LOOK AFTER EACH CHAPTER IS READ. --- ENJOY GOING DEEPER . . .

CONTENTS

ONE
NOBODY FROM NOWHERE - 1 -

TWO
ASHER'S MISSION - 55 -

THREE
HIGHER GROUND - 88 -

FOUR
COMING TOGETHER OR FALLING APART - 108 -

FIVE
BAD DREAMS OR SILENT SCREAMS - 130 -

SIX
COME UNDER THE BANNER - 146 -

SEVEN
GEMS FROM HEAVEN - 155 -

EIGHT
WOLF IN SHEEP'S CLOTHING - 169 -

NINE
FINDING A PLACE TO BELONG - 184 -

TEN
SNOW PACKED - 191 -

ELEVEN
BROKEN CHAINS - 201 -

TWELVE
READY, SET, BREAK! - 220 -

THIRTEEN
UPON THIS ROCK - 238 -

FOURTEEN
SUMMIT TRAIL - 251 -

FIFTEEN
WINDS OF CHANGE - 282 -

SIXTEEN
SUMMER OF SURVIVAL - 298 -

SEVENTEEN
SEEING THROUGH THE SMOKE - 338 -

Recommended websites, types and shadows feature, map

SPIRIT WINGS
THE ACADEMY

CHAPTER ONE

NOBODY FROM NOWHERE

On a windless winter day high above Spanish Harlem, New York, intricately perfect six-sided flakes form in the water vapor before gently tumbling toward the earth's surface. A flash of feathers, armor, and a glint of metal disturb the serene atmosphere, causing the flakes to swirl in the turbulent air left behind.

Anton, the Guardian angel, tucks his wings to increase his descent toward Spanish Harlem and his assignment: a sixteen-year-old boy named Jesse. The Guardian extends his wings to their full position, like a plane's wing flap slowing its landing speed. As light as a

snowflake, Anton touches the ground — target acquired –
– assessing opposition. The eight-foot angel with flowing
brown hair observes multiple dark slippery imps hovering
around Jesse's head. Watching over Jesse since his birth,
Anton rarely gets to intervene on his behalf. His visit just
now to the throne of the Most High God, [1]Yahweh, was
not his first, nor will it be his last. The angel needed
refreshing in the presence of Yahweh, because Jesse's life,
so far, is taking a toll on his Guardian angel. The
supernatural being is now ready to continue his task.

Five Latino intercessors have prayed together for
an angel to bring them the [2]Chosen One, Anton is
appointed to complete the task. He is sharply alert, all the
while fingering the handle of his sword in readiness to
protect. One prayer from a saint and he can scatter the
small imps in a thousand directions.

The young man braces against the cold air before
walking into it, hunched over, appearing more like a feeble
old man. He is alone on the sidewalk because it is just too
cold for any reasonable person to be out. Cupping his
hands around his face, he tries to thaw out his stinging
nose. As he trudges through the crunchy snow, he spots a
kid's fast-food meal box poking out the snow. He stops.

---

[1] Yahweh- Hebrew, from YHVH; also Jehovah, God
[2] Disambiguation:
Psalm 89:3 You have said, "I have made a covenant with my chosen one; I have sworn to David my servant: The ultimate Chosen One is Christ Jesus, people become chosen ones when they enter the Kingdom of God.

The warm food inside carries the aroma of fries and hamburgers that quickly consumes his senses. He reaches for it just as a snarling mottled dog runs up, baring his teeth. They both have plans for the food. With his heart beating out of his chest; Jesse holds his ground. How hungry is he? Is it worth a mauling from such a fierce canine?

"GO AWAY!" he yells. But the dog remains in attack position and growls, hair prickling upon its neck. Jesse kicks snow at it, but it does no good.

Just down the street, a man steps out of his doorway calling for his pet. Hearing its master the dog turns instinctively, darting away to go back inside the apartment building. The man locks his eyes on Jesse, who is kneeling alone in the snow. The pet owner gazes at the teenager and his cold, dark, sad eyes with straight black hair hanging in his face. Jesse's soiled coat and his position over the discarded food exposes his desperation as he just freezes in embarrassment. Finally, the man slips back inside, and Jesse drops to his knees in the snow to grab the red box. It feels good on his numb fingers. Even better, with a quick inspection, he discovers a few fries and a portion of a hamburger.

Walking into the alley next to the apartment building, he intends to enjoy his victorious meal. As he rounds the corner he discovers in a pile of dirty rags next to a heap of cardboard, a stray grey mother cat with her litter of mewing kittens. There are notches on the scrawny mother's ears from fighting.

"Aw," Jesse loves animals. Sliding down the brick wall next to the cuddling batch of kittens, he is glad the momma doesn't run away. The kittens' eyes are still closed, having been born only a few days ago. The mother rubs against his leg.

"You're tame . . . must've belonged to someone once."

Opening the box again, he takes a big whiff, "This smells so good!"

Then he looks at the mother cat. She is painfully thin, her big amber-colored eyes gaunt.

"Okay, here ya go . . ."

He pulls the meat off the bun and drops it in the snow in front of the cat. The hungry feline gobbles it down as Jesse eats the empty bun and remaining fries. He virtually swallows what little remains without really chewing. Hunger grows even more now that the young runaway has tasted something. Stroking the cat, he tries to warm up against the rough brick wall.

"You and me are both on the street. Maybe our luck will change, huh, grey kitty? That dog is lucky; he has a place to stay and plenty to eat," complains Jesse to himself and the cat.

"If I find more food; I will bring you some, okay Smokey? You look like a Smokey to me."

Realizing the need to move on, he gets up and braces for the cold breeze that awaits him past the alley. The park's view is like a Christmas card, a blanket of snow, untouched, except for his footprints. The morning sunshine causes the snow to be glaringly bright. He squints through loose fingers just to gaze ahead — every color possible sparkles in wondrous shades of pastel on the cottony blanket of white. On top of the old-style lampstands are Christmas decorations poking out of the fresh snow. As he huffs frozen breaths, the images blur around him. Jesse presses his boots into the pristine snow, leaving muddy brown footprints.

Pausing for a moment, he mumbles despairingly, "I can even ruin snow by just walking on it."

Jesse is skilled at brooding, and today he is planning a marathon. The morning sunshine causes the snow to be glaringly bright. He squints through loose fingers just to gaze ahead — every color possible sparkles in wondrous shades of pastel on the cottony blanket of white. As he huffs frozen breaths, the images blur around him. On top of the old-style lampstands are Christmas decorations poking out of the fresh snow. Jesse presses his boots into the pristine snow, leaving muddy brown footprints.

At this point, Anton focuses on the haze of depression that clouds about Jesse's head. He is not authorized to clear the air. The darkness is drawn to the boy by his continual thoughts of dismal gloom and doom. The muscled angel has watched the dark mist hover over Jesse off and on for years; however, this is the strongest it has ever been.

Now, Jesse isn't aware of what day of the week it is. It doesn't matter since he isn't in school anymore.

However, he does like weekends when school kids leave more food behind at the mall than adults. The last three years have been grimly cruel for Jesse, and his eyes have seen a lot in his young life. This reality would be tragic for anyone, and for the young Jesse, it was most cruel. As he walks on, he tries to stop clenching his fists by intentionally releasing his grip and shaking out his fingers. It just made his hands ache more in the cold December air. As a city kid, he longs for large open spaces with grass, trees, and sunshine. But that's not where he is; instead, he is nobody from nowhere. At least, that is how he feels. After passing through the park, he walks in front of a humble café. Now he is deep in Spanish Harlem. He sees his reflection in the café's old French windows.

"I hate you," he says to the reflection of his cold face in the window.

He is a survivor but hates what he has become as a result. He talks to God often; however, he never waits for a reply. He just wants God to know how he is suffering. The day his parents left to tour with a band; he was left at his Uncle William's. The habit of talking to God started during this lonely time. Jesse calls his uncle, "Bill." His uncle is always too drunk to know the difference anyway.

The smell of coffee captures Jesse's attention. In front of the café is an outdoor table and chairs with a cup of coffee and some food wrapped up in wax paper. Both abandoned in the chilly air. Glancing left and right, Jesse seizes the two items and walks briskly away. *Who would eat outside on a day like this*? Jesse wonders, considering the food as unwanted by its owner.

Due to plenty of cream and sugar; he manages to down the coffee. Feeling the warmth of the coffee, he opens the wax paper to find some sort of tortilla rolled around some sort of meat. Without hesitation, he takes a large bite. After a few chews; the sensation of jalapeno peppers begins to burn like fire in his mouth. He spits it out and paces around in pain. People from the store next door stare at him in his panicked state of "fire mouth." The remaining trace of the coffee does little to calm the burning.

"Aw man, that's hot," says Jesse, as he fans his open mouth. He even considers shoving some dirty New York snow in his flaming mouth. Earlier, a man dug in his car for his bookstore keys and left his lunch on the table. The bewildered man stands with his gloved hand on his head; *I was sure I left my food right here on the table.*

People walking past Jesse make no eye contact, giving him that invisible feeling from what he calls the "normal" people, with places to go and people to meet. The neighborhood's atmosphere is tense due to the terrorist threat being orange in New York City these days. Orange stands for "high"; the only color above that is red for "severe."

Due to an unprovoked beating, he took from "Bill" on Halloween night, Jesse has missed school being a runaway for the last two months. He climbed out his bedroom's second-floor window, down the old tree, and launched out on his own. Uncle Bill's house was too terrible to talk about; so, Jesse promises himself he will never tell anyone what happened there. Unfortunately, now on the mean streets of New York, things are worse.

Jesse's bangs have grown over his eyes; and he continually pushes them back. He is muscular but small framed like his father. His soiled clothing is a dead giveaway that he is not part of a loving home.

Looking down at his stinging palms, he realizes they are bloody again after clenching so tight his nails cut into the skin. To worsen things, he hears the distant sound of Christmas music.

Since he was about nine, Jesse has disdained the Christmas holiday season. His parents always joked that they were Jewish and didn't observe Christmas, but he knows it is not true; *we are nobodies, even less than nobodies*. The holiday reminds him of what he doesn't have: a house with a tree, Christmas presents, and a family who loves him.

He kicks a small piece of loose concrete and watches it roll down the street. As he walks with a downward gaze, he is not aware that two people are coming toward him. He looks up at the last second and almost bumps into one of them. Two smiling faces are looking at him, a man with a red scarf and a teenage boy that almost bumped him. The boy is brawny about his age. He stands holding out a candy cane and says with a slight Spanish accent, "Jesus loves you."

Jesse stares at him nervously. Then he grabs the

candy cane and runs, leaving the guy with his hand out and a bewildered look on his face. Anton also stands with his mouth open; he expected great power to flow from the encounter with the two servants of God.

The boy looks one more time in Jesse's direction before getting in the van. From behind a large bush; Jesse watches the two of them climb into an old blue van. *They look like father and son; the resemblance is unmistakable.*

Anton stands behind the bush as well. It is too soon to go running back to the throne of Yahweh, but he is already feeling weary.

Shivering and cold, Jesse feels embarrassed that he panicked and ran away. He angrily argues with himself; *I am not gonna cry, I'm sick of it . . . Tears will only burn my face, and someone will see me and look at me as though I am crazy. I'm not crazy; I'm not crazy — not yet anyway!*

After peeling back the clear plastic on the hook of the candy cane, he bites off a piece to suck on. It is glorious! A few good memories with his parents flood his mind until a cold blast of wind burns at his cheek. Now he needs to find real food; even though his stomach doesn't bother to grumble anymore.

Taking the long way to the shopping mall, the cold wayward teenager avoids the local gang hangout. Peering through the entry glass doors, he scans the food court looking for leftover lunch trays. The security guard recognizes him and points to the door. Jesse rushes in and grabs a sack left on a table and bolts for the entrance. He doesn't look inside till he is well into the parking lot.

"A half-cup of orange juice and a hash brown; not bad."

Content with his breakfast; he decides to head to the usual homeless spots.

Next on my list is getting warm. Today all the crazy people are out in numbers; and I'm too scared to stand beside them at their trashcan fires. The thought of the warm flames is tempting, but their strange expressions freak me out.

So, he decides to return to his newfound cat and her kittens. He feels happy when he sees them. In his pocket, he has five creamer packets he managed to lift from the mall for Smokey. Just then, he spots the old blue van again and wonders what they are doing.

The father and son have parked in front of an old Victorian style building that is full of character.

I don't know much Spanish, Jesse thinks: *but; that is a Spanish church.*

The sound of a piano playing emanates from the church's front doors with bay windows on either side. Walking closer; he hears *Silent Night* coming from the building. Cupping his hands around his eyes, he presses his face up to the frosty glass to look inside. The people are practicing a play. Jesse sees the boy from the park that gave him the candy cane; he is singing the loudest and, mostly off-key. The adults seem to be humored by his loud off-key singing. His voice is low, but his singing is much too high. Jesse laughs out loud; it feels good to laugh. Suddenly everyone stops and turns toward him. The young man points toward Jesse, and the man with the red scarf starts to walk toward him. Jesse steps back from the window and freezes.

Anton strengthens Jesse to not run from the very church Anton is assigned to get him to. Also, Anton hushes the voices of fear that tend to dominate Jesse's thoughts. Waves of power like rings of white light pour from Anton's hand, floating into Jesse's chest. As a result, Jesse doesn't run. Instead, he simply halts in place. As the man opens one of the glass doors, a piece of paper in the shape of a Christmas tree un-tapes itself and drifts like a feather, landing at Jesse's feet. Jesse slowly reaches down for the paper and hands it to the man. As the man takes the green craft paper tree from his hand, he smiles anxiously at him. He is a short Latino man with a bushy mustache and the bright red hand-knit scarf still around his neck. His son peers out curiously from behind him.

Guardian angels all over the church lean in to watch the unfolding scene. They are assigned to serve the saints, but rarely get any action. Various slimy creatures begin to squirm their way out of the area. Anton notes the smell of the Spirit of Religion, causing a staleness in the air of the church. He wrinkles his nose in disgust.

The Spirit of Religion looks like a Medieval Crusader knight with a giant leather book belted to his waist, a shield, and a war hammer. Anton is aware that he might interfere, so he stands in a defensive position.

The man continues to hold the door open.

"Come on in and warm up, you look frozen to the

bone," the man says with a distinct Spanish accent.

The young man motions him in as well. Jesse trusted people before and always regretted it.

Anything is better than freezing to death; I guess, he tells himself.

It is risky, but Jesse is too cold to play it safe.

They call him up to the gas heater on the stage; everyone steps aside so that Jesse can get close. Jesse feels awkward with all eyes on him, but the heater's red and orange flames call him. His toes especially are burning from the cold. Jesse assesses his situation; people standing all over and the pack of youngsters in a circle on the stage. There is whispering in Spanish from the back of the room that he may be the one from the prophecy.

A lady with kind eyes and a slow accent asks, "Wwwwhat's your name?"

She hands him a sandwich off a tray as a group of toddlers fidgeting at a bench on the stage stare at him.

"We are just stopping for a snack," she tells him, her Spanish accent is charming.

The young man steps up to him, holding out a paper cup full of hot chocolate. Jesse tries to eat slowly, but he can't help but wolf it all down, burning his lip on the cocoa.

"Whoa . . . easy there, man, no one's going to steal it!" he says. "I'm Manuel, my dad is the pastor here, and this is my family, all of them!"

Jesse looks around; there must be twenty people. He is amazed that they are all related. His own family is small, with only one uncle and one elderly man he called Poppy.

Jesse swallows hard and says, "I'm Jesse, but you can call me Rocky." (See "Types and Shadows" 1)

When the group hears his name; they begin to respond with delight.

It is as if all the air is sucked out of the room, as they gasp. To Jesse's surprise, they begin to weep and walk around with their hands in the air saying, "Gloria a Dios" (Glory to God). Jesse starts to slowly step back to make a break for it.

Okay, this is turning bad fast.

He is getting freaked out.

"Jesse!" the pastor puts his hand on his shoulder. "You are the one we have been waiting for . . ."

Jesse squints his eyes at him, "Waddaya mean?"

His heart begins to beat wildly.

The pastor wraps his red scarf loosely around Jesse's neck.

"We were told by the Lord that one would come whose name means 'God is'. Jesse, that is what your name means! We are going to take care of you; you are the Chosen One!" the pastor declares.

Jesse steps away from the heater's warm glow and moves closer to the steps that go down from the stage.

"No, I am no one; you got the wrong guy." He pulls the red scarf off his neck and holds it out to the Spanish pastor.

I don't like mind games, and I don't want to play.

What does my name mean anyway? For all I know, they can be making this all up.

The lady with the kind voice walks closer to Jesse, tears now streaming down her olive-skinned face.

"Jesse, just stay a while, that is all we ask. Stay through Christmas, okay?"

Her voice is quiet and tender.

Jesse surprises himself with a quick "Okay."

She puts the scarf back on Jesse.

Anton, filled with joy over this small victory, does a backflip and a victory dance like a football player after a goal.

Phase two: help Jesse trust the servants of God and allow them to help him, and ultimately get him born of the Spirit and part of the Kingdom of [3]Elohim.

Jesse sits on the front pew watching the practice; he feels like an outsider, not understanding all the Spanish conversation. It is not long until the Christmas play practice is over, Manuel's aunts, uncles, and cousins leave, and it is just the four of them: Jesse, Manuel, the pastor, and the lady with kind eyes, the pastor's wife, Ana. Jesse tries to return the scarf to the pastor.

"Oh, no. You keep it; my gift to you," the pastor insists.

"Jesse, this is where we live!" says Manuel, as he directs him up the noisy, worn wooden stairs.

---

[3] Elohim-Hebrew for God

Jesse notes: *Gonna be hard if I have to sneak out with these squeaking steps.*

Manuel shows Jesse above the church where they have their home. The Latino youth has wavy brown shoulder-length hair, and his eyes show compassion that Jesse has never seen before.

They all gather around the kitchen table for supper. "Well . . ." the pastor talks softly but with a serious tone. ". . . you can call me Papa. Everyone else does! This wonderful cook is my lovely wife Ana, and our son's name; you know already, Manuel. Now, God bless this food."

Ana has baked cinnamon rolls, and beef stew simmers on the stove. Jesse is ecstatic. The smell of warm food makes him feel grateful, and he, finally, is not so cold. Joyfulness swells up inside him like a water fountain. It is all he can do to keep from blubbering over his bowl of stew. The sensation of the soup in his mouth gives him overwhelming delight. He wonders if they notice that his hand is shaking when he takes a cinnamon roll. It is a big deal to eat this well. It is a shift in his complete outlook. Maybe things can turn around for a guy who has no family that loves him.

Don't cry, it's just food, please eyes don't tear up. I am in heaven right now, pure heaven.

He succeeds in keeping his composure during the meal, but the feeling of gratitude grips him.

"Thank you for the food; it was delicious," he manages to say.

Inside he is screaming to God, "I AM SO THANKFUL FOR THIS FOOD." The room falls silent after everyone has eaten, and Jesse gorged himself to the point of a stomachache.

Okay, this is awkward; Jesse thinks, looking at the wooden panel door that leads downstairs.

He considers bolting again, also wanting to feed Smokey the cream in his coat pocket. He feels out of place, plus, everyone looks at him as though he is something special.

The family notices the scar on his nose and cheek and that his hands look like a mechanic's — banged up.

"Soo . . . ," says Ana, "tell us about yourself."

Leaning in, she looks in Jesse's dark brown eyes. Jesse sees her graying hair betraying her age, braided, and rolled into a bun. Her expression is so tender that it causes him to have hope for the absence of any more drama.

Is this what a grandmother resembles? I wish I knew.

"Like I said down there in your church a little while ago, I'm nobody," Jesse speaks out of the coldness of his heart. "I am *really* nobody from nowhere."

Jesse looks at the old dark wooden walls that are plain and aged, with modest furniture scattered around the room. The place is spotless, however. There is some vintage charm to the old building. Taped construction paper decorations are everywhere; some have glitter glued on them.

"Check it out! I made the decorations because I got

bored being out of school this week. I took art this year and my teacher says I need to explore my creative side," Manuel says, with a smirk.

Jesse can tell they are close to the same age. Jesse smiles.

Ana stands up from the table and walks toward Jesse. She brushes his hair out of his eyes and says, "Let's get you cleaned up!"

Jesse tenses up, and his heart starts to pound again. In the aging white tiled bathroom, she shows their special guest the shower, turns on the little heater for him, and then points to the towels.

From the hallway, Manuel holds out to him a pair of his sweatpants and a t-shirt.

"They may be kind of loose on you, but you can sleep in them anyway," Manuel treats Jesse like some kind of VIP.

As Ana leaves him alone in the room and shuts the door, she says, "Tomorrow I'll cut your hair for you, won't that be nice?"

Jesse leans against the wall; it is so nice and warm.

So far, so good, a hot shower is going to feel so good, Jesse tells himself. Then he whispers to God, "Hope these guys don't turn out to be freaks. I have had my fill of freaks. Good ol' normal people, for once, would be nice."

After Manuel and Jesse have washed the dishes, dried them, and put them up, Jesse finds that the evening went by fast. Now Jesse finds himself standing in the hall in front of a bedroom door with Manuel. He can sense that Manuel's mood changed to somber.

"This is your room, Jesse," says Manuel as he opens the door across from his.

A room of my own, a bed, a nightstand, and a lamp. What a wonderful thing!

To Jesse, it seems like forever since he has slept on a bed. Two months is a long time to be homeless and alone. Jesse walks over and pushes on the mattress.

"Feels soft," Jesse comments.

He wants to say thanks, but it just won't come out. He is still waiting to see what the catch is.

"Buenos noches boys," says Ana and Papa as they pass by, off to their room.

"Oh, yeah . . . um . . . goodnight," Jesse speaks up after remembering what buenos noches meant.

Manuel waves as he leaves the room and shuts the bedroom door behind him. Jesse goes over and opens his door just a crack to the hallway. He finds himself alone with his thoughts while staring at old buildings through the only window in the humble bedroom. Knowing it is cold outside, Jesse thinks of Smokey and her kittens still out there, braving the winter night. He determines to get the cream packets to her tomorrow.

Why didn't I run today? My feet froze to the sidewalk . . . and, what do they mean I am the Chosen One? That could be a problem.

He plops down on the bed puts his hands behind his head and lies back, looking at the ceiling. Hearing the washing machine down the hall as it runs with his clothes makes him amazed at how everything is so different from just that morning.

How long will this good streak last? His thoughts are interrupted when he hears the door creak open, and Manuel pokes his head in the room.

"I can't sleep, too excited you're here."

Jesse motions him over as he sits up in bed.

He leans forward with an intense look on his face and asks, "Manuel, what does it mean, I am the Chosen One?"

Manuel plops on the far end of the bed and thinks for a second before he answers.

"Well, it's like God gave us a mission to fulfill, and He will bless us for it. You will bring us a blessing, comprende?" explains Manuel, as best as he can.

"Doesn't make any sense to me," Jesse says, looking out the bedroom window.

He feels strange that they have all these expectations of him.

"Well it's like . . . blessings . . . you know, like, blessed or cursed, good or bad. Something like that," Manuel says. "Why do they call you, Rocky?"

"I dunno."

Jesse's memories still carry too much pain to talk about, even to a really nice guy like Manuel.

"Oh," Manuel stares out into the night.

"Do *you* think I am this Chosen One person?" Jesse gets some boldness to ask.

"Sure, the Lord told me when I gave you the candy cane."

"So, you hear God talk to you?" Jesse asks in surprise.

"Yeah. Can't everyone?" Manuel responds casually, as he stands up to leave.

"Well, see ya in the morning. Sleep well, Jess," Manuel whispers as he tiptoes back to his room across the hall.

"Yeah, good night," Jesse calls back softly. *This Chosen One thing could become a problem, but for now, I am going to give them a chance . . . I can't believe I am this excited over sweats and a t-shirt. Things have been very crazy for the last three months. I hope Uncle Bill doesn't find me here.*

Jesse's emotions rocket back and forth from sheer joy to morbid dread, but at least his feet and hands have fully warmed up under the blanket and handmade quilt. Trying to calm himself down, he examines the thick heavy quilt on his bed. (See "Types and Shadows" 2) The cozy blanket consists of squares cut from men's plaid shirts. He can tell it took someone a lot of work to make it. Little yellow ties of yarn are at each corner of every square. It isn't long before he is overcome with drowsiness and quickly falls asleep.

At three o'clock in the morning; a voice startles Jesse, and he nearly jumps out of his blankets. He sits straight up in the bed and looks anxiously around the dimly lit room. A scratchy voice rumbles loudly and deep like someone who has smoked all their life.

"THERE IS A RAT IN THE HOUSE, AND IT IS YOU . . . STREET RAT! YOU HAVE NO BUSINESS BEING AMONG NICE PEOPLE; MAKE A RUN FOR IT, GO WHILE YOU CAN. GET OUT OF HERE NOW!" the voice yells through the darkness.

Jesse opens his eyes; his heart is pounding so loud he can hear it, then he realizes it was only a dream. He puts his hand on his chest as if it will help keep his heart from bursting out. Looking around, Jesse is still alone. He drops back down on the pillow. He has never had a nightmare like this before.

Now I am hearing voices. I guess going crazy happens all the time to street rats. I must have got it from that mean bag lady in Central Park. She hears voices and talks back to them all the time. God, if You are real, I want to ask You for something. I have never asked before, cuz You were more a pretend friend. But now I am talking as if You're real, so . . . if You are, please don't let me go crazy in front of these nice people.

Jesse pushes the thoughts out as each one gets heavier in his head. He slips back into a deep sleep.

Anton manages to muffle the imp that startled Jesse, but he does not have the authority to send him away. Jesse's thoughts are food for it, and it is growing stronger.

Anton remains by Jesse's side as the imp cowers in the farthest corner away from him. The two supernatural creatures do not mince words. Angels see imps as traitors and mutants, and all imps disdain anything pure and holy.

In Jesse's deep slumber, another dream unfolds. He feels a breeze and the smell of pine trees, the sound of the wind in the trees grows stronger. He finds himself on a bridge in the mountains over a rocky crevasse with a tiny stream at the bottom. Before him is an open gate between two massive stone towers, stone walls to each side, and a deep ravine below the bridge. Sitting on each side of the two tall buildings on the perimeter walls are four stone creatures. On one side is a lion in full roar, along with a massive ox statue. Conversely, a stone eagle sits on the wall next to a figure of a bearded man in flowing robes.

"Jesse, son of Allen, wake up!" Jesse hears a deep male voice and feels a hand touch his shoulder. He rolls over and opens his eyes, leaning up on his elbow.

"No one here . . . fantastic . . . I *am* going crazy," Jesse whispers. Looking down, he notices a big feather by his pillow.

"Hmm, that's too big to come out of this pillow."

He puts on the jeans that Manuel lent him; they fit well enough, just a little on the loose side. His jeans are just now rolling around in the family's old dryer. It is the sounds of home; sounds he has long forgotten. He puts the feather in his back pocket and follows the smell of eggs and tortillas to the kitchen, where he finds the family sitting around the table already.

"Sleep good, Jesse?" Papa asks.

"The bed felt great," Jesse replies, not wanting to

think about the threatening voice he heard last night. He sits down at the table and is about to dive into the fried potatoes with sausage and eggs when the family bows their heads. He quickly places the plate back down.

"Father, thank you for Jesse, bless our food, bless Jesse today. Help him to hear Your voice above all others, in Jesus' name, amen."

Papa grins at Jesse, who still has his arm out over the platter.

"Now, Jesse, now we can eat!" Papa says with a spark in his eyes.

Everyone puts the food in the tortillas and makes burritos out of their breakfast, smothering it with grated cheese. Jesse simply piles it all on his plate, wishing he knew how to fit in better. He tries to eat like them at first, slow and polite, but he finds himself gulping down Ana's good cooking.

"Jesse," Papa speaks up, "have you heard from the Lord today?"

Jesse swallows hard, thinking, *Okay, now it starts, it's gonna get weird. I just know it. What do they want from me?*

Jesse reaches into his back pocket and pulls out the feather. He looks around to see if this will freak them out or not, waiting to see what they will do. He holds out the feather, but instead of being freaked out, all three of them seem delighted with it. Ana's eyes well up with tears like the day before.

"This is an angel feather, Jesse. An angel visited

you! And what did the angel say?" she asks.

Jesse draws the feather back and looks at it closer.

"You mean this isn't something Manuel decorated for Christmas?" says Jesse avoiding the question. "It's covered in some kinda fine gold dust stuff!"

Manuel focuses on his dad's question.

"So, did you hear anything from God?" Manuel keeps on the subject.

"Umm . . . well . . . I . . . uh . . . I did hear a voice just say, 'get up, Jesse son of . . . of Allen'. My dad's name is Allen. Did I tell you that?"

Jesse doesn't tell them about the terrible voice or of the dream in the mountains. He keeps them to himself. Not trusting them entirely, he is not ready to tell them his dad's last name, just yet.

What if I get sent back to Uncle Bill's?

"Can I touch your feather Jesse, son of Allen?" Ana asks with a serious tone, as her hands tremble slightly in awe of the feather. "This is real gold dust Jesse; it was an angel of prosperity that woke you up."

Jesse doesn't say anything; he just watches them admire the feather, trying to decide if they are serious, or just playing with him. Papa gets a plastic zip-lock sack and puts the feather in it for safekeeping.

"Here, this is yours," he says, as he hands him the sack with the feather.

"And this is, too!" Manuel says excitedly.

He hands Jesse a box, wrapped in pastel blue tissue paper. The thin decorative paper is wrinkled as though it had been used before.

Jesse flashes back to yesterday when Manuel stood before him with a simple candy cane.

"Is this for me?" Jesse fingers the top of the pretty blue paper.

"Jesse, this is a Bible. You will need it where you are going." Papa grins encouragingly.

"Where . . . am I . . . going?" Jesse braces for the potentially dreaded answer, which he fears will ruin everything.

Ana stands up from the kitchen table, unties her apron, and begins to exclaim with excitement, "You . . . are . . . to go to Spirit Wings Academy (SWA) in the Rocky Mountains! We have it all arranged! You will start this fall. The Lord told us to save up money and be ready to send you."

"A school . . . that far away? Is Manuel coming with me?" Jesse feels dread come over him.

Papa leans over to Jesse. "No, Manuel isn't. We can only afford one, and you are the Chosen One."

"It's okay, Jess," Manuel speaks up. "I hope to live there when I graduate and be on staff as a counselor."

Manuel's parents both nod with approval.

"No need to worry about that so soon. We have time to tell you everything. August is eight months away. We are just so excited," Papa says.

Manuel wants to settle Jesse's nerves. He can see he is alarmed at the thought of being sent off to an unknown place. After all, he barely knows them; and they are already planning his future for him. They show him a pamphlet with photos of grandeur castle-style buildings, pine trees, and six-story towers with arched windows. It is unreal to Jesse. The leaflet says: "Spirit Wings Academy" Warriors **In God's** Service. **(WINGS)**. The front photo on the brochure shows a bridge leading to a twin tower with stone walls. There is a photo of four creatures on the walls, just like in Jesse's dream.

Jesse freezes, examining the image closely.

Is this Your way of telling me this is Your plan for me to go here? He asks the Lord. Silence . . . *It has to be a sign from You, right?*

"Spirit Wings Academy, is this a flight school for pilots?" Jesse asks innocently.

The family suppresses giggles and Papa elaborates on the school.

"This is a high school for radical Christian youth. They teach spiritual warfare, prayer, and fasting. Powerful young leaders like yourself go there to learn the ways of the Lord and grow closer to Him. You have a purpose, Jesse, a calling. The Lord instructed us to pay your way because He chose you to be a warrior in the last day's army."

"Looks like a resort or something, all these fancy castles." Jesse is amazed. "This is all just for rich kids, right?"

"No, Jesse, it's for all young people, many from all over the world. They say a rich eccentric millionaire built it. It's in the Rocky Mountains of Colorado. The Lord told us you are to go there, and that you will bring us a great blessing. All we know is that your name means 'God is'. We looked it up in Hebrew; JESSE means 'God is' — You are our Chosen One, Jesse!"

"How can I bring a blessing? I barely know what a blessing is — and a warrior? What am I fighting?"

Papa pats Jesse's hand, "You are fighting against the [4]rulers of darkness, wickedness in high places. You are fighting to bring light and truth to a lost and desperate world. We all are doing our part."

Jesse wants to be something special for them, but he knows he is not.

Jesse looks at Ana; she is beaming with joy. He wants to make her proud; he wants her to always look at him just like she is doing right now.

Manuel stands up from his chair and leans down on the table toward Jesse.

"All we have to do is send them your parents' full names so they can get permission. We know the Lord will work it out for you, Jesse. Just trust the Lord with this — Jesse, trust Him," Manuel says with urgency in his voice.

Then Jesse's thoughts flip, and all his focus is on the chance for things to go wrong.

But find my parents? Are they dead somewhere? Why did they not call for three whole years? What if they make me go back to live with Uncle Bill?

Questions like these are a heavy chain around

---

[4] **Ephesians 6:12**

Jesse's youthful neck. It is all he can do to keep himself from bolting out into the cold streets again.

Manuel picks up on Jesse's mood and decides to break the tension. He knows they can still lose Jesse.

"Come on, Rocky, let's see the rest of the church, and I'll show you the bell tower on the roof!"

Manuel leads Jesse to his dad's office. In the ceiling is a pull-down ladder leading to the roof. The boys climb up the old wooden ladder to the open-air bell tower. Pigeons flutter noisily away as the hatch door swings open. It is cold up here, and the wind is brisk.

"This bell came from Spain, and it is a hundred years old."

Manuel looks at the bell with pride, knowing it is a part of his heritage.

"Do you ever ring it?" Jesse asks, gazing out over Spanish Harlem.

"Yeah, Christmas Day, Resurrection Day, and stuff like that," Manuel says, jumping up and down to keep warm. "It's cold, let's go back down!"

Manuel climbs back down the ladder, and Jesse follows. As they shut the spring-loaded hatch to the tower, Papa is sitting in his antique upholstered chair. The chair's faded fabric of landscaped scenes of fields and trees appears quite worn.

"Jesse, it's time for our daily devotions," Papa says as he opens Jesse's new Bible and motions for the boys to sit in the fold-out chairs. Jesse panics slightly not knowing what 'daily devotions' are.

He notices the intense look on Papa's face, and sees how passionate the Spanish pastor is about the Bible. Papa opens to Genesis, chapter one.

"In the beginning, Elohim . . ."

Jesse finds the Bible mystical and exciting. Elohim, Jesse learns, is Hebrew for God.

After lunch, Papa and Ana are busy with their project, so the boys have some free time. Papa needs to get ready for the Christmas play that night. Jesse feels like a normal person again. He is keeping track of time and eating regularly. Joy swells in his heart, but still, in the back of his mind, there is the possibility that it all will end. He is expecting the bad that always shows up in his life to ruin everything. For now, things are good; and he is going to make the most of it.

The boys go outside and walk toward the park; it is cold but sunny out.

"Hey Manuel, there is a mother cat and kittens in the alley across from the park, wanna see?"

Jesse checks; the cream packets are still in his ragged coat.

"Sure," Manuel is game.

They find Smokey and her brood huddled in the heap of old rags.

"Look what I have for you, Smokey, cream!" Jesse peels back the top, and she eagerly laps up the first little packet.

"I want to feed her!" Manuel puts his hand out for

one of the packets.

Jesse hands one over.

"I know mom will let us keep them in the garage in back," Manuel suggests.

He knows his mom's tender heart couldn't turn the cats away. The boys find a box and move the kittens inside it. Jesse carries Smokey out of the alley, and Manuel follows with the box of mewing kittens. An older gentleman is in the park feeding the birds.

"Ola, Mr. Hernandez," Manuel greets the neighbor.

"What have you got there, boys? A mama cat and her litter of kittens?" the man, bundled up to his nose with his scarf, pets Smokey. "Aren't you a proud momma? Now make sure you don't handle them too much; the mama might abandon them. Hurry and get them settled."

The man's eyes light up, talking about the cats. Jesse senses Mr. Hernandez is lonely and would love to have them.

"Can you give them a good home? They need a lot of care from someone who knows what they are doing," Jesse says.

Manuel nudges Jesse with his elbow and whispers under his breath, "Jesse, what are you doing, giving away *our* cats?" Manuel tries to keep his lips from moving. He is already attached to the feline family.

Mr. Hernandez claps his hands in surprise. "You mean it? My apartment allows pets, and it is so empty since I lost my wife Rosa," the elderly man says as he leads the boys to his apartment next to the park.

"Just set them down anywhere. I will get these cute little furballs comfy as bugs in a rug. Don't you worry — and you can come to visit any time! Any time, you hear?" He rambles on with joy and excitement.

"Goodbye Mr. Hernandez," the boys say in unison and set back out into the cold park.

"Jesse, I thought they were *our* kittens. Why did you give them away?" Manuel wants to be charitable, but he is enamored with the cute fuzzy kittens.

"He is lonely. Did you see how his eyes lit up? He needs them more than we do," Jesse explains.

Manuel is impressed with Jesse's kindness to the older man. He senses Jesse is someone special. *If this guy is the Chosen One in our church's prophecy, then his integrity is real.* He is also quick to forget about the kittens as Ana calls the boys inside. "Jesse, come to the kitchen and let's cut your hair. We have church tonight; you should look your best."

After supper, everyone goes down to the ground floor to the church to prepare for the Christmas program. Papa and Manuel have put on dress shirts, and Ana changes clothes too. She has put Jesse's clothes on his bed to give him something that fits him to wear. His bangs no longer hang over his eyes, thanks to Ana.

"Tomorrow, we'll buy you everything you need," Ana promises him. "We've been saving up money for some time now. Everyone at church has given offerings just for you when you would come to us."

Jesse remembers yesterday when everyone reacted emotionally upon seeing him. The pit of Jesse's stomach becomes queasy again. He feels a sharp pain in his side, the kind of ache he has felt before, off and on, in the last few months. But he thinks it will go away now that he is eating regularly.

Downstairs, parishioners drift in through the front door, out of the cold evening air. Most of them are family members. The atmosphere is nothing like Jesse expected. No organ music, no whispering somber conversations, no dignified silence. Everyone prays out loud at the same time, and walks around as they pray, and some even weep. Jesse sits on the front pew with Manuel and Ana. Papa stands behind an old pine pulpit.

"We are Pentecostals, Jesse," Manuel tells Jesse quietly.

"Plenty-cost- what-als?" Jesse doesn't know the word.

Manuel just smiles and starts to pray. Jesse just watches him. Suddenly Manuel turns toward Jesse and lays his hand on his shoulder.

Manuel says, "God, bless Jesse . . ."

Jesse doesn't hear the rest of the prayer, but he feels a hot liquid flow over him, even though he knows there is no water on him.

Jesse shuts his eyes. *God, if this is You, lay it on me!*

The sound of music and singing draws Jesse's

attention, and he opens his eyes. To his surprise, he and Manuel are sitting on the edge of the stage.

How did we get from the pew to the stage? I don't remember walking over here.

People are singing, playing guitars, drums, and tambourines; some are dancing. Jesse feels his face; he has been crying, and so has Manuel. Jesse uses his shirt to wipe the tears off his face.

Then he glances and sees a lady leading the songs at the old piano. The music is simple, but Jesse finds it sincere. A young boy strums a guitar awkwardly. There is an older man on the violin, and a teenage girl plays the drums. The songs are in Spanish, so Manuel tells Jesse what they mean.

Anton is still beside Jesse when he spots the five intercessors that prayed for Jesse to come to their church. Anton recognizes that they are devout women but not too developed in the faith. They are all elderly widows living in the same apartment building. He surveys the Spirit of Religion as it tries to whisper accusations to one of the intercessors. She is ignoring the legalistic, critical spirit for now; Anton is relieved.

We are a meager fellowship of angels in such a dark region. Anton is aware that everything could soon change, and the rafters could fill with Guardians.

Everyone sits down on the well-aged wooden pews with nicks, chips, and rounded edges; that look as though they were made by hand many years ago. Papa says a few words before the Christmas play starts. He explains that he will speak in English on this occasion, and Ramón, his brother, will translate for the older people who only speak Spanish. Little giggling toddlers in angel costumes are taking their places at the back of the stage.

"Stand for the reading of the word," Papa speaks, pausing for his brother to translate. **Acts 2:38 and 39:**

> **"Repent and be baptized . . . every one of you . . . in the name of Jesus Christ . . . for the forgiveness of your sins, . . . and you will receive the gift of the Holy Spirit . . . For the promise is for you . . . and for your children . . . and for all who are far off, . . . everyone whom the Lord our God calls to himself."**

Papa José pauses, "Today, we celebrate the birth of the Savior."

Jesse closes his eyes and feels the same hot liquid love flowing over him as before. There is a flash of red and a vision of a man. It is Jesus on the cross. Then comes another blast of light . . . It is Jesus coming out of a stone grave.

"Jesse, son of Allen, believe in Me and be saved."
I do. I believe in You now.

"Jesse, oh Jesse," someone is touching his shoulder again. He expects it to be an angel, but it is Papa. He doesn't know whether to call him Pastor or Papa in church.

"Jesse, you were out in the Spirit; tell the people, tell them," he urges.

Jesse realizes he is flat on the floor of the stage. Everyone is sitting quietly in their seats, and the music has stopped too. The little angels still stand in the choir seats on stage, peering down at Jesse. His face flushes with embarrassment.

He sits up, feeling a newness inside; the embarrassment quickly fades.

Papa urges him again, knowing something powerful has happened in the spirit realm. "Tell us, Jesse."

Jesse steps off the platform and walks down toward the first row of seats as all eyes are on him. The Spirit of Religion begins to pace desperately about the stage, looking for a way to shut Jesse up.

Anton has a grin a mile wide. From birth, he has been with Jesse, and finally, now a testimony will be his. He rejoices; *Jesse is now a child of the Most High Yahweh!* Anton runs around the room, giving all the other angels "high fives." All the demonic creatures now are aware that Jesse is instantly a member of the Kingdom of Elohim. The Spirit of Religion is starting to panic. He is losing his influence in the church and shrinking in size.

"You're looking at me as if I am somebody, I'm nobody," Jesse states. "It's Jesus who is somebody great. I saw Him suffer for us . . . I saw Him; it is beautiful and terrible at the same time. I saw the love in His eyes. I know what it is to feel His love. I will never be the same."

The congregation reacts with emotion and exhilaration; quickly, they get still again to hear more from the Chosen One.

Jesse feels empowered and paces back and forth; he feels power and energy run through him. The Spirit of Religion begins to cry out in anguish. Anton expects it to leave altogether; unfortunately, several elderly ladies still cling to the stale dark influence.

"I did some really bad stuff . . . but Jesus loves me . . . He is *so* real to me now. He changed me on the inside, you know?"

Jesse gets light-headed again and sits down.

Papa stands up and says, "We were expecting a young man of God, a prophet of reputation. We see dimly as in a glass. God will not share His glory with another; through this boy, God receives all the glory. He is the Chosen One prophesied to come to us; he sees both the good and the bad in the spirit. Our assignment has just begun, and we are ready! His nickname is Rocky, like Peter the Rock of Revelation, isn't that wonderful?"

Papa knows Jesse sees things in the Spirit; he just doesn't know *what* Jesse sees. It is something Papa has not experienced himself and longs to. It gives the Latino pastor hope for encounters and experiences in the Lord.

The church breaks out in excitement and worship again, and Jesse sits on the pew — a new creature, the old has passed away, all things have become new **(Second Corinthians 5:17).** Anton knows Jesse is now one step closer to fulfilling his calling as a child of Elohim.

Phase Three: Training. Anton anticipates it with joy.

Jesse looks back at the front entry doors and sees leaning against the doorway, a small imp-looking creature with deep burrowed angry eyes. Jesse's heart begins to pound. Their eyes meet, and the imp points at the door for

Jesse to leave, and then it vanishes. Jesse is starting to make sense of it all — the Bible will show him, and the Holy Spirit ([5]Ruach HaKodesh) will teach him. He shakes off the surprise and trepidation the imp gave him to keep from embarrassing himself in front of the nice people. No one saw the demon but him. He cannot see the Spirit of Religion, but he can smell the stale air as Anton did.

Anton observes that the musty smell is almost completely gone; only a remnant of people embrace the Spirit of Religion. It is small now and fading from sight. Anton hears it moan as it struggles to keep its place in the church. Religion's ornate war-hammer is now larger than it is, and the dark spirit has to let it go. Its large white shield has a red cross in the center; the shrinking spirit abandons it as well. The entity now just stands on its colossal book, with "the Letter of the Law" inscribed on it.

The Christmas play goes off without a hitch. Manuel doesn't sing loud like in rehearsal, which relieves Ana. Jesse sits on the front row, taking it all in. Joy and peace are new to Jesse; it makes the humble Christmas seem like a grand event to him. Every family receives a paper sack with fruit and candy, which the church has done for years, even though it is costly for the small church. Papa and Ana filled the bags earlier that day, and the scent of oranges flooded their humble home all day long.

Jesse gets a sack too. Simple things are now a great joy to him. He scrounges through the bag and finds mini

---

[5] Ruach HaKodesh- Hebrew for Holy Spirit

candy bars, old-fashioned ribbon candy, one apple, one orange, and nuts still in their shells.

Too cool!

Later that night, Jesse lays on his bed on the second floor of the pastor's house in the heart of Spanish Harlem. The day has been full; and he is exhausted. His eyes are still hot from crying. He has peace and a sense of how he fits in the world. He spreads the ribbon candy out like a display on the bedside table.

"There, now my room is ready for Christmas."

He thinks of the crazy lady who is a 'bench dweller' in Central Park. *Can God fix her? Sure, He can.* Jesse is ready to sleep.

Will the dark voice torment him tonight? He only wants to hear from Elohim (the Lord).

Tomorrow maybe I can learn how to make those devils shut up.

"Thanks for the pillow and this blanket, God, and the Bible is nice, too," Jesse whispers to the Lord.

He feels guilty for loving the bed more than the Bible, but he knows that will change in time. There is no moonlight from the window tonight, making the room pitch black. A cold breeze wafts across Jesse's face. He notices a red glow in the corner of the room, and he forces himself to look in that direction.

A voice whispers from the corner.

"You're a fake. These people are using you, just like the rest. You're making a fool out of yourself. Jesus doesn't want a street rat like you."

The voice is cold and indifferent.

Anton sees several fallen creatures, gray hairy imps that slobber around Jesse. Anton shoos them away.

Vile creatures, Anton thinks. *Their master must be near.*

Belial's dark workers return to their commander in defeat, accusing each other of the failure. Like flies, Belial's tiny mosquito-like imps whisper twisted tales in the ears of humans. He is a king with minions all over the earth that do his bidding.

The red glow fades, and Jesse closes his eyes . . . *back to . . . sleep . . . too tired to be freaked out right now.*

During devotions the next morning, Jesse finally decides to call the pastor, Papa. He and Manuel sit down with Papa to read:

> **The fool says in his heart, "There is no God." They are corrupt, they do abominable deeds, there is none who does good. The Lord looks down from heaven on the children of man, to see if there are any who understand, who seek after God.**
>
> **Psalm 14:1-2**

"So," Jesse frames a question, "a fool says there is no God, so I'm not a fool, right?"

Papa responds kindly, "No, Jesse, you are no fool."

Jesse leans back in his chair and Papa continues. "No matter what others say, you must believe what God says above all others."

Afterward, Ana takes the boys in the old blue van to buy Jesse some new clothes. He feels weird at the East River Plaza Mall when security officers do not run him off. Some plain white t-shirts, jeans, and a pair of boots are all Jesse will let her buy. But then, with some convincing from Manuel, he also picks out a new coat. Jesse is not disturbed by the festive Christmas music anymore. The mall's decorations match Jesse's upbeat mood, and he takes in the atmosphere of the holiday with newfound joy.

"Your old coat is trashed, dude. We need to bury it in the backyard," Manuel jokes with him.

"Sure, if we can put your shoes in there too," Jesse retorts.

"My shoes aren't that bad," says Manuel, wishing that he had put some powder in them today.

That afternoon, after returning from the mall, Ana hands an old cardboard box to the boys from the attic. The box jingles with Christmas bells inside. Manuel is excited to unwrap antique ceramic figures and set them inside a manger made of sticks and straw. Jesse examines the old newspaper crumpled inside the box; it has yellowed with age. All the writing is in Spanish, but he finds a date of 1950 on the corner.

Manuel interrupts Jesse's inspection of the paper. "Put Joseph, Mother Mary, and baby Jesus in the middle," Manuel feels the need to instruct Jesse on all things 'spiritual'.

"Joseph is Mary's husband, right?" asks Jesse, as he makes the lamb run across the cabinet. "This lamb has lost its leg!"

The ceramic figures are old, and several pieces need to be glued back together because Manuel played with them when he was just a toddler.

"Remember . . . even though Joseph marries Mary, he's not Jesus' father, Holy Spirit is, got it?"

Jesse nods.

Jesse can't help but think how badly he wants to be back with his parents. The fact that his family abandoned him always haunts him. Even now, when things are looking up, his heart is with them. Sure, he had some issues with his dad being mean and controlling, but Uncle Bill was a nightmare.

"Manuel, you got some paper I can draw on?" Jesse asks as he unwraps a king perched on a camel.

"Sure . . ." Manuel jumps up and opens a cabinet with art paper in it. "Here are some pens, pencils, and markers. You want glitter?" Manuel asks jokingly.

"No glitter . . . that's your department," says Jesse with a playful smirk.

Jesse takes a pencil, eraser, and paper to the kitchen table. He draws for over an hour without saying a word and then finally he leans back. He sketched portraits of his parents, as he remembers them from three years ago.

Jesse can remember his dad's eyes; for some reason, it remains a clear image in his head.

"Jesse," Papa picks up the drawings. "These are

good."

"It's my mom and dad," Jesse replies, looking down at the table. The room falls silent. Everyone realizes Jesse is sad and withdrawing. He wants to belong somewhere, but he is not ready to be a part of Manuel's family yet. Jesse still has a hard time trusting people. His father's angry eyes fill his mind.

Why was Dad mad all the time? What's so wrong with me that they don't love me? I wonder if they even know I ran away. Uncle Bill may not even care that I am gone; he is so stoned all the time.

Jesse has to shut down his train of thoughts, or he will be enraged. He likes the calmness of Manuel's home. He is getting to like Manuel and his family quite a lot.

After supper, they all go down the block to get a Christmas tree. Holiday lights are all around Spanish Harlem, and the snow reflects cheerful colors. Jesse feels as though he is in a new world; the old part of town is charming at Christmas. Snow has a way of hiding peeling paint and aging buildings.

The boys throw a few snowballs at each other as Papa and Ana pick out a fresh-cut Christmas tree. Manuel takes cover behind the Christmas tree booth's fence to make more snowballs while Jesse lies in the snow catching his breath. The smell of fresh pine catches his attention.

"Dude, do you smell that?" Jesse calls out to Manuel in the chilly night air.

"Yeah, I love the smell of pine. The whole house is gonna smell like that when we take our tree home!" Manuel calls back.

The family stuffs their new tree in the back of the van and heads home.

They manage to get the tree on a stand and place it in the living room. As the boys admire the tree, Ana and Papa pull out boxes from the attic. They unpack the Christmas decorations, and Jesse finds brass angel ornaments with names engraved on each of them inside one of the boxes. He sees the engraving of Manuel, Ana, José, and Rudy. Jesse curiously hands the ornaments to Ana. A larger one reads "Perez Familia".

Jesse looks up and asks, "Who are José and Rudy?"

Ana replies sadly, "José is Papa of course, and Rudy is the son we lost after he was born five years ago. You are staying in his room."

Jesse now understands Manuel's mood change when he first showed Jesse the room. Ana leans her head over on Papa's shoulder, and he wraps his arm around her.

"We have another son. He is waiting for us with the Lord," Papa says softly.

Jesse wants to ask how the baby died, but he doesn't feel it is right. Everyone is happy, and so he wants to protect this holiday atmosphere. Still, it is sad to think that this remarkable family has lost a child.

I'm not lost; my family just forgot me.

His thoughts are distracted by the smell of pine that fills the air. Jesse never wants it to fade.

Papa sits in his easy-chair and reads.

The boys look at the manger scene, lost in the feeling of the holiday, as the delightful smell of sugar cookies in the oven fills the room.

Jesse is treasuring the simple things, and gratitude fills his once desperate heart. Now he knows Elohim for himself. *Maybe I can finally accept that the Heavenly Father told the Spanish church to take care of me, and maybe . . . Yahweh does love me after all.* It is a lot to soak in, but he is getting there. Jesse will think about that for a long time: *Jesus is not like my parents; Jesus loves me the way I am.*

Ana pulls out some little candles and some brass pieces from a star-shaped blue velvet box. Manuel knows just how to put it together, four angels with horns to their mouths cut out of thin brass spin around in a circle as candle flames move a fan on the top with their heat. A tiny bell rings as each angel turns and taps it with their trumpets. Jesse sits and looks at it for a long time, with the colored lights of the Christmas tree in the background. His heart is warm and full. He wants to jump up and say, "You guys are the best!" But he sits in the comfy living room of a modest church family, maintaining his newfound dignity. The frozen cold of two days ago is a fading memory. The thought of his troubled family causes Jesse to be grateful and enjoy every moment of kindness and consideration the Perez family shows him.

Tonight, for the first time, I will pray for mom and dad, Jesse purposes.

To pray for "Uncle Bill" is out of the question. Jesse hopes he is frantically searching for him and regretting what he did to him. He never tells the Perez's much about his Uncle Bill, his brutal past, the beatings, or the details of his old life. Stretching out on the nice bed, Jesse looks out his window. Frost takes up most of the glass, but he can see a few stars between the winter clouds up at the top. Christmas day is almost here. For the first time in a long time, he likes Christmas, and he likes himself. Large fluffy snowflakes drift silently down through the night.

Jesse makes it all night without any bad dreams or demonic encounters. That morning, he looks at himself in the mirror as he brushes his teeth.

You are going to be alright; after all.

Holding out his palms, he looks to see if it is healing.

Hope these don't leave scars.

Jesse is nervous about giving presents; *I can't buy*

any. What if they give me something, and I can't give them anything in return?

That day everyone is commenting on the beautiful Christmas Eve snowfall. The windless night caused it to pile up like cotton outside. Manuel and Jesse shovel snow off the sidewalk out in front of the church and sprinkle it with salt to keep it from making icy patches. A shop owner from next door sees their good job and comes over to hire the boys to shovel in front of her store. She happily gives both boys twenty dollars when they are through, giving her the same superior service.

"Wow, thanks," Manuel says. "Christmas snow and Christmas money!"

Jesse stands looking at the cash in his hand, stunned because he has never earned that much before. Usually, people just gave him food or candy when he worked for them.

Jesse is excited! *Now, I can run to that variety store down the street and look for gifts for the Perez's.*

For months Jesse had no one to be accountable to, so he feels funny asking Ana if he can go to the discount store. Ana says, "Okay," and the boys dash off to the store. Jesse wants to get a gift for all three of them.

Manuel whispers to Jesse, "Don't forget, God gets ten percent, so that's two dollars out of the twenty. It's called tithes."

"Okay. I have eighteen dollars to spend. I don't know what tithes are, but I will pay it just in case," Jesse states.

Manuel smiles, feeling that he is making an impact on Jesse's life.

The boys walk up and down the aisles in the store. Many of the items' colors and labels are fuzzy under a layer of undisturbed dust; as they have sat on the shelves for a long time. Jesse finds a yellow glass rose; *this is pretty, for Ana.* Jesse picks up a metal lighthouse in the office supply area that has a button to turn on a little light inside. Jesse gets that for Papa's office. Manuel is harder to shop for, plus he is in the store with him, and tougher to surprise. Manuel picks up a soccer ball and bounces it a few times. He remembers how ratty Manuel's ball they play with is, but it is twelve dollars, and Jesse just has six left.

It is Christmas Eve night, and Jesse is wrapping his gifts in his room. He uses a paper sack from the grocery store, a red marker, and tape. Jesse draws Christmas scenes on brown paper bags and uses it to wrap the gifts. For Manuel, he places the six dollars he has left in an envelope and wraps it up. Then he takes his little presents and puts them under the Perez family tree.

There is that beautiful pine smell again!

Jesse sees shiny gifts in fancy foil paper.

I see two with my name on them! I can't remember the last time I got Christmas presents. The ones from Uncle Bill don't count; they were always board games to the whole family.

Jesse remembers how his mother's uncle, "Poppy,"

as they call him, always took them out to eat for the holidays. Poppy raised his mom when her parents died in a car wreck; it was as close to grandparents as Jesse got.

Jesse and Manuel lie on the floor by the Christmas tree while they listen to the Christmas specials on TV. Ana makes more treats in the kitchen, and Papa naps in his worn-down recliner. Jesse's heart swells with love and joy, and again he wants to shout, "This is great!" but he fears he will cry and doesn't want to embarrass himself by showing emotion.

The night grows late, and all the shoveling from the day has drained his energy. Fighting to focus through weighted eyelids, Jesse gives in and goes to his room. As he crawls in his bed, he pulls out a paper he had written on during daily devotions with Papa. He begins to read and pray:

> **Pray then like this:**
> **"Our Father in heaven,**
> **hallowed be your name.**
> **Your kingdom come,**
> **your will be done,**
> **on earth as it is in heaven.**
> **Give us this day our daily bread,**
> **and forgive us our debts,**
> **as we also have forgiven our debtors.**
> **And lead us not into temptation,**
> **but deliver us from evil.**
> **Matthew 6:9-13**

His eyelids are getting heavy again. "Father God, send an angel to tell my parents about You, okay? And please don't let Uncle Bill find me." Then Jesse thinks: *Where are you, Mom and Dad?*

He watches as another white feather falls by his feet, but this one is longer than the other. He puts this feather with his other one in the plastic bag.

Does this feather mean an angel is going to my parents? Jesse wonders, his faith, building.

He feels a stirring in his heart but shakes off the emotion before it can fully develop. It requires more strength than he has right now.

Tomorrow is Christmas, and Jesse experiences happy dreams that night due to a recent peace in his heart.

Jesse hears the bell ringing above him in the bell tower. He figures it is barely dawn, based on the dim light of his window.

"Wake up, Rocky, wake up!" It is Manuel shaking Jesse. "It's time to open presents, dude, hurry!"

Manuel is halfway down the hall as Jesse steps down onto the cold wood floor. Papa is just coming down from ringing the old bell.

In the living room, everyone comes together and joins hands; and Papa prays.

"Father God, thank you for sending Jesus to earth and sending Jesse to us. Today is a special day that we will never forget."

Suddenly Manuel bolts to the tree and grabs some presents. He makes sure everyone has one and then finds one for himself.

Papa says, "Okay, go!" and everyone tears open their first gift together. Jesse opens a drawing kit with different pencils, a sketchpad, and erasers in a beautiful wooden case. Manuel hand-painted Jesse's name on the top in fancy lettering.

Jesse hears himself saying, "Thank you very much." Then he realizes he said it out loud without crying — *good deal*.

When Ana opens her present from Jesse, she gasps and says, "Oh Jesse, how did you know? It is beautiful."

Tears run down her face again, as she is known to tear up a lot.

"Yellow roses . . . ," Papa explains, ". . . were the flowers we put on Rudy's grave. They mean HOPE, the hope that we have of seeing him again in eternity."

Ana adds, "And now you are a son to us also!" Ana hugs Jesse for what he feels is a long time. Jesse isn't used to being hugged, so he just stands there feeling awkward.

Papa opens his next, from Jesse.

"Oh José, a lighthouse!" Ana exclaims, looking at Papa's gift.

Papa tells Jesse, "There is a prophecy that our church will be a lighthouse to help people find safe shores from the darkness. Jesse, has the Lord told you?"

Jesse just shrugs his shoulders. *Did the Holy Spirit lead me to buy these things*, he wonders?

Jesse is about to apologize for just giving cash when Manuel cuts in.

"DUDE! Six bucks, thanks, Rocky. Now I can buy that new soccer ball!"

Manuel continues, "Jesse, you didn't have to spend that money on us. That is very unselfish of you. You really are someone I admire and look up to."

Jesse looks deep into Manuel's eyes, trying hard to accept the compliment.

"You look up to me? Wow!" Jesse says, his voice trailing off with emotion.

The gifts are now all opened, and Manuel's family fills the house with joyful voices as they come for Christmas dinner. One of Manuel's uncles, Ramón, kisses Jesse and Manuel on the forehead. Jesse thinks that Manuel's family is very passionate like the Italian families he'd seen in the movies. He imagines large families in dress suits all at a wedding, hugging, and kissing and showing emotion. He thinks that is so opposite of his own small stoic family.

Papa tells everyone how Jesse's presents to them are so meaningful, and he and Ana carry on about it all during dinner. There are about twelve cousins to hang around with Manuel and Jesse. The little parsonage is full, like Jesse's heart. They eat downstairs in the fellowship hall, as the small kitchen couldn't contain all the Perez Familia (family).

As Jesse rests in his simple room that night, he begins to pray with conviction and knowledge. His faith blossoms and Jesse is using it the best way he knows. Manuel hears him praying and comes in to join him.

As time goes by, Jesse grows attached to the Perez family. There are days when he fears it will all end, and he will be homeless again, but those days are getting farther and farther apart. After a few weeks, he finally tells them his last name so that they can search for his parents.

"Logan . . . I'm Jesse Logan, Allen and Dana Logan are my parents' names."

He has trusted them with his parent's names; it is a considerable breakthrough for Jesse. Still, in the back of his mind, he is afraid it will come back to bite him.

That night Jesse decides to read the Bible on his own. He heard Papa say Psalms is a good book of the Bible to read every day, so he randomly opens up to a chapter in Psalms. Jesse is moved by what he reads.

> **Give ear to my prayer, O God, and hide not yourself from my plea for mercy! Attend to me, and answer me; I am restless in my complaint and I moan, because of the noise of the enemy, because of the oppression of the wicked. For they drop trouble upon me, and in anger they bear a grudge against me.**
>
> **My heart is in anguish within me; the terrors of death have fallen upon me. Fear and trembling come upon me, and horror overwhelms me. And I say, "Oh, that I had wings like a dove! I would fly away and be at rest; yes, I would wander far**

away; I would lodge in the wilderness; Selah I would hurry to find a shelter from the raging wind and tempest."
Psalm 55:1-8

"Wow, it seems this is written just for me as if God knows ahead of time what I will be going through." What Jesse reads enthralls him. He reads on down the page:

But I call to God, and the Lord will save me. Evening and morning and at noon I utter my complaint and moan, and he hears my voice. He redeems my soul in safety from the battle that I wage, for many are arrayed against me. God will give ear and humble them, he who is enthroned from of old, Selah because they do not change and do not fear God.
Psalm 55:16-19

"This is amazing, and You speak right to me from it . . . So You heard all my complaints, this whole time? Thank You, Jesus, thank You," Jesse tells the Lord.

He reads the last verse in the chapter:

But you, O God, will cast them down into the pit of destruction; men of blood and treachery shall not live out half their days. But I will trust in you.
Psalm 55:23

Emotion wells up inside, and he lets a few tears run down his face. His heart is softer now. It wasn't long ago that he was cold inside, feeling nothing but dullness. Now that he knows what it is to be alive on the inside, he realizes how awful it was to be dead inside.

The verses deeply move him. The Bible becomes a great joy to him, as he reads for hours at a time in the peaceful Perez home in the heart of noisy New York.

He is now somebody with somewhere to go!

ASHER'S MISSION

Jesse not only stays for Christmas, but he remains into the New Year. After Christmas break, it is time to start Public School again, so they enroll Jesse at Manuel's.

Papa sits Jesse down in his office to talk to him about finding his parents and contacting his uncle.

"Jesse, we have found out your uncle had a nervous breakdown and was admitted to a drug rehab center just about a week after you ran away. We could not find your parents, but they finally called your Uncle Bill at the rehab and he had them get in touch with us."

At this point, Jesse has a knot in the pit of his

stomach, having to deal with the prospect that his parents still do not want him. He realizes his hands are in tight fists, and he intentionally forces his hands to relax.

"Jesse, your dad signed the permission form for you to go to Spirit Wings. Here is a note your mom wrote for you."

Papa places a crumpled piece of paper with coffee stains on the desk in front of Jesse. Papa knows that Jesse wants some privacy, so he leaves the office so Jesse can read her letter.

DEAR JESSE,
YOUR DAD SAYS HE IS ON THE VERGE OF A BIG RECORD CONTRACT, AND HE WILL BUY YOU A CAR WHEN THE DEAL IS FINAL. ALL OUR DREAMS ARE ABOUT TO COME TRUE! WE WILL MAKE UP FOR THE LOST TIME WHEN THE RECORD LABEL PAYS US. UNTIL THEN, STUDY HARD AND DON'T BE A BOTHER TO THE NICE PEOPLE.
LOVE MOM

Jesse lets a single tear roll down his cheek. *Is it worse to know they are alive and don't want me or not to know anything?* It is as if an invisible knife is between his shoulder blades, and he can't reach it to pull it out. He lets out a heavy sigh and stares out into space. Then his eyes focus on Papa's Bible which is open and facing Jesse's direction. Jesse reads the words underlined in yellow:

For my father and my mother have forsaken

me, but the Lord will take me in.
Psalm 27:10

As he sits in silence, tears roll down his face. After another heavy sigh, he gets up, wipes his face, and goes to find Manuel.

As he opens the office door, he bumps into Papa, standing right behind it along with Ana and Manuel.

Jesse looks at them there in the hallway and smiles a feeble sad smile. Papa is the first to grab him and hug him.

"I'm sorry, Jesse, I know it hurts. It will get better in time. You will see," Papa assures him.

Jesse presses his face into Papa's shoulder and holds on to him. He looks up to see Manuel bursting into tears.

"Aw . . . you big lug," Jesse turns to him for a hug.

They embrace like brothers. Manuel is still crying, feeling concerned for Jesse. Jesse finds himself comforting Manuel.

"It's okay . . . I'm okay, man . . . I'm okay," Jesse reassures him.

Ana has that proud look on her face that Jesse loves, her handkerchief over her mouth.

"You dear boy, I know we can never replace your parents, but you are part of our family now," Ana says, still drying her eyes and pulling Jesse over for a hug.

"Yeah, Rocky, we got your back," Manuel states, regaining his composure.

During the rest of Jesse's stay at the Perez's, he begins to open up a little to Manuel, and they grow close. Manuel knows Jesse still has some walls up. He is aware that Jesse carries some dark secrets, and he is willing to give him all the space he needs. Manuel tells Jesse all about his childhood, so much so, that Jesse feels he has known him his whole life.

On the first day of school; Jesse isn't nervous.
Compared to being homeless, this is a piece of cake; he assures himself.
Jesse's excuse for not fitting in with Manuel's Latino friends is that he can't understand Spanish. He never really gets to know any of his classmates that much. He is content with reading his Bible and living a life free of drama.

There are days when Jesse will get quiet and pull away to dwell on his painful past by himself but not very often anymore.
In six months, he is aware he will be leaving New York City and going to Colorado to the Spirit Wings Academy. He doesn't know what to expect, but he knows he is no longer alone, no matter where he goes. He is leaving his troubled past far behind, hoping it will never again catch up with him. He is righteous now, and the enemy will not shake him. At least that is his hope.

Half a year passes without incident, just the way

Jesse hoped it would. However, he is unaware of the heavenly activity that is buzzing on his behalf. Father God looks to Asher to set things in motion concerning Jesse's transition to Colorado. One mile directly above Jerusalem, the Principality Angel looks out from the watchtower known as North Gate or Eagle Tower, his long straight white hair blowing in the hot breeze of an Israeli August. White hair is an honor; it represents wisdom in the spiritual realm. Asher is a high-ranking angel called a Principality; Michael is his captain. Asher is responsible for the tribe of Asher. Thus, his name carries the weight of responsibility. Elohim created all the angels on the same day He created the stars; hence, they are of the same age. Some are honored above others.

Asher has earned his white hair, having seen some real action well beyond the last seven thousand years. Thick, white leather straps are bound around his muscular forearms stopping at the wrists, much like the bands Jewish men wear at prayer. His white metal chest plate with an emblem of the House of Asher, easily reflects the sunlight, is across his back with similar white leather. His tunic is not fabric, but rather a force field that runs down to his white leather thigh-high boots. The force field is beautifully transparent with a pastel rainbow hue. The colors continuously spin in circles, much like soap bubbles do. His pants are the color of pure snow, reflecting a myriad of tiny sparkles in pastel shades. Asher holds a long gold staff with a diamond the size of a grapefruit on the top. The staff is a rod of authority given to him when the earth was formed. Incased inside the diamond is the word "Asher" in Hebrew made of sapphire. His thick velvet looking white cape tied about the neck continuously moves as if a breeze blows around the angel. The cloak's edge is trimmed in three braids of gold, making the braid one inch thick.

There are still a significant number of Hebrew people scattered from the Diaspora. The ten "lost tribes of Israel" are in no way lost to the eyes of Adonai. He keeps His eye on each one. One of the largest Jewish settlements not in Israel is in New York. Asher's troops are among the people of Asher's tribe, part of the House of Israel (also called House of Ephraim or Jacob, and the Ten tribes of the North), wherever they may be. Battle-worn angels continually return to the throne room to recover in the presence of the Most High as other angels take their place until their return. Asher knows that Elohim will someday restore all the tribes to one house. He also knows Yahweh will make "One New Man" from all the people of the Kingdom of Elohim.

To the humans below, Eagle Tower is undetectable. Only those in the spirit realm know of its existence. However, this realm is very real and very eternal. Glorious pointed arched windows and carved white columns are translucent white stretching through the clouds down to Jerusalem's walls. The bright popcorn clouds, contrasting with the deep blue sky, fade into turquoise where the horizon meets the land.

Lost in thought, Asher is alerted by the sudden powerful voice of Ruach HaKodesh (the Holy Spirit).

"Asher, come."

Michael, the Archangel, arrives to take over Asher's watch as Asher bows in respect and then leaps from the crystal white tower. He shoots up through the clouds and ascends beyond the earth's atmosphere to the third heaven in a matter of minutes. He passes by the New Jerusalem and sees that it is almost finished. It is a spectacular structure with twelve foundations of precious stones. It has twelve gates, one for each of the tribes of Israel, made from large pearls. He glides by the walls made of a gemstone called Jasper. Looking inside the city, he can see structures made of pure gold, so pure that it is clear as crystal. The earth does not have such pure gold with a transparent appearance; it is only in heaven that such purity exists. There is the noise of construction and much activity in the Holy City.

Asher rushes into the throne room with joy and presents himself before the Father and Son. Bowing low in reverence, he presents himself before Them.

"Adonai, I have come, as You bid me."

Asher warmly basks in the glory around him and the love of the Father and Son. Streaks of light shoot out from the throne, as do bolts of lightning. The power of the light brings healing to the many weary angels who have returned for refreshing. The glory of Yahweh (also known as Jehovah) and [6]Yeshuah (Jesus) continues to glow, causing worship to rise from all in the heavenly throne room. The smooth crystal floor perfectly reflects the splendor within the magnificent chamber.

The voice of the Father penetrates Asher's very being as he receives his latest assignment. Each divine word from the Lord of Hosts absorbs into the very fiber of Asher's being, changing him somehow.

"Asher, My strong and faithful Prince, I am calling you to escort Jesse Logan of New York City to Spirit Wings Academy of the Rocky Mountains. The Adversary (King of Babylon, commonly referred to as Lucifer) is watching Jesse, My new servant, in whom I delight and whom I treasure. The Serpent of Old desires to keep Jesse from joining the great army of young warriors I am preparing at Spirit Wings Academy. There are many demonic assignments against him, which is why I send you. You have the resources to get the job done. Stay on your toes. This is not as easy an assignment as it sounds," speaks the thundering voice of the Father to Asher.

Yeshuah (Jesus), who sits at the Father's right hand, releases virtue from His open palm in the form of a blue shaft of light; it glides to Asher and fills him with grace to dispense to Jesse. This power propels Asher to New York, where he will replace Anton for a season. A flash of light in the spirit realm occurs as Anton and Asher

---

[6] Jesus in Hebrew- Yeshuah (Lord who is salvation) or Yehoshua (Salvation) also Yeshuah

meet. Clouds part over them; and the heavens open up. As Anton begins to ascend to Elohim's throne, Asher is setting foot in Anton's place. They make eye contact, and without a spoken word, they exchange information. Anton the Guardian bows in respect to the Principality Angel and is gone. Just as suddenly, the spirit realm returns to its former state. Imps, demons, and strongmen of the enemy in the area flee from Asher's presence. Asher keeps his gaze on Jesse. Jesse is still thin but muscular. He has jeans that are slightly worn and wears a plain white t-shirt, a blue plaid shirt, and black boots. Asher memorizes all he can about Jesse to make it easy to keep track of in case of a battle. It is good to be back among humans again, face to face.

This very day Jesse is to start his three-day trip to Spirit Wings Academy. As Jesse steps out of the front church door and onto the sidewalk, Asher releases through the palm of his hand the grace of Yeshua into Jesse's chest. Jesse feels a surge of Ruach HaKodesh within him but is not aware of the fresh glow of blue that now surges in his inner being.

Ana is softly weeping as Jesse stands in front of the old church on the sidewalk. She brings out the quilt from Jesse's bed, rolled up like a sleeping blanket. Manuel carries Jesse's backpack out to the sidewalk. Jesse takes the bag from Manuel and looks at the quilt Ana has under her arm.

"Jesse, I want you to have this quilt from off your bed to take to Spirit Wings Academy. My mother made it for Rudy just before she passed away. You have helped to bring us healing and filled some of the emptiness we felt. So, I want you to have it. The top side is from my father's old work shirts and Papa's. The green and blue fabric square is from one of Manuel's shirts. You have brought joy back to us, and I am ready to stop mourning all the time. I can move on."

This time Ana's tears combine with joy as a slight smile brightens her face. She hands the quilt to Jesse and kisses him softly on the forehead.

Ana says, weeping, "Bye-bye, mijo."(Pronounced "Meehoe" slang meaning baby boy.)

Papa pulls Jesse to his side for a quick hug, while Manuel uses all his energy not to get emotional. Jesse is like a brother now. The house is going to be quiet again. Jesse feels a shudder run down his spine; the old fears grip him from his troubled past.

Manuel steps in front of Jesse, "Rocky, I just got a word from the Lord for you . . . I don't know what it means. He said: 'Cling to the red ruby and cling to your beautiful destiny that I set aside for you.'"

Manuel has been prophetic before, like when he heard Adonai tell him to give Jesse the candy cane.

"You promised to write and tell me everything, don't forget! Tell me about the gem and your destiny." Manuel hopes, but knows better, and doubts whether Jesse will write back very often, if at all.

Manuel and Jesse hug, and Jesse gets in the waiting car.

"Grace and peace be multiplied to you, Jesse Logan," Manuel softly prays. The prayer causes a blue glow in Jesse's chest to double in size. Papa tells the driver something in Spanish and shuts the car door. Jesse watches his beloved Perez's out the back window until they are out of view as the car heads for the interstate. At one time, Jesse dreamed of leaving town, never to look back, but now things have changed. The Perez's are good people; he is safe there and even loved. His rational thoughts conflict with his actions: leaving a perfectly good situation to go off into the unknown.

Okay, this is different; I am in the will of the Lord. Going to SWA is His plan for me. Man up and trust Him, don't be such a wimp. A red ruby and a beautiful destiny await . . . focus on that. What in the world does a ruby have to do with me? What is my destiny? Papa José talked about spiritual war; I don't know enough.

He tries to encourage himself, looking over at the quilt rolled up on the seat next to him. He spots an old ink pen on the floor and picks it up. He gets the acceptance letter for SWA out of his pocket and writes on it, "Cling to the red ruby, beautiful destiny." He leans back in the seat and looks at his backpack containing all his worldly possessions, clothes, art set, Bible, and angel feathers. That is all he owns. Yet, somehow it seems more than enough. He is full of Ruach HaKodesh of Yahweh, and His word. He feels a gentle peace and inner strength that is new. Jesse deals with passing waves of nervousness and anxiety, but he manages to discipline his thoughts, not to wander toward dark imaginations of potential mishaps. He remembers how he dreamed of the four creatures that adorn Spirit Wings Academy entrance.

Okay, Father . . . looks like I am going to see this place for real. I will find my destiny there, and some red gem? I have more questions than answers, Lord!

Jesse clutches the acceptance paper rolled up in his hands.

Asher monitors Jesse as he gets into an old gray car that is to take him to Colorado. *The tires have little tread*, Asher notes with his regular attention to detail.

This boy has great determination, with a mix of confusion and fear. He doesn't trust people, but his spiritual sense is more developed than most mature believers.

Asher sits on the car's roof and settles in, watching for anything that might develop. He is delighted with this young believer.

A subordinate of Asher's drops in, "Sir, do you want me to call in the troops, do a sweep of the area, or face off with the local strongmen?"

The military angel somehow resembles a bulldog; Asher tells him, "Sergeant, I will call you in when you are needed. Return to base and stay on alert."

The sergeant's countenance falls, "Not getting any action again today, I suppose."

Asher salutes him and the warring angel salutes and then zips away.

Jesse slumps in the back seat with his backpack under his arm. The driver is from Puerto Rico and doesn't speak a lick of English. Thinking he may have to use them at some point, Jesse looks over a paper with Spanish phrases on it like "How much farther?" or "Can we stop for food?".

Asher checks out Juan, the driver. The guy is in his forties with curly short cut hair graying on the temples. This Spirit-filled believer has some depression and deception, but well versed in scriptures. Asher nods in approval as he hears Juan praying for traveling mercies as they leave the Perez home and Spanish Harlem.

"Good," Asher says, "that makes things easier."

A force field forms around the car like a bubble blown from soapy water. The rainbow colors swirl around in the circle of protection, which matches Asher's tunic perfectly

As the first few minutes pass, Jesse watches all the familiar landmarks pass by. He thinks about Manuel's prophecy, *a ruby, and a beautiful destiny . . . strange*. The thought lingers off and on all day. He is in new territory, both physically and emotionally. Meanwhile, hunger finally makes its presence known, and Jesse begins eating his homemade tortillas and tamale for lunch.

"Go easy on the food, son of Allen!" Asher says into Jesse's spirit, knowing it has to last him three days.

Whoa, I better save the rest, Jesse tells himself.

Full, but not stuffed, Jesse relaxes into the drive

and the new scenery. Juan seems to live off coffee and sunflower seeds; he is continuously sipping coffee or spitting sunflower shells into a cup. Jesse snickers a little when Juan accidentally spits shells into his coffee.

"Hijole!" Juan exclaims. (Pronounced: "Eee hoe lay.")

Spotting a distant farmhouse off to the right, Jesse smiles at the humble beauty of an old white house and red barn centered between fields of newly plowed soil. He loves it when they drive past such rural areas with farms and ranches. imagining that the families there are happy and have no problems makes Jesse feel good. He also speculates that there are no crimes, drug abuse, or dysfunctional families. To him, country life is a fantasy of perfection. That is why he likes going to Central Park, to dream of better days. Central Park is long gone now, and Pennsylvania and Ohio signs flash by his car window, only reminding him further.

Juan begins humming; he hums a lot and genuinely seems happy. He asks Jesse a question from time to time amidst his humming, but Jesse cannot understand him, so they accept not to talk for the most part. Juan drives till midnight, by which time he can't keep his eyes open anymore. They have been on the road for sixteen hours. He pulls over and tells his passenger that they will sleep right there in the car beside the road, in Spanish. Jesse thinks he understands, but when Juan turns the engine off on the side of Interstate 70 just fifty miles past St. Louis, Missouri, and begins snoring, the message is clear. Juan's 1958

Chevelle holds up well, although the back seat is not the most comfortable bed.

Asher's twelve-foot body lifts off the car's cab, and he goes up to look around for any trouble. A few red eyes glare from the bushes, but they are not showing themselves. Asher rechecks the tires; they are okay.

Jesse lies in the back seat listening to Juan sleep soundly. His breathing is steady, so Jesse relaxes. There is no funny business with this stranger yet, but Jesse still doesn't allow himself to fall completely asleep. For him, the night will be long and tiresome, listening to cars and trucks go by occasionally and wondering if other travelers will disturb them.

Asher catches a Belial demon whispering in Jesse's ear.

"Just make a run for it, you're better off hitchhiking on your own. Go before anything bad happens, like it did in the past. Everyone hates you, you're street trash," the small insect-like imp suggests to Jesse, in his sleepy state of mind.

"Voice of . . . the enemy," Jesse whispers half asleep.

Asher identifies the little imp and sends him flying out of sight with one swift swat.

"How did he get past me? Those little ones are fast," says Asher.

Jesse doesn't brood as often as he used to, not much to keep an imp hanging around. The enemy is making planned attacks on the new servant of Yahweh.

Asher hovers over the car, checking all four directions. Above him, the heavens open, and the spiritual environment changes while Asher is there. Spiderlike demons scatter away from Asher in twenty directions, and for several miles; they flee. Only a few stronger dark spirits remain at a distance under rocks, in shrubs, and in dead trees.

Asher's sergeant sits at his base in the second heaven drumming his fingers, waiting for a call to action.

As the sun comes up, the red eyes in the bushes disappear. Juan starts the car, and they travel on. Asher suspects that there will be more attacks against Jesse, so he stays more vigilant. Juan asks for traveling mercies again, and the force field remains in full strength. Jesse prays today also which causes Asher to feel a surge of power sweep over him.

"Go, Jesse, go!" Asher pumps his fist.

They cross over into Salina, Kansas, around lunchtime. They are making good time. When they stop for fuel, Jesse goes inside to buy a grape soda. He has five dollars left in his pocket. There is a commotion outside by the gas pumps. He looks out the gas station's glass doors and sees Juan getting arrested. The arresting officer pulls a handful of tickets out of the glove box of Juan's car. Juan has accumulated quite a pile of unpaid speeding violations over the last six months. Not a good thing for a man with no passport to have. Jesse's heart begins to pound.

Should I go stick up for Juan to the cops? Is there

anything I can say that will keep them from arresting him? It is useless.

He feels helpless, watching Juan getting in the police van.

Man . . . I feel sorry for Juan; he treated me real nice. Even though we didn't talk, he wasn't like others I trusted before who turned out to be real jerks. Was that immigration that arrested him?

Jesse looks around at his surroundings. Jesse has little hope that Papa could do anything for him at this point. They could barely afford the gas money for Juan.

How can I get to Colorado now? Why did I have to leave my backpack in the car? Stupid! Relax one minute, and this is where it gets you, Jesse rebukes himself. *And Ana's quilt, what do I do? The police may have me listed as a runaway; they will send me back to New York or worse to juvey.*

"Oh no!" Jesse feels for his Spirit Wings Academy acceptance letter in the back pocket of his jeans.

"Whew, it's still there, thank you, Lord," says Jesse out loud.

Jesse builds up some nerve to get his stuff out of Juan's car. He loves his art set, and the angel feathers he found on his bed are priceless, not to mention the special quilt.

I bet other kids going to Spirit Wings Academy aren't having this kinda trouble. Why couldn't I be part of a normal family? I really let Ana down, losing her quilt. Maybe I don't deserve to be a part of a real family. Maybe.

. . .

Jesse stops his line of thoughts. He is getting himself all stirred up.

Sorry Lord, sometimes this anger just bubbles up out of nowhere.

He watches the immigration van drive off with Juan, and a tow truck backs up to hook up Juan's car. The mechanic takes the backpack and quilt and throws them in the cab of his wrecker. Jesse decides to ask the guy if he can get his stuff. He approaches the mechanic who is ratcheting up Juan's car to the hitch on his truck.

"Hey, that is my stuff from the back seat. Can I please have them?" Jesse tries not to look like a scared rat in front of a cat.

"Ya got any proof this stuff is yours? An ID, driver's license, any form of identification there, young man?" the mechanic says with a wad of tobacco in his lower lip, causing it to stick out.

"Um, no, not really; just my acceptance letter for school," Jesse says with a sense of defeat.

"Well, then you will have to go down to the impound with the proper paperwork to claim your belongings. I go by the book, and that's the rules, kid. Hey, you should have shown yourself when the police came. You an illegal too?" The mechanic begins to glare at Jesse as if he were an immigrant with no papers.

Jesse steps back and then takes off behind the gas station, running past several buildings before stopping to catch his breath. The grape pop is too shaken up to open.

He tosses it aside and watches as it spews out on the ground from a hole poked from a chunk of gravel.

Asher covers Jesse with his wings.

"We are well over halfway there," Asher acknowledges. "Sarge, do a sweep of the area, and then stand by." Angelic communications travel in milliseconds, and Asher's command arrives in the second heaven over Jerusalem.

Sarge pumps his fist and stands up, making his chair fall backward. "Yes, sir!"

With no awareness of Asher or his myriad of troops, Jesse thinks of his options and takes a phone number out of his pocket.

If I call Papa on a payphone, he will tell me to go with the authorities. No way I'm going to risk being sent to juvie for being a runaway. If my parents were around, this wouldn't be happening. That just makes me more determined, Jesse thinks. *It seems the enemy is trying to stop me from getting to the academy. It's just You and me now,* Jesse tells the Lord and refocuses on getting to Colorado.

Sliding the phone number back in his pocket, Jesse walks up across the overpass and sticks his thumb out. Always keeping an eye out for the tow truck since he didn't see which way it drove off.

"I'll get to Spirit Wings Academy or die trying."

Hearing that remark from Jesse makes Asher groan. Multiple cars with demonic influences fill the westbound highway of Interstate 70. Asher keeps the demonized cars from stopping for Jesse by ordering Sarge, who makes it happen with the troops. Within five minutes all is clear of demoniacs on the Interstate for hundreds of miles. An elderly couple heading to Denver is seen by Asher a mile away. Asher wants them to pick Jesse up, but they are afraid to pick up strangers on the road and pass by him.

Vehicles whiz by as Jesse has his thumb out. He feels like a freak again, just like when he was homeless. Cold stares and curious glances from all who pass by make him feel rejected by every car and truck.

Are people that cold and uncaring? Or is it my fault they don't stop? This is just like the old days . . . no wait . . . God is with me now.

Jesse walks for about an hour and then stops to pray.

"Father please get me a good ride to Denver and the academy. Don't let anyone evil stop for me, okay?"

A truck driver sees Jesse on the roadside, and he reminds him of his own son. The trucker stops for him. Asher approves of the driver seeing he has two guardian angels assigned to him. The angels exchange information in a nanosecond. Asher now knows the man's life history.

As Jesse cautiously gets in the passenger seat of the semi, a flood of memories run through his mind of people who took advantage of him on the mean streets of New York just about a year ago. The trucker looks to be a kind man in his forties; his Denver Bronco cap is stained with sweat that has seen as many miles as the man. He is potbellied, dressed in a soiled t-shirt, and he talks up a storm.

"Where ya headin' son?" the trucker smiles as he merges back on the highway.

"I am going to a school in the Rockies, Spirit Wings Academy," Jesse says, wanting the man to know he is not a runaway, even though technically he now is.

"Never heard of it. Is it a school for pilots?" the man wonders.

Jesse has to laugh inside himself; he had thought the same thing at first. The trucker loves to chat; he carries on all about himself and his own family in Denver. Jesse just listens and nods, staying alert and cautious. Jesse is glad he does not have to say much about himself.

The truck driver buys Jesse a hamburger and fries, and they continue down the highway. Jesse feels a little more relaxed while the man talks about his son and his dear wife. The Semi finally pulls into Denver around nine-thirty at night. Jesse is now just three hours away from the academy. Jesse tries to see the mountains, but it is too dark; he can only see a few lights in the foothills, and a black silhouette of the mountain skyline. No moon out, the air is chilly, and a sharp breeze cuts across Jesse's skin.

"You sure you're eighteen? You don't look a day over sixteen to me," says the sleepy chubby driver named Mac as he scratches his belly and yawns.

"Well, thanks for the food and the ride. I don't have far to go now. Don't worry about me," Jesse assures him.

He lets Jesse out at the edge of town at a large truck stop. Semis are parked all over the parking lot, with drivers getting some sleep.

"Thanks again, and the Lord bless you, and keep you, cause his face to shine on you, and give you peace!" Jesse tells Mac, the trucker, before heading out to find a safe place to sleep for the night.

The trucker meets all kinds of characters on the road. Mac thinks to himself, *nice boy, kinda on the strange side, though.* The trucker says a quick prayer for Jesse as he goes into the truck stop café.

Jesse finds a grassy spot under an overpass just past the truck stop and tries to sleep a little. He can see a few high-rise buildings, but it does not compare to the skyline in New York City. Lights on the hills from the suburbs and housing divisions are barely visible. He realizes how brilliant the stars are here in the high altitude. Jesse is captivated by the Milky Way's densely packed stars. He has never seen such a vast array of stars.

As he lies in a patch of weeds, he doesn't let himself get fearful by controlling what he thinks about under the overpass. He tries to imagine what it would be like to live in a castle and be in the mountains. It is a stretch for his imagination. As his mind gets fuzzy, he allows himself to sleep for short periods. The sound of vehicles occasionally buzzing past him echo in his head; engines go from quiet to loud and then fade in the distance. For Jesse, it is a tense night keeping his fear in check while trying to get some much-needed rest. He wants to stare at the brilliant sky, but his eyes are too heavy. He wonders what bugs may be crawling around in the grass under him.

My red ruby and my destiny . . . at . . . SWA . . . he dozes off.

Asher pulls his sword out and paces around Jesse all night. As Asher swings his sword, demonic clusters up to fifty miles away stir and flee the region. The angelic Prince causes quite a commotion in the population of the dark creatures in the area. He assigns Sarge to work on Jesse's next car ride for the morning.

The morning sun casts an orange haze on the Rockies, shining brightly enough to awaken Jesse. When Jesse sits up, he notices the mountain range in the west. It is dramatic and beautiful.

"Wow, I couldn't see the mountains in the dark; this is amazing!"

The mountains in the distance appear blue where the sun does not reach them yet, except the snow-covered peaks, which catch the sun's first rays and intensely display the pure white virgin snow. The view so stirs Jesse that he drops the awkwardness he feels of being alone on foot and aggressively runs up the overpass to catch a ride on the Interstate. The mountains have a powerful effect on Jesse, making him feel like he is in a glorious new place.

It takes four more car rides to get Jesse to Eastcliffe, the small town below the academy. From the foothills to the base of a mountain, the landscape has significantly changed.

The air is thinner, it takes more effort to breathe, but I really like Colorado. I can't wait to hike and climb rocks.

Just past the small town of Eastcliffe, tall pines, boulders, and a steep highway now surround him. His last ride is with a family of tourists who stop at a campsite just outside the academy. As they unpack their picnic; Jesse begins to walk up the road toward the campus; eating an apple they gave him. His nervous anticipation builds with the elevation of the mountainside.

After a few minutes of walking, he finds himself the only human around, just at the base of the pine-covered mountain. The campground disappears just behind him on the curving tree-lined road. He still feels hungry, but he is happy he is almost there. He tosses his apple core in the ditch.

Father, I feel I'm in a dream. SWA is so different from the Big Apple. Your creation does show Your glory. I just wish Manuel were here with me.

"Am I not enough for you, Jesse?" Elohim speaks back.

"Whoa, is it the mountain air, or this special school? I just heard You, Lord. Loud and clear . . . Oh, sorry, Lord, You are my strong confidence," Jesse answers back, hoping his heart will believe his words. His heart pounds with exhilaration. "Am I gonna hear You every day and stuff? Being able to hear You is great, more than I ever hoped for. Lord, I purpose to really obey Your voice, Your wonderful, beautiful voice! Have You been talking all this time, and I am just now listening?"

"There are some battles ahead, but you are not alone. I will show you how to fight, Jesse. We will have great adventures if you continue to listen and trust Me," Elohim tells him.

Jesse turns his head toward the side of the campsite behind him; something rustles in the brush along the road. Jesse picks up his pace. No cars, no one in sight. Thoughts of bears, mountain lions, and snakes almost cause Jesse to panic into a full run, but he chooses a slower pace. A brisk walk and thinking about what the Lord said keeps Jesse from getting too overwhelmed. He feels a twinge in his stomach but ignores it, knowing it never gets too bad.

You are my strong tower, and I run into You, and I am safe.

Jesse now knows to pray **Psalm 91** when he gets fearful. It always worked at the Perez home. Now he is a city boy in the heart of a wilderness with just a single road leading upward.

Asher is aware of a snake poised to attack Jesse, hidden in the underbrush by the road. It sees the high-ranked angel and lunges toward Jesse very quickly. Asher knocks the snake off course quickly pulling his shield off his back. It slithers back underground. Asher doesn't pursue, standing a moment with his sword pointed toward the snake hole; he signals the unseen angelic troops to be alert. Jesse turns around, hearing a sound.

"What was that, Lord? I heard something in the ditch!" Jesse knows there is something around, but he didn't see anything. A cold chill runs down his back. Asher returns to Jesse's side, keeping his sword drawn as they walk up the campus road. Now Jesse can see the large stone sign that reads, "Spirit Wings Academy." He focuses his attention on getting past the gate just ahead, where he will be safe. There is a huge brass eagle on top of the stone sign; its talons grip the stone sign, and its wings are outstretched to cover the full length of the stone. The paved highway meanders up to a massive concrete bridge that angles up to the mountainside beyond the campus, lying on two large rocky plateaus. Two tall spires decorate the bridge on each side, making a dramatic entrance. Four long white Spirit Wings Academy flags on the spires majestically mark the territory. A sizable rocky cavern lies below the bridge.

Jesse peers over the stone rail and thinks: *whoa, that's a long way down! Lord, what am I doing here? This looks more like a king's fortress than a school.*

A tiny stream of water trickles below. Up at the top of the road is a three-story stone gate tower. It guards the opening to the campus and has two tall square buildings on each side. As Jesse walks toward the gate, four massive stone statues loom majestically above him on the thick stone wall that surrounds the campus. A roaring lion, an ox, an eagle, and a figure of a man; all have their eyes heavenward. He saw these in a dream eight months ago; it is a mystery to him.

What does a lion, eagle, ox, and a man have to do with the Kingdom of God, Lord?

Just then, a screech from a bald eagle echoes against the rocks. Jesse glances at the stone eagle; he wonders if it has come alive. No, the statue is still a stone-cold rock. Then he sees the shadow of the flying eagle in front of him on the road. Jesse laughs in surprise. He looks up and sees a majestic bald eagle; it swoops low enough for Jesse to see its sharp dignified eyes as it glides through the air above him.

"Lord, what's up with the eagle?" Jesse laughs.

For the first time, Jesse is truly experiencing Adonai talking back. He has often spoken to Yahweh, mainly to complain about his hard life. Now things have changed. Yahweh is more than an imaginary friend. He has a real relationship with Him, and on this day, he is getting to know the voice of Yahweh.

Jesse walks past the stone creatures in silence. There is no revelation from Yahweh yet about them. However, Elohim seems to be incredibly excited about the eagle. He anticipates that he will learn more, as Elohim reveals it to him. It is very exhilarating — this new closer walk with Yahweh.

The big city kid feels small and humble as he walks by the massive creatures frozen with heads looking upward. He passes them and goes through the large gate at the tower's opening. An iron grill (portcullis) hangs ominously overhead within the gate tower. *Do they ever close this entrance?* Cobblestones make up the road now, planters with flowers and signs welcoming cadets dot the courtyard entrance.

Is this a school or a fortress? Walls all the way around, like a castle, towers, flags, statues!

After crossing the gate tower, Jesse finds himself looking upon the campus grounds. Everything feels different, as though he is walking into a new country with air that is electric with energy. Greeting Jesse as he walks are long white banners with "Spirit Wings" on them. They flap in the breeze along with a gentle whoosh of the various pines as they gently sway. Small signs on stands are everywhere, giving directions to dorms and some others say, "Welcome Cadets."

Ahead of him, long steep stairs lead to the tallest buildings on the top level above the pine trees in the campus's back. The view of the majestic towers causes Jesse to stop so he can take it all in. Also, on the top level, a magnificent cathedral is nestled. Jesse is amazed.

The pamphlet didn't do this place justice. Do I belong in such a remarkable place?

Asher begins to rejoice as they have made it to Spirit Wings Academy. Several bald eagles coast in the wind currents above the campus, as Jesse walks towards the campus center. The Spirit of Adonai dances around him, and he feels energy on his skin and a witness in his spirit that the presence of Elohim is upon him.

Asher's troops and Sarge, one of the troop leaders, rejoice over Jesse's arrival. They dance and whoop it up above SWA.

The Regional angel in charge of Spirit Wings

Academy greets Asher. ([7]Hierarchy for Heavenly creatures are found in the back of this book.)

"Prince Asher, we are honored to have you here. We rarely see a high-ranking angel in this remote part of Colorado," says the lesser angel bowing.

"Greetings in the name of the Lord. This believer is very dedicated, and the enemy seeks to keep him from learning the ways of the Kingdom of Elohim. He will be a real threat to the Kingdom of Darkness if he continues to mature in Elohim," Asher tells the Regional angel.

"Yes sir, we will assign him extra forces. We have the most anticipated group of new students coming. This year Adonai has called to Himself some mighty young warriors as the battle over the earth is coming to its fullness. Any news from the Holy City?" he inquires.

Asher's eyes fill with excitement as he reports: "Over one thousand of Abraham's seed have found the Messiah just last week alone. I must get back now, though. Watch out for Beliel's workers (the accusers of the Brethren); they have attacked Jesse, son of Allen, several times already."

"Yes, sir, we have lots of mosquitos this year," the lesser angel replies.

"Baruch atah Adonai" (blessed is the Lord), Asher declares in Hebrew as he leaves.

---

[7] **Colossians 1:16 For by him all things were created, in heaven and on earth, visible and invisible, whether thrones or dominions or rulers or authorities—all things were created through him and for him.**

"Baruch atah Adonai," the Regional angel responds, watching Asher soar out of sight.

The meeting between two angelic beings takes only a millisecond; however, they can hear each other's thoughts — no need to speak aloud.

Asher signals all his sergeants and the angelic military to return to Eagle's Tower as they are worshipping Adonai. With a distinct sound from Asher his subordinates race back toward Jerusalem.

Anton has now returned to Jesse, empowered from the throne of Yahweh, and full of zeal. He sees the Spirit Wings Academy and immediately feels the power of the place.

With Jesse's arrival, things are getting good, phase four: equipping and empowering, thinks Anton, from the top of Levi lodge, where Jesse is assigned.

The Guardian is invigorated with the prospect of Jesse being at SWA. Jesse's guardian angel announces to the other angels that Jesse has made it to the academy!

Jesse checks the worn-out brochure's map of the campus from his back pocket. Then he locates his dorm and sits on the steps outside the main entrance of Levi lodge. He pulls out the acceptance letter and looks at the prophecy he wrote down from Manuel.

A red ruby and a beautiful destiny cling to them, he ponders.

Then Anton flies from the roof of the dorm and joins Jesse on the steps in the heart of the campus. Anton has his sword across his knees for quick access. He looks

Jesse over, no worse for wear. Of course, Prince Asher has taken good care of his saint for him.

Jesse smiles a faint smile.

"Lord, is there an angel beside me right now?"

"*Yes*," Elohim confirms.

"Cool," Jesse answers back, suppressing a grin. He doesn't ask to see or talk to the angel. He knows Elohim will give him supernatural sight if it is called for.

The noon sun cuts through the pines and warms the stone steps of Levi lodge. This lodge is unique in that only one tribe resides here. The other dorms house up to three tribes each. The expected arrival of the students is between one and four in the afternoon.

"Wow!" Jesse gasps at the grandeur of the campus he is looking over. It looks like a spot out of Europe, not like a school for youth. The authentic sixteenth-century Gothic Sanctuary dominates the area over the other buildings. The sanctuary is a cathedral with carved stone arches with large glass windows, and massive wooden beams. Two six-story academic towers also rise above the trees, being the highest buildings. The aristocratic atmosphere of the campus intimidates Jesse.

"Thank you, Lord," says Jesse with gratitude, "for getting me here safely. I know there are a lot of bad things that could have happened to me out there, but they didn't," he tells Adonai. "Okay, I want to be ready for my gem and my destiny! But, seriously, are You sure I am supposed to be here?"

Jesse reaches for the paper in his front pocket with

Psalm 55 written on it; he is memorizing it. Jesse admires the beauty around him, tall evergreens, large rocks jutting out of the mountainside, and a few wispy clouds painted in the sky.

For now, he musters all his courage to be on the campus of Spirit Wings Academy, a place for dedicated young believers to sharpen their skills in the service of Yahweh. He genuinely wants Manuel's prophecy to manifest; he purposes to stay alert and watch for it. He feels if this is his fate; it is more significant than anything he could ever have imagined for himself, a street rat from back east.

The warm sun on Jesse's skin makes him sleepy, but the sound of a car coming up the road startles him from his drowsiness. No one else seems to be around; just a few staff cars parked behind the Academic Towers and the dining hall.

Tall pines surround the back of the campus like a wall of green cutting into the mountainside. Hiking paths dot around the area leading into and out of the dense forest. The sound of the breeze in the pines and their scent fills the air; Jesse remembers the smell of Manuel's Christmas tree from over eight months ago. Being here is another crossroad; this is a big jump for a street kid. For the most part, he is also unaware of the hundreds of kids on the same journey as him, leaving their homes for the first time to serve Elohim through prayer and fasting. They will be a zealous generation, separated for the battle against the works of darkness. Time is short, and the last days generation marches toward great conflict for the hearts and minds of the earth's vast population. Signs of the last days are all around them: earthquakes, floods, volcanic eruptions, famines, wars, and rumors of wars. The world of these young students is in turmoil. Also, another one hundred and fifty second-year students will arrive today and settle into life on the campus.

Jesse leans down to pick up a small evergreen stick that lies on the steps. He breaks the branch in two, causing sticky sap to stick to his fingers.

Why do I always seem to destroy things?

The sap causes dirt from the branch to stick to his fingertips. He tries rubbing it off on his jeans, but it is not coming off.

By now, two people are approaching him.

CHAPTER THREE

HIGHER GROUND

Three hours earlier, across the Sangre de Cristo Mountain range from Spirit Wings Academy in Denver, it is a gorgeous fall day. Various maple trees variegated from yellow to dark red stand on each side of the Alvarez home. White popcorn clouds occupy the Colorado sky as Ruby and her dad load the car and prepare to drive into the Rocky Mountains. School is starting at Spirit Wings Academy; and this is Ruby's first year. Professor Ruben Alvarez, Ruby's dad, has taught at the academy for ten years now, right from the first year the school opened.

Silently Ruby Alvarez prays, *Father, go before us and prepare the way*. After saying goodbye to Ruby's mom and older brother, they drive off in her dad's convertible. She hopes her hairstyle makes her look older. She is the youngest student to be accepted into the academy, being just fourteen. Being short for her age doesn't help her confidence much, either.

Ruby doesn't have far to go; she has lived an hour away from the Rockies all her life. Her dad has his red convertible top opened, so her long red-brown hair blows in the wind. She has to put it in a ponytail to keep it under control. She has a round face, full lips, and a cute nose wrinkled just enough for her dad to recognize her frustration. She will turn fifteen next month, and she knows her father doesn't want her to grow up any faster than she already has. After all, he always says she looks too much like a grown woman when she puts her hair down. For him, the convertible is a perfect choice.

West is easy to find as the Rocky Mountain range is always there in the west. Ruby is proud to be a native of Colorado, and prouder to be on her way to Spirit Wings Academy. She expects to be one of the first to arrive at the campus. She is glad for a chance to get settled in before all the other kids come streaming in. Having her dad as a teacher at the school is the best part of all. She feels pressure to excel, though. Most of all, she wants to please Jesus. As she watches the pine trees flash by in the car window, she hums worship songs cheerfully. This young Latina is just less than three hours to her new life. Her mom and older brother, Arlo, will remain back in Denver.

So, it will be Christmas the next time I see mom and Arlo. I don't want to think about missing mom. I need to concentrate on . . . the Lord.

Ruby tries to focus. She scans the roadside for bald eagles; they are something special to her.

Up into the early morning sunlight, an enormous white angel's wingtips grab the air and he streaks across the Colorado sky. The angel elegantly spreads out his wings to slow him down as he drops silently onto the roof of the Shekinah Sanctuary of Spirit Wings Academy. He steps to the roof's edge and begins his watch, with a sword on his belt and fire in his eyes. His eyes are blue, the color of the hottest flame.

Tucked into the mountainside, an old VW car is parked at the small campground, the night before, at three o'clock in the morning. Spirit Wings Academy is up the road. A young man in a black robe has built a small fire; he throws a fistful of powder and some odd articles into it. It sparks and gives off poisonous green smoke.

Nearby, in an isolated cave, a small neon lime green imp is curled up and whining with his long sharp fingers clasped over his bulging yellow eyes. He is a member of the local demonic stronghold. The Fire King Abigor has many dark creatures under his dominion in the caverns underground near the campus.

"I don't want to go to school this year; you can't make me!" the green imp's shrill voice whines annoyingly.

Pulling his long-pointed ears over his panicked face, like a dog reprimanded by his master, he cowers as he waits for impact. His master kicks him with great force into the air. The little imp screams all the way and never looks out, but flies curled up in a spinning ball as he reaches his highest point and feels his descent toward the academy. In full shriek, he falls to the earth, hitting the back of the massive white angel who just arrived. The angel turns slightly to see what hit him. One of the imp's wings is bent back from the impact. The imp picks himself up, manipulates a smirk, and scampers away into the forest. With no saint to rebuke him, the little imp is allowed to remain for now. The angel does not leave his post, but remains on the peak of the roof, watching.

On the same morning, Devin Simmons gets on a charted bus at the Wichita bus depot, traveling to Spirit Wings Academy, leaving behind a teary-eyed mom, with the words, "We are so proud" on her lips. The words linger in his mind. It is five in the morning; Devin's head is still groggy with sleep. It is an honor to be accepted into the Spirit Wings Academy, but Josh and Trey are not going.

Will we still be friends two years from now? Sure, they seemed glad that one of us is going, but we have done everything together, and now the gang is breaking up.

Devin has known his friends since they were toddlers in the church nursery. He has no better friends than them. They were called "The three musketeers" at church. He feels his own brown eyes welling up and decides to play a fast-paced song to change his mood.

"Don't come around with your chemical highs,

your cocaine; it just don't fly," the lyrics go. Devin's studio-quality headset covers his ears. The headset's band is under his chin so as not to disturb his perfectly groomed black hair.

It isn't the same without the guys, but his emotions settle into quiet nervousness; it is better than tears. He is content to think about what it will be like in the mountains of Colorado, with kids like him. To be with kids who are radical in their walk with Elohim excites him. Devin wonders if there will be any other African American kids besides him. He pushes his shiny black hair out of his eyes, making sure he still looks good in the reflection of the window of the bus. Devin feels the Holy Spirit stirring inside him. He knows there is something big that is going to happen up there on that mountain. Zipping up his sweatshirt, the teenager drifts off to sleep. He expects it to take eight hours to arrive at Spirit Wings Academy. He figures it will be around lunch when he gets there, and that is when his life will forever change.

Eric Sinclair has the same destination; he slumps down in the back seat of a luxury car with his earbuds on. He is hoping to avoid all the mushy talk his parents do at times like these. He just has to survive three hours through the mountains to get from Aspen to Spirit Wings Academy. His brown hair is just over his ears and covers his eyes slightly. All the guys are wearing their haircuts that way. He almost wishes he were using public transportation as the other kids do; then, he can get his heart ready to be on his own for long periods without his mom and dad. His mom keeps turning to the back seat of their Rolls Royce to pat him on the knee and smile reassuringly at him. He doesn't want to smile back in a cheerful grin, but it is automatic, always taking other's needs over his own. Eric's light hazel eyes hide his worry; to keep his mother from being too concerned for him; she is a mother after all. Eric just prefers to settle into a deep mood of thought, thinking of his dedication to Elohim, which led him to this commitment of two years at Spirit Wings.

He needs just one more touch from Ruach HaKodesh.

Is this really God's plan for sure? Well, no turning back now. It would be too embarrassing to quit. Ingrained in his brain are his dad's words: "Sinclair's are hardworking forerunners, trailblazers, we lead, not follow. We finish what we start."

Eric turns up the volume on his music a little too loud and closes his eyes. The song cranks out the words "I live for You, I live for Your embrace, let me see Your face." Distortion effect on guitars, and a driving beat, can be heard from the tiny speakers all the way in the front seat.

Merely by looking at the campus of Spirit Wings, a person can't tell it is a controversial place. It was built by an unknown man, with four dorms, a dining hall, and the Shekinah Sanctuary with Levi lodge off to the side. There are two round Academic Towers made out of stones and log beams, six stories high, with massive glass windows reflecting the pines and rocks. The builder designed the campus after European castles, as he was of Welsh descent. Spirit Wings campus is lavish and immaculate, every inch groomed, with cobblestone paths and lush landscaping. The builder is a mysterious recluse millionaire; he may have gotten his wealth from the music industry. The man has gone to extreme lengths to keep his identity cloaked. The school has a reputation for its Christmas light displays; many people drive through to see the decorated Gothic cathedral that took five years to build. The holiday lights make it even more spectacular.

Many on the outside label it "New Age" or a cult. Many radical Christians love the idea of it — teens from all over the world journey to this remote place for training at SWA. In the end, the cadets learn the ways of the Kingdom and get missions that will last them the rest of their natural lives. These kids are used to being misunderstood by the world. *Will they find common ground and bind together as a powerful force to shape their world?* Professor Ruben Alvarez wonders the same thing every year when the new groups of cadets arrive. There is a global battle going on, and many are entirely unaware of the great conflict in the spirit realm.

Eventually, Ruby and her dad arrive at Spirit Wings Academy and park in Ruben's usual staff parking place. They walk toward Ruby's dorm. Ruby pulls on her suitcase; it is stuffed and heavy. Her dad, "Professor Alvey" as the kids call him, has his hands full with his own. Ruby wonders if the next two years will be like this; if her dad will have time for her, or will she just be another student in the class. Neatly maintained cobblestone pathways connect all the buildings, and potted plants are placed all over the grounds along with park benches and shade trees.

As they take the rather long walk to the Levi dorms, Ruby has forgotten the pines' fresh smell; it is overwhelming and rich. Just being there takes her to a place in her heart of joy and fresh hope. She is going to soar to new heights in this place, and it will be nice to have others that want the same thing. Looking up, she spots three bald eagles, almost like dots, circling very high in the partly cloudy sky. Their screeches echo down upon the campus. Ruby grins. (See "Types and Shadows" chapter 4)

The four dorms framing the outside perimeter at SWA are called East Gate, North Gate, South Gate, and West Gate, but are also known as Lion, Eagle, Ox, and Man lodges — taken from examples of the Jewish camps in the Bible. (See "Types and Shadows chapter 3) Each dorm has two levels with two towers on each end, and a grand stairway and attic study hall. Stonemasonry and wooden beams align to make majestic structures. The students assigned to the Levi tribe don't live in the four main dorms but are assigned to live in the campus center next to the Shekinah Sanctuary in Levi lodge. They are the priestly tribe, appointed to serve all the other tribes. Levi lodge is styled the same as the cathedral, just on a smaller scale, thus; making it most spectacular.

Ruby and her dad have walked past the administration building, the dining hall, and up the long stairs. At the top of the stairs on the final level is her dorm Levi lodge, the Sanctuary and two more dorms, and the twin Academic Towers. The Sanctuary is the most impressive structure on the mountain. It is only five years old but looks as though it has been there for hundreds of years. Its massive wooden arched doors, curved rooflines, and ornate windows are the school's joy and pride. Ruby is glad her dad is there to help her get settled in. None of the kids are due to start arriving for another hour.

As she and her dad walk past the giant evergreen tree, a person slumped on the steps of her dorm comes into full view.

Professor Alvarez goes up to Jesse on the steps and stretches out his hand to him. Jesse looks up at them awkwardly.

"I'm Professor Alvarez, and this is my daughter Ruby," Ruben puts his hand out.

Jesse's face turns bright red, and he drops his acceptance letter. He tries one more time to wipe the sap off his fingers and shakes the Professor's hand.

Ruby? Did I just hear him say "Ruby"? Cling to a girl?

Jesse shakes off his surprise and picks up his letter.

"Hi," says Jesse softly. "I'm early. My name is Jesse, but everyone calls me Rocky."

"Come on, Rock Man, let me see your admission sheet. We will find your dorm." Professor Alvarez puts his hand out for the sheet.

Jesse stands up and hands him the barely legible tattered paper.

"I'm assigned to Levi lodge," answers Jesse, pointing behind him.

"Okay, sure, the same dorm as my daughter here, groovy Ruby."

"Dad!" grimaces Ruby with a red face to match her hair.

The professor grins, "Let's go in. Where is your bag, Rock Man?" Professor Alvarez enquires, looking around.

"Uh . . . I . . . kind . . . of lost it," Jesse says, looking down, and pokes his boot into the doormat. "And they call me Rocky, not Rock Man," Jesse points out.

The professor grins at the nervous new student. The oversized arched wooden double doors squeak as the three of them step inside the Levi lodge dorms. The entrance awes Jesse.

"Whoa!" Jesse exclaims quietly.

"Yeah!" Ruby responds with excitement. Their voices echo off the carved gray stone walls.

Professor Alvarez smiles, enjoying their reaction to the view inside.

Stone floors with massive ornate rugs lay about the space. There are fireplaces on both ends of the lobby. Elaborate sets of stairs in the center lead to the second floor, one for the girls' side and one for the boys'. Tall arched windows line the sides with vaulted stone arch ceilings. At the end, a set of two-story windows frames the pines that cover the campus.

Jesse chokes back the tears. *I went from homeless to Spanish Harlem; to this mansion in eight months. You are so good, God. Did I already find part of the prophecy? Is that professor's daughter going to be important in my future? How do I fit in this amazing place?*

Within Levi lodge, there are two dorm rooms for girls and two for boys, with the floor leaders having their rooms. Jesse is assigned the first boys' room.

"Okay, Rock Man, if you need anything, just tell your floor leader, and he will get it for you."

Professor Alvarez has a hint of a Spanish accent and looks compassionately at the lonely boy who stands before them. Jesse finds it comforting to hear the professor's Spanish accent. Manuel and his family sent him off, and now he is greeted by the same Spanish accent here.

Jesse opens one of the giant arched wooden doors of his dorm and peers inside.

"See ya later, Jesse. After I get unpacked, I'll show you around the campus. You'll like it here, Jesse, you'll see! Lighten up and relax! My dad is just giving you a hard time about your nickname," Ruby tells Jesse as she heads across the commons area and then to the girl's side.

Letting her dad lead the way, Ruby also tells herself to relax, but it isn't working.

Ruby glances back at Jesse; he looks anxious and alone standing in the doorway, looking into the room that will be his home for the next two years.

I really feel that guy is very anointed and great in the Lord. I hope we get to be friends.

Ruby feels a strange spiritual connection with Jesse that she has never known before.

Each dorm in Levi lodge is two levels high; the top is open to the ceiling and windows, making a glorious view. This level is the living area with a fireplace, surrounding bookshelves, and plush leather couches — the bottom level houses three sets of bunk beds, carved wood armoires, and a shower room. The smell of leather couches and firewood adds to the ambiance. The dorms are very inviting, with rocked walls and oriental rugs on the floors.

Ruby hurries to put her stuff up. She puts her sweatshirt on one of the top bunks along with her satin pillow, hoping the other girls don't all take the top beds.

I wonder what the other girls will be like that will live here with me.

Before she leaves her new dorm, she takes in the incredible view of the posh living space. Ruby stops everything, zips up the wrought iron spiral stairs, and sits on the oversized leather couch looking out on the top floor. She marvels, *it is so pretty here!*

She stretches her hands to the air and says, "Oh, Lord, thank you for getting me to this point. Help me every step of the way. Put me where you want me, not where I think I should be, but I really do like the music program here, you know."

With joy, she spins playfully around her room, and then her thoughts turn to Jesse.

I feel the need to check on that guy. He doesn't have anyone here, and I can make him feel comfortable. Besides, I find him interesting; there's something different about him.

Ruby leaves her paperwork on the desk in her quarters; none of the floor leaders are around due to staff meetings in the Academic Towers. With a smile, she heads out to find Jesse. The professor's daughter exits her dorm from the top floor and takes the massive staircase down to the commons area. Then, she makes her way through the multiple sets of tables and chairs for studying, and groups of couches spread out through the center area between the girls' and boys' sides.

Devin wakes to the hum of the bus. He has slept till noon. In the full daylight, he now realizes he is deep in the mountains. High rock walls on one side of the bus; and a forceful flowing river full of river rock and more granite cliffs on the other side, squeeze the road. His heart races a little when the bus flies around the curves, and he can no longer see the edge of the road, and the view is straight down, way down. He swallows hard and, instead, chooses to look straight ahead at the road. His attention turns to his destination. At this pace, he's sure he will be there in time for lunch.

Devin wonders if anyone else on the bus is going

to SWA. He asks the Lord, waits, but gets no answer at the moment. Soon, the young traveler will know. Just then, he spots the sign out the window. A large metal eagle with its wings in full flight cradled over the large rock sign that is swinging on huge chains declares: "Welcome to Spirit Wings Academy, home of the **Warriors In God's Service**. **(WINGS)** Devin envisions in his imagination the sign dropping on top of the bus and smashing it in two. He shakes his head to wake up. Reality is here; and it is in God's hands; he has arrived!

The campus is even fancier than the pictures online. I can't believe this is where I am going to live now! I'm gonna take pictures and send them to the guys back home.

Earlier, when Eric and his parents stop for breakfast in a posh pancake house, he notices a man eating next to them. He is alone and cowering in his booth. Eric thinks as he asks the Lord, *"How can people get to look so creepy?"*

"It takes years to get that way or many bad things all at once. He is just looking for some good news from someone with a kind word," says the familiar voice in his head, which he knows belongs to the Lord.

What can I say to him? I'm a kid; adults don't like kids that much; I think, unless they know them.

Eric glances into the tired eyes of the man. He appears to be about thirty, but his eyes look like that of an old man's, cloudy and dull. In an instant, Eric sees a vision of smoke and drugs, with people around a glass table. What is the razor blade for? Eric's heart pounds wildly, and suddenly he is back at his booth. Mom and dad are busy with their pancakes and coffee. He looks for the guy with the cloudy eyes.

Still there? Good. I have got to give him hope somehow.

Eric doesn't believe it; he walks right by the guy and doesn't say a word. Their eyes meet, and Eric tries to convey all he knows about the love of Yeshuah in one look. The man looks down, stirring his coffee with a faraway look in his eyes.

Stupid! Eric tells himself, *If I don't get a backbone at SWA, I never will.*

Back in their luxury car, Eric bundles up in a blanket in the back seat, feeling the weight of guilt for missing the opportunity to help the poor man. He silently vows never to blunder that chance again. The Rolls starts up, and soon enough, they are well on their way once again with two more hours to drive. With his thoughts mixed in with the hum of the road, Eric again questions whether people will treat him differently if they know his family is wealthy. The shiny Rolls Royce turns, heading up the curvy mountain road and disappears into the pines. There is not much that states wealth more than a Rolls Royce. So, with the arrival of this rolling luxury car, he is about to find out.

At almost noon, Ruby expects to find Jesse outside

in the great weather. But he is nowhere to be found. Ruby simply chooses not to believe he'd still be in his quarters on such a gorgeous day in a place like this.

Where can he be?

Jesse *is* in his quarters, asleep. His bunk has no bedding yet or pillows, his jacket is rolled up under his head, and his wrinkled acceptance letter lies next to his head on the bare mattress. He had a hard time hitchhiking to get to SWA, and it is his chance to sleep without worrying about being safe. Still, in his sleep, he jerks and tosses as his dreams take him places he does not want to go. Demonic faces yell at him. Snakes and bugs show up in ordinary places such as suitcases and laundry baskets. He struggles to get the words out, his face freezing in a panic: "*In . . . the . . . nnname . . .* he tries again, *IN THE NAME OF JESUS!*"

Each word grows in volume and strength as they come out. The area clears of threat; peace enters, and it is okay again. Jesse finds himself sitting up on the bed, sweating and breathing heavily. He worries that he just yelled out loud. *If this happens around my dorm mates, I will simply crawl under a rock.* He lets himself drop back down; he can sleep now. He never has two bad dreams at a time. He feels safe and needs to find the strength to face all the challenges of his new life, here in the mountains of Colorado.

"Thank you, Jesus," slips from his lips as sleep comes once more. Sunlight is streaming into his room, warming the stone surfaces and rugs on the floor. Ruby stands in his doorway; she backs into the hall quietly.

Why does he have his door open if he is sleeping?

As she turns around, she runs into the boys' floor leader; he has his head down and is muttering something.

"Oh, sorry, I didn't know anyone was here yet," Ruby says.

She steps back, looking at the blonde young man's muscular build in his early twenties with an SWA cap on.

"Girls' dorms are on the other side," he points to the other side stoically. "The signs clearly show —" Jamie, the floor leader, is interrupted by Ruby.

"You're new here, aren't you? Well, I know you are going to love it here! Welcome to Spirit Wings Academy." Ruby tells him, turning quickly to head across the commons area to the girls' side.

Jamie thinks: *That is my line, Welcome to, blah, blah, blah....*

Ruby stops in the middle of the commons area she scolds herself: *I sound like a silly schoolgirl, going on like that!*

She listens . . . *a bus? Classmates finally!* Ruby runs out to check out the new arrivals. It is quite a distance to the front entry where the buses unload. Posted everywhere are signs pointing to all four dorms that spread out in all four corners of campus.

Floor leaders in SWA caps with clipboards stand in front of the bus, taking enrollment papers and pointing out the dorms. There are roughly three tribes per dorm; girls' first floor, and boys' next floor. The exception is

Levi tribe with their dorm next to the sanctuary. Ruby can't believe all these kids are her age and follow Jesus. *There are more people here than go to my whole church!* Professor Alvarez has his SWA cap on, too, as he puts his hand on Ruby's shoulder.

He smiles and says, "Have you ever seen so many radicals in your life, Groovy Ruby?"

"Dad," says Ruby rolling her eyes, "don't call me that here!"

"Excuse me, please," Jamie steps down to take his place with the other floor leaders.

"He is new, Dad. I just know he will be a great asset to SWA," declares Ruby.

"He seems a bit cold to me," Ruben tussles Ruby's hair.

"Not the hair, Dad! Not the hair."

Watching for anyone that might belong to Levi lodge and will be in her tribe, she nervously straightens her bangs.

To Devin's surprise, everyone on the bus is cadets going to the academy. Devin gets down from the bus and starts looking for anyone else who is dark-skinned. Tucked under his arm is a black leather duffle bag.

I hope I am not the only black dude here. I see Asians, and Latinos; I hope they don't treat me differently.

A black Rolls Royce pulls up next to Devin.

"Now, that's what I'm talking about!" Devin smooth's his hair in the car's reflection as the back door opens. Eric steps out and looks around.

"Another skinny white boy, just what I need," Devin says as he walks toward Jamie, the counselor Ruby saw. Jamie is from Minnesota: fair complexion, blonde, with blue eyes, and a weightlifter — not so skinny. Embroidered on his SWA polo shirt is his name.

"Hey counselor guy, am I the only black dude here?" asks Devin, playing up his attitude.

Jamie just points to Audrey, a beautiful Afro-American student. She is standing in line to hand in her dorm assignment. She is Jamaican. Several chartered buses are just pulling in. The first has arrived, bringing fifty-five first-year and second-year cadets. Students will continue to come in over the next few hours.

"I think I am going to like it here," Devin says as he walks toward Audrey.

Eric is in a hurry to get out of his parent's luxury car and unload before anyone sees him in it, missing Devin using his door as a mirror.

"Just hug me and let me go. I will be fine. Love you, mom, dad, later!" says Eric trying to hurry them off.

Oh, man, Eric thinks; *I miss them already!*

Jesse sleeps through lunch. Everyone else enjoys the beauty of the angled glass ceiling in the dining hall. Great decorative bentwood beams divide the glass panels on the ceiling that bend and run the wall. Tall evergreen trees hug the sides outside, giving shade, as the second-year students check out the "Newbies". The staff sits at their tables, looking over the student body. The General will soon greet the new cadets and gather them to their tribes. He is known to sit randomly with the kids in the dining hall on occasions.

Scarves and plaid shirts are fashionable among the SWA crowd. Most have Christian T-shirts and caps. Cross necklaces and bracelets can stay on all year, but the rest will have to go for SWA uniforms: hiking boots, polo shirts, t-shirts, and jeans.

CHAPTER FOUR

COMING TOGETHER OR FALLING APART

That afternoon, all the new students gather for their first assembly at SWA. The sanctuary fills with nervous happy youth.

Shekinah Sanctuary is not like any church Jesse has ever been to — which is a limited number anyway. Two funerals and a wedding are the extent of churchgoing for Jesse. Except for José's church of course. To him, the massive building looks like a museum or a courthouse. It has Gothic cathedral architecture; with massive stone columns, and twelve hand-woven flags; with Israel's twelve tribes on them that hang on the outside walls in each of the twelve alcoves. Massive arched decorative columns are the main pillars that hold up the structure. Multiple sets of arched windows line opposite walls over forty feet high, where light pours in, leaving arched shaped sunshine in the interior.

The chatter of young voices subsides as the General walks up to the podium. The cadets are dwarfed by the immense grey fluted pillars that run in two rows through the sanctuary; and the lofty ceiling of bentwood and stone. All eyes are on the General as he adjusts his notes and prepares to address the new recruits. "Newbies" as they are referred to by the older students. In his early thirties, the General is a trim man, having shoulder-length, straight, light brown hair with well-trimmed facial hair and blue-gray eyes. He always wears plaid shirts, jeans, and a wedding ring.

Jesse and Ruby stand off to the side waiting for the speech, along with the rest of the first-year student body. Twelve rugs lie on the floor while all the pews are stacked up and placed off to the sides for today's event.

"Where are the birds?" Jesse asks Ruby in a whisper.

"Birds, what birds?" Ruby leans over to say.

"Isn't this a sanctuary?" asks Jesse, confused.

Ruby grins, "A sanctuary is a safe place; the worship area of a church is called a sanctuary. What do they call it in your church?"

"I dunno . . . everything is in Spanish most of the

time," Jesse blushes. A few girls giggle next to them. Jesse's face turns red.

To Jesse's relief, the General begins his address:

"I am the General. That is what you will call me. I have no need for a name here; my identity is all wrapped up in Christ. I must decrease that He may enlarge. Pride, you will find, is your biggest enemy, the enemy — in all of us."

"Let us begin with seeking God's favor on this gathering. Father God, here we are seeking Your favor and will. Let Your Spirit fill every cell of our beings. Bind us together as one. We will not go any farther without You."

There is complete silence, Ruby's heart pounds.

Does the General expect one of us kids to give a word of knowledge right away? She wonders.

She wishes she had the peace to seek for a word, but young Ruby knows she does not. Everyone holds their breath till a firm voice rings out and echoes through the Shekinah Sanctuary.

"Some of you will not complete your term; some of you, even now, think you are ready to be sent out. A few of you the enemy will try to use. They that seek Me will find Me. You know My voice. Your compassion is the key to the anointing. I am with you always even unto the end of this age."

Ruby knows that voice; it is Jesse's. She looks over to the right. He is shaking with his head bowed, and he doesn't look at anyone.

Wow, she thinks: *he's got guts.*

The General speaks up, "Good; now it is your job to discern. You may take council in friends and leaders, but your heart must be connected to the Spirit of Truth to decide. You are not here by accident; this is a day of destiny."

Jesse gasps, *day of destiny! You have my attention, Lord. Is my red ruby a . . . girl? I thought I'd find an expensive gem or something. Yesterday, when I promised to obey Your voice, I didn't expect to give a word of knowledge to the whole assembly on the first day. What are You doing to me?*

Jesse wipes the sweat off his brow.

The General continues, "Before me, I see a mighty army. You are not yet all arrayed with advanced armor or weaponry. But this I know . . . the Lord of Hosts handpicked you and deep inside you He instilled the militant desire to fight. The world is full of violence and injustice. We will cry out to the Righteous God to stop the earth's great injustices and judge the wicked. [8]We cry out for the peace of Israel. They shall prosper that love thee! We fight to redeem the hearts and minds of the lost, waiting for the final battle when Jesus and His bride take the earth back from the Dragon. **Revelation 17:14**; and **Revelation 12:17.** We fight for a single soul; we fight for the souls of entire nations. **For the weapons of our**

---

[8] **Psalm 122:6** Pray for the peace of Jerusalem! May they be secure who love you!

warfare are not of the flesh but have divine power to destroy strongholds. II Corinthians 10:4. Here you will learn the ways of our God, learn to be a team; and most of all, to love. If we fail to love, we fail everything. The ways of the Lord are righteous and true. Jesus is our bright shining light. He will always be faithful. He holds us together and makes us one. For Him, we fight the darkness, love the unlovable, and die to our selfish ways. **Blessed be the LORD, my rock, who trains my hands for war, and my fingers for battle; Psalm 144:1.** Father God will one day set His throne on the earth and call it home. New Jerusalem, His glorious city, will come down. In these, the last days, you cadets; you have been born to see Revelation play out in your lifetime.

"Now, when I call your name, come and take your place on your tribal rug. Your tribal captain will assign you to a three-man cell group; pardon the expression MAN, girls . . . As you know in the Bible, the word man often refers to ISH or the seed of Adam. We are a family and a war unit; we are a family first; this is your home for the next two years." (See "Types and Shadows 5.)

Ruby's name comes right away, just another benefit of being an Alvarez. Since they are both assigned Levi lodge, Ruby knows Jesse is in her tribe. The *other* tribes' placement is not forthwith as they only know which lodge, not their particular tribe. (The Levi lodge, only houses Levi tribe as the priestly tribe that serves the others.)

There is more to that boy than meets the eye; Ruby

realizes as she heads over to the tribe of Levi rug.

Eric, Devin, and Jesse eventually take their turn and step onto the Levi rug. The words "day of destiny" still echoes in Jesse's head.

Why are those guys on the Judah rug all giving high fives to each other and acting as if they won the lottery? Jesse wonders.

He can't help frowning at them, as if he can put them in their place with his eyes.

"What's their deal?" Jesse finally asks the guy beside him.

Eric tells him, "The tribe of Judah are praise and worship majors; they are the best of the best in this place."

Eric's shirt is a purple and white geometric print, his brown hair touches his collar, and his eyes are kind, making Jesse comfortable with him.

"They don't look that great to me," Jesse observes.

Devin leans over, "They lead worship, pick the songs and everything. I hope they have guitars and drums, or else I'll just prefer silence."

"Give me rowdy or give me silence!" declares Jesse.

All the boys nod.

After the assembly of first-year students is concluded. A British female voice on the loudspeaker announces, "First-year cadets meet in your Tribal homerooms for orientation."

That voice will soon be as familiar as their moms', as the next two years as announcements come every forty-five minutes during school hours, and sometimes on the dorm speakers. It is a very prim and proper voice and somewhat perky even to the point of being annoying to some.

All the new cadets join all the second-year cadets on the campus on this day. There are also numerous angels and some dark creatures here and there.

Both Academic Towers are six stories high, with eight sides, making them round in an octagonal shape. A bridge walkway attaches to the set of towers. On the top level of both towers is a prayer room open day and night. It provides the best view of the campus. There is even access to the roof when weather permits.

Adora White is Ruben Alvarez's younger sister and the SWA dance teacher; she is the Levi tribe homeroom teacher. Her classroom is the dance room. A strip of mirrors reflects the arched windows. She comes out in a flowing ballet outfit, sweeping gracefully to the podium and addressing the twelve new cadets of the Levi tribe. Her electric blue hair flashes in the sunlight.

"I am Professor Adora White, your tribal captain. The selected ones of this special tribe are the student body's backbone, radicals, and leaders. That is your identity; perceive who Elohim says you are — not caring about being scrutinized in many religious assemblies; as to your intentions and purity. Many outside this campus think the Devil is the only supernatural power on the earth, and if you have power, it must be of the Devil. You may not feel spiritually gifted; but you have spiritual gifts, freely given by the Spirit. By tomorrow I want you to find in your Bibles the verse that speaks of the gifts of God, given with no repentance. Now, Levi is the priestly tribe, a servant to all; there is no room for pride or arrogance in this tribe. To be joined, like a wreath of flowers joined to make a circle, woven in and out. That is what Levi is in Hebrew."

Professor White gracefully illustrates with her hands and arms.

"You should strive to keep unity among the cadets and pray that the Lord will reunite Judah and Ephraim. Your homework tonight is to read **Ezekiel 37**. Your floor leaders have prayed and fasted before making up your class schedule and cell group assignments. There will be no changes — Worship is at seven o'clock in the morning, leaders will be doing worship for the first week. Until the loudspeaker dismisses you, remain here; and welcome to Spirit Wings Academy newbies . . . I mean, cadets!" Professor White ends her orientation.

She gracefully walks over to hug her niece, Ruby.

"Congratulations on getting accepted this year, Ruby; it's going to be a good year," Professor Adora tells her. "I will leave you to get to know your classmates."

"Okay, Aunt Adora, I will see you around!" Ruby tells her.

Ruby nervously looks around at all her new classmates. *Who should I talk to first?*

Everyone mingles around the room, some sitting in the deep-set window ledges of carved stone. Devin quickly glances in the full-length mirror to check his hair. He sees Ruby doing the same and asks her, "So . . . did Judah and Ephraim break up? What is she talking about?" Devin has no clue.

"I believe it is about the lost ten tribes of Israel, or maybe about the Gentiles and Jews becoming 'One new man' in the Messiah," Ruby responds.

"Clear as mud," Devin answers back.

Eric too, asks Ruby, as she seems to be the one with all the answers today, "Do we have to do ballet here? Is it mandatory?"

Ruby smirks, "Don't worry; I think the boys get to do mime and clowning; for street ministry!"

"Oh, great. I feel so much better!" Eric suggests, "Let's compare schedules and see if we have any classes together. I got Cell Groups, Science and the Bible; Demonology 101 after that."

They all shake their heads, yes. "Umm . . . Law and the Prophets is the fourth period?"

"Yep," they all chime in.

"Last are Spiritual Warfare, Prayer and Fasting Principles 101 and Introduction to Mimes and Clowning - Street ministry."

"Oh, no, I've got Prophetic Dance - Street Ministry. That's my aunt's class, but I can't dance," notes Ruby.

"Looks like we're stuck together all day; except for

the last hour," Devin comments happily. "Since all three of us are in the same cell, I guess we should hang out together, okay?"

Ruby is glad they are put together, but not ready to admit it.

The question is, who is in Jesse's cell group? Where did Jesse go? He was here just a minute ago. Ruby scans the room for him.

She wonders if he hates his cell group assignment.

The loudspeaker squeals as the British woman's voice comes over it, "Free time is now in effect till supper. Welcome to Spirit Wings Academy. Use your time well; little soldiers!"

The woman's British accent is sickeningly sweet, but all welcome the news of the free time.

With a "Yay!" kids begin to scatter all over campus. Some are dancing, playing guitars, climbing trees, or just talking in groups. The older second-year students tend to keep to themselves.

All members of the Judah tribe gather in the attic study hall of their dorm, Lion - East Gate.

"I feel the need to seek the Lord," states Aurora Oliver, captain of the Judah tribe and worship leader. She is a strong-featured twenty-something woman with compassionate eyes. Besides leading worship and being a floor leader, she teaches worship classes.

"We have a lot of others counting on us to create an atmosphere of praise that will open the heavens," she adds.

Many nod in agreement. Others look envious of the fun below. They get on the floor and begin to call on Elohim, first and second-year cadets together. Outside there is laughter, and kids are running around.

Jesse is alone at the back of campus, where he has found an outcropping of rocks. If his floor leader sees him, he will surely get in trouble for ignoring the caution sign warning of a steep cliff. Jesse needs to be alone with the Lord. He is aware that he should get to know his cell members, but he just has to get away and get his head together. He was never much of a team player. At the Perez's, Jesse didn't know anyone else. He didn't make any friends at school. He begins feeling Ruach HaKodesh, bringing peace to his heart; he is ready to go on now and face his cell group. He hopes they will like him.

Why am I stuck with two girls in my cell group? Ruby is cool, but some girls giggle too much. I need understanding on this red ruby thing . . . is it a person? Is it Ruby? I think she is way above me spiritually.

Jesse misses Manuel back in New York; they understood each other. He wishes he could ask him if he thought the red gem prophecy was about a person.

During supper on the first day, everyone is seated according to tribe and cell group. Ruby looks for Jesse; there he is sitting two kids down. He looks as though he doesn't want to be there. Everyone around him chatters away. He just sits there; Ruby catches his eye and gives a little wave. He waves and smiles slightly.

Everyone notices that Judah's table is served first.
(See "Types and Shadows" 5)

Figures, boy, sure smells good though! Jesse thinks.

Jesse is delighted with the steak and rolls.

I never had food this good my entire life! Well, maybe Poppy's Christmas dinners at his swanky restaurants. He is a strange old man with an accent, but I like him.

The loudspeaker cuts into Jesse's memories.

"The staff will reward cake and ice cream to the cleanest dorm every Friday, so let's make those beds spiffy, shall we?"

Kristen is in Jesse's cell group. However, she wears flashy clothes and talks way too loud for Jesse's comfort. Kristen is used to getting her way, and she is not beyond making a scene if it suits her purpose. Her red hair matches her angry red face.

"How can you stick me with these underachievers? I want to talk to someone in charge!" she yells, standing up, waving her fork.

The kids respond mockingly with a loud "OOOHHH."

Kristen glances around to see who is paying attention to her little fit. The room falls silent; even the tinkling of silverware stops for a small moment. Kristen remains standing up, puts on her best frown. No leaders acknowledge her; soon; she sits back down, and the dining hall is back to normal.

"No offense; you two. I just belong over there," Kristen points to the Judah corner of the room. "I have a prophecy that I will do great exploits for the Kingdom of God. That must mean Judah tribe, not Levi."

No one comments on her statement of greatness.

Jesse and the other cell member, Audrey, keep their eyes on their plates. To Jesse, each bite of food takes forever to chew. The sooner supper is over, the better.

Audrey whispers to Jesse, "I bet she will be out of our cell by morning."

"Fine with me," says Jesse.

After the students leave for their dorms, the General turns on the large TV in the dining hall. The adults watch the evening news as the world is enduring wars, natural catastrophes, and terrorist acts in diverse places. Terrorism in the nation is almost a weekly event. Authorities are dealing with attempted car bombs, attacks on national monuments, and even food tainting. Each day a specific color is shown to represent the level of the terrorist threat. This week the color is yellow for "elevated." It has been six months since it was a lower threat of blue for "guarded" or green for "low." They keep up with the latest news on Israel so that they can pray for her effectively.

The next day classes begin. First-year students soon learn all their classes are in the East Academic Tower. First-hour cell groups assemble in their homeroom.

Jesse, Audrey, and Kristen, the raving screamer, are stuck together for half an hour. Jesse has his arms crossed and is leaning in the opposite direction of his group. The floor leaders go from cell to cell with instructions, as Professor Adora White looks on.

"Well, we better have all these questions answered by the time Jamie gets here. I, for one, don't want bad marks on the first day," snorts Kristen.

"Okay, then, what are you two's favorite place in the world, and why?" reads Jesse from their devotional sheet.

Kristen answers first.

"My favorite place in the whole world is over there, where the Judah tribe meets. Lion lodge, that is where a person can go to high places."

Her eyes glaze over with images of glory.

Audrey answers next, "Oh, I don't know . . . the mall, I guess. I don't care about places. It's the people that make a location attractive."

Audrey feels her answer is better than Kristen's any day.

"And you, Jesse, what is your answer?" Audrey knows they have to know each other better in cell class.

"I . . . uh . . . right now, I guess it's behind the campus. There is a rocky cliff; you can see way down. I can feel so close to God there."

Jesse's face flushes; he has just said something personal about himself to two girls.

Why has God punished me with this cell

assignment? Have I gotten prideful or something?

Audrey is alarmed, *Is he crazy? Close to death is more like it, these mountains are dangerous. In Jamaica, I know what to be scared of, here I'm scared of everything.*

Jamie Gerard walks up to the three. "Okay," he says, marking in his clipboard. "I am Jamie, as you know, your counselor; and boys' floor leader. Have we gotten acquainted yet? Kristen, despite your scene at supper yesterday, I feel this cell is a good fit for you."

Good for puking, Jesse thinks.

"Do you know everyone else's name, where they are from, and their majors?" asks Jamie.

Jesse, Kristen, and Audrey look at each other. "No," cell group ten all say together.

"Everyone else in the room is going on to the next step, you guys better get with it," Jamie tells them as he heads for the next table.

"Okay," Kristen takes over. "Majors," she demands, ready to write it down.

"Deliverance (casting out demons)," replies Jesse, "and everyone calls me Rocky."

"Prophecy," Audrey answers, "and to be called Aud is not my favorite; it is too close to odd, as in weird."

Jesse recalls when people called him hurtful things. He can relate to Audrey in that instance.

"And my major . . . ," says Kristen in a boisterous voice, "is street ministry." [9]All the world's is a stage; it is

---

[9] Quote from Shakespeare, *As You Like It*, scene 2, act 5. *"All the*

my calling and my home." She dramatically looks off into the distance, her hands poised in the air.

Jesse wants to roll his eyes, but he knows how he feels when people put him down. The last thing he wants is to be critical and harsh, even if it is Kristen the screamer carrying on. Jesse glances over to his new friends Eric, Devin, and Ruby, in cell group nine. They are laughing and having a good time.

Science class is next for Levi and Benjamin tribes. Doctor L. Luz gives his usual philosophy demonstration to the twenty-five or so kids in the East Academic Tower's second-floor lecture room. The classroom has eight walls with three huge beveled leaded glass windows on each wall and is covered with heavy velvet curtains. The classroom is dark, with the curtains drawn for a dramatic atmosphere and just a few dim lights on.

Everyone sits at the long half curved tables and benches. Doctor Luz addresses the new group of cadets.

"I imagine you are all passionate about your Bible classes. Every class will contain powerful spiritual subjects. I will show you God in science, and that science is in the Bible. Here in my hand is a crystal that represents you."

He holds out a diamond-shaped crystal about the size of an egg.

"In this condition, it is plain, or dull to the human mind. By exposing it to light, its refractive properties cause

---

world's a stage...

light to split into a rainbow spectrum. The light represents Ruach HaKodesh; you are the crystal. The Bible, without the influence of Ruach HaKodesh, is not understandable, plain, or dull to the human mind. I welcome Ruach HaKodesh in this room as the greatest teacher; I am his instrument."

Devin, in the front row, raises his hand.

"Sir, what is Ruach HaKodesh?" Devin is confused by the term.

Doctor Luz writes it on the board, "Not what, but who? Ruach HaKodesh, Hebrew for Holy Spirit, also means Holy breath or wind."

Ruby tells Jesse, "I knew that."

Jesse smiles.

Now, Doctor Luz nods to his aid Jennifer who is standing by. She pulls the heavy braided cord, and all the curtains draw back, bathing the room with direct sunlight and thousands of little rainbows. The leaded glass windows are beveled, and the morning sun is hitting them full on. The kids gasp with delight. It is dramatic and beautiful.

Doctor Luz smiles. He tells Jennifer, "I never get tired of doing that!" Then he divulges to the class, "Every one of you who graduates will get a crystal just like this one from me at the end of your second year."

"God is light. This week we will study natural light properties and references to God and light in the scriptures. There are seven colors in the rainbow and seven spirits of God. Now, in the light spectrum, there are wave energies unseen by the human eye, yet they are very real and affect our natural world, just like the unseen world of the spirit!"

The doctor's eyes flash with excitement as he shares these delightful revelations with his class. Most don't know the Dr. is a medical doctor.

"Okay, kids keep quiet about what you just saw so that you don't ruin the surprise for the next class," Jennifer says, as she pulls the curtains closed. She is simply dressed in jeans and an SWA shirt and has a wedding ring; however, she has a pair of elegant tan pumps. They seem out of place in the rugged mountains, but Jennifer is known to have many pairs of sleek footwear. She always manages to get all over campus in her heels.

Everyone grins and nods in agreement as they leave the dark lecture room. The cadets also realize Jennifer's voice is the one they hear over the loudspeaker all the time. She is young, in her early thirties, and calls cookies, biscuits.

She announces, "Period two is over, and period three will begin in ten minutes. At the end of the week, uniforms will be ready, and street clothes will be off-limits at that time. Just a few more days, kiddies and those flip-flops will be gone. That is all."

However, Jennifer will not lose her glamor heels, wearing them all year, except for snowstorms. Her voice is getting on Ruby's nerves.

Someone should show her some professionalism.

The first day of real classes is over. Everyone

settles in for the night.

So here we all are in our jammies, thinks Ruby excitedly, looking around her dorm room. *Yay! Oh, I sound perky like the loudspeaker lady; I just need the accent. I need to be less judgmental.*

All the girls have jockeyed for position on the top bunks. So far, Ruby is stuck on a lower bed. One bed is empty, waiting for a student who has not yet arrived.

Milagros, Millie for short, has on headgear for her braces, black hair, and big brown eyes. Gloria's short blonde hair is falling on her face, and she has painted her toenails hot pink. Faith is refolding her clothes and talks about her favorite singers at SWA. She wears a shiny black shirt that Ruby admires; her medium-length hair is blonde with brown, wavy, and multi-layered streaks. No one knows who the sixth girl is; she hasn't shown up yet. Ruby notices everyone has spiritual names, except for her and Audrey. Even Milagros; is Spanish for "miracle." Audrey has brought a pile of books to school with her; she is lovingly setting them inside her armoire. Ruby wonders if the others notice the coincidence in the names.

If the sixth girl's name is GRACE, I am gonna freak out! I wonder how Jesse and the guys are doing. At least Jesse got in the same room with the gang. He really lost out on the cells thing! Audrey is nice, but Kristen is a handful. Kristen is stuck with the second-year girls in her dorm, serves her right! There I go being critical again.

Eric, Devin, and Jesse are comparing music tastes. Yosef, the boy from Israel, is still in the shower. There is a knock on their big double pine doors; Jesse goes to answer it. It is Jamie with a sack. Jamie stares at Jesse in the doorway; Jesse glares back. Neither one speaks. After a moment, Jamie shoves the bag into Jesse's chest, leans over, and whispers to Jesse so that no one else can hear.

"This is for you; don't lose it this time. The General says you have a history of being a runaway, and that you hitchhiked here without telling your host family. I am supposed to keep an eye on you, Jesse. Don't blow it; this is not a place for flakes that don't have any loyalty."

Jamie drops his stare from Jesse and walks on down the hall.

Everyone is looking to see what Jesse has.

Jesse just says, "Lost my backpack. Jamie had to come up with some stuff for me until uniforms come in."

"Bummer," says Devin.

Jesse doesn't respond; he looks a million miles away.

"Hey," says Eric. "I have two of everything. You can borrow some stuff from me."

Eric goes to his over-stuffed armoire and pulls out a ski coat.

"Here, I hear it might snow soon," says Eric as he holds the coat out to Jesse.

Jesse still doesn't say a word. Eric shrugs his shoulders and tosses the coat on Jesse's bed. Yosef shows up, his hair dripping from the showers. He is Israeli, and everyone treats him like royalty, being a Messianic Jew. His accent makes him hard to understand at first, but the boys are now helping the adults understand him. Yosef senses the tension in the room and asks what is going on. They tell him Jesse is upset and they don't dare ask him why; his eyes say back off. Jesse places the coat in the nearly empty armoire along with the sack Jamie brought him. He doesn't bother to put things in drawers or hang up the nice new jacket.

At nine-thirty at night, Jamie comes through to shut out the lights, and the boys are alone with their thoughts. Jesse begs the Lord to keep the tears from his eyes. They simply can't learn he was homeless ten months ago. He wants to save what little pride he has left.

Everyone settles in their bunks. Eric can hear Devin's music player from the top bunk. He wishes Jesse didn't go to bed in a bad mood. Every time his body moves, Eric's bed squeaks. Lying motionless on the top bunk proves to be painful. He lies in one position till his back hurts and finally rolls over. Tomorrow Eric will take another available bunk bed. There are only four guys in Jesse's dorm; fortunately, there are six beds in each room.

Jesse smells the fresh, clean sheets on his bed; *this is high living. I'm sorry, Father God, for not being more thankful. You do so much for me, and I do so little for You. I'm gonna change that, though. We are going to have great adventures, You and me. I plead the blood of Jesus over my dreams. Jesus, You are wondrous to me*, Jesse prays. *I am ready for my gem and destiny, whatever or whoever they are.*

Jesse waits for the boys to sleep; then, he gets out

of bed and cracks open one of the double dorm doors. Now he can go to sleep.

On the girls' side of Levi lodge dorms, Ruby and her roommates are still fighting over the top bunks when it is lights out. For now, Millie and Ruby are stuck on the bottom ones. Tomorrow night they will see who sleeps where. Ruby has a plan, and she isn't talking. Millie is a Latino from Texas with five sisters at home; she is used to fighting for her rights. She is embarrassed to wear the headgear for her braces in front of the other girls. It makes her uncomfortable, but she manages to sleep her second night away from home.

CHAPTER FIVE

BAD DREAMS AND SILENT SCREAMS

The school day starts with a worship set in the sanctuary. After all, changing the atmosphere with adoration to Yahweh is a basis of spiritual warfare.

Ruby, Eric, and Devin find their way to class after breakfast. Breakfast is the topic of conversation.

"Best orange muffins I ever had," and "all the bacon I could eat," are comments heard everywhere.

Jesse walks alone to class; deep in his thoughts. Ruby wishes he was more social. All the new cadets feel a little anxious about starting their new life as a warrior in

Adonai's army.

After Doctor Luz's class, all of the Benjamin and Levi tribes are sitting in the East Academic Tower on the third floor. Ruby is grinning; her dear ol' dad is teaching Demonology 101.

"As I told you yesterday, my name is Professor Alvarez, and in this room; we will focus on the struggle in the unseen world of the spirit."

He points to the scripture carved on stone leaning in the corner of the lecture room.

For we do not wrestle against flesh and blood, but against the rulers, against the authorities, against the cosmic powers over this present darkness, against the spiritual forces of evil in the heavenly places.

Ephesians 6:12

"This year, you will memorize eighty scriptures to pass this class.

The class groans and the professor grins and continues without missing a beat.

"Ruach HaKodesh will teach you most of what you need. Without Him, all this will be meaningless. Discerning of spirits, the gift of faith, the helmet of salvation; there are many tools you can take advantage of. I intend to equip you with as many as you can possibly lay hold of. How far to go and how fast; is up to you — your dedication and zeal, or lack thereof. I will take questions for a few minutes then we will get down and dirty, so to speak."

A few hands fly up.

"Yes, you in the green shirt, what is your name and question?" Professor Alvarez asks.

"Eric Sinclair . . . can a Christian be possessed by a demon?" the young man asks.

"We open doors for the enemy, and that gives him access. That is where oppression comes in. Unclean spirits can oppress Christians, clear down to a cellular level."

"Oh," the kids respond.

"Yes, you on the front row," the professor says, pointing to the girl with a pastel scarf.

"Destiny Morris from North Dakota, if you see a demon does that mean you should cast it out?" she asks.

"Dark entities that manifest you have dominion over. You need to ask the Lord why He revealed this to you; and what He wants you to do. [10]If you cast it out and the person doesn't let God in their lives, seven stronger demons can come to take its place. Bringing down strongholds over regions and nations can be difficult, so you need to have a team, do not go solo. Understand? Well, we will define all these levels over the next two years. If there are no more questions, get your concordances out and

---

[10] Luke 11:24-26 "When the unclean spirit has gone out of a person, it passes through waterless places seeking rest, and finding none it says, 'I will return to my house from which I came.' And when it comes, it finds the house swept and put in order. Then it goes and brings seven other spirits more evil than itself, and they enter and dwell there. And the last state of that person is worse than the first."

get all the references for the words 'deaf' and 'dumb.' I want you to read and study them all by tomorrow so we can discuss them in class."

Books fly open as everyone slumps over their work.

Jesse gazes over at the girl from North Dakota.

Wow, that girl must be able to see demons like me. I have got to get the nerve up to talk to her. She is stunning, and I get thick-headed in front of pretty girls. Except for Ruby, I can dialogue with her. What was that girl's name? Something that starts with a "D". . . .

Jesse turns his thoughts to the demons in his dreams. He wishes he had the nerve to ask Professor Alvarez about them.

Across the curved wooden table, all the cadets work on assignments. Ruby and her cell are working together well; one is reading; another one is writing, and one looking up the next scripture. After fifteen minutes, Professor Alvarez interrupts the class's work.

"Jesse the Rock Man, what did the demons you saw in your dreams look like?" Jesse stares at the teacher in amazement.

"How did you know?" Jesse asks wide-eyed.

"Why, Ruach HaKodesh, of course. So please describe one to us, if it is not too personal," Professor Alvarez urges him on.

"Well, one had a wrinkled face, and it was angry. It yelled at me."

Jesse doesn't want everyone to think demons

oppress him, but he desperately needs some answers. "Did the Lord give me these dreams of demons?"

Professor Alvey (nickname for Professor Alvarez) leans forward and looks straight at Jesse.

"Did the dream scare you in any way?"

"Yeah, I couldn't even get the name of Jesus out; I was so scared." Jesse finds himself admitting it in front of everyone.

"Will everyone who has had dreams like Jesse's raise their hand?" the Professor asks.

Half the class raises their hand. Jesse draws a sigh of relief; he is not alone after all. The professor writes a scripture on the blackboard behind him.

-for God gave us a spirit not of fear but of power and love and self-control.

2 Timothy 1:7

"What does this say about scary dreams? Anyone?"

The Professor looks around for someone to answer.

One of the kids in the back by the door answers with a guess.

"So . . . if it brings us fear, it is not of God?"

"You will have to know the difference between Godly fear and the spirit of fear the enemy would put you under," the Professor says. "Daniel and others quaked in the presence of angels, and they were from the Lord. Develop discernment, people, discernment. Now! Take this scripture into account:

It is the Lord your God you shall fear. Him you

shall serve and by his name you shall swear. Deuteronomy 6:13

Professor Alvey sits down at his desk.

"So . . . why does He allow us to see these things?" Jesse continues.

Jesse is beginning to feel frustrated.

"Any demon the Lord reveals to you, you can take dominion over it, assuming you are right with the Lord, and not in agreement with the demonic entity. Answers will come in time. Some things we will wonder about for a long time. Sometimes we open doors by our own words or actions. Watching the wrong movies perhaps, buying a video game that has witchcraft, or even just being in a place where the demon has permission to be," Professor Alvarez suggests. "There are laws all spirits must obey, just like gravity is a law we experience. Some spirits are connected to a family line and have never been broken off the family; that is how many witches get their power. It 'runs' in the family."

The subject is riveting to the cadets because the professor is passionate about warfare.

"Period three begins in ten minutes." The loudspeaker cuts in on the class's discussion.

"Don't forget your reading assignments, people!" Professor Alvey tells the kids.

Ruby grins and waves to her dad as she heads out the door with the rest of the Levi and Benjamin tribes. Professor Alvey's next class is the Judah and Reuben tribes.

Jesse feels a load off his shoulders. Other kids have had the same experience. His heart swells with joy, over the beauty of the mountains and the whole Spirit Wings experience. His step is lighter, and he is in a great mood. He wants to tell the guys why he was so moody last night, but Kristen sets her hand on Jesse's shoulder just then. She is wearing a bright pink fuzzy shirt with feathers that make his nose tickle as small pink fuzz floats off her shirt into the air.

"So . . . Rock Man, did you get all sixteen scriptures down? I need a copy. Okay? Okay, good, later, Rock Man!" Kristen doesn't even wait for an answer; she struts off in her own little world.

"It's ROCKY, not Rock man." Jesse is left standing with his mouth open; there was no time to get in a word. Audrey nods at Jesse as they head for the third period Law and the Prophets class. Jesse nods back. He is content with his interaction; it is a start to fitting in, at least. Ruby runs to catch up to Destiny from first period.

"Hey, do you happen to be assigned dorm G2 Levi lodge?" Ruby asks her.

"Yes, how did you know?" Destiny asks back.

"I just did. We will be rooming together. Sorry, you are a little late to get a top bunk!" Ruby answers with a shrug of her shoulders. "Oh yeah, welcome to SWA, I know you're gonna love it here."

Destiny has fairly long dark brown hair, pretty features, and a mature strength about her. Destiny and her brother Jacob have been living in India as missionaries with their parents.

As Ruby walks away, she complains to God: *I guess you know everyone in my dorm room has cool spiritual names, but for me, and Audrey, of course. Destiny, Gloria, Faith, Milagros, and then plain ol' Ruby and Audrey.*

Ruby doesn't wait for God to answer; she is just complaining. Little does she know "Audrey" means noble strength.

Ruby steps into class; Destiny sits next to Gloria and Millie; next to her is Devin and Eric.

Jesse's thoughts are still on last hour's Demonology class. He wonders how he will have enough energy for Prayer and Fasting, Spiritual Warfare, and the Law and Prophets Class is just one floor up. He also wonders: *Is that cute girl that can see demons assigned to the Levi dorm?*

At noon everyone enjoys looking at the scenery around them through the glass windows in the dining hall.

Lunch was especially good today. Is it the mountain air or what? Ruby wonders.

Ruby catches her dad's eye at the head table; he winks at her.

Kristen seems quiet today, compared to yesterday, especially. She is always watching the Judah tribe; it is tiring for her cellmates: Audrey and Jesse. Faith looks pale, as though she is not feeling well.

After lunch, all first-year Levi and Benjamin tribes are on the East Tower's fifth floor. The view is breathtaking; the tops of all the buildings, the mountain range, all spread out before them. Often the professors have to pull the curtains to keep the cadets focused. The sister tower (west) is close enough to see inside the many windows — this too causes some distraction at times.

"Now, here is one thing I feel you need to be aware of in these last days."

The bald, muscle-bound ex-army professor writes on the board:

So everyone who acknowledges me before men, I also will acknowledge before my Father who is in heaven, but whoever denies me before men, I also will deny before my Father who is in heaven. "Do not think that I have come to bring peace to the earth. I have not come to bring peace, but a sword."

Matthew 10:32-34

"Due to the urgency of the hour, I feel the need to stress to you this major paradigm. Now . . . Peter denied Jesus three times and converted from self-centered to Christ-centered. The Anti-Christ, mark of the Beast, Armageddon, is nothing to fear; death is nothing to fear. if you are in Christ and He is in you. Never . . . I mean, NEVER deny Christ, even in the pain of death."

The Professor looks over his cadets. The girls are about to cry; the boys are wide-eyed.

The professor is concerned that he filled them with

fear and not empowerment, as he intended.

"But, my young warriors," the Professor then writes more on the board:

> **No, in all these things we are more than conquerors through him who loved us. For I am sure that neither death nor life, nor angels nor rulers, nor things present nor things to come, nor powers, nor height nor depth, nor anything else in all creation, will be able to separate us from the love of God in Christ Jesus our Lord.**
>
> **Romans 8:37-39**

"Okay . . . ," the Professor wipes his brow. "On with the lesson plan, starting with the Armor of God. Yes, wonderful thing is the armor of God. We can't go running around unprotected, now can we?" Professor Norman plops in his chair behind his large wooden desk and blows out a deep breath.

At the end of class, the new cadets somberly take the winding stairs to the top for their last course of the day. This room doubles as a prayer room during off-hours.

"Boy, I hope Prayer and Fasting is a little more upbeat," Jacob comments, plodding up the metal stairs. "I thought that one girl in the back was gonna faint!"

Jacob grins until he sees her right in front of him.

"I wasn't fainting. I am afraid of heights. I didn't hear a word that last professor said. I was hyperventilating. And now we are going up higher," Audrey exclaims, keeping her white knuckles on the railing.

"Oh, sorry, it's okay, just look down at the floor. Just a few more steps. Everyone is afraid of something. I mean, I . . . for example . . . am afraid of clowns; to this day I won't eat at Bubba the Clown's Chicken Shack. The wig and the nose give me nightmares. True story," Jacob says, to encourage her.

Destiny bops her brother on the back of the head. They find it awkward to be a year apart and be in the same classes. It's a compromise Destiny had to make to go to SWA. She is dedicated and focused, Jacob, — not so much.

Before they know it, their second day of classes is concluded. Everyone settles into their dorms for the night. The floor leaders are doing their checkpoints and locking up. Jamie walks through the boys' side. Jesse hears a hissing noise in the commons area, just outside their doors. He goes and opens the dorm door just as Jamie is walking past.

"Everything kosher here, Rock Man?" Jamie almost sounds as if he is taunting him.

"Yeah, it's all good," says Jesse, nodding his head and going back into the room.

Dismissing the hissing sound, he turns back toward the guys. Jesse notices that on his bed are his backpack and the quilt! He runs over and looks inside the pack; only his clothes remain. The paint set and feathers are gone. The authorities have sent his things on to him after they contacted the Perez's. Now the Perez's know he hitchhiked; it is considered a crime in some states. Jesse fears Papa is disappointed with him for hitchhiking or that the authorities will charge him with a crime. The thought of disappointing Ana is more than Jesse can bear at this point. He figures the tow truck guy helped himself to the missing items. Jesse shakes off the trace of anger, knowing the dark side of people very well.

He needs to get some things off his chest. Jesse decides to come clean to the guys about how he lost his backpack.

"Hey guys, I have a confession to make."

He waits till they all turn toward him.

"I lost my backpack hitchhiking here from New York. The cops sent my stuff to me. Around a year ago, I was homeless for a while, till a church took me in. I have only been saved eight months. My pride got the best of me. I didn't want you guys to know that I am not from a normal family. I am not . . . able to talk about stuff."

Jesse puts his head down, humiliated about his past. The boys stand in silence, shocked at his confession and history.

"You mean you have only been saved for eight months, and you can already give words of knowledge?" Eric looks closely at Jesse.

"Sure, can't everyone?" Jesse responds.

Everyone breaks out into laughter. It breaks the tension, and the dorm mates laugh more just to clear the air.

Yosef says, "Oy vey, crazy Americans!"

Jacob steps into the dorm.

"Yo, yo! I am your new roomie! Have I missed anything?" Jacob drops his suitcase down and looks around.

The evening continues quietly in Jesse's dorm, as Jacob unpacks. Everyone is on the bottom floor, taking showers and getting ready for bed. After Jesse takes his shower, he brushes his teeth and tries to shake off the uneasiness he is feeling. He has on his sweatpants but no shirt yet. Yosef is just standing, staring at Jesse's back through the doorway. The room gets quiet again. Dropping his head, Jesse stops brushing his teeth and breathes a heavy sigh. He knows everyone is looking at the scars on his back. He knows he can't hide them forever.

"Don't ask!" Jesse finds himself yelling. He slams the bathroom door, leaving everyone standing in the dorm room silently. Leaning over the sink and looking in the mirror, tears stream down his face. Voices silenced after his salvation now echoes to him.

"Street trash . . . reject . . . good for nothing . . . damaged goods!" Mean-spirited whispers roll through his head.

Jesse looks for his shirt. He has left it out on the bed.

That's what you get when you let down your guard, he tells himself.

He stands in front of the bathroom door with his left hand on the doorknob. He takes a deep breath and walks into the room. Everyone pretends to be busy and doesn't look at him. He puts on his shirt and jumps into bed, leaving his backpack and quilt at the foot of his bed and waits for 'lights out' to be called by Jamie.

Eric walks over to him and says, "Goodnight, Jesse."

Jesse nods and smiles a feeble smile, knowing if he talks, his voice will give away the fact that he is about to cry. Jesse saw compassion and concern on Eric's face, much like he saw on Manuel, back in New York.

Then Jamie yells, "Lights out!" and opens their door to flip the light switch off.

Jesse looks over at the moonlight through the huge thin arched windows facing the mountainside and the campus buildings. He feels sick in his stomach.

"*Tomorrow will be better,*" the Lord assures him.

Jesse begins to thank Yahweh for everything he can think of. It is a habit he started at the Perez house.

Thanks for bacon, and toothpaste, and Eric.

"Jesse," Eric calls down from the bunk above Jesse. "We won't tell anyone about your scars," He assures him.

Everyone else agrees with a round of yeses.

"Thanks; guys . . . Sorry I yelled."

Jesse tries to sound cheerful. He waits for the guys to go to sleep so that he can crack the door open to the hall.

The mood is different in the girls' quarters with five girls and three top bunks. Ruby, Faith, Gloria, Milagros, and Audrey are assigned to the room, leaving one bed still empty. Ruby plans to go to bed early to get a top bunk.

Top bunk ownership will be set in stone by my roommates in the next few days. It is now or never. Ruby is getting comfy in her top bunk with her homework scattered on the sheets when Destiny comes in with her bag.

Destiny is glad to see faces she recognizes.

"Hey Ruby, where do I put my stuff?" says Destiny casually.

"The armoire over there is yours, Dest." Ruby points without leaving her claim on the top bunk.

Suddenly Destiny freezes, her eyes fixed over Faith. Faith looks back at Destiny. Her gray-blue eyes look dull; she is sitting on the oriental rug.

"Do you see that?" Destiny says, frozen in place.

"See what?" Faith asks, getting nervous.

Destiny keeps her eyes over her head.

"That big wormy thing, there!"

Destiny points at Faith's head.

Faith says, "I don't see anything!"

From the other side of the room, Millie stands and declares: "Wait, wait, the Lord says Faith is experiencing high altitude sickness."

"Ooh, make it go away, make it go away!"

Faith thinks that for sure, she is going to throw up. She flips her hands back and forth as if she has gook on them.

Gloria steps up to Faith and says, "Sickness be

gone in Jesus' name."

A red glow comes on her hand; she puts it on Faith's stomach, and the light fades away.

"It's gone; it shrunk and disappeared," reports Destiny.

"I was dizzy and sick to my stomach all day! Thank you, Lord, thank you that Destiny is in our dorm." Faith hugs her. "Here, you can have my top bunk!"

Ruby is still trying to see the worm.

"Okay, that was fun," Ruby comments. *Okay, Lord, all these girls have gifts and spiritual names. All I have is the top bunk. What gives?*

Again, she doesn't wait for an answer; she is just complaining. She cannot pout for long; she still has three scriptures to read for her dad's class tomorrow. Audrey is documenting all the unusual events in her journal. Tonight, she has some writing to do.

CHAPTER SIX

COME UNDER THE BANNER

Today, the student body must wear SWA embroidered shirts, blue jeans, and hiking boots; and optional are; accessories like chokers, scarves, and bracelets. Hundreds of caps with tribal names are on young heads; the caps are not required but quite popular. Worship is in full swing; the bass and drums are heard two levels down the campus to the dining hall. Judah tribe is now doing all the worship instead of the professors. Aurora leads worship, as she has since she graduated seven years ago. Inside the Shekinah Sanctuary, the room is full of students with their arms swaying in the air. (See "Types and Shadows" 6) The sizeable Gothic building echoes with music, and the arched beveled glass window streams in sunlight. Levi tribe stands front and center of the stage. Ruby loves it there, but Jesse hates it, and he wants to be in the back where no one can see him. He looks back toward the big doors where Jamie stands with his arms folded. Jesse catches his eye. They both look away.

Aurora Oliver has gotten the new worship team up and running. It is all second-year cadets so far. Judah tribe is showing their colors, with singers, musicians, and dancers; giving it their all. The young worship team changes to a slow song:

> Oh God, rain your righteousness down
> Break up our fallow ground
> Have mercy, with your love so profound
> It is time to seek you, Lord
> Till your righteousness rains upon us all around

Weeping sweeps through the room. Kids sit on the floor; some lie face down, weeping under the hand of Adonai. It is humbling for all in the building. Only a few kids stand unaffected by the move of Elohim. The workers in the kitchen come see why the kids have not come for breakfast. They, too, find themselves crying out to Elohim. The eggs get cold, but, no one cares. All the guitar players' fingers start to hurt from playing so long, and the singers soon feel the need to be quiet before the Lord. The sound of a single piano echoes through the hall. A new voice begins to sing. It is Ruby singing without a microphone. It is so quiet that her voice echoes throughout the massive room.

> Come under the banner, Come into the fold
> Come to the anointing that makes you whole
> It is here that He led to this very place
> Come . . . seek His face
>
> Now is the promise of a better day
> Now is the Word working, quickened by faith
> Your whole life you've waited, to see His grace
> In such a manner, in such a great place
> Come . . . seek His face
>
> The enemy has noticed; he cannot prevail
> With the sword of the Spirit, in prayer, we travail
> It is God who is exalted; it is God that we feel
> Touching, and saving, and keeping us still
> Come . . . seek His face
> In this place . . . Still . . .
> Before His grace, come

Aurora, captain of the Judah tribe, nods her head to Ruby. Ruby smiles.
Wow, she acknowledged me!
Ruby has found her gift; it was there all along. She sang at church all the time, but not like this. The youngest cadet at SWA is thankful to the Lord for making her voice supercharged. She feels she can knock down walls with her

voice today.

As the last few kids head out for breakfast, Ruby wonders why Adonai used her after she has been so selfish about the top bunk back at the dorm. In fifteen minutes, classes will start.

The General comments to Professor Norman, "This group of kids are the most anointed we ever had. Jesse and Ruby stand out the most."

"Agreed."

Professor Norman, ex-military with a shaved head, is a man of few words.

Ruby grabs her jacket and heads for the door. She bumps into a guy with blue streaks in his spiked hair. A new face in the Levi tribe talks to Ruby as the students walk to breakfast.

"Hey, dude! Nice voice, ya got there. I'm Jacob," says the boy putting on his jacket.

She wonders how she has never noticed him before, with the blue hair and all.

"I'm not a dude, but thanks on the voice part. Are you in the Levi tribe?" Ruby asks as they head out the door into the nippy fall air.

"Yeah, my sister Destiny and I got here yesterday," Jacob says, pulling up his collar to block the sharp breeze. She is a year older, but they let her in anyway.

"Oh, she is my roommate. I see the resemblance, now that you mention it."

Ruby wishes she had her gloves about now.

"Cool," Jacob says, putting on the charm; at least

he thinks he is charming. Jacob and Destiny are experienced missionaries; SWA has allowed them to come late. Ruby has more respect for Destiny now that she knows she has already done foreign mission work. Jacob is hard to take seriously; he is always making everyone laugh.

It is cell group period; and Eric, Devin, and Ruby are trying to decide what each other's strengths and weaknesses are. Jesse, Audrey, and Kristen have all the weaknesses written down; the strengths part is another thing altogether. Yosef and Jacob are the only two in their cell group. Gloria, Destiny, and Milagros are chatting cheerfully.

"This can't be right; you wrote I am impatient, stubborn, and self-centered. No, what do you *really* think?" Kristen's voice is lower than usual. Almost pleasant, Jesse thinks.

"And on me; you guys put moody and withdrawn, isn't that a little strong?" Jesse questions their description of him.

Jesse is surprised he cares so much about what these two girls think of him.

"Shy and quiet? Yuck! Who would like to know someone shy and quiet? Boring!" Audrey protests their assessment of her also.

She is just as unpleased as the other two. All three sit there being upset.

When Jamie comes to check their progress, he

notes their expressions and decides to sit down and try to fix the situation.

"So . . . let's turn these weaknesses into positive strengths. For example, stubbornness can also be inner fortitude; stick to it, and never give up in hard times. Moody, well, that can also be meditative, deep thinking, and conservative. Shy, well, turn that into a great listener! Okay? I hope you wrote that down, so I am not repeating it. BYE-BYE now."

Jamie is up and on his way to the next table. The three look at each other and say, "Hmmm." Pencils are buzzing. They have what they need to finish their assignments, and they don't feel insulted anymore.

By the time Jamie checks on Eric, Devin, and Ruby, they are at a standstill. All their papers are blank.

"What's the matter? Are you afraid to hurt each other's feelings? You can be honest if you are gentle and sincere. Start with the positive first if you need to."

Jamie is up and on to the next table, leaving them sitting with blank looks on their faces. Devin takes a stab at it.

"I'd say Ruby is passionate, good at communicating. Eric is confident. Okay, I did mine, your turn."

Devin is pleased with himself; he leans back and relaxes.

Ruby jumps in next.

"Okay, Eric, you are so confident; it comes off as cold sometimes, not all the time, just once in a while.

Devin . . . you act tough; but you are really a nice guy — a teddy bear actually."

Ruby looks into their faces to see how they take it. She thinks it went rather well. Eric thinks intensely, and then he takes a deep breath and speaks his mind.

"I act as though I am confident. It is just an act . . . I am actually not. I worry that people will come and talk to me and I will sound stupid, so I put up a wall, you know? Devin, you love people, and they pick up on it. That is why they are always telling you about their problems. It's not because you're so wise; they just know you care. I admire that — I really do. Ruby, people feel comfortable around you; I feel as if I have known you for years. You are casual and upfront with people; that is something I could never do. That is why God put me with you two. Just being around you has shown me some things."

Eric's honesty blows his cell members away. They get busy filling in the blanks of their assignment, deep in thought.

Suddenly a ruckus is heard in the corner next to the windows.

"Jerk!" yells one girl.

"Snob!" responds another.

All heads turn to the corner table. The two girls suddenly become embarrassed and slump down in their chairs. Jesse's table starts laughing; Jesse stops snickering when he looks across at the boys. He tries to ignore the girl's laughter, but then he bursts out laughing again.

Jamie tells everyone, "Next week, you will send

one member to another table to learn more about other members of your tribe. Good work today, cadets. I trust everyone had a productive time."

Jamie is looking at his watch as though something else is on his mind.

"Next class is in ten minutes, little warriors. Wash your hands and eat your veggies at lunch!"

Jennifer, the loudspeaker lady, is perky as always, her "Brit" accent still a surprise in the mountains of Colorado.

By now, everyone knows their place at the tribal tables. The Judah table is earning respect from the other cadets; they are living up to their reputation. Aurora Oliver says "hi" to Ruby, suggesting Ruby's song should be written down and used as part of the song list as SWA. All the gang goes, "Ooh," teasing Ruby, and she grins. She is feeling better about who she is and not having a spiritual name. *Destiny can see in the Spirit, Gloria glows with anointing, Millie can discern spirits, and I can sing in the Spirit, loud and strong!* This place is all she hoped it would be and more. Her dad often came home with stories of how Elohim used the teens in supernatural ways. Four worship bands have formed through the years, and three worship albums have done very well. SWA has become well known in Christian circles.

"It is supposed to snow tonight!" Gloria has brought her snowboard to school; she has the perfect hill picked out for the first opportunity to go snowboarding.

Ruby's dorm room is toasty warm. The girls have decided to rotate sleeping on the top to keep from fighting about it, and it is Ruby's week to sleep on the bottom.

"So, let me see if I have this straight," Ruby is sorting out her roommates. "Destiny can see demons and is Jacob's sister, the crazy guy with blue hair. Faith loves popcorn, Audrey has glow-in-the-dark pajamas and Millie talks in her sleep. Have I missed anyone? Oh yeah, Gloria, she is the snowboarding queen."

Ruby looks around the dorm; Audrey is writing away in a journal while eating Faith's popcorn. On the floor, Millie makes friendship bracelets in tribal colors. Faith and Gloria are busy fixing each other's hair. Faith has a feather in her hair. Milagros's hair is now dyed a dark blue that enhances her dark Latino skin.

Of all Ruby's roommates, she is drawn to Destiny the most.

Destiny is two years older than me; she probably won't want to hang around with me. So far, she is really nice, though.

When they finish, they gather together to make posters on the upper level of their dorm. The signs have their names on them and will soon hang all over the room.

"Hey, look, it's snowing!" Ruby plops down on the window seat with her face pressed against the glass.

Tomorrow, she hopes that beautiful white snow surrounds them.

CHAPTER SEVEN

GEMS FROM HEAVEN

By lights out, Jesse's dorm room is already deep in sleep. No TV to watch, and six-thirty in the morning comes all too soon for these teenagers. Jesse prays that Yeshuah will visit his dreams for once. If the devil can hassle him in his sleep, certainly Adonai can show up more often. He drifts off thanking Yahweh for one thing at a time as it comes to mind.

Now Jesse is dreaming that he is climbing a rocky mountain with no vegetation on it. Tucked in between a few rocks, he finds a hand mirror with thousands of human faces in it. The images fade from face to face continually. He is amazed by his find and tucks it in his back pocket.

Next, he finds a ruby gem the size of an egg. He puts it in his pocket also, knowing it must be prophetic. The sky fills with winged angelic beings with swords that glow in many colors, as they drop jewels down to the rocks below. Jesse climbs higher, picking up more gems as he goes. The view, as well as the treasures, and his ascent to the top invigorate Jesse. Suddenly, his heart stops when a large man appears on the summit, his hands on his hips and an angry look on his face. Jesse stands there looking up at him, wondering if he can get by him or not. He takes the mirror out of his pocket and the jewels, not wanting them to get broken. He knows Yeshuah is waiting for him at the top; he is determined to get there. (See "Types and Shadows" 7)

He figures the giant has to be a demon, so he tries saying, "In the name of Jesus." Jesse feels his body propelling through the air straight up to the large figure.

He can now see the massive man's eyes; they are empty and black. Jesse knows he is in for a fight. Up close, the man with muscled forearms and fisted hands looks more like a giant to Jesse now. The man draws back his hand and swings at him, striking him violently, knocking him down several feet till a rock stops his fall. The giant follows and kicks Jesse's jewels and mirror off the edge; they are gone; this angers Jesse. He struggles to stand up because of the pain, but he gets up and says again: "I said, IN THE NAME OF JESUS!"

Jesse's voice is as loud as Ruby's was that day she sang at worship. This time, the giant whooshes backward. He falls against a rock and doesn't get up. His hollow eyes follow Jesse as he walks by the fallen giant. Jesse now wonders what type of creature this man is. When Jesse gets to the top, he forgets his pain; as the sun gets so bright his eyes hurt. He has to shade his eyes with his hands.

He tells Yeshuah at the top, "I got up here, but I lost all my treasures in the fight!"

Jesse is heartbroken about losing the mirror with images in it and the big ruby gem. Yeshuah tells him to look in his pockets; he finds the mirror and the red stone. Again, the mirror shows faces one after the other; they are all lost and desperate people. The light intensifies to the point Jesse has to squint his eyes almost shut. He drops to his knees in awe of the overwhelming presence of Yeshuah. Next, the sleepy Jesse opens his eyes and sees the sun shining on the new snow through the dorm window. He realizes it was all a dream. He sits up on the side of his bed, adjusting to the fact that this is reality, and the other was a dream. *It seemed so real.*

"Rock Man . . . are you okay?" Devin asks Jesse.

Devin already has his headphones going. He is rocking his head to the music's beat.

"Yeah . . . just tired. I feel as though I have been up all night, and it's Rocky, not Rock Man."

Jesse is mourning the loss of the treasures in his dream.

How can they be gone, and what does the dream mean? Cling to the red ruby and the beautiful destiny, what does it mean? Is it Ruby? I don't know for sure. The prophecy is essential; I have to get it right. God . . . what are you doing to me? All of this is so uncomfortable.

"Last one out in the snow has to do all the laundry!" Devin declares as he runs out the door. We have five minutes to throw snowballs before worship."

Outside, Jesse realizes that the borrowed coat of Eric's is very warm and fits well. He reaches down to make a snowball, as one flies past his head. He scoops a handful of powdery snow but drops it when he sees something shiny on the ground; it is a small round mirror and a chunk of red glass, faceted in a gem shape. Jesse stands there looking at them, ignoring the snowballs impacting his back. Devin looks over Jesse's shoulder at the flash of light in the snow.

"It is just trash, Jesse, don't let it cut you. The red thing is pretty, though."

Devin rolls in the snow like a commando.

Jesse walks toward the dining hall, putting the items in his pocket.

He feels like yelling, "I was with the Lord last night!"

But he doesn't. It is too holy and too personal. All through breakfast, the dream lingers in his mind; the images still fresh and clear. Jesse thanks Elohim for strawberry pancakes and last night's dream. He feels silly putting pancakes and a powerful vision in one heap, but both are a big deal to him. Out of habit, he rolls four pieces of bacon in a napkin for later. On his way out of the dining hall, Jesse accidentally runs into Jamie. They both stand there looking at each other. Jamie is in good shape being a weightlifter, and his upper arms are thick with muscle. Jesse feels a threatening sense of darkness that he cannot explain. Jamie looks at Jesse as if Jesse knows something about him that is a secret. Jesse can discern dread in Jamie's eyes. Jesse doesn't know if Jamie is depressed or is in some sort of demonic bondage to something. Something is definitely wrong.

"Getting to the early breakfast, you must really be excited for worship today?" Jamie inquires with a skeptical scowl on his face.

"No, just the normal zeal for our Savior," Jesse examines Jamie's stern expression.

They drop their gaze; and walk on past each other.

During worship, Jesse feels heaviness and drops to the floor. His dream so impacts him that he gets lost in the power of the Lord. He can hear the altar workers say to each other, "Don't touch him; the Holy Spirit is all over him!"

Ruby feels she should kneel by him and make sure he isn't in some crisis or something. Jesse is glad not to be the only one at the altar. At his small Spanish church in New York, he was often the only one there. Ruby sees Audrey's devotion to worship; it moves her. Ruby feels dizzy and finds herself under the anointing. She drops to the ground, her body heavy under Ruach HaKodesh's presence. Destiny joins them on the floor. Judah tribe plays slow and rich sounding songs with stringed voices on the keyboards, a real harp, chimes, and many acoustic guitars.

The harmony sounds exceptionally beautiful this morning as they sing of drawing close to Yahweh and wanting to know Him more. The dancers gracefully drift across the stage with ribbons and billowy fabric that flows through the air. Many cadets have tears dripping down their faces. No one notices too much because this is normal and expected, not just of the girls. One of the banners in the rafters reads, **"God is spirit, and those who worship him must worship in spirit and truth." John 4:24**

When the loudspeaker announces the end of worship, Jesse, Ruby, and Destiny are given a hand up by the altar workers.

"What was that all about Jesse?" Ruby knows Adonai did something, but she doesn't know what.

It isn't unusual for kids to lay before Adonai, but the three know they somehow changed. They feel connected in some way.

Jesse doesn't have an answer for Ruby. All he knows is that Elohim is changing him from the inside out, and he feels drawn toward Destiny in a profound spiritual way. He is drawn to Ruby too. He studies their faces looking back at him.

I have never felt a connection like this. Lord, what is this? I don't know if I am ready to be close to people. I still have trust issues. I still don't know the pretty girl's name; it is driving me crazy.

The first chance Jesse gets, he decides, he will ask Ruby what the new girl's name is.

The loudspeaker interrupts with an announcement:

"Ten minutes until cell groups. Please stomp the snow off your shoes before you enter the buildings. Thank you."

She is happy about the snow too.

"Hey, do you smell bacon? Cuz, I sure do," Eric says, sniffing the air.

Ruby shrugs her shoulders.

Jesse discretely stuffs the bacon deeper into his pocket.

In Demonology, Professor Alvey is five minutes late in starting class, which is very unusual. He has his head down as if he is talking on the phone or something.

As the professor lifts his head, he asks the class, "Who had the closed vision last night?" Then he walks up to the rows of kids.

Jesse raises his hand slowly, trying not to look shaken.

"Very well, Jesse," says the professor, "can you tell the class about this dream, or is it too personal?"

Jesse tells them about his dream, even though he finds it hard to put into words what he saw, but they get the overall idea. Jesse pulls the mirror and red glass out of his pocket and sets them down on his table. Everyone gasps; Devin leans over to see if he can see faces in the mirror. Then the professor gives further instructions.

"God gave Jesse natural items to confirm this, so it must be imperative. A natural manifestation of the spiritual. There is a parallel. Okay, everyone; be still and ask God for the meaning of Jesse's dream. You will have five minutes to receive the interpretation. Go."

The class is still except for the sound of people fidgeting in their seats. Jesse's heart is pounding; he isn't used to this much attention, but he very much wants to get an interpretation of his dream. He knows if Elohim can tell the teacher about it, He will certainly have an answer for him. He waits nervously, looking at the red glass and mirror.

"Okay, God gave Joseph and Daniel in the Bible interpretations of dreams. Does anybody have an interpretation for Jesse's dream?" asks Professor Alvey as he stands at the chalkboard ready to write.

Eric shyly raises his hand. "I got some of it, Professor Alvey. The rocky mountain is your time here at SWA, Jesse, and the winged creatures are angels of provision. The gems, the things they dropped, are kids here at school, Jesse. The ones you picked up and kept are your friends here. The giant was not a devil; his eyes were empty cuz he was not 'alive'. He was your own fears and hang-ups. You had to put down all your treasures to fight because your anxieties make you pull away from your friends to feel safe; it was your defense mechanism. You were so busy getting as many friends as you could. You were not taking the time to form real and deep relationships, but the ones God gave back to you are. The mirror is Destiny, and the red glass is Ruby, of course. They are o work with you as a team in the future after you graduate. You are drawn to the rocks in your dream because of the verses you memorized in Psalms."

Jesse's face flushes. *Is the new girl named Destiny? Is this all about two girls?*

Eric sits back down. Professor Alvey writes all the symbolic meanings on the board from Jesse's dream. He writes the passage from Psalms on the board, as Jesse quotes it for him.

For God alone, O my soul, wait in silence, for my hope is from him. He only is my rock and my salvation, my fortress; I shall not be shaken. On God rests my salvation and my glory; my mighty rock, my refuge is God.

Psalm 62:5-7

"Professor, there is more," Jacob speaks up.

Professor Alvey motions for Jacob to comment also.

"Jesse, the items that you found on the ground, the little round mirror and the red glass gem there on the table . . . They are more than just a confirmation of the dream; they have a meaning of their own. You thought you were a throwaway kid; before God found you, right? Those are to remind you where you came from; so pride won't get a hold of you. Also, it is prophetic that you are part of the Levi tribe. You have joined with friends, with the body of Christ, and to a team. You are no longer a lone wolf. Yes, God confirmed His will to you last night. That is all I got, Sir."

Jacob gives his buddies a high five as he sits down, pretty proud of himself.

"Okay, Jacob, now don't you get prideful either,"

the professor teases.

Destiny's face looks like her brother has embarrassed her again; it was not the first time. His blue spikey hair and loud voice are bad enough. Destiny always wears neutral colors. She is also a girl of few words for the most part. She doesn't know Jesse that well yet, but she knows Jacob is good at understanding dreams. She takes the dream interpretation seriously. She writes notes in her notebook and then gazes over to look at Ruby and Jesse.

Jamie, the teacher's aide today, hands Jesse a written version of all Eric and Jacob have said. Jesse is amazed he had time to write it all down already.

Jamie leans in to discreetly tell Jesse, "I know for a fact you belong in the Asher tribe, I . . . for the life of me don't know what you are doing in Levi."

Jamie has a cold expression; Jesse stares at him blankly, as a bead of sweat rolls down his temple.

The professor moves on with a short lecture, and Jamie returns to the front of the class.

"Today," begins Professor Alvey, "we have seen words of knowledge, visions, interpretation of dreams and prophecy all at work. What you just experienced is the introduction of the works of the Holy Spirit, people. By tomorrow I want a scripture for all four gifts, showing where God established them in His word. Get out your concordances and get busy. Good job today, tribe of Levi. And remember the enemy will try to copy the things of God with poor imitations; we will explore this tomorrow."

Professor Alvey winks and grins at Ruby. They

haven't seen that much of each other. Ruby thinks: *I should spend some time with my dad, but I am in this new dorm life. Maybe tonight, if I can get my homework done, there will be time left over to spend together. I want to talk to him about Jesse's dream and us becoming a team. The whole idea thrills me. I really like the idea of being connected with Jesse and Destiny.*

Jesse has a lot to think about: *So . . . Ruby is Manuel's red ruby prophecy, and Destiny is my destiny . . . Teamed up with two girls? Why didn't I notice Destiny's name earlier? Cling to Ruby and my Destiny? What if they don't cling back? Does the word destiny have a double meaning? I think so . . . I still don't know what my purpose in life is . . . exactly.*

Joy and worry grip Jesse simultaneously.

After class, a bunch of kids tell Eric all about their dreams. He can barely get out the door.

Finally, he yells, "Go ask Jacob what they mean!"

Jacob, of course, loves attention. Destiny glares at him with her big sister's eyes.

"Okay, I can see you during lunch and you between the third and fourth periods. The rest I will see tomorrow. Don't crowd dudes," Jacob says, as they leave the classroom.

Jamie, who is leaving the building also, walks up close to Jacob and whispers in his ear, "Ya otta charge five dollars a dream, my man. No reason not to. The psychics do, why shouldn't we? Just between you and me."

Jamie gives him a wink and goes on his way.

Jacob has a puzzled look on his face. *Charge money? What an odd thing coming from a floor leader.*

Jacob puts it out of his mind, distracted by all the cute girls walking by. It is hard for him to concentrate on anything else.

Jesse walks up to Destiny, trying to look calm.

"Hi, I am Jesse," Jesse smiles nervously.

"Yes, I know. Glad to officially meet you. It seems there is some future for us together . . . somehow; I mean . . . the Spirit was powerful in worship today, and then your dream. It's overwhelming sorta," Destiny says, stammering over her own words.

She finds herself nervous and flushed in the face. It is rare for her; she has gained confidence and maturity during her time in India.

"So, do you think they are right? About my dream, I mean," Jesse breaks out in a sweat.

"Jacob is usually right about dreams; I think it would be exciting — from what little I know about you. That is to say . . . exciting to work with you and Ruby," Destiny says awkwardly. "I guess we will know when the time is right."

"Yeah, in two years . . . well . . . see you . . . around," Jesse is getting too flustered to make sense and so he cuts the conversation short. He has a lot to process in his mind, and he wants Ruby's reaction to the prophecy of the dream as well.

He catches up with her before the next class going down the metal spiral staircase.

"I think it's cool. We will make a great team. I have no problem with it. Why, do you not want to work with us as a team?" Ruby is beginning to love probing him for answers.

"Right now, I am a blooming idiot around Destiny; she may not even like me for another two years . . . until we graduate."

"You like her . . . you really, really like her!" Ruby says in a whisper, picking up on his affection for Destiny. She is grinning and pointing her finger at him.

"I am not ready to like her. I will have to think about it for a while," Jesse states as stoically as he can manage. "I thought we were talking team partners, not like . . . like — as in girlfriend . . . like."

Jesse pulls the collar up on his shirt, hoping to hide his blushing face. Ruby grins at him, as they walk on to the next class.

The rest of August settles into a routine: classes, worship, free time, and weekends. The grandeur of the campus is almost getting to feel commonplace to this group of students. The second-year cadets have classes in the other academic tower; they still don't mingle much with the underclassmen.

Ruby, Destiny, Gloria, Milagros, Faith, and Audrey will spend two years as roommates. Jesse, Eric, Devin, Yosef, and Jacob also will get to know each other well in the next two years. Ruby and Jesse are now talking often; Jesse turns into quite a talker after all. Everyone in the gang seems to listen to his excited recounting of how Yahweh is revealing Himself. Jesse has more encounters and experiences with the Lord than anyone else they know.

The girls love to hear Yosef's accent, and soon everyone can understand him. Destiny seems quiet and more dignified than the other girls. Ruby enjoys being dorm-mates with her. She is proud to be thought of as in a team with Jesse and Destiny; she admires both of them and wonders what value she will be to the team. Jesse retreats to his rocky cliff at times, finding it a great place to "get his head together." He spends hours pondering the future and his ability to connect with the girls or anyone for that matter.

WOLF IN SHEEP'S CLOTHING

September melts into the next month, and Ruby is now fifteen. Students are in the groove of classes. It is snowing again, not that unusual for October in the Rockies.

The campus does not celebrate Halloween, but they are aware that October thirty-first is a time when witchcraft is very active. Jesse reflects that it was a year ago when he ran away from his uncle Bill. The day brings Jesse grief, and he wishes it would pass quickly. Ruby wonders what is up with him being so quiet today. She feels like he is in a crisis but doesn't know what that crisis could be.

However, what is unusual on this Halloween evening is how all the staff gets up from supper and goes out of the dining hall into the chilly air. They look at no one in particular, but all pray in their supernatural prayer language with the most serious look on their faces.

Back inside, the room settles down again, and everyone resumes eating until the kitchen staff also leave through the front doors. With stern expressions and prayers on their lips, they go out without taking the time to get their coats. At this point, the cadets curiously stream out into the front courtyard of the dining hall, some eating their rolls as they go. The General is out there as well. He begins to shout orders, something to Aurora, then to the Simeon tribe. People are moving here and there in very determined ways.

All the cadets are now outside on the snow-covered grass. The wind is picking up, and the clouds are moving unusually fast in the evening sky. The adults are praying and quoting scriptures.

Destiny turns and looks up across the sky.

She points and yells, "I see a storm with red lightning! It is rolling this way and takes up the whole of the sky — and I see lights of all sorts of colors on us, each of us has glowing lights over our heads! They are beautiful and frightening at the same time."

Everyone hears her and stops to find out what to do now. All the Guardian angels stand by their saints with swords moving back and forth, unsure of what direction an attack will come. They stand vigilant and in a defensive position. The wind picks up and knocks over some potted plants and park benches as the sun sets. A Spirit Wings flag ripped by the wind from the gate tower drifts across the walkway in front of the dining hall.

By now, the Judah tribe is on the scene per the General's instructions. They have drums and guitars in hand. The Simeon tribe is surrounding the rest, kneeling, and praying for the scared cadets. Three others confirm that they see the red lightning Destiny mentioned. Many of the younger girls begin to cry, and a few scream.

Jesse keeps saying, "Yes, Lord, okay, yes."

Then he looks out at the group and says, "Someone from SWA has summoned a demonic hoard. There is a servant of darkness working among us. He is not alone; he belongs to a large underground cult with sects all over the U.S. The Lord says that dark spirits are here to hinder the moving of the Holy Spirit. Their purpose is to divide the Spirit-filled believers; from the rest, so the rest will not learn of God's power, so they reject speaking in a supernatural prayer language and the moving of the Holy Spirit."

Suddenly a muscular young man in a red satin hooded cape is spotted on top of the Shekinah Sanctuary roof. It is some distance away, and he is just a silhouette to their eyes. How he managed to get up there is shocking. High on top of the cathedral, the man holds up a scepter. The scepter has a glass ball on the top surrounded by a crescent coming out under the ball; red lightning sparks off it into the air. The rod is a carved wooden snake; its mouth holds the glass ball. His blonde hair blows in the breeze; he has on a black shirt and blue jeans. He steps up to a candle and papers with incantations written on them. He feels power surge through him and the hordes of demons coming his way. Filled with pride and self-indulgent confidence, he gloats over the people below. He believes himself to be superior to the Christians he sees below him on the academy's grounds. No one can make out who he is from this distance. (See "Types and Shadows" 8)

Below, the drums begin a call to battle with their beat. Then, the words of the song echo through the campus like a whisper with hope and strength. All the kids recognize the worship song.

Oh, grant us help against the foe, for vain is the salvation of man! With God we shall do valiantly; it is he who will tread down our foes.
Psalm 60:11-12

Then the musicians change the beat. It is fierce and militant, and the staff is quiet now. Everyone waits on Ruach HaKodesh.

Demonic spirits manifest on the roof with the man. They fly down and streak by everyone, glowing with a sickening green tone. Their faces twist with terror. The demons push down anyone who cowers. A group of kids crouch on the ground, with their hands on their heads, screaming. Professor Norman runs to them. The drummers stop playing and look around at the ensuing chaos.

Unseen by humans, the Guardian angels swing at

the demons; they elude the angels' blades, screaming in fear. Still, the demons do not flee. Shrieking spirits attack only the people who yield to fear. Those who are in faith only cause more torment to the evil spirits.

"Come on, people, don't let fear grip you! God is with us!" Jesse yells at the mayhem in front of him.

Jesse's words cause Ruby to feel the presence of the Lord all over her; the cold air makes her shiver. She begins to beat on one of the conga drums and sing:

> BEHOLD OUR GOD IS FIGHTING FOR US AGAINST ENEMIES UNSEEN,
> THE CAPTAIN OF HOSTS GOES OUT BEFORE US
> AND WE SHALL SEE THE VICTORY . . .
> BEHOLD OUR GOD . . .
> HOW HE LOVES YOU AND ME

The drummers pick up Ruby's rhythm and start to play in unison. Destiny yells, "It is shrinking, and the clouds are breaking up."

She shakes in the nippy air, her beanie and gloves not keeping her warm enough.

The man on the roof releases a final attack, muttering and swinging his arms, scepter in hand. He holds up his scepter, the glass ball beginning to produce smoke and then a sizeable shaft of red lightning. The lightning coming off the staff in the man's hand glows over them. He is laughing, drunk with power, and has disdain for the people below.

The warlock on the roof looks down and hears the song Ruby is singing. The lightning begins to run down his arm, causing him enough pain to make him cast the staff down. He is alarmed that the lightning strikes him; his face is full of pain. The scepter rolls down the roof and shatters on the ground in front of the sanctuary doors. The man's cape blows off violently. His candle goes out, and the powers he conjured up strike him as they abandon him and flee the area. It is Jamie, the floor leader.

"Nooooo," he yells in anguish.

He stumbles around, leaving all his implements of sorcery to scatter.

Jesse begins to explain, "It is the love of God that destroys this attack, our love for one another. This storm is big enough to have affected three states around Colorado, but it won't anymore. We aren't leaving SWA, none of us!"

All the cadets feel moved and stand to yell, "We are not leaving SWA!"

Jesse looks toward the sanctuary, "The one who opened the door in the spirit realm for the enemy's device is now opening his car door to leave this Academy. Jamie, will you continue to serve darkness even with all this light around you?"

At this point, Jamie supernaturally is on the ground and peels out as he drives off toward the school entrance. Everyone begins to notice how freezing they are. The General tells everyone to return to the dining hall. Some kids are dazed, but no one is seriously hurt — just a few bumps and bruises. The sky is clear now, and all the demonic manifestations are gone. Many cadets did not see the demons at all; they just felt the fear and the wind. No one will let the event influence them to quit the academy.

Everyone trails inside, but Jesse lingers, looking out into the night. He knows Jamie is out there somewhere and somehow feels an urgency. Ruby comes and pulls him in. Destiny also urges him out of the cold.

Spirit Wings Academy has pulled together into a close group tonight. Four hundred plus souls have gone to battle and won; this is a night of victory. Destiny, Jesse, and Ruby taste what it is like to work together as a team. All three were pivotal in turning the situation around. Everyone knows of the prophecy by now and expects them to be a close-knit team.

Inside the warm dining hall, the kitchen staff prepares hot chocolate and coffee to bring out to the chilled gang of warriors — the youth huddle around their hot cocoa. Everyone feels the love of Elohim stronger than ever before in their lives. Many who rejected speaking in a supernatural prayer language are ready to embrace it and be filled with the Spirit. Jesse, Ruby, and Destiny have become a valuable part of the student leadership. No longer does Judah have all the "bright lights" in the halls of Spirit Wings Academy. Supper is cold, but no one complains. They indeed did something tonight, something recorded by Heaven and taken notice of by the powers of darkness. Most of them had felt rejection of some type from other Christians and churches. Now perhaps this will change how they are perceived, and things will be different. Maybe after today, the Holy Spirit will flow in a more significant measure.

Professor Norman thinks of a phrase from the *Star-Spangled Banner*: "Land of the free, home of the brave."

He wipes a tear from his eye as he looks across the group of young cadets.

All the angelic Guardians return to their rooftops and other strategic locations while people talk excitedly about the night's events. Anton is thrilled; the atmosphere is changing in the region.

"Dude, you should have seen your face when that lightning came out!" Jacob jokes with Devin.

"I seem to recall you screaming like a girl!" Devin retorts back, laughing. The girls laugh, listening to the boys bantering. They all can't believe Jamie is a warlock.

Jesse doesn't join the conversation but continues to stare out into the dark of night, cupping his hot chocolate around his cold fingertips. Jesse knows fear and confusion all too well. He feels compassion for Jamie and doesn't want to see him come to ruin.

Jamie drives just outside the academy, and then he parks in the picnic area. He looks at himself in his rear-view mirror — the image of himself in a red cloak flashes through his mind.

"I thought hate was stronger than Your love. I

thought the power I was using was greater than the power of those kids. I have blown it; YAHWEH HAVE MERCY ON ME! What a great rip off! I bought into all those lies – – hook line, and sinker! Have I gone beyond the point of no return?"

Jamie slumps over the steering wheel, shaking, and hiding his face. It is dark now, and he feels the darkness cover him like never before.

"I have really messed up my whole life. What am I going to do?" Jamie wonders.

A dark winged figure lands silently on the roof of his car. It is a thin grey creature covered in short fur about three feet high with long steely claws.

"Now. . . end your life . . . it's over. Yeshuah will never forgive you; you are tainted, defiled, corrupt to the bone," it whispers as it drools; its voice scratchy from thousands of years of shrieking.

Professor Alvey stops suddenly in the dining hall, sets down his coffee cup, and has a distant look on his face.

Professor Norman asks him, "Ruben, are you there?"

Professor Alvey shakes the glare off of his eyes and says, "I have to go for a ride down the road a few miles. Tell Jesse and Devin to meet me in the parking lot. Let the General know. We still might be able to reach Jamie for the Kingdom of God; I have to try."

He is in a dead run by the last sentence.

Jesse and Devin run out to the professor's car, "What's up?" Devin asks with a serious look on his face.

"I feel that Jamie may commit suicide if we don't find him in time. Let's go," their professor tells them.

As they get in their teacher's convertible, the boys start to intercede for their deceived and fallen floor leader. Jesse remembers what he learned in Spiritual warfare and Demonology and begins to bind and loose.

"Spirit of Suicide, I send you away from Jamie in the name of Jesus," Jesse prays.

"Father, I know You love Jamie; make a way for him, where there was no way," prays Devin.

About that time, an angel swoops down and knocks the imp off Jamie's car. It shakes its head, gets up, and gets in a position to fight. The angel stands on the hood of the vehicle, staring down the demon in a fighting position. Tears stream down Jamie's face at this point; he hasn't cried in years. Tears are a strange event for Jamie; anger and ambition have controlled his heart for many years.

"If You can forgive me, Adonai, send a messenger to me, or I know I am lost forever. You are the one and only true God, Yahweh. Even the demons fear You and tremble; I don't want to suffer Your wrath. PLEASE!"

Jamie's shoulders slump down, and his chest heaves with sobs. He feels his chest will burst open at any moment. The angel and the imp wrestle in the air over the top of Jamie's car.

"There he is!" Professor Alvey points to the small foreign car parked by the picnic tables.

The boys wonder how he can see Jamie's car in the darkness. There is no lighting in the park. They pull up next to Jamie and shut off the engine. Jamie never even looks up; he is in his own world, talking to himself, deep in regret and anguish. A wave-shaped dagger sits on his console.

Devin taps on Jamie's car window. The two spiritual beings stop and look to see the humans below them, waiting to see which one of them will be allowed to proceed.

"Jamie, it's Devin. Open up!"

Jamie is startled as he sees who is outside his car. He is gripping the ceremonial knife in both hands, but now he discreetly drops it below his seat. Looking away and wiping tears from his eyes, his hands are trembling uncontrollably. He manages to roll down his car window.

"MY OLD MASTER DEMANDS MY LIFE, IS THERE ANY WAY TO BREAK THIS BLOOD COVENANT WITH HASATAN? (Hebrew term for Satan)"

For once, Jamie is straight up with his floor members. He regrets the spells he cast and feels great remorse. Only an hour ago, as a warlock, Jamie set in motion a demonic storm poised to hit the academy and the surrounding three states. He has changed his way of thinking since he saw Yahweh's power working in unity in the dining hall yard. Jesse stands next to Devin, looking in at Jamie.

"Look, Jamie, the blood of Jesus will set you free," Jesse explains.

They are all very concerned for Jamie, the situation

is at a tipping point, and Jamie must accept Jesus to stop the destruction that now lies before him.

"Demons, you can't have Jamie. I claim him for the Kingdom of God! Release him and let him go!" Jesse demands.

These words make the demon tumble headlong into a tree branch. The angel lifts his sword higher.

"I bind you, you Spirit of Blinding Deception. Come off of Jamie's eyes. Father, God of Glory, open Jamie's eyes. I pray that he may see the glorious light of Jesus and be redeemed from [11]darkness and translated into the Kingdom of Your dear Son."

Jesse takes more authority over the enemy, looking out into the darkness of the pine treetops.

"Spirit of Suicide . . . release him and let him go! [12]Jamie, hear, know, perceive, and understand what the Lord is saying to you! Don't be rebellious or turn back," Devin says as he joins the battle.

Jamie stops sobbing and looks up, his expression changing from torment to somber alertness.

That is just what the angel is waiting for; his sword begins to glow, and he strikes the dark spirit. The Spirit of Suicide gets tangled in a branch and starts to wiggle furiously to get free. Its eyes are bulging in panic. The angel swings again; there is a flash of light. The demon

---

[11] **Colossians 1:13**

[12] Paraphrased from **Isaiah 50:5** from the Amplified version

cries out a horrendous scream that only Jesse and the angels hear. Green slime drips from the branches in the spirit realm. Jamie is less fearful and clear of many unclean spirits that have accompanied him for many years. Still, all the forces of darkness have not fully released him.

The air in the area blows out a fresh breeze, like wind clearing smoke out of a valley and causing a rustle in the pines. Jamie opens his car door and falls out in front of the three Christians. His t-shirt is black with a grey skull on the chest.

"Tell me what to do, servants of the Living God! I will be your servant if you will let me." Jamie presses down into the forest floor with all his energy spent.

The way Jesse and the others sent all the unclean spirits packing has Jamie shook up. Devin and Jesse sit down on the grass next to him as Professor Alvey intercedes with his prayer language. Jamie still has ties with darkness; it isn't over yet.

"Jesus says the only way to hell is by rejecting His sacrifice on the cross, and that He rose again the third day. Jamie, repent of your sins, renounce your blood covenant with darkness, and accept Yeshuah as your Lord and Savior. Jesus' blood is stronger. It will annul the contract you made through witchcraft. Serve the Master . . . God loves you, and the blood of Yeshuah brings forgiveness for everything you did against Him and His people," Devin says, as he puts his hand on his shoulder, feeling kindness for Jamie. He can feel Ruach HaKodesh dealing with Jamie.

Jesse speaks softly and gently to him, not as he did before to the demon in the air.

"Hey, man, we forgive you; you can make it right. God can turn a curse into a blessing, Jamie. He became a curse for us, so we wouldn't have to be cursed. Come on; yield your spirit to His. You will never regret it."

Jamie tries to speak but begins to choke. The dark spirit guide Jamie used to control now whispers threats in his ear.

"You belong to me, sinner boy; we have a blood covenant, remember?" Jamie hears the terrible voice in his head. He still struggles to speak.

"Say the name Jesus, Jamie. Say His name!" Jesse urges.

"Je . . . Jes . . . Jesus, in the name of Jesus," Jamie manages to speak the words.

A rush of air pulls away from Jamie, and he is free to speak. No more voices in his head.

"I can breathe; I can breathe! I am a wicked, miserable fool. My parents are pastors. I always scorned them as weaklings, sentimental, emotional, and old fashioned. I was so stupid."

Jamie holds his head in his hands.

All four of them pray together for several hours, there in the park. The stars are brilliant tonight. The high altitude makes for a clear view of heaven. Jamie confesses many things he did to achieve power, renouncing his covenant with the dark forces. He gets delivered from several unclean spirits who have been affecting his mind and emotions. It is almost mid-night when they head back to the school, including Jamie. Jesse rides with him in his car.

Jamie expects he will have to step down from his counselor position. Even so, he looks to the future with a newfound joy. The former warlock is free like never before, and even if Jamie has to leave the academy, it will be alright. Elohim is with him, and he will never be alone again. It has been a long time since the young man has looked for his parents' number on his cellphone. He takes a deep breath and hits "call". There in the front entry of the Levi lodge dorm, Jamie contacts his weary parents in Minnesota with good news.

"Hello dad?" says Jamie, his voice echoing through the massive room.

Jamie came home to the arms of Yeshuah.

By midnight, Devin and Jesse fall into bed, not realizing how tired they are until they lie down. Angels minister to them as they sleep. Instead of the red thunderstorm of darkness, an angelic host hovers over the area. Light and truth charge the atmosphere while the humans below go about their lives, consumed with the cares of life. Many students at the academy have little awareness of the activity in the spirit realm. Tonight was a wake-up call for them.

"Thank you, Jesus," rolls off Jesse's lips as he slips off to sleep, resting in the Lord.

Ruben Alvarez dials the phone to call his wife in Denver, "Honey, the Lord saved a warlock tonight . . ."

CHAPTER NINE

FINDING A PLACE TO BELONG

The next morning, as the kids stream into breakfast, all the talk is about Jamie, how last night he was exposed as working for the enemy. Someone broke the glass with his picture in it in the hall, where the staff is featured. By now, everyone has heard how Professor Alvarez and the boys had gone out and brought Jamie to Adonai. A few are unsure of his conversion, and Jamie experiences more than one cold stare at breakfast.

The loudspeaker breaks into the morning's conversations, "There will be a special assembly today during first period. All students and staff are required to come. The boys in East Gate/Lions' dorm one, have won this week's cake. Girls, the boys have won five more cakes than you so far. Better spiffy up girls."

It is surprising to all how many cakes the boys are winning. Could it be they are neater, or just more motivated to get cake? Jamie and most of the teachers leave breakfast early.

Audrey comments, "Everybody is wondering what the purpose of the assembly is. Maybe it is about the demonic storm and Jamie?"

Destiny tells her, "We will all know soon enough."

Everyone heads to the sanctuary.

The Shekinah Sanctuary is packed, with the student body present in full force. It is impressive to see everyone in their tribe's section, staff on stage, teachers, and aides; even the kitchen staff is present.

The General stands at the podium and announces, "I feel it necessary to address some concerns you may have about Jamie Gerard. The best way to deal with them is, to begin with, Jamie telling his story. Whether he stays or not will be left up to leadership, but we want you to understand some things. I commend Jamie on his willingness to make amends and face the critical eye that some may give him on campus. Jamie has been through the fire, and it has burned off some dross. (See "Types and Shadows" 9) Okay, enough of my words, Jamie; I give you the floor. Cadets, I expect you to listen with the ear of Ruach HaKodesh. Jamie, come on up."

Jamie has no notes, no prepared speech. He has prayed, and Adonai promised to give him the words. The room is still as if all the air is sucked out of the atmosphere, waiting in anticipation.

"I have been up all night, confessing my terrible mistakes before Jesus and the Father. I think I will spend many more days this way as my sins come to mind, and the horrible things I have done are relentlessly before me. I was so sure of myself, bold and unashamed, until last night when I saw you all in unity, with one mind, one purpose, and one God. I have never seen God move like that before. I thought your worship was just mindless emotion, that the love of Jesus on old antiquated religion. I thought witchcraft was true enlightenment. I was a fool. The Bible says: [13]For a fool says in his own heart, there is no God. I was wrong, dead wrong, blind, proud, arrogant, and self-assured. Now I am sure of only one thing, and that is Jesus and His cross.

One thing have I asked of the Lord, that will I seek after: that I may dwell in the house of the Lord all the days of my life, to gaze upon the beauty of the Lord and to inquire in his temple.
Psalm 27:4

"No one can take that away from me. I do ask for your forgiveness. I have lied to you, gave you bad advice, wished you evil . . . I did some bad stuff. I am . . . so sorry; I was *so* wrong."

Jamie's voice begins to falter. He drops his head down, his hands shaking. His past actions now disgust him.

---

[13] **Psalm 53:1** paraphrased

He regrets what he did as a warlock.

"I know forgiveness is necessary to live in the Kingdom of Adonai, and that trust has to be earned — I can live with that. I expect if I stay, I will get demoted. I submit to the SWA leadership. I respect you all here, as I have never respected anyone else in my life. I have much to learn. I have head knowledge, but my heart is just beginning to wake up to the experience of the love of God. I know what it is to walk around half dead inside. Christ has brought me to life, and I commit to serving Him all my days. There are consequences to sin, and whether I feel them or not is up to God. I submit. He is Lord."

Jamie suddenly falls to his knees because the power of Adonai is so weighty on him. He finds the strength to continue: "Adonai the people here are in truth Your disciples . . . whom You have handpicked and called and are equipping. Please blot out the sins that I have committed against them by the blood of Yeshuah. Your mercy renews every morning, or surely, I would not be here today. I wouldn't have made it through the night, but I'm still here . . . so I got mercy over judgment. . . right?"

"Now I ask this school if I can learn from you, if I can serve you. Please forgive me; I was wrong . . . *so* wrong."

Jamie submits to the school and the Lord. Kneeling on the stage, feeling the love of Yahweh surround him, he is silent. No one in the room moves, several of the students weep, and a few look skeptical on the whole affair. The power of Ruach HaKodesh remains heavy on him as he simply lies face down on the stage. Pride drains from Jamie, and a new humility has come in its place. Elohim took all this hatred and malice and replaced it with deep compassion and devotion. Jamie never does anything halfway, and he is going to yield to his newfound master wholly.

Aurora stands up to say, "[14]Whom I have cleansed let no man call unclean. Whom I have called, let no man turn away. I have turned a curse into a blessing and the cursed into the blessed. Rejoice in Me, for I have done great things here this week, and if you continue to walk in love, you will see more great things. Compassion is the key to the anointing."

Aurora sits back down. Jamie gets a hand up from Jesse and Devin. Many people come up to hug Jamie and show their support.

Another voice rings out, "Jamie has been broken before My face, and I have raised him up. There are some here that have pride puffing them up. Beware; your pride will bring you down if you do not master it. The person who broke the glass in the hall of pictures, repent, or you will be judged as you have judged. [15]Judge yourself; and you won't be judged by others. [16]The high and lofty will be brought down, and the lowly put in his place."

The General stands at the podium with Jamie under

---

[14] **Acts 10:15**

[15] **Matthew 7:1-3**

[16] **Proverbs 29:23**

his arm. Devin and Jesse by his side.

Jamie admits, "Uh . . . that picture needs to stay down, cuz . . . I was making a hand gesture that represents the pitchfork of Satan." Jamie is now embarrassed by it.

Everyone gasps at the thought that he was so brazen, and they were so clueless. Ruben Alverez puts his hand on his head with alarm.

"Okay . . . good to know," the General is also surprised by his admission about the picture. He continues with his message to SWA. "This young man is now in a position to learn from you; you are the teacher and he the student. Will you teach him how to love? We sing a song that asks: what will we do if we don't learn to love?"

The worship team begins to sing the song, and Ruby goes to sing with them, as a guest of the Judah tribe.

Kristen and Audrey get the broken glass out of Jamie's frame in the hall of pictures and put it back up on the wall. Kristen puts black tape over the part of Jamie's hand that makes the satanic symbol.

Audrey prays, "Lord, keep Jamie on the wall, and don't let him fall from grace."

When the assembly dismisses, the snow outside is coming down, it stacks up over five inches high on everything. Jamie feels it snowed just for him. The bright white covering everything is how he feels inside.

"Come now, let us reason together, says the Lord: though your sins are like scarlet, they shall be as white as snow; though they are red

> **like crimson, they shall become like wool.**
> **Isaiah 1:18**

Being reassigned to the groundskeeping crew means today Jamie is shoveling sidewalks. For the first time in his life, his pride is not easily hurt. He has joy, piles of it. He greets everyone he sees, whistles, and works hard. He is going to show them all that what he has is real. He has seen the hand of Yahweh, and it is a hand of love. A new photo takes the place of the old one; Jamie is smiling in it. The new policy states for staff photos: only head shots will be allowed.

CHAPTR TEN

SNOW PACKED

By noon classes are canceled for the day. It is too hard to get to class due to the snow levels at over one foot. Kids gather in groups everywhere, the dining hall and dorms. Moving between buildings is kept at a minimum. Now that the wind is picking up, the snowdrifts are at five feet. Everyone manages, however, to get to lunch. The stone floors are slick with the melted snow on them, and many giggle; as they watch their fellow students slip and slide. During lunch, the lights begin to flicker.

Audrey continually stands in front of one of the fireplaces; she can't get warm enough, even wearing her coat and scarf inside.

The grounds crew has been outside all morning in the snow, dealing with problems brought on by the snowfall. Along with Jamie, they trudge into the dining hall at noon, all bundled up and cold. Jamie keeps his head down, not looking around. He is trying to sense if people still hold him in contempt. Many tell him and the crew to keep up the good work. Professor Norman seems to be the main one who is still skeptical of Jamie's conversion. The weary team sits down to hot soup and cinnamon rolls when the lights go out entirely. The crew leader motions to his group; they gather up their gloves and gear and head back out into the cold, cinnamon rolls hanging out of their mouths.

Floodlights on the walls come on. Emergency generators kick in.

The loudspeaker announces, "We are on generator power. Minimize all use of electricity at this time, as mentioned in your SWA handbooks, page 114. We will all remain in this building until further notice. No one is to leave; due to the severe weather."

The loudspeaker lady has nothing perky to add, as she usually does.

Professor Gerald Norman stands up at the main table and yells, "It's Jamie! He caused this storm. We should send him packing right now! How can we trust him after what he did?"

He is visibly upset. The other teachers disagree with him and speak with him in hushed tones.

The wind continues to pick up; the howl of it is

heard even through the thick walls of stone. Some of the dining hall's glass windows have snow so high that they might give way to its weight. Volunteers help the ground crew clear off the glass windows that are at risk. Eric goes with them. He always wants an excuse to wear the new ski suit. From the yard of the dining hall, the crew can see the downed electrical lines. There is more than one. Now with minimal power, the weather forecasters claim it is not going to let up for hours. One of the frozen workers comes in to tell the General that a snowdrift has caused one of the long-arched windows in the Ox lodge entrance to break. He reports that it is just glass and water damage. They are starting to mop the wet floors and boarding up the window. The feel of the room turns more serious. At first, everyone is excited about having no class, but this is getting too dangerous. Professor Norman communicates again to the General that he feels Jamie is a security risk and demands that he deal with him differently.

All the workers, wet with snow and sweating from hard work, shuffle into the dining hall. The room comes to a standstill when Jamie takes off his ski cap and scarf.

The General takes advantage of the stillness.

"Simeon tribe gathers for prayer by the kitchen. Judah get us some music to minister. People, we have work to do."

Everyone is responding to the General's orders when someone passes out by the front doors. It is Jamie.

Doctor Luz or the nurse over here!" the crew leader calls out. "He's burning up with a fever, I guess."

Professor Norman speaks up, "Could be the Lord has judged him, and this is God's hand on this deceiver."

Jesse stands up and glares at the professor, his hands clenched.

"No, you weren't there; you didn't see what God did!" Jesse defends his new friend.

Ruby puts her hand on Jesse's shoulder, worried that he is going to lose his temper.

"Time will reveal all things. We will not jump to conclusions here," the General tells the crowd of confused young people.

They lay Jamie on a nearby table. The nurse and Doctor Luz are busy taking vital signs and looking over the stricken young man. They need to get him out of his snowsuit and boots.

The nurse writes on a clipboard. Male Caucasian, in his early twenties, stomach pain, fever.

Jamie stirs; they question him about his symptoms. He tells them he felt ill last night after the red storm broke up, but he just thought it was from being upset. Now he wonders if the cult leaders have cast a spell on him. Jesse, Eric, Destiny, Kristen, and Ruby let Jamie know they care about him.

"Rocky," Jamie reaches out for Jesse's arm when he sees him. He knows Jesse's nickname from the dorms. "I didn't cook up this snow, you know." (See "Types and Shadows" 10)

Jamie feels everyone is accusing him with their staring eyes.

"No man . . . don't sweat it. Some people are just freaking out a little. Most of us have never seen more than four inches of snow in our whole lives. Just relax and let these guys do their work," Jesse tells him.

Jamie grabs him with both hands; his face is pale with pain. "No, Rocky, you pray. I can't; it hurts too bad . . . can't think. Pray for me, man, okay?" Jamie asks with his eyes welling up.

He drops back down on the table, and the nurse tells him to lie still.

"What if it's his appendix?" the nurse says with concern. "We can't get him to a hospital in this storm, and we are not equipped to do surgery here on campus."

Jamie closes his eyes and braces as a wave of pain hits him. He holds his stomach and moans a little. Jesse and the small group step back as Dr. Luz and the nurse observe him closely. Dr. Luz is very concerned that he didn't plan for this type of situation. Jesse is unnerved a little. He looks down and begins to ask the Lord what to do. He grabs Destiny's hand, and soon the small group of friends is in prayer. Suddenly Jesse lets his hands go from the prayer group and spins around toward everyone else.

"General, may I speak?"

Jesse gets a nod from the General.

"Wasn't it just last night that we all had warfare on the lawn, in unity and full of praise and power? What has changed? Is it our love that has failed us? Are we going to sit around and argue, or are we going to be the Body of Christ, equipped to do God's business? If we don't have love, we don't have anything. I know what it is to have nothing, and believe me, you don't want to go there. Didn't Judah sing about it just this morning? The song asks what you will do if you do not learn to love. Didn't God call us to show Jamie how to love? Wasn't that God's last word to us? Why seek a new word when we haven't done the last one?"

Jesse looks around, his eyes like fire. Simeon tribe tells the General that was also what the Lord told them in their prayer group.

"So, it is love that we need to break this natural storm also. Everyone, let's pray for Jamie's recovery," the General recommends.

The room erupts with a compassionate prayer for Jamie. As the tide of voices subsides, everyone notices the wind has quit. It is evening now; the stars are out, and it is cold. Jamie's fever breaks, and his pain mellows. Peanut butter and jelly sandwiches are served for supper. Electricity is expected to come on in the morning. All of SWA will be sleeping in the dining hall; it will be an interesting night. The school is ready for this, arctic sleeping bags come out of storage.

Jamie is diagnosed with the flu, complicated by exhaustion and hypothermia from working outside. Pneumonia is a cause for concern now. He is doing better but very tired and weak. They have found a cot for him and placed him near the fireplace. The grounds crew suits up one more time to check the campus for the night. Jamie is resting. Students sit all over, playing games, playing guitars, or talking. Professor Norman stands up and determinately walks toward Jamie. Jesse and Eric notice and step closer to Jamie. The Professor shakes the feeble Jamie on the shoulder.

Jamie opens his eyes dimly and says, "Yes, sir?"

Norman leaves his hand on Jamie's shoulder. From Jesse's angle, it looked bad, as though the teacher would do Jamie harm. Jesse bolts his way to the cot, ready to defend his new friend.

"I spoke out of turn today; I was too quick to judge you. Will you forgive an old military man?"

Jesse still looks unnerved.

"Easy there, Rocky, we are just having a friendly chat," Jamie says, very quiet and precise.

He closes his eyes, too tired for any more activity.

The nurse shoos them all away.

"Sorry Sir, I thought . . . I mean . . . it looked like . . . ," Jesse stammers.

"It's alright, son, everything is alright now. Have a good night," Professor Norman tells him.

The teacher's eyes are kind again, not like they have been earlier. Ruby puts her hand on Jesse's shoulder.

"Down, boy! All you need is to lay your hand on a teacher to get suspended."

Ruby studies Jesse's eyes for signs of his mental state. She can see he is in control and reasonably calm. Professor Norman is ex-military and can be intimidating. Devin is now off to look for something soft to sleep on now that things have calmed down. Professor Alvey is ministering to Jamie. He prays with his hand on Jamie's chest.

"Father God, thank you for bringing us through the day, now safely bring us through the night. Give Jamie strength and peace. Don't let him lose heart now; after all that he's experienced. Thank you for preserving him from death and the attack of the enemy. We pray for protection over this campus. Help us to dig out tomorrow and give us electricity for the buildings soon. We are thankful for these fireplaces. We would be in much worse shape if they were not here. In Jesus' name, Amen."

Jamie whispers a faint, "Thank you." He is unsure of his position on campus. The ex-warlock may still have to leave. He doesn't want to, as he knows of no other place like this one. The presence of Elohim has become the most important thing to him. Now he knows why his parents rush off for church all the time. He has tasted of Yahweh, and it is good. He is addicted.

The over-sized fireplaces crackle and glow in the winter night — it is a nice feeling. Everyone at SWA sleeps on the floor, teachers and all, with one side for girls and one for boys. Jamie is one of the few to get a portable cot, the others are the General and his wife, Jennifer. The kids find out she is the General's wife. The General protects his privacy; he is somewhat of a mystery. The students only know him as the General.

"Who'd a thunk it? Jennifer is his wife?" Jacob comments.

Tomorrow will be all about digging the snow out

and getting the campus back to normal. Ruby and Jesse are learning that normal is a thing of the past.

The fireplaces produce a flickering glow on each end of the room, as the glass ceiling reveals that the stars are very bright in the cold night. Everyone has their polar sleeping bag and pillow. Hushed voices mellow as the night goes on. Most everyone is lying down, trying to sleep.

Jesse thinks Eric will never quit talking. Eric gets chatty at night, but Jesse wants some quiet time with the Lord. Eric is finally out of things to say. They both lie down and close their eyes. Jesse just gets his head on his pillow when there is a flash of blue light. He knows it isn't the emergency lights; they are red. He sits up just in time to see that there are two angels over Jamie. They both touch him with one finger. Jamie is still asleep, but he twitches, and a smile comes on his face.

Over by Professor Norman, Jesse discerns two little insect-like imps with tiny wings that flutter furiously. They are chattering things into his ear. Their voices buzz with disturbed and upset tones.

Across the eaves of the dining hall, Jesse can see angels sitting everywhere in all directions. Some have swords, while others do not. They are looking around and staying alert. Many of them look as if they are looking far away into the distance. Others focus on people in the room. Jesse catches the eyes of one large all-white angel at the peak of the ceiling; his eyes are piercing and intense. He nods at Jesse; Jesse nods back, a little intimidated by the robust and powerful angel.

"Hey, Rocky, want some jerky?" Eric asks Jesse. In one nanosecond, the angels and the tiny imps are nowhere. However, Jesse knows they are still there. He takes a piece of jerky and lies back down. Over on the other side of the room, Jesse sees Destiny sit up suddenly and look up at the peak of the ceiling where the big angel is. Jesse recognizes that she, too, is getting a glimpse into the spirit realm. She has the same look on her face that Eric saw on Jesse. Destiny gives a wave to Jesse from the other side of the room. They both can see demons *and* angels. It is late, and the two are getting very drowsy. If Jesse wants to walk in the Spirit, is he going to be able to see in the Spirit all the time?

"One step at a time, Jesse," Ruach HaKodesh tells him.

That is okay with Jesse. It is a lot to take in. He is glad Destiny is learning with him; he knows she is someone special. Tomorrow he will ask Jamie if he remembers the visit by two angels.

Please, Lord, don't let the enemy hassle me in my sleep. I plead the blood over my dreams and mind; Jesse prays before he drifts off to sleep.

Ruach HaKodesh tells him, *"When you see in the Spirit, you see both sides, not just the good. You will get used to the spectacle so much that it won't throw you. I need you to be calm in many situations. Faith and fear don't fit in the same bottle."*

(See "Types and Shadows" 10)

CHAPTER ELEVEN

BROKEN CHAINS

The snow is melting, and eventually, mud will take its place. Power returns at some point in the night and everything is close to normal again as everyone emerges from their sleeping bags.

It's not long until the cadets trudge one by one into worship in the morning after the blizzard. It is good to see the sunshine. Judah has some new songs to try out today. Christmas decorations are starting to be put up, here and there, on the inside of all the buildings. It will take all month for the grounds crew to hang lights and put up Christmas tree displays. The academy is known for its beautiful holiday displays.

The first song starts with just a strumming acoustic guitar and then vocals, and finally, the rest of the musicians join in. Everyone is enjoying the new song; the words are forceful and run deep with honesty and emotion. Aurora Oliver wrote most of the songs in the past, but Jamie wrote this one. His name is on the overhead projector with the lyrics. Jesse looks around for Jamie. Did he come to worship, or is he still sick? Kristen spots Jamie on stage with a guitar. No one knew he played. In the dorm, no one saw him with a guitar. Yet here he is with the worship band. His strength has returned miraculously.

The song is earthy and natural. Jamie leans up to a microphone and sings:

> Life has changed overnight
> I was fighting the wrong fight
> Still, I'm singing,
> Father, take me to your secret place
> I don't see the old man on this face
> Still, I'm singing,
> Father, take me to your secret place
> Too many reasons to admit I was wrong
> Still, all my excuses aren't that strong
> I'm not giving up,
> When you're changing me from the inside out

The words are insightful. Ruby notices Jacob has a distant look on his face. She waves her hand in front of his face; his eyes don't focus. Ruby grabs Jesse by the arm and points to Jacob.

"Oh, he is in a trance in the Spirit. Don't bother him," Jesse says so casually that it takes Ruby aback.

"Huh?" Ruby wonders if Jesse is right.

Jesse sees the look on her face and adds, "You know . . . like John on the isle of Patmos? **Revelation 1:10,** Duh!"

Ruby shrugs her shoulders and heads out for class as Aurora thanks Jamie for sharing his new song.

"Everyone is leaving worship, and Jacob is still sitting there, blinking, breathing," Eric says with concern.

Destiny comments, "There will be no living with him after this."

Her brother is cocky, no doubt, Ruby thinks.

By this time, several teachers have come to see why the group didn't go to class. It isn't the first time someone has gone out in a vision for long periods at the academy. They tell the others to go on to class. Several adults attend to Jacob while he is in the Spirit.

A lady from the office gives Jesse a note at the doorway. Jesse reads: "Your parents are here; please meet them at the front entrance of your dorm."

Across the room, Ruby glances at Jesse, wondering what the note from the office is. Jesse's face gives no clue as he heads towards Levi lodge.

Over the sizable piles of snow dozed up in the parking lot, Jesse sees an old jalopy van, rusted with stickers all over it. The back seat full of junk. Jesse knows it belongs to his parents. They are embarrassing him already, and he hasn't even seen them yet. He takes a deep breath and steps inside the lodge entry. There, standing in the commons area is the General and his parents. Jesse has mixed emotions seeing his parents after over three years. One urge is to punch his dad, and another is to hug them both and weep. He puts both on hold till he knows what is going on.

His parents grab Jesse up with hugs and say, "Oh, look how big you are!"

Jesse loves his parents, but he knows they are always bad news. He greets them guardedly, waiting for the bomb to drop. A thousand questions pile up in his head. He was around twelve when they left him with Uncle Bill.

Why are they here? It's been over three years. What do they want now?

The General puts his hand on Jesse's shoulder.

Wow, the General is talking to me.

Jesse feels honored, even if it is bad news. The General's voice is compassionate toward Jesse as he begins to fill him in.

"Your parents have come for you, Jesse." The General's voice is low and quiet.

His mother stands excitedly with her medium length hair pulled back and unkempt; no makeup, baggy sweater, and a simple long shirt, she can barely contain herself. She is very "organic," as she calls it. Turning to look at Jesse, her eyes light up as she tells him, "Yes, Jess, we are going to take you on tour with us. Isn't that great? We will give you a minute to get your things."

"See you at the van," Jesse's dad, Allen, says with little expression as he and Jesse's mom walk toward the front door.

Allen is thirty-eight, but his face shows evidence of a hard life. His deep-set eyes are piercing. He has a faded blue denim shirt and jeans with long black hair running down his lower back. Rhinestone studs decorate his over-worn shirt. Jesse's eyes look panicked as he focuses on the General.

The General sits Jesse down on the couch in the common area as Jesse's parents wait in the parking lot. The General speaks in hushed tones.

"I know this looks bad for you, Jesse, but just give God a chance to turn it around. I still feel you will be able to finish out your training here. The prophetess said they would come for you, but you would return swiftly. I understand they abandoned you in the past; you need to let God put your broken family back together. God has a plan; we just have to hold on for the ride."

Jesse nods — he is still soaking it in.

The General gives him a cellphone, "You get in danger, they get drunk and drive, anything; you call me."

Jesse never had a cellphone before. That was something "normal" people have. Jesse puts the phone in his pocket as if it is a gold treasure. The General is younger than Jesse's dad, but he is more of a father to Jesse than his own dad. All the cadets look up to the General. Jesse feels the General genuinely cares about him, that he somehow understands him.

"Thanks," Jesse says, still stunned by it all.

"Can't I tell everyone goodbye?" Jesse isn't ready to go so suddenly.

"No, it is better this way. I am hoping this isn't final, and the Lord will have you back by breakfast. Go with God, Jesse, the prophet."

The General gives him a long hug, and Jesse heads to his room to pack his things. He places Eric's coat on his bed and slowly walks out into the common area. Looking around at the beautiful dorm, he sighs.

I have such mixed emotions seeing my parents after over three years. Leaving here doesn't feel right, God. What is going on? Please, God, don't let me have to leave here. Please. Jesse begs Adonai. *How can I cling to the girls if I am drug away? I have to stand on the prophecy; I have to keep the faith. Why can't I have my parents and this school too?*

"Trust me, Jesse, trust me." Jesse hears Ruach HaKodesh in his head.

Down at the van, Jesse's parents are digging through the back seat to make room for him. Jesse comes over to the van with his backpack containing his few possessions.

"Where is your coat, Jesse?" his mom questions.

"Don't have one," Jesse wants them to know life has been rough. They don't have a clue. (See "Types and Shadows" 11)

"You won't need one in California," Allen tells

him.

"I want to stay here; this is my home now. No offense, but I am almost seventeen now. I have a life here," Jesse confronts his parent's wishes.

Allen walks over and quietly says, "Get in."

"But," Jesse stops when his dad's arm goes up as though he is going to hit Jesse.

Jesse knows his dad is a hard-core disciplinarian. The discussion is closed; this causes Jesse's anger to well up on the inside. The prophetess said he would return swiftly — he holds on to that hope.

Jesse feels as if it is at the last minute that they decided to come and get him. Pop cans, candy wrappers, and music equipment are scattered all over the back seat. Jesse squeezes in and sits on the stained cloth upholstery. The smell of drugs and beer brings back memories of early childhood. He fingers the phone in his jacket pocket, next to his ratty old acceptance letter. Jesse's mom is giddy and happy; Allen lights up a cigarette from the driver's seat. Jesse smiles weakly at his mom. Allen looks back at Jesse through the rear-view mirror as they start out of the parking lot, his cigarette smoke dancing around the rear-view mirror.

"We gotta get you out of this Jesus freak place. It would have ruined you, son. You are with us now, so no more of that touchy-feely love talk, you hear? I'm gonna make a man out of you, despite yourself," Allen lectures him. "Billy had a nervous breakdown when you ran away. What were you thinking?"

Jesse looks back at his dad's angry eyes in the mirror. Jesse's mom turns up the radio, and Jesse sees the SWA entrance disappear behind him.

Oh, God; how can this be happening? Maybe the car will slide off this snow-packed road, and we will have to stay. Why can't I have my parents and this awesome school too? I have a prophecy with Ruby and Destiny; this can't be happening.

In his mind, he thinks of where he would be about now in class with his friends. His parents always pulled him in and out of school. When they left him with his Uncle Bill, he thought he would never see them again.

How can they pretend everything is okay? Where have they been for over three years? What about all the big talk of record contracts and making it "big"?

Jesse feels rage stir in him; he manages to stuff it deep inside for now, but he clinches his fist till they hurt. To his surprise, they stop in town. They jump out and head to the front door of a bar. The bar sign squeaks on an old wood slab, wired to the building, "The Crow's Den." It is an old tin warehouse with few windows.

Jesse's dad yells, "This is our first stop, Jess, come on. Because of all this snow, we're stuck in this pathetic little town."

It is ten o'clock in the morning; are my parents going to hit the bars already?

Inside it is dark and dirty. Jesse can sense demons in the place. He feels so alone even though he knows that he isn't. His mom brings him a hamburger and fries from the bar's grill. He had breakfast on campus, and he isn't hungry yet. She smiles and pats him on the head. They are making a deal to play there tonight. Jesse will have to run the sound for them as he did years ago when he was only ten or eleven. *Maybe being in a bar is enough to get them in trouble and get me out of this arrangement.* Adonai says, "*Wait*," so Jesse settles in and puts the phone back in his pocket. He goes out to help his dad carry in equipment.

Jesse stands outside the bar, waiting to carry in guitars. There are broken beer bottles in the grass jutting out of the melting snow. Jesse's eyes glaze over, recalling memories of New York and darker times.

Allen suddenly backhands Jesse in the mouth and splits Jesse's lip open. Jesse puts his hand against his lip to stop it from bleeding.

"Hey, boy, wake up and take this inside!" his dad yells, holding out a guitar case.

You're just like Uncle Bill, Dad . . . you are just like your brother.

Jesse is shaking, more in rage than anything. He walks past his mom, who sees the split lip. Her expression changes as she goes out to Allen.

Anton, the Guardian, is with Jesse all the time. He couldn't stop Allen from hitting Jesse this time. He remains vigilant and helps Jesse not to get overwhelmed. A tear runs down the mighty angel's face.

Back on campus, everyone asks about Jesse. The word has gotten around that his parents have come for him.

During third period, Jacob, still in his trance, yells out, "The stone sign is falling on the bus, better fix it fast."

A few adults who are attending him jump up and call the grounds crew. The grounds crew drives out to the front bridge gate to check it out. Sure enough, the giant chain attached to the rock over the road is rusty and about to give way. A field trip bus is returning from town. The workers flag them down. The bus will have to wait until the sign is safely secured. The crew gets a ladder up to replace the chain. One guy is slipping a second chain loop on the rock when the old one breaks from rust. The colossal rock sign swings down, being hooked only on one side. Everyone at the gate watches it as it smashes into the pavement. It could have wiped out the entire bridge rail, but it only tears up some of the pavement, and no one gets hurt. Everyone on the bus is glad it didn't come down on them. The metal eagle keeps its grip on the stone sign, lying sideways with one end jabbed in the pavement and snow.

The bus rolls on up to the campus, and the crew begins to re-attach the sign to its spire. The crew leader radios back to the main office that Jacob was right.

Back at the Shekinah Sanctuary, Jacob is still somewhere else in his spirit. What else is Jacob going to reveal?

"Destiny, Jesse is gone; his parents came for him," Ruby breathlessly exclaims.

"No way! I am going to fast and pray. Ruby, you should too," Destiny advises.

"No, I am going to panic and pout — seriously? Jesse can't be leaving!" Ruby is too overcome with dread to pray or fast.

After class, Ruby goes straight to her dad's classroom. He explains Jesse's situation to her and reminds her of the prophecy that they work together after graduation.

"You will see him again; he will be just fine. Just you wait and see," he assures his panicked daughter. "Let's pray, and you will feel better," he tells her as she gives him that look of disbelief.

Back at the dorms, Eric and Devin find Jesse's things gone.

"It's true. His stuff is gone. Here is the coat I let him borrow." Eric feels terrible that he is gone. They all feel sad, and the room becomes quiet. They feel awful for Jesse being ripped from the beautiful school and miss not having him around.

Destiny is crying in the dorm room. No one realized she cared that much for Jesse.

"It is just that he is an exceptional person and such a blessing to the school," Destiny rationally justifies her tears. It makes Ruby start crying.

Destiny keeps off by herself in their dorm. Ruby cries off and on all night.

The night is not at all quiet for Jesse. The Crow's Den Bar is full. Jesse's parents are on the small stage, playing rock and roll at full volume. They are both skilled singers/songwriters and musicians. Their playing doesn't hinder them from drinking. Jesse sees that it is ten-thirty p.m. He is used to being asleep by now. Tonight, he doesn't know where he can sleep. By now, Jesse's lip shows swelling; no one seems to be concerned for him. By eleven-thirty, Allen stops giving Jesse commands to adjust the sound, so Jesse just slumps down behind the counter. He finds a pile of bar towels to use for a pillow. Jesse feels like the only one in the room that isn't drunk. He is too young to be there, but no one seems to care. The music pulses in Jesse's chest, but the words don't move him. It is all noise to his ears. He rehearses the conversation he had with the General. How did the General have a cellphone ready to give him? It gave Jesse some peace to know Adonai is up to something, but he just doesn't know what. Jesse is getting very sleepy. He pulls out the crumpled SWA acceptance letter and clutches it in his hand. He watches the demons dance and throw what looks like dirt on people for a while.

Hey Lord, the General called me a prophet. Wow.

With that thought, he falls asleep on the floor behind the counter in Crow's Den Bar. The acceptance letter still gripped in his hand, and the hand-written prophecy still legible, just tattered.

Jesse's parents sing the words, "Will you still love me tomorrow?"

Jesse wakes up stiff on the floor the next morning;

it is quiet. The clock on the wall shows it is five-thirty in the morning. Surprisingly the sound equipment is gone from the counter. His parents rarely get up before noon. Peering over the counter, Jesse sees a lady mopping the floors; she ignores Jesse altogether. It seems she has issues of her own.

"Hey, are we the only ones here?" Jesse asks sleepily.

The woman has frazzled hair, and her makeup has smeared.

"We are the only ones here; I have to clean the entire place by myself." She breaks down and cries over her mop bucket.

"Oh, don't cry . . . I will help you. Don't cry. Here give me your mop, I'll finish this floor," Jesse hates to see her cry.

With surprise, she passes the mop to him.

"You will do that for me? Oh, I see by your shirt, that you are a cadet from the academy. You are so nice. Thank you. Now I can finish on time to see my son play the violin at his recital! It is at eight o'clock sharp; no way I can get all this done by myself. He is just nine, but he is really good!" she wipes her face and scurries around to finish up the last few details.

He finishes the mopping, grabs his backpack, and goes outside to see if his parents are there.

Where's the van? Did they get arrested?

The only vehicle is the cleaning van. He feels for the phone in his pocket . . . it is gone! He finds a napkin there instead. He pulls it out along with the SWA letter. The sun is so bright; it takes a minute for his eyes to adjust. They have left him a note on it:

DEAR JESSE,
WE FEEL THE NEED TO MOVE ON WITHOUT YOU. HAVING YOU AROUND DAMPENS OUR STYLE. THINGS JUST DIDN'T WORK OUT. WE TOOK THE PHONE; YOU WON'T NEED IT. WE'LL CALL YOU AT CHRISTMAS. GO ON BACK TO SCHOOL.
LOVE,
MOM AND DAD
WE HEREBY GIVE SWA AND JOSE PEREZ ALL AUTHORITY FOR JESSE'S CARE UNTIL HE REACHES EIGHTEEN.

Jesse sits on the steps of the bar; as the cleaning lady locks up. Someday he hopes his parents will be able to love him. The weary Jesse figures that his mom decided to protect him from his dad's flare-up of violence. He imagines his mom is just looking out for him. He mainly wishes she loved him enough to stay around. Today marks the third time they have abandoned him. Grief over his parents' actions hits him, and he puts his head on his knees as he feels the deep pain that abandonment brings.

The lady is concerned, "Oh, honey, are you okay?"

"Yeah, yeah . . ." Jesse gets a grip on his emotions to save his pride. "I just got shook up for a minute. Family

— can't live with them — can't live without them."

"You miss your parents cuz you are at the academy . . . well, that will pass. Can I run you up to SWA? It is only four miles from the campus. I still have time, since you did the floors," she offers.

"Why were you sleeping in the bar, anyway? I know the General would disapprove, young man," she says in a motherly fashion.

Jesse smiles, "It was my family's idea of a reunion. I really need to get back before classes start."

She can see the sadness in Jesse's eyes. She realizes she does not know his situation all that clearly.

"Well, I will run you up there, *real* quick, don't forget your backpack." The lady unlocks her cleaning van, and they both get in.

She drops him off in front of the General's office and insists he go straight in, to make sure Jesse is on the "up and up."

Jesse waves goodbye to her as she drives off to her son's recital. Jesse steps inside the office; to his surprise, the secretary knows who he is.

"General, Jesse is back! Just like the prophetess said!" she announces through her office phone.

The General runs out of his office, and down the stairs to the lobby; he sees Jesse and his sad eyes and swollen split lip.

"Welcome back, Jesse, tell me what happened." The General shows deep concern. Everyone in the office hovers around Jesse. They all are upset seeing Jesse's lip and broken demeanor. Soon all the office staff is standing in the lobby to hear his story.

"My family is still a broken mess . . . but I know my mom cares for me, in her own way."

Jesse pulls out his parent's letter and hands it to the General. The General reads it.

"I'm sorry Jesse, I wish I could've spared you the grief," the General pats him on the shoulder.

"It's okay, this is home now," Jesse is ready to get back to the gang.

Jesse tells them about getting backhanded by his dad, how his mom probably talked his dad into letting Jesse come back to school, and that they had the General's phone.

"If you don't mind, I am pretty hungry. Can I go now?"

Jesse wants to move past the trauma and get back to the routine.

"Your parents will be there for you someday, Jesse. Give the Lord time to turn things around for them. Broken families are His specialty," the General says with a smile.

Then he gives Jesse a short hug and dismisses him. All the office workers tell Jesse they are glad he is back and return to their desks. Jesse nods and heads to the dorms.

The General comments as Jesse walks out the front door, "The prophetess was right, that was fast."

Jacob came out of his trance in the Spirit about

eleven-thirty last night and ran late for breakfast. Jesse runs into him in the dorm commons area; they are both heading for breakfast.

"Hey Jesse, how'd ya bust your lip? What did I miss? I have been out of it for a while."

"Nothing really; you didn't miss much," Jesse says with a smile, split lip and all.

Jacob sees a twinge of sadness in his eyes.

They both go to breakfast together; as they step into the dining hall, everyone applauds.

"Welcome back, boys," says Jennifer, who is standing by the door.

"Hey, where did *you* go?" Jacob asks Jesse.

"About four miles away. Where did *you* go?" Jesse asks back.

"I went about four miles up," Jacob says as he points up with his finger and grins.

All the gang gives high fives to the boys as they sit down — all except Ruby, who grabs Jesse and gives him a big hug. Then Destiny runs up, hesitates, and then gives him a long tight hug as well. He rises to meet her in the hug.

Everyone oohs, till Professor Norman cuts the hug short with an "ah-hem."

As Destiny sits down, she notices his lip but doesn't want to embarrass him by asking about it.

Ruby studies Jesse's face and notices his swollen lip as well. She will have to wait until he is ready to tell her about it. His emotions are fragile right now, and she knows she has to give him time.

As Ruby finishes breakfast, she thinks: *I'm sorry Lord, I didn't have faith that You would bring Jesse back. I can be so double minded at times. I just turned fifteen, and all these things have happened to us already. What can possibly happen to beat the last month?*

For now, there is still enough snow outside for some sledding before the first period. All the cadets are gulping down their food, so they can go outside except Audrey, who is freezing and does not want to go play in the snow. Gloria is joyfully snowboarding on a small incline.

"So glad you're back, Jesse," Destiny tells him in passing.

"Me too. I mean, I'm glad to be back."

Jesse stumbles through his words. He still gets nervous around Destiny and is embarrassed by his split lip. Jesse and Jacob remain to eat alone, with just a few teachers at their table and the kitchen crew cleaning up.

The General comes over to the boys.

"I thank the Lord you are both back. Jesse here is your note from your parents. I am glad your parents can now be reached by phone. I hope they stay in contact."

"Don't hold your breath," says Jesse in monotone.

Jesse is bitter, and he knows it. He doesn't know how else to be. The General pats his back and leaves to talk to a professor, and the boys are left alone to eat their breakfast. They can see their classmates outside, throwing snowballs, and running around on the big snow piles and drifts. They feel different from what they did yesterday, and both feel a connection they did not have before. The Lord has taken them both on a short journey, and it has changed them somehow. They don't say much. They just feel the commonplace the Lord has put them in. As they step out into the campus's snowy playground, they look at each other and wonder if they are spiritually mature enough for all this? They run after their friends until time for class.

As November progresses, everyone at SWA is thinking of Thanksgiving and Christmas break. Four months into the semester; the kids know the campus like their own backyards. Christmas is just around the corner. Some kids will be taking their first holiday home, while many are counting the days, others dreading it. Jesse has no plans for the holidays; his church cannot afford a bus ticket to bring him home. Several staff members stay every year to be there for the ones who remain on campus.

CHAPTER TWELVE

READY, SET, BREAK!

In only five days, it will be Christmas break. Everyone is buzzing with conversations about their holiday plans. Some are going with their families on faraway trips; others are looking forward to just being home.

Ruby tells Destiny, "Just a few more days of classes to get through. This year, we will stay on campus; it's dad's turn to stay with the kids who don't go home for the holidays. I have many happy memories of Christmas on the campus. My mom and my big brother Arlo are coming up."

Destiny says, "I am excited to go home. I just want

to see my parents and then get back to school."

Ruby has been working on a song for two months. She has dance steps choreographed to it and everything. The last night before Christmas break, the academy has a big talent show. She is signed up. Jacob has a comedy routine to do. Gloria plans to do a version of *Silent Night* set to techno music; she won't let anyone hear it. Judah tribe has eleven entries, along with all the other tribe's entries. It will be a night to remember. Even the staff and teachers participate. Professor Alvey is known for his outrageous skits that spoof famous Christmas movies. One of the cooks does a mean breakdance.

It is hard for the kids to concentrate on their studies, nevertheless, all the tests demand that they buckle down. Oral reports are due on the subject of spirits of addiction and complacency in Professor Alvey's Demonology class.

The holiday lights on campus are lavish. Decorated trees light up every dorm lobby, hall, classroom, and the dining hall. The night glows with all the lights on the buildings and large pine trees. Several people have candy canes in their mouths, even Professor Norman. Spirits are high, even for this busy week.

Jesse has mixed feelings about the holiday season. He likes Christmas now, but he misses the Perez's. His parents come to mind often this time of year as well. Conflicted emotions swirl in his mind due to their erratic behavior, having abandoned him three times now, plus he feels angry about the violence from his dad. If he dwells on it too long; it will bring him to tears. He checks out the small scars on his palms from his nails being in a tight fist in fear and frustration. He wonders if his dad has scars like him. The split lip his dad gave him also left a scar, inside and out. *They promised to call, but I don't think they will.*

One door down, Kristen is heard singing Christmas carols at the top of her lungs. She is forbidden to sing *Jingle Bells* anymore, for she has worn out her floor leader's patience. Kristen has a plastic holly headband that lights up and flashes in her red hair. It is very festive.

Ruby tells her, "I am determined to win the cleanest room of the week. This week it is not cake and ice cream, it is cookies, chocolate cherries, and a huge load of holiday sweets!"

Kristen responds, "Yeah, everyone wants to get their hands on the prize for Christmas week. My roommates are not neat, so I gave up on winning a long time ago. For second-year students, they are not very together."

Jesse's dorm room is not holding out much hope to win either. They just acquired a new roommate, Steven. He is moody and messy. Steven's hazel eyes seem very sad. His black hair contrasts with his fair skin and makes him look pale, even sickly. Steven has not finished writing his oral report, and papers are scattered all over. Eric and Devin are wrapping presents. Tape, ribbon, and all the wrapping paper clutter the bed. Snowsuits are drying in front of the big window.

Yep, no hope for this room, Yosef resigns himself

to the fact.

Yosef can see nothing but clutter. He fears his Hanukkah menorah will only get broken in the chaos, so he sadly leaves it in the drawer and never takes it out to light the candles.

In Kristen's dorm next to Ruby's, the girls put up lights hoping to edge out the competition. A glow of blinking lights flash in the doorway of their room. Others put out "bribes" for the judges: a plate of cookies, the Bible opened to a passage of Christ's birth with a nativity scene on the side.

It is Wednesday, and it is Ruby's turn to read her report in her dad's class. She just wants to get it over with so she can relax and enjoy the season. She gets up and steps behind the podium, her head disappearing behind it. There is a big laugh. She is too short, so they find something for her to stand on. Everyone else is relaxed, but she is nervous.

"First, I studied about the Spirit of Complacency. I thought about this topic and decided it is just not that important. I mean, how much damage can this particular spirit do? Everyone is complacent about one thing or another; what is the big deal? For instance, I don't really need straight A's; I can relax instead. Okay, get my point?"

Ruby speaks way too fast because her nerves are getting to her. She continues, her foot wiggling on the wood box.

"Eighty percent of all the students polled on

campus don't listen to any news on a daily basis. They only listen if there is a chance of classes getting canceled due to bad weather. Fifty percent of all adults polled on campus don't know their cholesterol number. Only twenty percent of all Christians pay tithes; they are the group that keeps the churches running and the missions supplied. Only one in four people get their flu shots. Half of all cars in the area have flat spare tires. Complacency is a blanket of fuzziness that settles over a person, lulling him or her to feel as if everything is okay, whether it is or not. It can cause a Christian to skip praying, calling on the sick, and checking on the elderly. It can cause the lost not to be concerned about eternity. This spirit moves slowly, but it can develop into a stronghold if left long enough. Complacency can mask itself as a peaceful spirit. The difference is, however, that one spirit gives assurance, and the other gives excuses. Once complacency has been renounced or cast away, the person must replace it with God's will and dedication, or it can return bigger and duller in the life of that person."

Ruby's voice trails off as Jesse's mind wanders onto the coming holiday break. He is daydreaming. Though many in the class actually listen to this report, truly absorbing Ruby's wise words, Jesse does not. He simply fades from the sounds around him, falling deeper into his own thoughts.

Who else will be on campus for Christmas? He wonders. *If my friends get me gifts, what will I give them? Do I have time to draw a bunch of portraits? Why can't I have a normal life and parents that are stable?*

"Addiction," Ruby begins her next subject. "Addictions can be inherited, learned behavior from living in an environment, as a result of dysfunction, a painkiller of sorts. Regardless of the cause, Jesus has made a way out. The consequence of bad behavior may still have quite a bite to it, however. Tobacco, gambling, controlled substances, eating addictions, shopping; the list is endless. Humanity has an endless appetite, Jesus being what we all need to be satisfied. Somewhere along the way, people lose control, and the addiction calls the shots. Marriages, jobs, friends, health, and reputations, all lost to feed the need. Sin is a cruel taskmaster. We, as ministering agents, can recognize and deal with addictions. Many victims will deny their addictions strongly. Denial is a hurdle to jump over. In fact, denial itself can be an addiction that turns to habitual lying. Lying to self is the start: "I can quit any time," "Just one more, and then tomorrow I will change." Repentance is the key to God's deliverance. Other strongholds often must be dealt with first.

"In conclusion, I must stress that the ability to convey the love of God is the best and greatest task we can undertake. Love bears up under anything and everything that comes; it is ever ready to believe the best of every person. It causes hope to survive under all circumstances, and it endures everything. Love never fails. **I Corinthians 13:7-8a**. As we go out into the world, it is so important that we walk in the Spirit and in love. What are we if we don't learn love? Thank you."

Ruby's friends stand up and applaud the loudest as

she steps off the crate and takes her seat. As Professor Alvey smiles and calls for the next student speaker, Ruby slumps to her chair, her heart still beating hard.

It is over. Now I can concentrate on Christmas.

Kristen has bells on her boots today, and she jingled them for Ruby. After the first hour, everyone knows Kristen has the Christmas spirit. She is passing out candy canes to everyone she meets and hums Christmas carols incessantly. Several people wear Santa hats, even a teacher or two, but Kristen's blinking lights in her plastic holly are just too much. One teacher insists that she turn off her holly during class.

On the stairway to the next class, Kristen continues doling out mini candy canes. She is surprised when she hands Jesse one; his hands shake, and his eyes well with tears.

Not quite the reaction I was going for, Kristen thinks. *I don't get boys*.

As the days go by, everyone feels more festive. Eric is in the Christmas mood by now, ordering all his gifts from expensive catalogs. The delivery truck knows by routine where his dorm is. Others take the Saturday bus to the only department store in the little town of Eastcliffe, just below the campus. Jesse, of course, has no cash for presents. He can't knit like Gloria, but he can draw portraits; he has all his friends drawn. Only Professor Alvey and the General are left to sketch. He created caricatures of his friends and serious portraits of the adults on his list. He looks for a card in the mail from his parents, although he knows there is little chance.

Wednesday is a blur of tests, Thursday a few more. Snow falls on Thursday, making the night light displays even more dazzling as they reflect on the snow. Jamie thinks how the white snow resembles the purity of his redeemed heart. It glistens and sparkles in the cold night air. He feels new inside and has peace in his heart. Joy envelopes him as he works with the ground crew.

By Friday, all classes are over for the semester, and the talent show is all the talk. It is a time to celebrate and enjoy the season. Jamie is doing well, and people seem to accept him now.

The Shekinah Sanctuary dazzles with all the decorations. The talent show is finally here. Judah tribe opens the show with a parody of *The Twelve Days of Christmas*.

On the first day of Christmas, my Savior sent to me
-The truth that set me free
On the second day of Christmas, my Savior sent to me
 -Hope and faith
On the third day of Christmas, my Savior sent to me,
-Power in the Spirit
On the fourth day of Christmas, my Savior sent to me,
-Life abundantly
On the fifth day of Christmas, my Savior sent to me,
-Joy in the Lord
On the sixth day of Christmas, my Savior sent to me

-Fruit of the Spirit
On the seventh day of Christmas, my Savior sent to me
-Health and well-being
 On the eighth day of Christmas, my Savior sent to me
 -Living water springing
On the ninth day of Christmas, my Savior sent to me
 -Heart full of singing
On the tenth day of Christmas, my Savior sent to me
 -Promise of His coming
On the eleventh day of Christmas, my Savior sent to me
-Peace that passes understanding
On the Twelfth day of Christmas, my Savior sent to me
-All of Abraham's blessings

    Jacob does his comedy skit like a pro. As usual, he loves attention and doesn't seem to be nervous at all. Gloria's techno of Silent Night turns out quite pretty after all. There are dance numbers, Christmas songs, and of course, Professor Alvarez's running skits that appear without intros, off and on all night in between acts. Ruby's song is emotional and fresh; the crowd loves it. After the show, the dining hall is ready with hot chocolate and cookies. Most people happily exchange gifts then. Jesse gives out his presents to everyone that is leaving campus for Christmas. Kristen loves her caricature sketch; so does Jacob, Eric, and Steven — the new kid.

    Yosef likes his caricature also.

    "My mother will love it."

    Yosef will travel to Israel for the holidays.

    After the program, Ruby walks to the dorm. Her

watch glows "eleven-thirty p.m." as she hears the snow crunch under her feet. She feels Yeshuah rise up beside her, and they walk together through the beautiful scene of lights and snow. Her heart is full of joy and emotion.

I never thought I would sing in front of everyone or do a solo!

The first semester has been awesome. "What do You have in mind for next term?" Ruby asks the Lord.

"*Wait and see, Ruby, wait and see.*"

Saturday morning finds the dining hall with a handful of people. Most students are picked up or take the bus out by eight-thirty in the morning. Destiny is excited to go home for the holidays. She gives Jesse and Ruby handmade cards with pressed flowers on them. She wrote them personal letters about how much they each mean to her and how she values their friendship. Jesse rolled up her portrait he drew with a blue ribbon. She has it in her hand as she gets on the bus alongside her brother. Jesse sketched her face and wrote words that described her, and some things she is known to say off to the side. He made one for Ruby as well.

Ruby feels the gifts she gave them are inferior.

I just gave them worship music. I wish I had something meaningful to give, like what Jesse and Destiny gave me.

During Christmas break, everyone that remains on campus is sitting together now: teachers, staff, and kids alike. Mrs. Alvarez and Ruby's brother Arlo have arrived. Ruby and her dad are excited to see them. Arlo is in his twenties; he looks very much like his dad. Ruby mostly resembles her mom, Yolanda.

A few days later, everyone on campus will join together for a Christmas Eve service, with candlelight, communion, and prayer. Jesse knows the Lord has big plans for that night; he can feel it.

Ruby invites Jesse to spend the day with her and her family. Together they are going back to the Alvarez cabin to make cookies and watch movies. The small log home is cozy and perfect for a Christmas atmosphere. There is a small porch with firewood stacked on it.

Jesse loves to watch families; they are a mystery to him. He especially loves to see Arlo and Ruben together. He has trouble calling Professor Alvey "Ruben" for the holidays, but it is growing on him.

Everyone except Ruby's mom Yolanda goes outside. Arlo starts a snowball fight. Jesse throws one that hits Ruben smack on the forehead . . . everyone freezes a second.

Ruben calls out, "Now, you're gonna get it!"

He runs and chases Jesse into a snowbank.

Ruben grabs Jesse's hand that holds a snowball. He is about to pile snow on him when Arlo comes to Jesse's rescue and tackles his dad, allowing Jesse to climb free of the snowbank. Jesse stands, catching his breath, watching Arlo and Ruben laugh and wrestle in the snow. Ruby laughs, and her mom grins from the kitchen window. Laughter fills the air.

The rest of the day is like a dream for Jesse; baking cookies, popping popcorn and doing family type stuff. Arlo elbows Ruby in the ribs and kids her that Jesse is handsome and a real catch.

Ruby will always turn red and say, "He is already caught, and I'm not fishing."

Arlo still finds great joy in teasing her. Ruby asks Jesse if he is sad about his parents not contacting him for the holidays.

"Well, it bothers me a little, but I try not to dwell on it," he tells her, scarfing down his seventh cookie with milk.

Arlo comments that it doesn't seem to dampen his appetite. Everyone laughs.

On Christmas Eve, Ruby shows Jesse three presents under the tree in the living room with his name on them. Jesse still needs to draw a portrait of Arlo and Ruby's mom for Christmas. Jesse is nervous about giving handmade gifts, though he is relatively sure that the drawings are suitable. It is good to have something to occupy his time. Just like last year in Spanish Harlem, his presents are wrapped in plain white paper with sketched snow scenes. He remembers back then when Manuel's family took him off the streets and brought him into their family. For a year now, he has walked with the Lord.

Things have turned around for him. His old life seems like a vague dream. He feels guilty for not writing Manuel, but not enough to sit down and actually write to him.

It is time for the candlelight service, and Ruby's heart swells with joy.
This is the best Christmas ever!
As the Alvarez family and Jesse come into the Shekinah Sanctuary, they see that all the decorative candelabras are lit all over the room. It is stunning. Dramatic shadows from the candles play with the architecture of the columns and arches. A lady is playing the harp with dignity and emotion, and a student plays the violin with skill. The music echoes through the massive cathedral space as if they used speakers. It is more than just candles and the small group; Ruach HaKodesh fills the empty spaces. Professor Alvey starts with prayer. As musicians play softly, Ruby notices her dad's voice is trailing off. She opens her eyes. She is floating out in endless space with stars among beautiful pinkish-blue clouds. There are others there too, floating, caught up in the Lord's presence. She can sense that everyone in the group is there and others also. The harp and violin continue their song of worship. Ruby can hear Hebrew words singing:

  Kadosh, Kadosh, Kadosh (Holy, holy, holy).
  Adonai Elohimtz'va'ot (Lord of hosts)

Everyone soaks in the Lord's presence. They are

propelled around in the vastness of space. They praise and sing to the Lord for what seems like hours. Angels are there also; they bow before the Lord and never rise at all. Ruby once again hears the voice of her father. He is singing the Hebrew words, and his off-key singing is annoying to her trained ear. They are back at the Shekinah Sanctuary, sitting around the candles. The two musicians end their song and rest. (See "Types and Shadows" 12)

Did they play the same song for over an hour? They started at eight p.m., and it is midnight already, Ruby wonders.

They all look at each other. It appears that hours have passed while they soaked in the spirit realm. No one speaks; some people wipe tears from their eyes. Ruby notices Jesse sitting with his eyes closed.

Is he still in the Spirit? Everyone else is getting ready to leave.

Ruby points out Jesse to her dad. By now, tears are running down his face. He doesn't wipe them off; it is as if he doesn't even notice them on his cheek. Her dad stops her from going to him. She is worried about him.

"Don't disturb him," he warns Ruby.

Abruptly, Jesse takes a deep breath, as though a glass of cold water hits him.

"Whoa!" Jesse looks around, getting his bearings. "I saw my mom and dad singing in a church, and worshipping, really worshipping. My dad is clean-shaven, and my mom has her hair all done up. I can see it now; God can reach my parents; it's not *too* hard for Him! Ruby, there was this endless sea; calm like glass, no waves . . . I bowed before this cross on my knees. I was on the sea; it held me up! That is when I saw the vision of my mom and dad. It was too beautiful to describe! The sky reflected blue and white on the glassy sea; it was awesome."

By now, he notices the tears and wipes his eyes. Ruby has never seen him grin so big.

At this point, the Alvarez's and Jesse return to the cabin to open presents. Ruben's mini log cabin is warm from the fireplace. Red and green Indian blankets adorn the walls, tables, and railings.

Jesse's drawings bring oohs and ahhs. The Alvarez's surprise Jesse with clothes, a sketchbook, and a ski hat. Jesse wears the hat all day, even in the house. He can't wait to hang up his new clothes; now, his armoire won't look so bare. His favorite gift, however, is Destiny's letter. He set it inside his armoire where he can see it every day.

Everyone reflects on how wonderful the evening was at the candlelight service. Arlo is sleeping in Jesse's dorm; Ruben's cabin has just one bedroom. Ruby stays at her dad's cabin, on the couch for the night.

Jesse and Arlo settle in the dorms. Jesse is now able to sleep with the doors closed. The days when his uncle used to lock him in his room for days with just a box of cereal have long faded. He rarely even thought about his painful childhood anymore. They turn out the light, and

Jesse gets in bed.

"Ouch. Ouch!" Jesse feels a few sharp pains in his side.

"Hey man, you alright?" Arlo asks in the dark.

"Oh yeah, sure. I always get these little twinges in my gut. They go away," Jesse made light of them. He has felt these pains ever since he was homeless. He ignores them as much as possible.

"Ya otta go to the doctor," Arlo suggests.

"Nah, I'm not worried about it," Jesse rolls over and drifts off to sleep.

Arlo lays there, worrying about Jesse.

What if it's an ulcer . . . or his appendix or something else serious? Arlo prays for Jesse, "Father, I feel worried about Jesse's stomach. I commit this situation to You."

The next morning is Christmas day. The sun is so bright on the snow that everyone considers wearing sunglasses, even in the house. Jesse takes a moment to go to his prayer rock. The sun has melted the snow off the rocks, and Jesse sits looking down at the cliffs. He wonders where his mom and dad are. He thinks about Poppy, his mom's uncle. They ate many Christmas dinners together when Jesse was young.

God, I don't know how You're gonna save my family, but I thank You for saving them.

"What about your uncle?" Adonai mentions his uncle's lost condition.

Jesse's heart turns cold.

You will have to change my heart cuz I don't feel anything for him. I know You want me to forgive him, but I don't want to even think about him on Christmas day.

Jesse doesn't want to get his emotions in an uproar, so he goes on to the Alvarez cabin for Christmas dinner, putting his family out of his mind. He can enjoy someone else's family for now. He is grateful to Ruby and her family for including him in their holiday.

Sunday service is small and intimate compared to the massive Gothic structure. Worship consists of acoustic guitars and vocals. It is earthy and raw, and the sound echoes off the walls. Ruby loves it; as she gets to lead the worship. Ruben speaks about how Mary, the mother of Jesus, told the Lord, "Be it unto me according to thy word, Lord." He points out that everyone has a word from the Lord about His plan for their lives.

Afterward, Yolanda makes Sunday dinner in the cabin. Jesse gets an invitation to the tasty dinner.

Can life get any better than this? Jesse wonders.

He asks Yahweh to forgive him for the things he did back before he came to know Yeshuah. He feels so grateful to Yahweh this time of the year.

During Christmas break, Jesse, Jamie, and Ruby earn extra money working for the school. They carry boxes of books to classrooms and help take down decorations. Jamie and Jesse enjoy their time working together. Jesse calls him 'little brother' because he led Jamie to Adonai.

Jamie is older and taller, and he and Jesse have a strong bond. Ruby imagines they will be friends for the rest of their lives.

Jamie spent the holidays with Professor Norman. The professor wants to get to know him better and be his mentor. They also workout together and lift weights.

CHAPTER THIRTEEN

UPON THIS ROCK

Yosef is the last one in Jesse's dorm to get back from Christmas break. He has just arrived and gives all his friends souvenirs from Jerusalem. Sadly, he lost a male cousin to a car bomb, and he attended the funeral over Christmas break. The two cousins were close, having gone to Haifa's Hebrew school together before Yosef came to SWA. Everyone is trying to find ways to cheer him up.

Ruby's bunk bed fills with new clothes, make-up, and a neon guitar wall art that she got from her family for Christmas. Milagros comes back with a new face retainer from the Orthodontist and bright blue hair. She is upset with the discomfort of her teeth. Everyone is praying for her when Kristen drops in wearing vintage clothes from her favorite boutique back home. Gloria puts up a poster of a snowboarder on her side of the dorm and is admiring it. Destiny is back from North Dakota. A new ski jacket and a picture of her mom tossed on her bed. Gloria prays for Milagros, but her teeth still hurt.

Ruby is tired of the SWA shirts. She wants to wear the flashy shirt her mom gave her.

"Oh well, maybe on Saturday."

January is routine at SWA: classes, snow, thawing, and more snow. Yosef starts the habit of staying up to hear the nightly news on his radio. His mom sent him to the U.S. to keep him safe, and he worries for her and the rest of his kin living in Haifa.

February brings warmer weather and melting snow. Everyone is talking of spring. After classes, Jesse heads to the back of the dorms to the rocks, where he likes to pray when it is warm enough. It is warming up again, and he loves the feel of the sun on his face. Guilt rises in Jesse, remembering more things from his past that can easily overcome him; some prayer time before the Father is necessary. His old life tends to dominate his mind if he doesn't take it to Elohim. Things that happened to him on the back streets of New York bring him grief and shame. He has never told anyone about all the abuse he suffered after his parents sent him to live with his uncle. Not even to Manuel.

"Jesse, the battle in your mind must be won so you can battle for others. Guard your thoughts, control your dark imaginations, and think about good things. Tear down your walls, let Ruby and Destiny in," Ruach HaKodesh instructs him.

Also, Adonai urges him to ask his friends to come and pray together. Jesse struggles with it. It is hard to let others see his vulnerable side, and it feels too intimate to share. Yet Ruach HaKodesh urges him all the more.

The enemy tells him, "Yeah, you get them back here, and I will push them down the rocks."

Jesse declares, "This is a holy place set aside for the Lord, so no evil shall prevail here. Let the angels of the Lord guard over all who enter here." (See "Types and Shadows" 13)

Jesse realizes he is learning to fight against the dark forces in the spirit realm. From Jamie's deliverance in October, he sees just how powerful it is for believers to take authority over demonic realms. The idea thrills and scares him at the same time. Jamie and Jesse spend time together; they are getting close, even though Jamie is older. They have some things in common that others cannot understand.

As the sun drops below the western mountain range, the clouds turn yellow to orange to pink. Jesse hates to leave the gorgeous view, but it is late and getting quite cold.

"Okay, Lord, I promised to obey your voice. I'll

invite the gang to come here for prayer," Jesse feels optimistic.

It is time to bed down for the night, as school starts up again in the morning. Milagros is still fidgeting with her headgear as Ruby drifts off to sleep. Her dream is dark and murky. In it, a girl about her age is walking around outside barefoot and crying. She has long brown hair and is in her pajamas. She steps on a sharp rock, and the bottom of her foot bleeds. Ruby senses she is distraught, and Ruby fears for her wellbeing. Ruby wakes up before she can finish her dream. She asks the Lord what she should do.

Sitting up in bed, Ruby puts her feet on the floor. She looks out the window, but she doesn't see anyone out there.

"I need to check behind Eagle lodge; that is where the rocky ledge is," Ruby decides. Jesse has told her all about his prayer spot.

Then she decides to tell the dream to Destiny.

"Destiny, wake up. I need to go to Jesse's prayer rock; I think there is a suicidal girl out there," Ruby says, shaking her.

"Okay, I'll go with you, but we should take Melody too," Destiny's groggy voice whispers.

Melody's room is at the end of the girls' rooms. The girls wake up their dorm leader, and they all bundle up and go outside to look and see if they can find the girl in Ruby's dream.

With flashlights in hand, they walk over and look

over the short retaining wall and see the girl in Ruby's dream, looking down the cliff behind the dorms. The girls have seen her on campus, but she isn't in any of their classes.

She is standing on the edge of a huge boulder right where Jesse always prays. The distraught girl is looking down and weeping, mumbling, and not making any sense.

Ruby climbs over the stone retaining wall and approaches her. "Let me help you," Ruby puts out her hand. Melody is calling for help on her cellphone. Destiny prays.

"I am just so tired of it all. I can't take the pressure," the girl mumbles.

Her foot is bleeding on the giant boulder.

A thin grey furry imp with long steely fingers is hovering around her head, whispering.

"Go ahead, and kill yourself," he slobbers.

"Aren't you freezing? Let's go warm up," Ruby suggests to the shivering girl.

"No . . . no," the girl appears as if she is not in her right mind.

Ruby whispers under her breath, "Spirit of Suicide, release her, let her go."

The imp looks shocked and very distraught. The small goblin wanders away, cursing and yelling, "I am so tired, I can't take this." Of course, the humans don't hear the imp, Destiny saw a shadow, but that's all.

By now, five adults are on the scene, and the girl runs to her dorm leader and cries.

"I was going to jump, but when I got here, I just couldn't. I wanted to, but something stopped me. I am ready to let God have control of my life."

The girls' dorm leader prays:

The Spirit of the Lord God is upon me, because the Lord has anointed me to bring good news to the poor; he has sent me to bind up the brokenhearted, to proclaim liberty to the captives, and the opening of the prison to those who are bound; to proclaim the year of the Lord's favor, and the day of vengeance of our God; to comfort all who mourn; to grant to those who mourn in Zion—to give them a beautiful headdress instead of ashes, the oil of gladness instead of mourning, the garment of praise instead of a faint spirit; that they may be called oaks of righteousness, the planting of the Lord, that he may be glorified.

Isaiah 61:1-3

The sobbing girl goes with her dorm leader to call her parents. Ruby thanks Adonai for what He did for the girl. It is midnight already. Ruby, Destiny, and their dorm leader begin to walk back to the dorms. Yawning and looking up, Ruby sees Jesse in the window above. He, too, has been stirred from his sleep.

Knowing the morning will be rough if she doesn't 'hit the hay'; she still feels incredible. She can't wait to hear how Jesse was part of the event. She knows he was, somehow.

Jesse meets them between their rooms in the common area.

"I couldn't sleep, so I got up to look at the stars and pray. You say a girl was out there?" Jesse says.

"She was delirious, and we thought she was going to jump," Destiny explains.

"Yesterday, I was there and prayed that darkness could do no evil on those rocks — that it is holy unto the Lord's use. Just now I saw a de —"

"Demon of Suicide" Destiny finishes his sentence.

The next day the weather is unusually warm for late February. At breakfast, Jesse sits with Ruby and Destiny. Ruby learns more about the girl from last night.

"My dad told me today that the girl is a straight-A student and anorexic. She is getting the help she needs now," Ruby reports to the group.

Jesse feels Ruach HaKodesh tug at him about prayer on the rock.

Okay, Lord, here goes, "If anybody is interested, I pray back there all the time, especially on Saturdays at about four p.m." Jesse speaks up.

Many nod and say, "Okay, cool."

"Destiny, do you and Ruby want to come?" Jesse asks sheepishly.

"We'll try, but no promises," Destiny tells him.

Jesse tells the Holy Spirit; *If the girls don't come, I will feel bad. Also, I value our time together more than anything. How can I share that? Leading a prayer session is out of my comfort zone.*

No answer. Jesse knows it is a 'wait and see' thing. That Saturday evening, Eric, Devin, and Yosef come to the "prayer rock." During prayer, Jesse feels like the guys are watching him. Lying face down on the warm rock, he determines to press past it and get with Adonai. As wind in the pines calms him, he finds the words flow from his mouth. Praise and prayer flood from him, mingled with tears. Jesse doesn't mind the tears as it is cleansing and healing, but it is still awkward around others. Elohim has told him about Jeremiah, the weeping prophet. He knows he must overcome his pride so Elohim can use him more. As the urge to pray lifts, Jesse sits up and wipes his eyes. As he focuses, he sees Yosef, Eric, and Devin lying there with him and praying. Eric especially is vocal and emotional. Jesse is impressed. Yosef sits up and lays his hand on Jesse's head and prays in Hebrew. Jesse thinks it is the most incredible thing he has ever heard. He also can tell he is praying for protection over him and rebuking the enemy.

This guy has his stuff together, thinks Jesse.

Eric joins Yosef and lays his hand on Jesse's back. Jesse feels the rush of Ruach HaKodesh on him, just like when his church prayed for him in New York. They hug and pat each other on the back; no one has a dry eye.

Good deal, it's not just me. The guys cry too when the Lord touches them. "Man, thanks; guys, that was great," says Jesse, standing up and brushing the dirt off his jeans.

"Hey Rock Man, thanks for inviting us. This prayer thingy is good. Can we do it again tomorrow, and I'll bring tunes, okay?" Devin says, straightening his clothes.

Jesse gives up correcting people on his nickname.

"Yeah, umm . . . I needed that! I was, uh . . . missing my parents pretty bad. I'm okay now," confides Yosef.

"Hey, if the girls come, you think we will still move like this?" Jesse throws out his concern to the guys.

"Sure, Rock Man, why not? God takes over, it's all good," says Devin with cool confidence.

Jesse nods.

Okay, God, I know You don't say I told You so. But You did. I can see now how important it is to gather small groups. [17]***Wherever two or three are gathered there You are in the midst of them.***

Yosef adds, "Um . . . too bad we didn't start this five months ago, aye?"

Meanwhile, Ruby and Gloria finish their homework in the dorm's common area, and Destiny is helping Milagros with her book report. It is due Monday. Audrey is reading a book, and Faith is just doodling. The girls are all together at a round table when Gloria checks her watch.

"I wonder if it is too late to pray at the rock," she asks the girls. They see Jesse and the guys come in, and they walk over to the girls.

---

[17]**Matthew 18:20**

Yosef asks the girls, "I um . . . thought you gonna pray with us today?"

Destiny points to the textbook, "Just finished. But tomorrow we will be there if you'll be there tomorrow too."

The girls know they have missed something; tomorrow, nothing will distract them!

"Oh sure, we are meeting again on Sunday if it is warm; same time," Jesse tells them.

"Judah tribe is known for breaking out in prayer groups and moving in the Spirit, that is why everyone wants to be in it. It's about time everyone else gets into it," Destiny tells the others.

Ruby nods in agreement.

On Sunday morning, it is snowing and too cold and slippery for prayer at the rock. The kids are tired of the snow, and they are ready for warmer weather and spring break.

"No prob', we can pray in the common area just like Judah does," Jesse suggests.

Everyone likes the idea.

Gloria jumps up in their dorm and says, "It's three fifty-five. Let's head out to the common area!"

All the girls head out except Destiny; she is not around. Jesse and the usual guys are there. Devin turns on the music. "I want to know You more," the lyrics sing.

Everyone huddles on the Oriental rug by the large windows in the back of the dorm, sitting, kneeling, or sucking carpet as they call it.

Jesse is disappointed that Destiny hasn't come yet. He decides he can't wait for her any longer.

He leads off with, "I feel that there are some difficult times ahead. We need to pray that we will be ready for these difficulties. I don't know what is ahead. I just know He said, 'the battle before us is one of survival and endurance. Let's start by praying for strength and wisdom and pray for protection and for God's will to be done."

He looks up and sees Jamie has come along with several dorm floor leaders.

All right! Jesse is glad to see them. Everyone feels moved by Jesse's talk of a battle for survival. Ruach HaKodesh gives witness to their hearts that it was an actual word from Heaven. Some begin genuinely praying in the Spirit with fierce intensity. It moves others to pray and focus harder. The common area of the lodge is filled with sounds of weeping and praying. Devin's music plays on with driving melody and scripture intertwined. The sound of prayer grows louder and louder.

Several new angels are drawn in by the prayer and gather on the roof. They are there to maintain the open heaven the prayers have produced. Jesse is making a difference and furthering the advancements of the Kingdom. The whole campus will soon be alerted for the "battle of survival."

Things are winding down after two hours. People are stirring from their prayer positions. Ruby looks up to see kids everywhere praying — on the stairs, on the floor.

"Must be fifty people," Jesse estimates.

"Wow, when did they all arrive? It was just a few of us when we started," Ruby says, amazed.

"I think you have started a movement of Ruach HaKodesh here, Rocky," Jamie says, putting a brotherly arm around Jesse.

Jesse is still getting used to being touched. Jamie doesn't loosen his grip. Jesse's family does not demonstrate affection.

He smiles up at Jamie, "Hey, little bro. Next week we can get in groups of four or five and minister to each other. We should be praying together in our dorms before bed and in the mornings."

Jesse sounds like a seasoned pro.

Oh, God, can't I go back into the crowd? Why do You have me out here like this?

Jesse doesn't like the attention being on him.

"You know God is going to push you, just hold on for the ride," Eric says out of the blue.

Adonai telling Eric surprises Jesse; he looks down and blushes, kicking his foot in the Oriental rug.

"I know . . . I know Eric."

Jesse asks the girls where Destiny is. They all shrug their shoulders. Professor Adora White comes to the dorm. She walks up to Jesse; he thinks he is in trouble.

"Rock Man, you have permission to hold meetings in the Academic Tower East; prayer room. I would like to get together with you to address any concerns you may have. How does that sound, Jesse?"

Professor White never called him Rock Man before. "Okay, yes, I would like that Professor White," Jesses stutters a little. He is in shock.

What just happened, Father God? Jesse is taking it all in.

Ruby gives him a big grin as if he had won the lottery or something.

"We get to be at the top of the tower and pray, and you get to be the leader of the session!" Ruby beams.

Destiny shows up. Looking around at all the people, she asks, "What did I miss?"

SUMMIT TRAIL

The gray grass turns a bright new green by late March, and coats forgo light jackets. Jesse's prayer rock sessions can be outside again. It has grown to over fifty people. Other tribes are starting prayer rocks modeled after Jesse's. There is something about being out in the fresh air; everyone is going outside. Yahweh is gearing His young army up for difficult times ahead, but today, in the warm weather, minds are on spring and hiking.

Professor White is mentoring Jesse with his prayer rock. She colors her hair dark blue but has a reputation to show up in any number of hair colors. Jesse loves their talks. Either the General or Professor Alvey joins the meetings.

The General and Professor White join Jesse outside at a group of picnic benches for his mentoring session.

"So last week you heard about a battle for survival and the need for endurance?" the professor asks Jesse.

"Yeah, that's all I got — kinda vague," says Jesse.

"Has the prophetess mentioned anything like this General?" asks Professor White.

The General leans back and looks out at the sky. The prophetess is a highly respected woman who lives up the mountain in seclusion.

"She has said to buy candles and lots of canned food, enough for three months. I guess that is an indication of trouble ahead. Hopefully, we are ready," the General comments. "She kept saying, 'look to the sky' over and over. I passed it on to the government officials. They, however, didn't take me seriously. Jesse, you are indeed a prophet now. I need you to report anything else you get from the Lord," he urges.

"Okay," Jesse feels honored and humbled at the same time.

"I will get with you next week, Jesse," Professor White says, getting up from the meeting.

The General pats Jesse on the back. "This is a very significant word, discerning the times and seasons is most important in these tumultuous days."

After the intense conversation, Jesse wants to get alone and think and talk to Adonai. Jesse still finds solace at his prayer rock behind the dorms. He loves looking down the cliffs. He doesn't have prayer meetings at that spot anymore. The General, no doubt, would not allow it. Only a few people can fit back there anyway. Jesse has his meetings in a grassy spot near the dining hall now or the top room of East Academic Tower if it rains.

With the great outdoors, there is no problem finding a place to be alone. Trails cut through the mountain. A specific trail is longer than most; it is Summit Trail. March is the month when all first-year students hike to the summit. (See "Types and Shadows" 14)

Part of the mystery of the mountain hike is the prophetess's cabin halfway up. She is only known as the prophetess, like the General, her identity is private. The staff highly esteems her, but her identity is mysterious at best. Students on their way to the top stop for a personal "visit."

The tribes of Levi and Benjamin hike to the Summit Trail first this year. Professor Norman is getting it organized as the two tribes stand waiting to start the hike.

Jesse stares at the trail leading to the summit. The Lord sweeps over him like a hot breeze.

What is it about this hike that excites You so? Jesse inquires of the Lord.

Silence. Jesse gazes up at the mountaintop. Several eagles play effortlessly in the wind currents.

Everyone is used to eagles in the area; they are a common sight. But not Ruby; to her, they are like a kiss from Yahweh. She and Yahweh have their own thing going with the eagles. She will step out the door and search the sky. Will Adonai show her eagles today, maybe three or more flying together?

Recently three eagles have always been seen, coasting so high they turn into dots. Ruby feels they are symbols of her, Destiny, and Jesse as a team. She turns her attention to Jesse, who looks zoned out again.

She tries to walk up behind Jesse without making any noise. Just as she stretches out to surprise him, he turns around.

"Oh . . . I was trying to sneak up on you!" Ruby greets him.

"You know how I hate that," complains Jesse.

"Yep, that's why I do it." Ruby grins playfully. "Are you ready to face the mountain, Jesse?"

Ruby studies Jesse's expression for clues.

"God is ready, that's all that matters, I guess," Jesse's voice trails off.

Ruby sees that Jesse is deep in thought; she doesn't question him further. She feels the warm sunshine and looks for eagles. They both stand lost in their own worlds.

"Okay, everybody, listen up!" Professor Norman yells out to the thirty or so kids gathered at the start of Summit Trail. "Remember; keep conversation to a minimum for the first tier of our trek. This hike is a God walk. There will be no listening to music this morning. After lunch, restrictions will lift, and you can talk and listen to music then."

Professor Norman adjusts his cap and backpack.

He adds, "Keep your trail leader in view as much as possible and try not to get too far away from your group. When we get above timberline, you can see for miles, but it is a different story while we are in the trees. Okay, let's head out!"

Professor Norman is in his seventh year of leading expeditions to the summit; this is his favorite job at SWA. He and six adults will carry the backpacks with lunch and supplies for the kids. Everyone starts on the trail. The other tribes will have their turn throughout the coming week.

Destiny loves the beauty on the trail; she picks a clover, a tiny river rock, and a wildflower to put in her scrapbook. She is spending more time around Jesse, listening to his every word. The three now hang out together often. Ruby is delighted.

Audrey is out of her element and is afraid of everything outdoors. She keeps looking for bears or other dangerous animals to attack her. She intentionally does not leave Professor Norman's side.

Ruby listens to the sound of hiking boots, birds, the breeze in the pines, and the smell she never tires of — the sweet scent of the forest. She sees Steven and Jesse ahead of her. Steven has his hands in a fist, *how odd,* Ruby thinks. Jesse looks at Ruby's unusual expression. She cocks her head toward Steven. Jesse shrugs his shoulders.

Steven just arrived around Christmas break, Ruby thinks to herself. *Oh, sorry, God, I have left you out of my conversation.*

Jesse is quietly laughing. Ruby knows how

Yahweh and Jesse laugh a lot. She worries that he will get yelled at for talking.

Everyone settles into walking and enjoying the view. It is beautiful with streams intertwining the trail that forces hikers to jump to keep their boots dry. The water tastes so good from the stream; it is so cold it turns their hands blue.

Ruby drinks from streams all the time; her family used to hike on weekends during summer break. She has her hands cupped together full of spring water when she looks up, and her heart leaps — three bald eagles! She lets the water drop back into the stream and wipes her hands on her jeans.

Wow! She listens for it . . . SCREECH . . . "Yes!" She says out loud.

Ruby claps her hand over her mouth. The majestic screech of the eagles thrills her every time. Over by the stream bank, Steven plays with some smooth stones he picked out of the clear water. Kristen is brushing dirt off her boots.

Okay, God, Ruby thinks: *let the adventure begin*! She takes the eagles as a sign that God will show His spectacular works to them today, on this hike.

Devin takes photos along the way. Eric is getting blisters; his expensive boots are new and not broken in yet. Jesse has never experienced anything as wondrous as this mountain.

It is even better than my mountain vision if that is possible. God, the works of Your hands reflect Your glory.

A scripture burns through his thoughts.

-and many peoples shall come, and say: "Come, let us go up to the mountain of the Lord, to the house of the God of Jacob, that he may teach us his ways and that we may walk in his paths." For out of Zion shall go the law, and the word of the Lord from Jerusalem.

Isaiah 2:3

Jesse studies the path that is worn by traffic, rocky, and winding. He passes several hikers catching their breath as the air is thin at this elevation.

God, I can imagine Your house, but Your mountain is still a mystery to me; Jesse keeps his conversation going with the Lord.

[18]**"It is the glory of God to conceal a matter and the glory of kings to investigate a matter,"** Ruach HaKodesh reminds him.

He finds himself grinning. He wonders if people regard him as odd. His face turns stern. Feelings of inadequacy flood his mind causing his shoulders to slump down.

From joy to despair in three seconds, that's a new record. Why do You feel so far away when I need You the most?

Jesse kicks a rock and walks for a while, feeling despondent.

My mom is melancholy, so do I have to be too?

---

[18] **Proverbs 25:2**

No answer, but he doesn't actually expect one. Things tend to get quiet with Adonai when Jesse gets moody.

Ruby looks back at Jesse, noticing his expression. She wants to see what is wrong but knows that there is no talking for now. Jesse keeps looking down at his feet, so she can't catch his eye. Audrey, on the other hand, is still afraid of everything that rattles in the bushes. For her, mountains are unknown territory, and she doesn't know what to be frightened of and what is harmless. The expression in her eyes cries out, "I am scared."

Ruby turns her head toward Steven, who is getting yelled at for throwing rocks too much.

Ruby feels the need to pray for Steven.

Why is he so uptight? Lord, I bring Steven before You. Touch his heart and heal him of whatever has him so upset. He loves you,[19] *restore unto him the joy of his salvation, uphold him with Your free spirit. Help Jesse to be free of that dark cloud that shows up sometimes.*

The aroma of the pines sweeps over her, making her smile; Elohim's creation is all around her.

You are awesome, God!

The group walks on in silence. The only sounds are of the forest and their boots pressing onto the trail. Ruby looks forward to lunch and talking.

Ruby tells Yeshuah, *I am sorry I am spending all our time together worrying about Jesse. I know I am*

---

[19] **Psalm 51:12**

supposed to have my mind on You. I didn't realize I can be so obsessed! Elohim, help me get free of this fearful feeling that grips me. I should be enjoying this hike, and not so sad and worried.

Suddenly an eagle screech is heard; everyone looks up to see it, but there is no visual. Ruby's heart swells with joy. She hears them at three o'clock in the morning when Elohim wakes her up to tell her things.

Professor Norman's air horn goes off. That means everyone is to stop to pray where they are for a whole hour. Ruby squints for a sighting of Jesse, but he is out of view.

If I could just see him, I would feel less worried.

The responsibility to pray settles down upon her as she snuggles to the forest floor next to the trail. She lunges into the grass to weep in Elohim's powerful presence. The familiar travailing power comes over her, and she gives in to it and cries and prays. Stopping to catch her breath, she listens for others praying . . . she hears none. Ruby feels alone with Elohim on the big mountainside. In a vision of a scared kitten clinging to Yahweh's leg, and then a majestic eagle perched on His shoulder with piercing eyes, Ruby understands the imagery.

Okay, I want to be the eagle, not the kitten. I will stop letting the enemy put thoughts in my head and think on good things.

Down on the forest floor, Ruby prays in the Spirit, and time flies.

Jesse is watching a boulder baking in the sunlight with heat waves rippling off of it. He feels dry, emotionless, and empty.

Father, I keep tripping on my past; it keeps coming up to haunt me. Will I ever be able to look beyond it and move on? I know I am a new creature in Christ, but I feel so bad sometimes. Ruby looks at me as though I should tell her stuff, but I just can't seem to trust anyone yet. She deserves a good friend; I just don't know what to do. Destiny is a great girl. I think the world of her, but I think they are better off if I don't get close. Are we supposed to be a team after graduation? I can't imagine it at all. Our destinies are intertwined, but I feel so awkward. What are You doing to me?

Jesse feels the power of Ruach HaKodesh flood over him, and he receives strength to reach out to the girls. At lunch, Jesse decides to talk to Ruby about how he feels about Destiny. He is excited again — the cloud over his head lifts, and the joy and peace of Elohim return.

The air horn sounds again, bringing an end of prayer time. Lunch and conversation are on the agenda next! Ruby is glad; she is hungry and anxious to see how Jesse and Steven are. Everyone gathers in a little clearing. Logs with the tops sawn flat for sitting are benches. The sun is warm and inviting after a harsh winter. Spring is refreshing. The smell of orange peels fills the air as everyone eats their lunches. Jesse, Ruby, and Steven sit on one bench. Jesse is talking away; the others just nod and listen. Ruby loves it when Jesse feels free enough to talk. She also knows he can draw away and be quiet for days. Today, Jesse talks of how Elohim revealed Himself to him with an incredible encounter. Ruby marvels at his experiences and decides Jesse must be some special guy to have such a special relationship with Yahweh.

Destiny always hangs on every word Jesse says. Steven seems miles away. He keeps kicking his boot into the grass, digging a hole. Jacob sits by his sister for once; they tend to fight too much. Everyone seems to enjoy the day so far.

Devin has a nervous look on his face, "I have a stupid question."

Destiny says, "We are all friends, go ahead,"

"Well, do I talk to the Father, the Son, or to the Holy Spirit?"

Jesse speaks up first, "Dude, they all hear it . . . I ask Father God for stuff like what Jesus said to do. I talk to the Holy Spirit a lot, and to Jesus when I am upset; He knows how I feel. They are one but asking the Father in the name of the Son; it's scriptural to pray that way."

Destiny adds, "As Jesse said, Jesus told us to ask the Father in His name, so if you are requesting things, go to the Father."

Devin shifts his position on the log bench, "Okay, got it. I worry about saying the wrong thing to the wrong one, ya know."

Everyone smiles.

Next is the visit to the prophetess's house. Ruby is unsure about this lady or what to expect, but she will still visit and hear what she might have to tell her. Steven isn't sure if he is going to see her or not.

"I will decide by the time we get there," Steven tells the others. Jesse pats Steven on the back.

"I think you should go for it. I am," Jesse says with a grin.

Back on the trail, the terrain is steeper and rockier from here up. The hikers leave no trash on the mountain; Professor Norman sees to that.

It takes about an hour to reach the prophetess's cabin. Ruby wonders how the prophetess gets along out here by herself. The logs of the compact cabin are smooth and varnished. The windows are spotless, not a thing out of place in her yard. There are flowers planted in pots that seem to greet the hikers as they drift in and out of her small home.

Destiny has already seen the prophetess; she waits on a rock for everyone else to go into the cabin. Gloria, Devin, and Kristen are already in line to see her when Ruby and the guys arrive. They join the waiting line, eager to go in. Ruby is the first of the three to go in. Kristen comes out the door, wipes tears from her eyes, and comments on how accurate the prophetess's word is.

"It's as if she read my mail; I mean seriously. I want to be a prophetess now, forget singing songs; this is real heavy-duty — God in your face type stuff."

Kristen is still talking as she walks on up the trail.

Ruby steps in, her eyes adjusting to the dim light of the cabin. It looks like a fairy tale house with a fireplace, log walls, and furniture made from logs and twigs. The prophetess sits by a small round dining room table, holding her hands out to Ruby. Adora is there helping the prophetess for the day; she stands behind her.

"Come my dear beloved and sit with me . . . ," the prophetess invites.

The prophetess is quite pretty with long brown hair and blonde highlights. Ruby sits and takes the lady's hands. *Beautiful dark gray eyes*, Ruby thinks. She has an English accent, and she is very articulate, using precise and deliberate words. She realizes that the prophetess looks like the General somehow.

"Oh, you are a warrior, with song and prayer. You don't realize the power you have over the enemy, but the enemy knows. Guard your prayer time. You have an idol in your life. Wrestle to get it out. It slipped in unawares, but now you know you must deal with it. Yeah? You love it more than Yahweh. You can more than overcome this. Let Yeshuah show you. Look straight into your own failure and deal with it. Yeshuah will show you. You don't want to look at yourself, but you must. And sweetie, I see great things in your eyes, wait for it. Don't get ahead of Adonai. It's my honor to minister to one such as you. You are a great one in the army. In this season, Yahweh is raising up a special army, and you can be part of it. Now go speedily and come out of this wilderness as a bright and shining one, soon you will have your hands full."

The prophetess has tears running down her face, and her hands shake with anointing. She uses Hebrew terms for God. The kids know these names from class, but don't use them in everyday talk like the prophetess does.

The prophetess adds one last comment, "Oh, and beware. The enemy will try many things to cause a breach between you and your partners, so hold fast to what you have."

Ruby wonders if she is that emotional with everyone.

"Thank you, thank you," Ruby bows out of the cabin.

She is moved and troubled, knowing it is true. Fear tries to grip her that she could lose her partners; they are most precious to her.

Soon I will have my hands full, full of what? She ponders . . . *Okay, wait and see.*

Jesse studies Ruby's face as he steps into the prophetess's cabin.

The prophetess stands up and walks toward Jesse. She waves her hand toward him, and a fiery airflow pushes him to the floor. The power force shakes him up, but he knows it is the hand of Elohim. He remains on the floor, his head bowed. The rock floor is cold against Jesse's arms.

"Your name means 'God is'. You carry the power to bring people to a deeper walk with Elohim. I can't tell you all that I see, but Elohim desires to mark your life with signs and wonders and tribulation. But I see you walking in a fog; two girls hold great lights, but you are walking away from them. The Adversary is trying to keep you apart from both, and it is up to you whether he succeeds. You have pride; you must subdue it. You will hurt the ones you love if you don't. Shame follows you like a stray dog. Threaten it with a stick, and it will run off like a mutt in an alley. You think it is a formidable monster, but it is just a mutt. Humility will make you great. Compassion is the key; Elohim does not want you to influence anyone until compassion rules in your heart. Let go of your past . . . you are a trophy of Yeshuah's salvation. Your past reveals Yahweh's redemptive power. It should not humiliate you for others to see your story. How will others have hope if you hide your journey? Rise up now and catch the wind; fly over the enemies' camp and see new things. See yourself as Yahweh sees you, a bright and shining one."

The prophetess adds one last warning. "Oh . . . and beware. Satan will try many things to cause a breach between you and your partners, so hold fast to what you have. Beware of the breach! And Jesse . . . don't be afraid to love."

The prophetess helps Jesse up by the hand and smiles tenderly.

"I have never been as blessed to minister to a group such as this. You are ones to watch, you are ones to do great things . . . great things."

She puts her hand on Jesse's shoulder as he stumbles out into the sunshine, squinting.

Jesse walks over to a rock to sit down and get his bearings. His head is fuzzy and spinning. He feels Ruach HaKodesh whirl around him like a whirlwind. Ruby and Destiny stand by him and pray, seeing how he is still under the power of Elohim. The door opens for Steven. He hesitates, but Eric pushes him in. Ruby and Jesse watch the door shut behind him. They smile at each other because they know he doesn't know what he is in for! Eric smiles too.

"He will thank me for pushing him in, just wait and see," Eric says, pleased about getting Steven in.

Jesse tells the girls how powerful his visit was with the prophetess.

Jesse looks to the summit trail and feels a stirring in his spirit. Ruby eats her orange and tries to get the stickiness off her hands. Without a word, Jesse takes off on the trail, just him and Adonai. He wanders in Yahweh's thoughts.

Ruby waits for Steven, Audrey, and Faith to get through the prophetic line. They talk about the word that the prophetess gave them as they head for the summit. Ruby has a burst of energy and lunges ahead of her friends. She feels vigorous and agile in the rugged terrain, alive and free in Elohim's grace, the sun warming her skin. Suddenly she stops and listens. It is "her eagle." The single eagle she sees most often is soaring high in the Colorado sky. Now there she is sitting on a rock ledge looking with distress down into a crevasse. She flaps her wings and jumps around, looks at Ruby, and then looks back down. Ruby looks around, but there is no one else nearby. The eagle takes flight and circles, crying above Ruby. Ruby heads toward the place where the eagle sat. It is relatively easy to climb there. As she gets close, she hears a rustling noise in the rocks, and then she freezes.

What if it is a rattlesnake or something else dangerous?

She listens for a second and then continues toward the sound. Still, no one else is nearby. Ruby peers over the rocks to see down the little crevasse. It is a baby eagle with a broken wing and in bad shape. The little eaglet looks up calmly at Ruby with big brown eyes. It is too young to know that it is supposed to be afraid of her. She reaches to pick it up and sees how dirty it is and draws back her hand. She hesitates to pick it up. The eaglet gives a hoarse screech. Ruby hears her own voice say "Aw" and pulls the bird up to her chest. Its breath is labored, it looks hungry and thin. Ruby's heart races a little, as she unzips her jacket and places the young bird inside of it, with its head poking out. It is all beak with big eyes. The eaglet's wing is hurt, so Ruby tries to walk as delicately as possible as she approaches the summit. Ruby spots a lonely nest at the top of a dead pine tree. She figures that is the eaglet's nest. Ruby feels the little fuzzy creature squirm. She hopes Professor Norman will let her keep it. Steven and the gang catch up with Ruby as she walks gingerly. Everyone oohs and ahhs over the eaglet peeking out of her jacket.

"Ruby, your knuckles . . . they're bleeding!" says Jesse with concern.

"Oh, yeah, I got scratched up when I got this little guy out of the rocks. Buzzards were circling, but the mother eagle kept them away!" Ruby says out of breath.

As they reach the summit, some of the hikers are in a circle singing:

Faith will rise as I fly on eagles' wings
You take me up,
and I can see the enemies' strivings
I catch the wind, and I ascend,
Caught in Your love, I fly
I catch the wind, and I will ascend,
Caught in Your love, I fly

The adult female eagle is still overhead, but she looks like a speck in the sky up so high. Everyone stops singing and sees the little head, peeking out of Ruby's jacket. In the stillness, they hear the eagle screech from her heights in the clouds. There is a hush that comes over the group. A cool breeze chills the high-altitude air.

Ruby blurts out with compassion, "It broke its wing!"

Hot tears roll down her chilled cheeks. Everyone feels Ruach HaKodesh's presence rise. Professor Norman has a tender look on his face that the kids have never seen before. He gently touches the bird on the head with one finger and talks to it.

"Aren't you a poor little eaglet?" He talks in baby talk, unbecoming an ex-military man. "Judging by the depth of beak and footpads, I say this is a female. Surely Yahweh has given us a sign. We are just like this bird. We were lost and broken, till Jesus took us up in his care, and brought us hope for life."

Everyone melts into tears. Jesse uses his t-shirt

collar to catch his tears, not wanting anyone to see him cry. Steven looks down, covering his eyes with his hand. Ruby doesn't see much emotion from him.

"Well, you will have your hands full; she will need night and day feedings, with a tube for probably four weeks." The professor rambles off information about eagles like an expert.

My hands full! Wow! Ruby recalls the words of the prophetess.

The group looks sheepish at the professor. He turned out to be quite a softy!

Ruby's heart soars like the mother eagle. Adonai made a way for her to care for the eagle: a local expert right in the group. Everyone lingers on the summit till all the hikers arrive.

Professor Norman stands up to address the elated group on the summit. His voice wavers, and he has to get composure to speak. The kids have never seen him this way.

"This is a day like no other; God has visited us. On our ascent, he has shown us the darkness we still possess, and we have grown from it. This little life in Ruby's pocket is just like us . . . ," the professor's voice trails off with emotion. He continues, "If God didn't pick us up and put us in His pocket, the buzzards would get us."

The professor's words are crude and unpolished but still cut to the heart of the group. Everyone is moved and weeps, kneeling on the rocky mountaintop. The Spirit is bringing to mind the lost condition they all were in before their salvation. Several experience healing. One girl from Benjamin tribe finds that her eyes no longer need glasses, and she joyfully removes them. Many are set free of depression and anxiety. Jacob and Destiny don't seem to hang around each other much as brother and sister, but today they are arm in arm on the summit. Milagros, Steven, Gloria, and Faith sit together on the summit taking in the expansive view. Devin takes more pictures, and Kristen cleans her boots again. Audrey feels a new strength; she has faced the mountain and conquered. Steven remains pensive and withdrawn as Steven always is.

The hike back to campus is sweet for Ruby; everyone looks at her special eaglet and talks about how the day is undoubtedly one to write home about.

Jesse is skeptical, "You gonna get up in the middle of the night to feed this little bird?" he asks Ruby.

"She needs me! She's not that little; about seven inches high. Did you know the females are bigger than the males are?" Ruby says with delight.

She can't wait to tell her dad about it. Ruby now has her hands wrapped in some paper towel where they were bleeding. She will not let anyone hold her eaglet. It will hurt her to take her out of her jacket. She knows the eaglet is close to death but believes she can speak life back into the little raptor.

Halfway down the mountain, there comes a yell echoing off the rocky cliff. Steven gets his foot stuck between two boulders and his ankle twists. Devin is the closest to him and rushes over to help him. Steven is in no mood to be messed with and curses at him.

"What's your problem? Are you going to stay stuck all day?" Devin doesn't appreciate getting cussed out.

"Just back off!" Steven looks down at his foot, keeping his head down.

Jesse hears the conversation and pulls Devin back.

"I know where he is coming from, let me handle it," says Jesse, as he approaches Steven.

Jesse sits down next to him, not saying a word. Devin gives them some space. Eric, too stands off to the side.

Steven wipes a tear from his cheek.

"This is just too much. I hurt my ankle with three miles of trail left. I think I am cursed."

"No, man, you're not cursed. If you were, it would be raining, and a bear would be chewing on your leg," says Jesse smiling.

They both laugh, a type of laugh that comes from stress and crisis. Professor Norman is now coming with a small folded out shovel from the back of his pack.

"This may hurt a little. Pull out your foot when I pry back," he instructs.

The Professor is quite strong. The little shovel begins to bend. Suddenly the smaller boulder gives way, and Steven pulls his foot out. He cries out in pain, grabbing the ankle and rocking on the ground. By now, half the hikers are on the edge of the trail where Steven is sitting.

"It's alright, people. Just look for small limbs to

make a splint. I think it's broke, but I'm not sure," the professor instructs as he takes off his flannel shirt.

The professor's t-shirt says, "ARMY," his muscles still toned for a middle-aged man. He still works out with Jamie in the weight room.

Steven holds onto the ankle with both hands, trying to squeeze hard enough to block the pain. The professor takes off Steven's boot and sock. The foot is purple and swelling.

"Anyone see a branch to make a splint with?" the professor calls out, holding Steven's aching foot.

About ten people step up with sticks and branches.

"Okay, I just need two. Everyone, stop looking for branches!"

About ten more kids drop their finds back down on the forest floor.

With his flannel shirt torn in two, the ankle is wrapped and supported with two tree limbs. Jesse and Devin hold him up on each side, and he tries to walk with one foot.

"Owe, Owe!" Steven shakes his head. "It's going to be a long walk down."

Steven feels sick to his stomach.

"You guys, Jamie is coming up with an all-terrain vehicle. He can get to the spring. We will meet him there," the professor tells them.

Everyone is worried about Steven. He hobbles along, the boys on each side helping him. Most of the youth from the Benjamin tribe pass them and go on down the mountain, but Levi Tribe walks together with Steven. He will have to stop every few steps because of the pain, his face grimacing. The girls pray, but his aching remains. Ruby looks at her eaglet. She is so fragile lying inside her sweatshirt looking up at Ruby with big eyes.

Finally, the group makes it to the spring. Jamie is waiting on a four-wheeler, and Steven sits on the back, putting his hurt leg on the cargo bars. Each bump is painful, but they get Steven to the nurse's station much faster than on foot. Everyone else walks the rest of the way back.

Steven's ankle turns out to be fractured. He has a removable cast put on and has to use crutches. Everyone helps him with his books.

The whole campus is talking about the hike and the eaglet and how God moved on the mountain. The next two tribes due to hike tomorrow have great expectations. With Professor Norman's help, Ruby gets the baby eagle settled in a cardboard box with shredded paper. The professor shows her how to grind up the food and feed with a tube.

She keeps whispering to it, "You're gonna be just fine," and "live little eaglet, live."

As Ruby sinks into bed that night, she realizes how worn out she is. Her hands are sore and swollen, and her arms and neck ache from cradling the eaglet. She looks down into the box and declares, "Live little eagle, live."

It is four hours later; time to feed the fuzzy bird, all eyes and beak. Ruby talks to her softly. She has learned fast how to run the tube down her throat. The eaglet is too weak to struggle; those big brown eyes look up at Ruby. Ruby feels a deep connection with the eagle. It is as though Yahweh has brought them together for some reason. She feels honored to be allowed to care for a bald eagle. Ruby falls back in bed. Six o'clock in the morning is coming fast.

The next day Professor Norman calls the local Wildlife Center to get advice, and they say they have some medicine to help the eaglet survive and a permit for Ruby to keep the eagle.

At breakfast, everyone is asking about the bird. Is it still alive? Has it been named? All the students are curious and fascinated. Ruby is sure the bags under her eyes must be bulging. No one seems to notice, though, and if they do, they don't say anything. Jesse tries to talk her into letting him care for it tonight.

"No, not till she can stand and is more stable; besides, she will be afraid without me."

Ruby thinks of her little bird alone in the dorm; her heart feels a twinge. She wolfs down her food and rushes back for the morning's feeding. Every four hours, she feeds the little eaglet. Ruby pulls back the cloth that covers the box; her bird still can't stand.

"You have got to make it; you have got to!" Ruby needs a name. "Fight little one, fight." Ruby wipes a tear. *It would be terrible for such a great bird to die.*

Professor Norman drives all day to get the medicine from the Wildlife Center, and then he travels back again, giving up a day taking kids to the summit. He arrives that evening. Together they give her antibiotics and feed her. Professor Norman hands Ruby the permit from the Wildlife Center. The Professor is gentle and patient with the struggling bird. Jesse gathers up the gang, and they come to pray for the bird.

Jesse leads the group: "Abba 'Daddy,' we have all become attached to this little creature. She has become a symbol for us; please breathe Your life into her and raise her up."

"THAT'S IT!" Ruby exclaims in the middle of prayer. "Her name is Hope"

-but they who wait for the Lord shall renew their strength; they shall mount up with wings like eagles; they shall run and not be weary; they shall walk and not faint.

Isaiah 40:31

"She is a symbol of hope."

Eric confirms the scripture with a second reference.

May the God of hope fill you with all joy and peace in believing, so that by the power of the Holy Spirit you may abound in hope.

Romans 15:13

Kristen, teary-eyed, yells out, "Hope you can't die! Hope can't die."

Jacob makes a joke about the girls getting all

emotional.

"I noticed you choked up during the prayer, Mr. Calm, Cool, and Collected," Destiny responds with sarcasm.

It is two weeks before Hope stands up. One morning Ruby pulls back the cloth, and Hope is standing there like the proud bird she is, her eyes piercing and alert now.

Ruby shows up for breakfast, beaming with a huge grin on her face. The announcement comes over the intercom. "Hope is going to make it." The dining hall lights up with yells and applause. Professor Norman is grinning like a big kid with his hands in his pockets.

Ruby's dad comes over to hug her and tells her how proud of her he is.

Jesse puts his hand on Ruby's shoulder. "Good job Ruby," he says, a rare compliment from him.

"Next," Professor Norman says with a spark in his eye, "we can start to train her. We should take her in for examination; see if she will fly. We may have to give her up to the wild someday."

"I know," Ruby says as she looks down at her feet. "But for now, we have a lot of work to do," Ruby asks Elohim: *Will she fly away from me? I am so attached to her. And Jesse is quiet sometimes. I really don't know if he trusts me as a friend. I know he is hurting, and I don't know why. God, when I lost my kitten, I was such a wreck, and Hope is so special to me. If I would lose Jesse and Destiny,*

I don't know what I would do.

Ruby is always worried that Jesse is in some sort of a crisis. She has helped him a few times, but often he just stays off by himself.

"You may not always feel like you do now. Someday you will need to be free to do what I have planned for you, Jesse, and Destiny," Ruach HaKodesh says.

Elohim is always causing more questions with His answer! Jesse glances over toward Steven. He sees in the spirit realm many tiny demons like flies whispering to him. Jesse doesn't know what to do. He sees demons all the time, but not on his friends. He is going to see if Destiny can see it too.

The school day is over, and the sun feels warm in the Rockies. Almost everyone gathers together outside. Jesse finds Destiny sitting by herself reading for a class. He sits down by her. She smiles.

"Where are Ruby and Devin?" she asks.

Jesse says, "Ruby is getting raw hamburger for Hope; Devin is with Eric somewhere. I want to ask you a question."

"Shoot," Destiny replies casually, closing her book to look at him.

"Have you noticed any demons hanging around Steven?" Jesse's eyes narrow in intensity.

Destiny puts her book down in the grass.

"Steven is a complex kid. I guess I have seen some darkness around his head. Why, what did you see?"

Destiny leans in toward Jesse.

"A cloud of little mosquito demons whispering in his ears."

"Hmm," Destiny leans back, "Someone should fast and pray for him. Maybe we should get Ruby to do it since she seems to be able to fast more than any of us."

Ruby and Devin come walking up.

"Someone say my name?" Ruby asks with a bag of meat for Hope in her hand.

Destiny says, "We think Steven needs some intercession to move oppression off him."

Devin and Eric sit down on the tender new grass peeking through the pine needles.

Devin picks up a pinecone and examines it as he comments, "Yeah, Steven has been moody ever since he got here. Worse than Jesse ever was."

"Thanks a lot, Devin. Was I *that* bad?" Jesse says with a smile.

Ruby knows all about Jesse's moods, and so gets back to the subject.

"Steven seems to have a dark cloud about him. Plus, he's always angry and won't relax. He clenches his hands a lot! Will anybody fast with me for him?"

Jesse reluctantly raises his hand. Ruby nods.

"It's time to feed Hope, and it's getting cold out here! I'm going in," Ruby says as she dusts off her jeans.

The group breaks up, and they wander to their rooms. Destiny and Jesse walk to the dorms together. Steven is not around.

Hope is growing and being vocal. She wakes up the

whole dorm room with a loud chirp when she is hungry! Ruby lets her out of her new wire dog kennel, and she follows Ruby around the room. Hope is interested in what everyone is doing, very unusual for an eagle to care about humans. Professor Norman is seeing about getting an extra-large cage put out in the Levi dorm's big lobby. If Hope is comfortable with all the people coming and going, she can have more room to move as she grows bigger.

At worship, Jesse tells Ruby, "I am worried about Steven. His eyes are red, and he isn't amiable today."

To everyone's surprise, Steven goes up for prayer. Jesse and Ruby walk him up to the altar workers.

"I admit I have been drinking and getting high ever since I came at Christmas. I feel like such a hypocrite. I'm gonna quit SWA," Steven tells the gang and the altar workers.

Jesse encourages him to stick with it.

Ruby leans over and asks Jesse, "How can he be getting drugs and stuff here at school?" Ruby is shocked at it.

Jesse explains to her, "Drugs seem just to show up when people who use them need it."

Steven's pride is hurt most of all; Jesse knows how that feels. He wants to tell Steven he used to feel like quitting sometimes too, but he draws back. He'd have to think about it more. Steven gets a mentor from the second-year students.

Steven feels better, "I am happy my mentor is a

guitar player from the Judah tribe!"

The demons I saw are gone, but for how long? Jesse wonders.

Part of Steven's drug program is that he can get expelled if he is caught using drugs or drinking. Ruby gets rattled. How could she not have known, right in her own circle of friends?

God, why didn't you tell me? Ruby asks the Father.

"Be careful not to think yourself to be above falling. Anyone can fall at any time if they take their eyes off Me." Ruby's head echoes with the words of the Lord.

As Ruby lies down that night, there is a strange feeling in her gut, as though tomorrow will be different. She slips out of bed and sits down on the rug to pray in the Spirit, that her team won't split up, that Jesse will tell her what is troubling him. She grows tired and slips into her warm bed, falling asleep but feeling uneasy.

Jamie is no longer living in the Levi lodge, as he is just part of the groundskeeping crew now. He has a staff cabin all to himself.

As he starts to pray at ten o'clock at night, images of an ocean crashing over its banks and engulfing grass huts grip him. Next, he sees families running from rocket fire in a cement city in the desert. He travails in intercession because of the images. He bitterly weeps as he sees volcanoes, earthquakes, and then floods and wars. He prays till three o'clock in the morning. The visions leave him trembling on the floor. The Holy Spirit reveals to Jamie some of the shaking and birth pains the earth is poised to suffer. His last vision is of small planes crashing into power stations, with a misty trail of green smoke behind them.

"Have mercy," Jamie can only implore, "have mercy."

The Holy Spirit urges him to sleep now and get some rest as the daytime will require strength.

Aurora Oliver, from her dorm in Eagle lodge, also has a visit from the Spirit of Adonai. She sees suffering people in diverse countries crying out for justice and peace. The vision moves her to pray for them also, crying out to Yahweh for justice and peace. She knows peace will only come after the birth pains; this gives her more peace, as the Holy Spirit gives her the strategy for the season. Just as she puts her head down in bed to sleep, she sees cities with blackouts and a green mist in the evening sky.

CHAPTER FIFTEEN

WINDS OF CHANGE

    Ruby wakes up; it is Wednesday morning in early April.

    Good, church tonight! Ruby reminds herself.

    An announcement interrupts the morning hustle.

    "NO CLASSES TODAY, WE WILL MEET FOR PRAYER IN THE SHEKINAH SANCTUARY."

    Kristen yells, "Hey, my cellphone says no service!" Ruby feels her stomach turn; something is very wrong. She didn't tell anyone how she feels, not wanting to scare the girls.

    At breakfast, everyone is quiet.

    Jesse tells Ruby, "Looks as though we are in for

some battles."

Ruby nods; they have a way of communicating now. They have grown pretty close, and Ruby treasures their talks. Jesse still holds some things back from her, but he is opening up to her and Destiny. Destiny spends her time with Ruby and Jesse these days; Ruby is very excited to develop together as a team.

In the sanctuary, all the students wonder what is going on. No radios or TV's work that morning either.

The General walks up to the podium; his face says a lot. Everyone freezes. The room is still, no one stirs or shifts in their places. The General closes his eyes and bends his head up toward heaven, waiting for the emotion to subside so that he can speak. Ruby and the girls grip each other's arms. The boys look at each other and back at the General.

"The uh . . . the news stopped broadcasting early this morning. All we know is . . . Israel was under attack by sea, and our government declined to defend them. A few hours later, embedded terrorists secretly living on our shores for more than five years attacked us. They flew small planes with dust cropping equipment and sprayed an unknown substance all over the country. It is like germ warfare, and it was sprayed in the air by small planes."

(See "Types and Shadows" 15 part 2)

Everyone gasps.

"All traveling has been banned in the U.S. until they know the full ramifications of the substance. Most of the terrorists managed to fly their planes into electrical stations, and the rest are in police custody. Through Jesse, the Lord told us that a battle for survival and endurance was coming; well, this is it. The prophetess got a word for us to buy candles and canned food to last three months. The Gracious Heavenly Father had provided us with what we needed. Prayer for Israel is our assignment for today and the days to come."

Just then, almost on cue; the lights flash off and then on, and then stay off. A few girls scream, and the emergency lights come on. For a moment, everyone listens for bombs or some sort of attack to happen — nothing but silence. Three hundred kids, fifty staff, and fifteen volunteers in the shadowy sanctuary began to call on Yahweh all together. The bright streaks of sunlight contrast with the darkness of the rest of the massive sanctuary. (See "Types and Shadows" 15)

Leaders stand and lead prayer all morning. It is comforting and powerful. Some kids just cry out of fear; some cry in genuine intercession. Prayer for Israel and the United States rings out. The leadership also expressed gratitude that Heaven forewarned the campus, and the necessary supplies are in storage. Ira and Jesse were instrumental in that aspect. Stress and praying have everyone worn out — still, no power or cellphone signals.

After cold sandwiches for lunch, Professor Norman hooks up his police scanner to batteries. Everyone listens to the reports the government broadcasts on the emergency channel in the dining hall. Many bring batteries to help keep it powered.

Jesse slips out of the crowd and heads for his prayer rock. There are no planes or even vapor trails of aircraft in the sky. It is strangely quiet except for the breeze in the pines.

No classes for the day, so General Eli and the staff can adjust how to get by with no power. The academic towers have stairs and plenty of light so that classes can resume soon. For the moment, everyone is in a state of moderate shock.

Jesse climbs over the short retaining wall and settles down in his favorite spot. He feels the warm rock where the sun hits, in contrast; the other side of the granite boulder is cold.

"God, I feel like this boulder, out of Your light and cold. Father, what's going on? Why did I not take the words 'battle for survival' more seriously?" Jesse feels hot tears fall as he speaks out loud.

"Did you think your country is immune to crisis and calamity? Many countries go through great difficulties. [20]Be of good cheer; I have overcome the world. Your Prayer Rock group prayed, and the things needed for this crisis are all now in place. Even more, angels support arrived that very day. SWA would have been unprepared if you and the prophetess hadn't listened. I am well pleased with you, but you need to trust me for safety. Many idolize the nation and cling to it more than Me," Ruach HaKodesh

---

[20] **John 16:33**

tells him.

Jesse thinks about Yosef, about how he lost a cousin at Christmas to suicide bombs in Israel. Jesse sees a vision, of an explosion next to a tree in an Israeli neighborhood. Frantic voices cry out, and a family flees toward the hillside crying and in distress. Jesse decides he should go and see how everyone is doing, especially Yosef. He is unsure if the vision was about Yosef's family, so he keeps it to himself until he knows for sure.

Jesse finds Yosef glued to Professor Norman's police scanner, hoping for news. His cellphone has no signal; he is desperate for some information from home. Jesse remembers his vision but hesitates to relate it to Yosef. Ruby usually knows what his dreams mean; he will check with her first.

In the Levi lodge commons area, Ruby is sitting on the floor playing with Hope. The young eagle is roaming around looking for crumbs. Ruby looks up at Jesse and tries to smile. Destiny runs to Jesse's arms and weeps. Her sobs echo down through the dorm. It seems as though the whole world is crying, except Hope; her eyes are sharp and piercing.

Still, no electric service and night has arrived. Each of the dorms spread out bedding on the floor next to the lobbies' giant rock fireplaces. Girls cuddle up together. Candles are now the hot item to own, while cellphones are suitable for light until they go dead. The silence is almost ghostly. No air flows through vents, and there is no music or radio. In the silence, everyone listens; will more planes come with harmful substances? The uncertainty creates an undertone of tension.

Signs in all the dorms, dining hall, and other buildings state that the generators will power up for one hour in the morning and one hour at night, just for showers and cooking. One generator continually keeps freezers and refrigerators powered. Fuel siphoned from cars keeps the generators going for now. The hum of the loud monotonous generators outside the buildings is a constant reminder that things are not the same.

Thursday comes, and the General still hasn't resumed classes. Ruby and the gang hang out outside. Eric fills the others in on what he had heard.

"The word is that travel will not resume for three months or longer. The terrorists' fog was a form of germ warfare. No one is allowed to change locations until the government lifts the restrictions. The use of vehicles is minimal.

"Mail will continue to be delivered, while eighty percent of the country is without power. That's what I heard," Devin tells the group.

Jesse adds, "Yeah, the nation is at a standstill, no business, as usual, just survival. If you can find it, gasoline is thirty dollars a gallon. As food begins to run low, fear of chaos and riots is feared to break out in the bigger cities any day now."

Jesse thinks of the Perez family back in Spanish Harlem. *God, keep 'em safe,* he prays. Yosef is in the dining hall, glued to the police scanner. Jesse has a chance to tell about his vision to Ruby and Destiny. He describes what he saw.

"Oh, Jesse, I think that is about the people of Judea, fleeing in the Great Tribulation! Do you think we are in the Great Tribulation?" Ruby's voice gets loud.

Destiny is the voice of reason: "You are talking about **Matthew 24**, the abomination of desecration. We are not there yet; we are still in the part just above that. Here let me show you:"

> **And Jesus answered them, "See that no one leads you astray. For many will come in my name, saying, 'I am the Christ,' and they will lead many astray. And you will hear of wars and rumors of wars. See that you are not alarmed, for this must take place, but the end is not yet. For nation will rise against nation, and kingdom against kingdom, and there will be famines and earthquakes in various places. All these are but the beginning of the birth pains.**
>
> **Matthew 24:4-8**

"So, Destiny, what happens after birth pains?" asks Jesse wanting to know more.

"Let me read on down," says Destiny as she flips the page of her worn leather Bible.

> **"Then they will deliver you up to tribulation and put you to death, and you will be hated by all nations for my name's sake. And then many will fall away and betray one another and hate**

one another. And many false prophets will arise and lead many astray. And because lawlessness will be increased, the love of many will grow cold. But the one who endures to the end will be saved. And this gospel of the kingdom will be proclaimed throughout the whole world as a testimony to all nations, and then the end will come.

Matthew 24:9-14

"Gee, thanks Destiny, I feel so much better," says Ruby sarcastically.

"Wow, first, Destiny, you really know the Scriptures, and then, we have some wild future ahead of us." Jesse has never understood much about the last days.

"And then the end will come? End of what, life on the earth?" implores Steven.

Destiny smiles, "End of the age . . . End of the devil."

"All this discussion just because Jesse had a vision!" Ruby exclaims.

"So, false prophets and lawlessness are the next markers we should watch for," Jesse surmises.

"Yes, the battle to take back the earth is looming. We have prayed for the judgment of evil while our eyes look to the harvest," Destiny says with great conviction.

In deep thought, everyone nods.

Saturday is spent doing the usual things but without power. Most buildings have good lighting from the long-arched stone windows.

On Sunday, everyone gets up for service, longing for comforting words from the General. Acoustic guitars and a piano play for worship; no microphones for the singers. The worship is natural and gritty, and beautiful. The gang sits close together in the front pews. All the cadets huddle together; it is comforting. Many hold onto each other, groups of girls and groups of boys arm in arm, longing for their parents' comfort in all the chaos.
The General walks up to the center and stands in front of Jesse.
"Today, you are looking to the academy leadership for comfort and direction. But God has made another provision."
The General looks down at Jesse. Jesse's heart begins to pound.
God, what are You up to?
Jesse needs a response quickly.
"Today," the General continues, "Jesse Logan has the heart of the Lord, and he will share it with us."
The General motions Jesse to get up; Jesse flashes back to the days when he would speak at his home church in New York, but that was a little church, and he knew all of them. Jesse feels himself stand up and look into the General's eyes. For a moment, they are Papa's eyes. Jesse shakes off his feelings and gathers his thoughts together.
Jesse quotes the Bible:
I have said these things to you, that in me you

may have peace. In the world you will have tribulation. But take heart; I have overcome the world."
John 16:33

Jesse's voice echoes through the room; he feels the power and energy of the Spirit flowing through him.

"[21]Will the Father find faith on the earth? That is the question." Jesse walks over to the side where the Judah tribe always sits.

"Will this body of believers make the sound of triumph for the Lord, or will silent fear grip us? Didn't they teach us that the purest form of warfare is praise? How God swings his sword to the rhythm of the worshipers? [22]When our faith is tried, will we come forth as gold?" Jesse finishes by quoting:

And when he had taken counsel with the people, he appointed those who were to sing to the Lord and praise him in holy attire, as they went before the army, and say, "Give thanks to the Lord, for his steadfast love endures forever."
II Chronicles 20:21-22

Jesse motions to Ruby and Destiny, so Ruby goes to the piano and plays while Destiny stands next to her.

Ruby plays three simple chords and begins to sing in the Spirit. Destiny sings harmony as they both hear the words from Ruach HaKodesh.

---

[21] **Luke 18:8**

[22] **Job 23:10**

Rise…Je…sus…is coming…soon

Pra…ay, for our faith stands in power…. not just words

Fight, for what we know is right…against the night

Dan…ce …before His throne, for He, has made us worthy

Rejoice … for it won't be long…till He makes earth His home

Some dancers with ribbons get up and dance.

They sing it over and over as people pray and soak in the presence of the Lord.

Then the General gets up again, and everyone settles in their seats. He takes his place in front of everyone.

"We have prayed for Israel, always knowing that someday they will be surrounded on all sides. We also know the Lord will come as their Messiah to deliver them. What is next for us, rapture, the great tribulation, martyrdom?"

It is silent in the hall.

"You are chosen by the Lord to live in these times. He will not let you experience more than you can bear. HE IS YOUR STRENGTH; HE IS YOUR STRONG TOWER. Gold is purified by fire, as Jesse said. Let's pray that our faith fails us not! Now is a time of our influence on the earth. It is not a time to run off and leave it to the

Devil."

The General's voice echoes through the grand room.

Everyone is moved and stands up to clap and yell with zeal.

Jamie walks up to the General; everyone gets quiet again.

"Look at this man," says the General. "We helped him come into the Kingdom. Is this not our ultimate goal, to go out amongst the wolves and save? How many others are waiting for us?" He points to Jamie and says, "Jamie has something to say, and we need to hear it."

Jamie speaks casually but with confidence, "My old friends told me you were weak and ignorant, and that Satan was going to consume you with fire. My old friends, they are still so messed up." Jamie's voice cracks. "God has turned my cold stony heart to a heart of flesh that is full of love for those guys, but now they pray for my demise. I don't want to see them in the lake of fire! The world is ripe for harvest. How can we go on like normal, eating, and drinking, while people we love are lost and undone? How can we let days go by without standing in the gap and crying out for mercy? God, have mercy."

Jamie weeps, unembarrassed, the Holy Spirit flowing over him.

Aurora steps up to add:

"[23]If we have not love we are as a clanking of a

---

[23] 1 Corinthians 13, 2 Timothy 1:7

bell. If we fail to love, then we fail, for God is love. Let the love of God rule in our hearts. God has not given us a spirit of fear, but of love and power and a sound, controlled, disciplined mind."

Her thin face with high cheekbones and her determined eyes makes her look fearless and calm. Everyone feels emotion from her words, boldness, and zeal.

The sound of a police siren wails and grows louder until it is at the sanctuary's front door. The General and Professor Norman hurry over to meet a pair of police officers at the front doors. Everyone else remains seated in the sanctuary looking back at them.

The taller of the two cops hands the General a document.

"Sorry to interrupt your assembly, sir. But we are here to get some gas out of your vehicles. Emergency Regulations state you are allowed to keep enough fuel for five cars and enough fuel for your buses to transport everyone out in an emergency. We will need the rest of your fuel for the hospital generators. Here are the regulations from the Department of Transportation. The fog may be a substance designed to make men infertile. The good news, however, is that it is not a deadly substance. The list of people who died due to power station explosions or other unfortunate events is on this sheet for you to look for missing relatives. Nationally, the fatality list consists of two hundred names. If you need us, here is an emergency radio; you can use the handle on the side to power it. Listen to the news on it Tuesdays and Fridays at six o'clock at night only. Mail is running, so letters can get through to loved ones."

They hand Professor Norman the radio.

"Hey, we heard about the eagle you all have here. Can we see it? We think that is so cool!" Officer Barns, the tall one, inquires, keeping his voice lowered.

Professor Norman motions Ruby over, and they take the officers to her dorm to see Hope.

Jesse and Jamie tag along. Meanwhile, the General returns to the front stage to give the news to everyone.

After watching Hope walk around the dorm floor, Officer Barns asks, "Why did you name her Hope?"

"Well," Ruby begins. "I just felt she needed hope to give her the will to fight to live. Calling her Hope is like declaring hope over her; that gives her the will to live, which she desperately needed to pull through. Does that make sense?"

The second man, Officer Edward's eyes well up with tears, "We are dealing with so many people right now who have lost hope. I don't know if I can handle it anymore."

Jesse asks, "Can we pray with you?"

"Sure, we can't handle all this pressure. Everyone expects us to have it all together. We are just as scared as everyone else, but we can feel peace up here on campus. It is amazing," Officer Barns admits, which his partner readily confirms.

They both pray to Yahweh and accept Yeshuah's blood to make them worthy of the Kingdom of Elohim.

"We'll ride our bicycles to service next Wednesday evening," they promise. They felt at peace and empowered to help others now.

Now, everyone is looking at the deceased's names posted on the wall by the sanctuary door. Jesse worries about his parents out there somewhere, and Manuel and the Perez's in New York. He feels guilty for not writing Manuel more often for almost losing Ana's quilt and the whole hitchhiking thing last August. Jesse heads to the top floor of his dorm to write the Perez's a good long letter.

Oh, Father, are my parents thinking of me? Are they safe? Why is my family so messed up?

Jesse must concentrate on Manuel's letter; otherwise, his emotions would take him to places he did not want to go.

Yosef listens to the news radio every waking minute. He tells everyone, "The U.S. must prepare for the possibility of winter with no electricity. Less than half the power stations are repairable. Most have to be built from the ground up. Hospitals are the first to get electricity or gasoline for generators. Gasoline supplies are limited. Lives are interrupted by a single day of terrorism. 'Jihad' (holy war) is on everyone's lips here among the international community. The news coined the phrase;

'Great Terror Crisis of April.'" Yosef exhibits quiet strength during hard times; life had made him that way at an early age.

That night, everyone sleeps on the floor in front of the fireplaces. It is still cold at night. Most cadets worry about not getting to go home for summer break and are not sure what is happening to their homes and family members. The second-year students were looking forward to graduation and returning home. What if the traveling restrictions go longer than three months? Would they be able to start their new lives or be stuck on the mountain? These are trying times, and all the kids finally realize they are about to grow up fast.

Even with no electricity, SWA manages to finish the school year on time. Classes are over by the end of May. The academic towers have windows on all eight sides, so light is no problem. The two academic towers have winding metal stairs, not elevators — so no power is necessary. The graduating class has a small ceremony since most family members cannot make it to SWA, and the seniors remain on campus for at least a few more months. A summer without modern conveniences looms over the academy and the nation.

CHAPTER SIXTEEN

SUMMER OF SURVIVAL

Everyone talks about how they keep flipping light switches, even though they know there is no power. It is a sinking feeling to wake up and realize that all the modern conveniences of life are gone.

Officers Barnes and Edwards peddle their way up the steep road to the weekly SWA service, and most of the town also shows up. Up to a hundred people come from the community on Sundays. It is incredible to see the modes of transportation people are using. Horses pull hay wagons full of people while some walk the four miles. The sanctuary holds up to five hundred, and today it is close to maximum capacity.

The darker the times, the more light the academy gives out. Healings, deliverances, and miracles begin to increase on campus. The General teaches about the last days, and everyone takes in the message. Fear, confusion, and uncertainty are the battles in most hearts currently.

Steven wins a battle he has been fighting since he was thirteen. He never thought he would be able to be sober and drug-free, but he is. Professor Alvey simply lays hands on him one Sunday morning and says, "Be free!" and he is. Steven falls out on the floor in a blur of liquid love, the Holy Spirit filling the empty space in his heart. Steven writes a letter to his dad and tells him all about it. There is concern it may take at least a week for the note to reach home, if at all.

Summer finds the campus full of life. Typically, everyone goes home for summer, and the academy has only a small crew of maintenance workers. Nothing is normal about this summer. It brings more responsibilities to cadets since they have power for only two hours a day. Kids learn to cut firewood, garden, make candles out of old stubs, and even make soap.

Each tribe is assigned a skill to master. Some cadets get permission to change to another guild if their skills warrant it.

They set up the guilds by trades:
1. Judah-   Shows and comedies

2. Ruben - Farming
3. Gad - Metalwork and combat
4. Asher - Groundskeeping
5. Naphtali - Artwork, patterns
6. Manasseh - Food preserves, canning
7. Simeon - Books and science
8. Levi - Embroidery and sewing
9. Issachar - Leatherworks
10. Zebulon - Candle making
11. Benjamin - Self-defense
12. Joseph - Woodcutting, furniture

Not all them of Levi tribe want to sew, of course, so they made adjustments. Jesse and Steven join Naphtali because of their talent for drawing.

"I am joining Benjamin guild," announces Gloria. "They get to practice hand-to-hand combat; somehow, I think I will be good at that!"

Some farm animals are brought in, but they can't eat all the grass. Snakes will be a problem if the grass is allowed to get tall. It is odd to hear mooing and horse whinnies on campus. In a clearing near the entry, they build wooden corrals out of peeled pine logs.

"Now, all we need are cats. They can keep the mice away," Jesse tells everyone as he thinks of Smokey and her litter back in New York.

"I hear we are getting chickens and pigs next!" Kristen says, looking down at the newly built corrals.

"Great, this place is turning into a hippy commune," Jacob jokes.

"Jesse, I didn't know you liked cats." Destiny is intrigued.

Audrey contributes: "There has never been a cat who couldn't calm me down by walking slowly past my chair. Rod McKuen wrote that."

"Who?" asks Devin.

"Never mind!" Audrey gives up on explaining.

Everyone is encouraged to spend time in the garden. Ruby and Destiny have no sewing work today, so they go to the garden. Hope is allowed outside now, so she follows Ruby around while she helps. Hope's grey fuzz has turned to dark feathers now like her eyes, and her head has that majestic eyebrow. Her distinctive beak is also black. Ruby makes sure that Hope doesn't pull off the tops of the newly sprouted plants. She is three months old and measures a foot high. Ruby is afraid there are snakes in the plants. At the slightest movement, she jumps up off the ground. Hope stays nearby Ruby as if to protect her from threats.

"You're my feathered watchdog, aren't you, Hope? Yes, you are." Ruby's pet talk annoys other gardeners.

Yosef sits just over from Ruby and Destiny in a patch of squash pulling weeds. He mostly stares off into space. He is taking the crisis pretty hard. It has been months now, and he still has not heard from his Israeli family. Israel is still defending her borders and the right to exist as a nation. Everyone tries to cheer him up.

Yosef and Jesse decide to visit the prophetess and see if she can get a word on his family from the Lord. The General gives them the okay, as long as they are back by dark.

Back in the garden area, Ruby sees the boys leaving.

"I guess the boys are going alone. Jesse didn't invite us," Ruby says, feeling left out of the adventure of going to the prophetess's cabin. (See "Types and Shadows" 16)

"I figure Jesse wants Yosef to feel free to talk, and he might feel more comfortable with just the two of them," Destiny understands Jesse's motives. "Maybe his vision of the family fleeing to the hills is for Yosef, and Jesse wants to tell him about it."

As the boys disappear into the mountainside, the hot June sun glares down on the garden plants. Neatly labeled rows of vegetables thrive, cared for by the Ruben tribe and anyone else who wishes to attack the oncoming weeds. A patch of watermelon dies, but the rest of the garden does well.

Hope is particularly lively today, running and trying to fly some. It scares Ruby that she will surprise the veterinarians and actually take flight. Ruby wants Hope wholly healed, but she is so attached to her. As much as she tries, the young eagle can't fly any better than the chickens raised on campus. A slight breeze cools the laboring gardeners. The garden seems covered with a natural and simple atmosphere of peace. Gentle conversation and the scent only a garden can give; dominate the area.

Overhead, the screech of eagles is heard, which is typical for these parts, but today Ruby stops pulling the seemingly endless weeds in the carrot patch and looks up. To Ruby, it sort of looks like Hope's mother; Ruby isn't sure. Suddenly two eagles swoop down toward the garden. Ruby panics. What if they are going to attack Hope! The beautiful eagles land on the ground near Hope, where they all squawk together and rub against each other. They must be Hope's parents! They are jumping up and down while many other eagles fly in and perch on the tops of trees. The loud chirps and the eagles' movement attract attention, and everyone stops to see the excitement. Then just as quickly as they landed, the two eagles take off, joining the others in the sky. They are above the treetops for a moment, and then they take to the sky. Everyone's heads are tilted upward, watching them ascend out of sight. Hope is content to be earthbound, and from then on, she only flaps her wings when she is excited. She stops floundering and struggling to fly. The right wing was fine, but the left wing doesn't fully extend out.

During this time, Jesse and Yosef reach the rocky area where Ruby found Hope in March. Yosef is quiet on the trail as he and Jesse traverse up to see the lady prophet. Jesse worries that it will be a long day with little conversation. The breeze through the pines is still a little chilly; the boys button up their sweatshirts as they go higher up. A sudden wind comes up and is gone. Jesse sees a flash of white in the corner of his eye. Yosef sees it; also, they both stop. Yosef says nothing but points. Asher, the Principality angel, appears to them in a visible form.

The twelve-foot angel stands next to Anton, who is only eight-foot-high, and Yosef's angel. The boys do not see the others as only Asher is in the form of a "man." The glow of Asher's snow-white pants and armbands hurts the boys' eyes like sunshine on a pool of water. His chest plate and belt glow a deep electric green that sparks with electrical particles. Asher carries a shield, a long sword, and a golden staff; the massive diamond on top is unmistakable.

Jesse and Yosef become overwhelmed by his presence and drop to their knees in awe of the powerful prince.

Asher speaks, "Stand beloved of Adonai. I am here to walk with you for a while. I have been in Jerusalem fighting and have seen your kin. Be strong and walk with us."

They manage to stand up and continue to the prophetess's cabin.

As they walk with Asher on the trail, Jesse gets the boldness to ask, "Uh, are there more angels here with us?"

"Sure, both of your Guardians are here, of course." Asher is a little miffed they are not aware of their own lifetime angels. Anton is a bit alarmed that Jesse isn't cognizant of him, but he is content taking care of Jesse since birth.

Yosef begins to weep at the thought of having a guardian angel; his family didn't believe in angels much, and he and his mother are the only ones who have found the Messiah so far. Yosef rarely displays emotion, but he continues to weep as the Holy Spirit touches him deeply. The strong Principality angel pushes him on lovingly.

"Keep moving toward the prophetess's home; it is your destination."

Jesse and Yosef want to get a better look at Asher, but they feel it would be disrespectful to stare as they walk. Plus, they have to see where they are going.

Both boys just wait for the angel to speak, walking briskly, excited by the angel that remains with them on the trail. The sound of the large white angel's boots, armor, and his sword made a rhythmic beat on the path. The angel begins to chant a war song. The two guardian angels join the chant also, but the boys can't hear them. Yashab is Yosef's Guardian; his name is Hebrew and means to abide and stay.

The Lord utters his voice before his army, for his camp is exceedingly great; he who executes his word is powerful. For the day of the Lord is great and very awesome; who can endure it?
Joel 2:11

The boys will never forget the melody. Jesse intends to teach Ruby and Destiny the song. Time passes quickly, and the three arrive at the prophetess's cabin — the angel motions for Yosef to go to her. The Holy Spirit told her Yosef is coming, and she is ready to tell him what she has seen in the Spirit.

The prophetess calls Yosef to come and sit by her under a large shade tree. She delays greeting Jesse and the angels until after she delivers her message to Yosef.

Jesse stands with the muscle-bound being. The shield on the angel's back is silver with a braided gold border on the edge and a single Hebrew letter engraved in the center. Jesse doesn't know what the letter means, only that it is Hebrew. Asher notices Jesse's curiosity, so he takes it off and places it out for Jesse to see better. Jesse reaches out to feel it, and power surges through him like electricity. Jesse pulls back because he cannot endure the energy any longer. Jesse feels tingly like static electricity feels in someone's hair.

He stumbles back as the angel opens his mouth, "You don't use yours much, or your helmet; they are a beginners set, but you need an upgrade. You keep looking back; your eyes are on the wrong things. I have something for you, though," Asher says, his voice sounding like a giant's voice, deep and booming.

The angel reaches down with one finger and touches Jesse on the chest. Jesse watches in the Spirit as a chainmail tunic comes together on his upper body. It is a fine wire mesh but strong and lightweight. A delicate scroll pattern adorns the neckline.

Keep your heart with all vigilance, for from it flow the springs of life. Put away from you crooked speech, and put devious talk far from

you. Let your eyes look directly forward, and your gaze be straight before you. Ponder the path of your feet; then all your ways will be sure. Do not swerve to the right or to the left; turn your foot away from evil.
Proverbs 4:23-27

"Your heart can get full of pride, or even hardened by life and lead you off course, Jesse, son of Allen. And I warn you there is a dark cloud over your head trying to get a stronghold in you. Deal with the root of your fears, or they will cloud your judgment against the ones you love the most."

The stern talk of this majestic twelve-foot-high angel significantly moves Jesse, causing his hands to shake.

"So, is there anything *my* angel wants to tell *me*?" Jesse is full of questions but not bold enough to ask what is really in his heart — if he had a Guardian angel, then why was he so abused and beaten as a kid?

Asher glances at Anton and gets Jesse's answer.

"Anton wishes for you to pray for protection, use your armor every day, and petition the Father for what you need," Asher explains, smiling at Anton.

"Anton . . . his name is Anton? Is he Italian?" Jesse is fascinated with the angel realm -– demons not so much.

Asher chuckles.

"Anton is German/Slavic; it means 'precious,'" Asher tells Jesse.

The prophetess and Yosef finish talking. She

comes over and greets Jesse and the warring Principality angel; she calls him by name, Asher (meaning blessed). Her English accent resonates with authority. She asks him how things are in Israel.

"Israel is in travail," he responds, his voice wavering with emotion, and a single tear like a diamond runs down Yosef's face. The prophetess reaches for the teardrop, and it turns into a clear glass vessel. The angel explains.

You have kept count of my tossings; (or wanderings) put my tears in your bottle. Are they not in your book?
Psalm 56:8

The prophetess nods, "Tears to melt the heart of the people that they may look on Yeshua Ha'Mashiach (Jesus the Messiah). We are in a season of tears; Adonai give us strength."

Yosef seems peaceful again, and there is a spark in his eye. *Much like an eagle's eye,* Jesse thinks. The angel bends his knees and jumps straight up out of sight. Jesse and Yosef are sad to see him go.

The prophetess tells the boys, "He must be at the battlefront; we can't delay him any longer."

Feeling bold, Jesse asks the lady prophet, "What's your name — may I ask?"

She looks him in the eye and takes a deep breath.

"My name is Ira, which means watchful. I am the General's mother, you know. We tend to stay out of the spotlight. My son values his privacy, and I expect you to keep this between us for now."

"Yes, ma'am, I didn't mean to be nosey. I just thought you deserved to be known by your name." Jesse stumbles over his words.

"The General and I desire for Yahweh to have the preeminence. We are content with mere titles that point to Yeshuah. Humility is vital in this walk, you know." Ira glances over at Anton and Yashab.

Jesse wonders if she knows all that is going on in the world. "Have you heard what has happened —"

She interrupts, "Yes, I know." Her voice is soft and laden with emotion. "You should be heading back now; it is getting late. Have them send me some canned meat if they can spare it, and some coffee."

"Okay," Jesse calls out as they head back down the trail.

"Well, what did she tell you?" Jesse asks.

"She says . . . uhm . . . my family has moved to the hills . . . where it is safer. She says I would see them all saved . . . if I would just hold on to the promise and not doubt," Yosef says with his thick accent. "She says, according to **I Corinthians 10:13,** Elohim would not put me through more than I can bear; Elohim is faithful."

The boys walk back deep in thought of all that happened that day. Jesse's vision of the family running to the hills seems to be matching.

"Yosef, I had a vision, but I didn't have the confidence to tell you what it was. I saw a bomb fall in an Israeli neighborhood; all the buildings had tan-colored stucco-type stuff outside. There was one tree in the middle. The bomb blew up the tree, and I saw a family rush for the hills," Jesse relates his vision. It remains firm in his mind.

"Oh, Jesse, my family lives in a place just like that. There is only one tree around the houses. Me, and my cousin that died, we used to play in that tree all the time. Next time Jesse, just tell your vision and let others figure out if it is for them," suggests Yosef.

"Yeah, I guess you're right, sorry," Jesse says.

"It's alright; we would have never seen Asher if we didn't take this hike to the prophetess," Yosef says.

"It is almost dark; the boys should be back by now." Destiny gazes at the trail.

She and Ruby sit on the large rocks by the Summit Trail sign and wait for them. Hope is piling sticks up between some rocks. The girls have run out of things to talk about when Ruby breaks the silence as she sees the boys emerge from the trail.

"Hey, you guys really missed it today!" Ruby announces.

"No, *you* missed it," Yosef retorts, his joy restored.

Jesse just smiles, "I'll never tell . . . if you won't, Yosef," Jesse kids Ruby.

"No fair, Jesse, you always tell us stuff!" Ruby feels put off a little by Jesse's joking. She knows something extraordinary happened. She is upset that Jesse pulls away at times. It feels like he is rejecting her, and the prophecy that they will be a team after graduation is at risk of failing.

Meals happen according to the daylight, so supper comes at seven at night, leaving an hour for everyone to eat and get to their rooms. Ruby and the gang sit in their usual places in the dining hall. The evenings cool off, making it necessary to wear a lightweight jacket. Food is simple now, but the hard work outside makes it taste even better. As the sun goes down, there is mostly candlelight or lanterns. Their lives are dictated more by nature than before. They get up by the sun and go to bed by the sun. Power comes on for one hour, twice a day now, as generator gas is on a tight ration. Letters from home are under pillows; **Psalm 91** is prayed in the dark, as the kids in their dorms face a new day with unknown challenges and an uncertain future. The General continues with the guilds' many projects to keep structure and order and the feel of "normality." The graduated students, especially, are antsy and need something to occupy their time while waiting for travel to resume.

Tonight, Yosef prays for protection over his family in Haifa, calling the angels to camp around them and that they would believe in Yeshua Ha'Mashiach. Yosef has acquired his own wind-up radio that gets the news. News programs are now twenty-four-hour broadcasts. All stations that remain on the air are news formats, no music or talk.

Yosef has the volume down to a whisper and lays

it on his pillow next to his head. The male voice puts Yosef to sleep every night. On this night, the news does not mention Israel:

"There are to be no more than three hours traveling distance and no crossing state lines at this time. Scientists say they need to do more testing on the mysterious fog. They see more results pointing to the sterilizing effect on men exposed to the fog, but still not enough conclusive evidence. An effort to get enough fuel for cars is still months off. Soup lines are forming in the larger cities, just as in the Great Depression." The muffled voice of the newscaster is void of emotion, much like Yosef's tends to be.

The peace of Elohim supernaturally settles on the campus of SWA. The young people find a way to rest in the presence of the Lord. It could be months before they see their parents again.

By late June, everyone seems to have somewhat adjusted to the new lifestyle. School is out for the summer, but there are plenty of demands on the kid's time. They will need to learn new things to survive through the summer. Because farming is a lot of work, there are two tribes now dedicated to it.

Ruby tells her roommates the happy news, "My mom and brother are coming in a government bus up to SWA. They are in the accepted range to travel. They're coming to live on campus! My mom's job is gone for now until things get back to normal if they ever will."

Ruby chatters away with excitement as the girls yawn, but they are glad for her.

"Arlo, that's my older brother's name, is a carpenter; he can help out a lot on campus."

Destiny gazes over at her mother's picture on her nightstand.

Along with Ruby's mom and brother, the bus brings medicine provided by the government and some other supplies. It will also take the first group of graduates back to Denver.

The government-approved bus arrives on campus, pulling past the gate tower. The driver is unloading boxes of medical supplies and mail when Ruby's mom and brother step out. Ruby feels guilty hugging her mom and brother, knowing most of the kids will not get hugs from their families this summer. However, the other kids are glad for her.

Arlo looks aged; a few grey hairs salt his brown hair at the temples. Ruby realizes the crisis has been hard on him, seeing him getting off the bus.

He is in his early twenties, a spitting image of their dad. Ruby's mom is so glad to see her and Ruben; they cry as they all hold onto each other. Arlo gives Ruby a teddy bear with armor, including a little sword, shield, breastplate, and helmet.

"You are growing up, Ruby," Arlo tells her.

"Yeah, I guess so," Ruby says.

Adora White, Ruben's sister, the dance teacher,

comes to greet her sister-in-law and nephew.

"Adora, I have brought you a large box of special embroidery threads for the Levi sewing guild," Ruby's mom excitedly says. "There are spools of silver thread and gold and gorgeous colors for you to use, and there are a lot of them," Yolanda says.

"Wherever did you find this?" Adora asks.

"Oh, the Lord caused it to cross my path," Yolanda responds.

Letters are on the bus; everyone stands around anxiously, listening to the names on the envelopes. Jesse knows his parents won't write, not even in a crisis like this. He is about to walk away when Destiny brings him a letter from Manuel.

The letter tells how food is in low supply and that riots have broken out. Manuel adds that they manage to find food by God's grace, but things are unstable in the big city.

A group of fifty graduates gathers to take the bus to Denver, their suitcases in hand. They all live within the accepted three-hour travel time. The General won't let them leave without a little ceremony. Everyone stands in the courtyard, Ruby arm in arm with her brother, and Professor Alvarez with his wife, Yolanda.

"Today, as we rejoice in Yolanda and Arlo Alvarez's arrival, we find ourselves saying goodbye to fifty of our SWA family. We have grown close this summer, working hand in hand for survival. I have never been so proud of a student body than this one," the General tells all the students and staff, including cooks and groundskeepers.

"We send these fifty warriors out to be a light in the darkness, to spread the Kingdom of God. Grace and peace of the Lord Jesus Christ be multiplied to you," the General says, as he sees everyone tearing up.

"Next week, fifty junior warriors will return to their homes as well. We wish them well, and we'll miss them dearly. These strange times have caused us to make many adjustments, and I applaud you all for your strength and endurance. Those one hundred out-of-state students remain for now. We are here to support you as you wait to move on with your lives and see your loved ones again. The rest of us will continue with the calling to pray and fast and prepare the Lord's army."

Everyone claps as Doctor Luz opens a box fresh off the bus. The doctor managed to get some Austrian crystals to hand out to the graduates. They have just arrived on the government bus. He hands them out to all one hundred and fifty seniors.

The Alvarez family is reunited. The whole campus seems renewed by it. In one week, the cadet population will drop down to two hundred. The Ox lodge is closed. SWA adjusts to the changes and stays busy with many new skills taught in the guilds.

The Levi tribe begins to make tapestries and become masters of embroidery; they patch clothes with beautiful embroidery patterns, even making a wedding dress for a local bride. They are setting some fashion trends in their area with ornately patterned embroidered clothing. Adora is a gifted seamstress; she made all her dance costumes and the worship flags in the past. Now Levi guild is patching work clothes for the locals and doing more practical sewing under her guidance.

Covert operations occur under the cover of night. Two tribes meet in the bus barn, after hours. The others do not know what their project is. Benjamin tribe and Gad tribe are led by Professor Norman to practice combative martial arts and gather guns. They are planning for the worst but hoping for the best. The future is uncertain, and they intend to be ready for it no matter what it would bring. They test the large iron grate to make sure it will lower and protect the campus. It was meant to be a decorative item, but now it proves useful. (Portcullis – a lattes grill of wood or iron.)

The professors are now wearing Guild Leaders' hats to teach cadets skills for working everyday practical things. Business owners, farmers/ranchers, and people from town share what they know with the youth guilds. A market is forming on the front lawn and courtyard of SWA with white tents to house different little businesses.

By mid-June, the Levi tribe is doing elaborate works of embroidery. Everyone is getting their t-shirts embellished with tribal symbols or crosses or doves. Their work is very much in demand.

The townspeople are coming to SWA to get things repaired, buy carts for horses, metal wheels, and leatherwork. Other tribal guilds at SWA make candles, gather books, and preserve historical records and information. One tribe cans food for the winter. Another tribe crafts leather purses and items that are more in demand.

Soon the cadets of SWA are known for their excellence in work and deeds of valor. With help from the professors, some cadets walk to town to give food to the needy: canned goods, fresh eggs, and home-grown vegetables. Other SWA students help locals paint their houses or do repairs. Guild leaders oversee community volunteering.

Each tribe contributes to the survival and prosperity of the campus and community. By June, the school has evolved into a village community. SWA does all activities as unto Yahweh. Elohim supernaturally blesses the young band of students as they work unto Yahweh. It is a form of worship to hoe in the garden, mend a work shirt for a man in town, or preserve winter peaches. The Naphtali tribe, the art guild, creates elaborate labels for the canned fruit, embroidery patterns, and other similar items. Jesse helps them; he sketches portraits that look incredible. Judah tribe puts on free shows on the weekends. They do comedies because laughter is a needed medicine that helps everyone. Jacob is a writer for the comedy shows. Even the townspeople come to see the performances. SWA is a full-time marketplace now where local people come to barter, make deals, and do business.

Surprisingly, Kristen shows her inner strength by giving other girls support and encouragement; she seems to thrive under adverse conditions. Faith and Gloria seem numb, still wrapping their minds around the changes. They call Kristen their rock. Audrey has found many books of knowledge to be collected to preserve if things go downhill and power remains down.

Steven is grateful to be free of his addictions. He creates patterns and designs for the embroidery guild. Many ask specifically for his designs. Jesse and two others are in demand to do portraits; one makes paintings with oils, and her work looks like that of the old masters. Soon, under the tutelage of Arlo Alvarez, the Joseph guild will learn to carve picture frames for the oil paintings.

Jacob has turned into a wheeler and dealer, connecting goods to buyers. He is good at it.

"If you can't find what you need, just ask Jacob," Professor Alvarez advises people as he oversees the market during the week.

Jacob has a small notebook in his pocket full of connections and contacts. He has set up a message board in the market where people can leave "for sale" or "wanted" listings. Jacob is a natural entrepreneur besides being a good comedian.

Devin turns into an inventor — his first device is a bicycle that powers a battery charger. He wanted to keep his music player going, so he rigged up a bike to recharge batteries. Now, it is catching on. It takes a while to peddle long enough to charge a set, so people peddle for exercise or barter points. Devin suggests people can charge their batteries if they want to peddle the bike themselves. For a reasonable fee, he recharges other people's rechargeable batteries. Audrey helps the Simeon Guild with her passion for books. She is documenting the summer events in her journal as a part of recording history. Devin joins the Joseph Guild of mechanics and woodworkers

Times are strange for Ruby; her roommate Gloria is acting weird, and Jesse is pulling away. Jesse spent hours talking to her; now, he tends to walk the trails behind campus or hang out alone on his "prayer rock." Gloria talks of adventure and is being secretive, gathering food in her armoire and writing a series of scriptures in her notebook about being a stranger in a foreign land. Ruby finds it not like Gloria at all.

Ruby begins fasting for Gloria and Jesse; she intercedes every day as Adonai had assigned her to do some months ago. Jesse has been sullen; Ruby doesn't know his birthday is in June, and he is missing his parents.

She shares her concerns with Destiny, "The Lord showed me a demonic force that is on Jesse and Gloria since birth. It is called "Baal."

"Baal? Whoa, Ruby, that is a heavy-duty force. You need a whole group to confront him," Destiny warns.

Ruby is disappointed. Destiny doesn't want to jump in the fight with the Demon King, just the two of them. She feels as though Destiny doesn't take her insight on Baal seriously. Inadequacy builds up in Ruby's mind, and so does fear that their prophecy as a team may never come to pass. Ruby waits anxiously for more understanding on the subject of Baal.

The more Jesse leaves Ruby out, the more a dark haze forms around her. The Spirit of Depression is trying to stay and create a stronghold, and Ruby isn't fighting it off very well. She remembers the prophetess speaking of an idol in her life; it is painful for her to look at her shortcomings.

Jesse spends hours thinking and reading his Bible, as he used to in New York when he first came to know Yeshuah. Today, Jesse is having a strange day; while he works on portraits of the local mayor and his family. Jesse keeps getting flashes of an angry face, and it is laughing at him. He tries to shake it off and keep working, but every time he looks at the mayor's photograph, a strange flash of the images comes up out of the paper. Finally, Jesse puts off working on it until tomorrow.

Adonai urges Ruby to get stronger in Him instead of concentrating so much on Jesse and Destiny. It is a wrestling match that Ruby is heading into for quite a while. No matter who she is with, she is lonely and misses being close to Jesse and Destiny, feeling like her partners were stolen by a demonic device of some sort. Adonai tells her to wait on Him, but the voices in her head torment her. (Belial is a tormenter that affects many as they yield more to him than in times past.)

"Fear and Faith can't stay in the same bottle." Ruach HaKodesh tells her.

She sees Jesse and Destiny walk by. Jesse barely nods to her, but Destiny is friendly enough.

Everyone welcomes the cool of the evening; it seems to bring a refreshing every night. Sleeping in the dorms is comfortable enough on the chilly summer nights. Jesse is tired from the vision of the laughing angry face he saw and is looking forward to a good night's sleep.

Ruby steps out of her bed and walks to the big window to see the stars. It is a clear night, and the stars shine clearly in the night air. She pulls out a paper full of scriptures and prays over Jesse and Gloria. As the presence of Ruach HaKodesh gets stronger on her, she continues to pray into the night.

As for Jesse, his sleep is troubled. He hears a fire blown by the wind. It is that face again, but this time words come out of the fire.

"You are fooling everyone but yourself. When your friends find out who you really are, they will all leave you," the horrific voice of King Abigor whispers in a scratchy voice that sounds as if it had been screaming for thousands of years in despair and loneliness. This fallen angel was a fiery minister unto Yahweh, but now he answers to Baal. He is a strongman (Powers, Exousia level) in the region, a Fire King in the kingdom of darkness, on an ancient iniquitous throne.

The sound of the crackling fire grows louder.

Jesse is now in a vast dark space with stars in the sky and simply dull blackness under him. Ahead of him, there is the voice with a body to go with it, tall and massive like a weightlifter, only ugly and larger than a man, with eyes that are empty with darkness. Fire dances around the creature's body like a shadow, and it moans in misery and then looks at Jesse and laughs. Jesse recognizes the face as the one he saw while drawing the mayor's family portrait. The fierce Fire King's eyes lock on Jesse, and his laughing becomes so loud that Jesse holds his ears. He tries to think of a verse to rebuke the enormous figure. The evil spirit comes up to Jesse and presses on his chest with his massive hand. Jesse can't exhale. He begins to panic, and his eyes water with pain. He can't speak at all. Suddenly a streak of light flashes above them, and the tormentor releases Jesse. The Fire King's eyes show pure terror in them, and he freezes in fear. Jesse hears Ruby's voice declaring:

When you pass through the waters, I will be with you; and through the rivers, they shall not overwhelm you; when you walk through fire you shall not be burned, and the flame shall not consume you.
Isaiah 43:2

Her voice trails off like an echo across a valley,
As King Abigor leaves, he threatens Jesse.
"I will have you and your children after you if you remain here. This land belongs to me; get out!" the Fire King's voice fades. A Belial spirit is behind him, and they both fade away.

Jesse remains on his knees in the darkness.

"Father, I don't understand. Why couldn't I rebuke it myself?" Jesse asks, still feeling remnants of despair.

The Holy Spirit touches Jesse and raises him up on his feet.

"*You need others, and others need you. It is My design that you trust and rely on others. How can you trust an unseen God if you can't trust your closest friends? Your pride has built walls, and your fear clouds your judgment. Will you hurt the girls to preserve your comfort zone?*" Ruach HaKodesh asks him.

"Jesse . . . beware the enemy desires to sift you as wheat," the voice of Ira the Prophetess whispers in his head.

Jesse opens his eyes; it is three a.m. sharp. He is not sleeping well these days. Devin's snoring irritates Jesse. It sounds like a deep sleep, one that Jesse can't seem to get. Jesse remembers the great time he had talking to Destiny today, and he falls back to sleep.

Ruby feels the heaviness of sleep pulling on her. She wipes her tears with a bandana and gets back into bed. By now, it is three-thirty a.m., and tomorrow will be a long day with not enough sleep. Hope shuffles her feathers in the big wire dog crate next to Ruby's bed. Hope's cage is almost ready in the big lobby. Soon, Ruby also is fast asleep.

The following day, Gloria, Destiny, Milagros, and

Faith are all doing needlework with the gold and silver thread Yolanda brought. Faith makes a lion head on an SWA shirt; she will trade it for cash or items at the open-air market.

Destiny mentions casually, "I'm thinking of joining Ruben's farming guild. I'm not good with sewing, and I don't have the patience for it."

Ruby doesn't say anything; she takes it personally that Destiny is leaving the Sewing Guild. Ruby is upset but doesn't want to show it. The Holy Spirit tells her only to believe and not to let her eyes lie to her. Unfortunately, her flesh is ruling the day and her spirit-man is in the background. Ruby gets lost in her sewing project.

"Bookbags are popular; I am making this one for the market." Ruby shows the girls her denim messenger bag with rows of ribbons hand-sewn across the top. She tries not to think about Destiny and Jesse.

Hope roams around at Ruby's feet, content to play with scraps of threads she finds on the ground. Ruby looks around her, remembering that this was her aunt's dance class a few months ago. Today it is full of antique sewing machines and tables of fabric. There is still space for dancing over by the mirrored wall, but the sewing guild takes over most of the room. The mirror proves useful, adding more light to the space. Gloria comes and sits down by Ruby.

"Ruby, I am leaving SWA. Don't tell anyone," Gloria whispers in her ear.

"What? That's illegal; you'll go to jail. What about

your Anna anointing and the call to a lifetime of prayer?" Ruby whispers back in shock at Gloria's news.

"I just feel a call to start walking. I will know as I go what I am supposed to do."

Ruby can tell there is no talking her out of it but senses it is not the Lord calling her away.

I feel as if I failed as an intercessor. Maybe I should have fasted more. Is Baal behind Gloria's leaving?

Scenarios of rejection and disappointment rule Ruby's thoughts: images of Gloria starving and lost and of Jesse in despair and loneliness flood her.

I will be an old lady with a house full of cats, talking about what could've been. Yep, sitting on the porch in a rocking chair, babbling about lost opportunities and regrets.

Jesse forces himself to finish the mayor's portrait job. It is due today; the mayor is coming to pick it up. Jesse looks at his drawing; it is almost ready. He hopes the evil presence doesn't appear today. Jesse waits, nothing. *Good*! He can finish the sketch of the mayor's family and move on to the next assignment. The drawing is intricate and impressive. Jesse is quite pleased with how it turned out despite the angry face that manifested. Jesse is anxious to leave the market, so he can pray about the Fire King and ask Elohim what to do about him. He wants to be alone where he can better concentrate.

The mayor arrives to pick up his commissioned

portrait. With him, he has a stack of papers to give to the General. It is handouts with the locations of fire evacuation shelters in Custer County.

"Make sure the General gets these distributed. It is a new list, and we have to prepare for anything," he tells Professor Norman, who is in charge of the market today.

The mayor sees Jesse and walks over.

"This is fine work, young man," says the mayor, as he looks the portrait over.

Jesse sees the Fire King flash behind the mayor, and the fallen spirit laughs at him. Jesse tries not to show his surprise. This time the fallen angel carries a staff, and Jesse can see a crown on his head. He watches the evil Fire King pompously follow the mayor to his car, and he is gone.

I should talk to the girls about this, but I'm going to pray first.

June is a month of simple living for SWA. The garden is growing well, and soon they can eat the fruit of their labor. Maybe they will even have some left to sell. Most of the extra is canned, though, for winter, just in case things are still not back to normal as the government predicts.

Jesse keeps to himself these days; for the most part, this makes Ruby upset. Destiny seems not to worry and gives Jesse space. However, Ruby takes it personally and continually looks for some indication that Jesse still wants to be friends. Jesse does not show any clues about his state of mind as he gets lost in his thoughts. When he walks past Ruby and doesn't even acknowledge her, her heart sinks.

That evening dinner is a fresh garden salad with hand-squeezed lemonade, steak, and baked potatoes. Everyone is proud of a complete meal grown on campus. New seven-foot trees grow in large terracotta pots in the courtyard; everyone loves the attractive potted trees. The lemon trees were expensive and will grow indoors for the winter.

Destiny loves gardening: she has pressed flowers in her Bible from her home in North Dakota.

Jesse drags through supper, just looking forward to sleeping. The portrait of the mayor's family has taken a heavy toll on him. Ruby notices that Jesse barely says two words to her; she feels tremendously grieved.

Ruby is also worried about Gloria wanting to leave; and if she should tell the floor leader or not. After supper, Ruby gets alone to pray. She asks Adonai what the real reason behind Gloria's desire to leave. Ruach HaKodesh tells her it is Wanderlust, a spirit that pulls a person out of their life looking for adventure, making them unhappy with everyday life. Discontentment and restlessness attach to the victim's souls.

Ruby begins to take authority over the wanderlust demon.

"I command you Wanderlust to release Gloria. I speak peace and godly contentment to Gloria and her calling in Christ! **II Thessalonians 1:11.**"

Ruby wishes she could see in the Spirit like Jesse

and Destiny.
I hope Gloria is free. I did feel the power in my words; that is usually proof the Lord is in it. It's late now; I'm crawling into bed.

Hope is sleeping in her new cage in the entryway of the dorm. The enclosure has a round stone base and a wrought iron top shaped like a huge metal dome that comes to a point. It is over nine feet around, giving Hope ample room to spread out her wings. A decorative tree branch made of iron provides Hope places to perch. The cage was created in Denver by a wrought-iron artist and delivered three hours out to SWA. SWA paid for the ornate cage. Professor Norman found the artist and designed its functional parts. Her new "nest" seems way too big for her, and Ruby is not sure she will like it there at night.

Hope is busy tearing up the shredded paper on her cage floor to make a nice bed as Ruby wanders off to her room. Gloria is in bed too.

So far, so good, Ruby thinks as she continues to whisper a prayer for Gloria as she gets under the covers.

As soon as Jesse lays his head down; he falls asleep, dreaming. The Spirit lifts Jesse straight up; they pass through a gate of stone and enter space. The stars are brilliant and vast; he realizes he is standing on a glass floor. He can see beautiful nebulas and all of outer space in its splendor. He hears a voice but sees no one.

"Lord, why do I feel this awful presence here?" Jesse asks the Spirit.

"Jesse, trust me, and do not fear. I am teaching you new things," the Holy Spirit tells him.

A voice other than Ruach HaKodesh's booms in the majestic space.

"You can't have this region. It is legally mine, so get out!" the familiar scratchy voice is yelling.

Jesse calls back to it, "Who are you?"

It manifests again: the fallen angel with thousands of flames around him. King Abigor either moans in misery or laughs with a mocking cackle.

"I am King Abigor; the mayor invited me," he cackles.

Jesse recognizes his face as the Fire King that kept showing up when he was painting the mayor's portraits. The evil spirit throws fire at Jesse. It makes Jesse angry and scared at the same time. He rebukes the effects of the fire.

Jesse tries to take authority, "In the name of Jesus whom I serve, I command you to release the region."

The fallen angel king smiles a maniacal grin, and suddenly a superior spirit manifests. A red dragon appears and morphs into a sun god, then into the queen of heaven. All the while, the entity stares at him with angry, intense eyes. The spirit returns to the form of a dragon and comes closer.

"Men are wood for me; those who do not abide in the Holy One, we devour them." (**John 15**) The Fire King hiding behind the dragon begins to swell and enlarge himself. Jesse feels intense heat coming from him. Anton braces holding his shield to block the fire.

"The voice of the Lord flashes forth flames of fire." **(Psalm 29:7)** Ruby calls out.

Jesse recognizes Ruby's voice. She felt her words were like iron going out of her mouth. She has never felt such power before.

The dark spirit begins to shrink and returns to the mayor's home. The dragon blows out smoke, laughs, and disappears. The laughter echoes out into space. Jesse stands on the glass floor in the massive cosmos catching his breath. As the power of Ruach HaKodesh subsides, Jesse feels exceptionally fatigued.

An angel comes to replace Anton so that he can be refreshed at the Father's throne. He says, "Jesse, you have persevered, now rest. Soon you will learn how to deal with this matter; this battle is not over. This conflict is a great one, and all the saints follow the Lord of Hosts into battle. [24]You must not isolate yourself; the enemy desires to sift you as wheat."

As he touches Jesse on the head, Jesse falls back to sleep. He feels the pillow and the bed under him, and he lets himself go back to deep sleep. Anton drifts wearily up to the third heaven; soon, he will return ready for the next battle.

Just across the lodge, Ruby now wrestles with a spirit of Wanderlust. Ruby is in the Spirit, on the roof of

---

[24] **Luke 22:31**

the dorm. The view is fantastic, and the sensation of being up there is magnificent until the demon manifests. Ruby recognizes the being as Wanderlust.

"I take authority over you; unclean spirit to leave Gloria and this area. In the name of Jesus, you must go!" Ruby waits to see a response.

The demon is see-through and gray; her hands and legs drift in the breeze and never stop moving like strips of thin fabric in the draft. She is always looking around. She flies up close to Ruby and stares into her eyes.

"No, you don't want me to go. You like me. I am pleasant to be with."

The demon uses her power to try and entice Ruby. Ruby does not give the spirit any place in her mind.

"No spirit. You are not allowed to remain here anymore. Wherever the Spirit of the Lord is, there is liberty, and you cannot bring anyone into bondage anymore. So, leave in Jesus' name. I call on the Lord of Host to send the angels of the Lord to chase you into the dark and slippery places where no man dwells until judgment," Ruby declares.

A scroll comes down from the sky in front of Ruby; it reads:

> **I do not cease to give thanks for you, remembering you in my prayers, that the God of our Lord Jesus Christ, the Father of glory, may give you the Spirit of wisdom and of revelation in the knowledge of him,**
> **having the eyes of your hearts enlightened,**

that you may know what is the hope to which he has called you, what are the riches of his glorious inheritance in the saints,
Ephesians 1:16-18

Ruby uses this to pray that Gloria will again know the hope of her calling, and the scroll changes into two silver angels with chains in their hands. They are so powerful their image would have taken Ruby aback, so she is not allowed to see them. They are fierce angels of judgment; their features are incredibly alarming with sharp teeth and intense eyes. Their skin has the appearance of chrome that reflects like a mirror. They produce the sound of metal scraping on metal as they move.

The demon screams in torment. Ruby can see her getting dragged away. She can't see the angels that hold the devil, but she can see shackles on the demon as she disappears. Once again, Ruby is alone on the roof. The breeze through the pines has the scent of perfume. It is the presence of the Lord. Ruby pulls it in deep; it is so lovely. Ruby feels herself lowering back through the roof, past the attic, down to her floor, and her bed. Her pillow and covers are so soft and inviting. Her sleep is sweet and deep. She is catching up with Jesse and Destiny, being able to see the spirit realm.

Just before this, in the General's room, the General receives a message from the angel that ministered to Jesse.

"You will pass through the fire, but you will come forth as gold."

Today is not the first time the General hears about going out "in a blaze of glory."

The General is shaken a little by the words of the angel. He will speak to his mother concerning it soon.

That morning Ruby finds Gloria still in the dorm. "Hey, you're still here!" Ruby puts her hand on Gloria's shoulder.

"Yeah, I had a dream last night. I learned that a demonic spirit was trying to seduce me away. I saw dome-like scales falling out of my eyes, and fire came out of my chest that turned to smoke. I don't feel like leaving anymore."

"Oh, good Gloria, good." Ruby gives her a big hug, and the power of the Lord comes down, and they weep in Elohim's presence.

Ruach HaKodesh tells Ruby to urge Gloria to look at why the demon could draw her away. She needs to realize how impatient she is with how slow the Lord is moving. She needs to learn how to wait on Elohim. Ruby shares the verse:

-but they who wait for the Lord shall renew their strength; they shall mount up with wings like eagles; they shall run and not be weary; they shall walk and not faint.
Isaiah 40:31

At that moment, Hope lets out a cry, like eagles do when they are sailing on the currents of wind in the sky. It echoes across the whole building, and several people come running to the lobby to see what is going on. Hope stands looking at them wisely and knowingly.

Someone says Jesse is not waking up; and Doctor Luz is coming. Ruby feels her heart pound in panic. She bolts toward Jesse's room straight across the commons area, throwing on her robe as she goes. His dorm doors are open, and several people are around his bed. Ruby rushes up to his bed and sees him in a deep sleep. Everyone seems very concerned that they can't wake him up. She puts her hand on his shoulder, and the Lord tells her Jesse had been in an intense battle, and He is giving him rest.

She whispers to Jesse, "You need to wake up long enough to let people know you are okay."

Jesse stirs and opens his eyes. Doctor Luz rushes to the bed and leans over Jesse.

Jesse mumbles to him, "Can't a guy get a little rest around here?"

The doctor checks his vital signs and is satisfied and sends everyone out. Jesse remains in bed for the rest of the day. He doesn't even get up to eat. He is just tired, and it is a peaceful, contented rest. Jesse knows the Fire King is out there, and Ruby has broken him out of another nightmare. He has to tell the girls about the dark king, but for now, sleep demands his time. Eric brings him his supper.

That night the campus has a worship meeting to thank the Lord for helping them do so well during the Great Terrorist Crisis of April. Everyone meets outside in the cool of the evening around a campfire. Jesse is up and looking refreshed, standing with the guys. Ruby gets a smile from him, but little else. She tries not to feel grieved over his coldness, but it bothers her a lot. She wonders if he is even aware that the Lord used her to pull him from another demonic attack.

It is rare to get visitors during this crisis time, but to SWA's surprise, a troop of Native American dancers drop by and join the meeting by dancing unto Yahweh with their drums. Ruby, Destiny, and others feel a blessing fall upon the campus as they dance; as if a curse just broke. The Native Americans dance before the King of Ages, redeeming their ancestor's dance to the Lord. The power of Elohim is more powerful than ever at SWA after that. The land is now redeemed; it is a significant event in the spirit realm.

The General stands after the dancing and addresses the dancers, SWA staff, and cadets.

"We honor the Native Americans as Host peoples. Adonai has a special blessing on the Host people. We acknowledge the wrongdoing of our ancestors towards yours. As an offering of repentance, we have bought you a new van to travel in. Forgive the sins of our forefathers."

The dancers' leader accepts the new van with joy; the group is deeply touched and receives incredible healing in the General's words.

The elder of the dance group speaks for his people, "We have never realized how deep our reproach ran until now, now that Yahweh has freed us from it. We had stuffed it deep within your hearts; now, our dance will be more joyful. Thank you, this is a reconciliation of great proportions. Thank you. Thank you. Now, all we need is for fuel to be available again, along with open travel."

The Native American group bows thanking everyone, with tears in their eyes. As they sit down, the General began to speak to everyone.

"Summer was a time that God manifested his blessings, amid the chaos of the nation. We thrived in a time of leanness and lack, and the academy had enough to give out to others. The local towns all gathered for the market on our front lawn. You cadets have learned and mastered new skills and vocations. Fall is coming, and the future is uncertain, all except for the faithfulness of God. That is a certainty."

The General looks over the SWA community gathered in the beautiful campus.

Have I done enough to equip these warriors?

He continues to speak.

"The tribal guilds have flourished, gathering together the like-talented and like-skilled individuals. We reached out to the community; we didn't huddle in our selfish circle. Now fall is coming; we cut firewood, preserved food, and made lots of candles. I commend you SWA family, and I offer thanksgiving to our Heavenly Father for His blessing, Yeshuah for His sacrifice that we have abundant life, and to Ruach HaKodesh for abiding with us still."

"This very night, Adonai has brought the Native

American dancers to break a two-hundred-year-old curse. I expect we will experience greater open heavens than ever before. We must learn how to dance our own dance before the Lord. For the Lord is the Lord of the Dance. To close, I will read **Psalm 149**,"

Praise the LORD!

Sing to the LORD a new song, his praise in the assembly of the godly! Let Israel be glad in his Maker; let the children of Zion rejoice in their King! Let them praise his name with dancing, making melody to him with tambourine and lyre! For the LORD takes pleasure in his people; he adorns the humble with salvation. Let the godly exult in glory; let them sing for joy on their beds. Let the high praises of God be in their mouth and two-edged swords in their hands, to execute vengeance on the nations and punishments on the peoples, to bind their kings with chains and their nobles with fetters of iron, to execute on them the judgment written!

This is honor for all his godly ones.

Praise the LORD!

CHAPTER SEVENTEEN

SEEING THROUGH THE SMOKE

The echo of axes splitting wood reverberates through the campus. A few cattle and horses in the stables whinny and moo. The burning pine in fireplaces leaves a small layer of smoke and the smell of pine in the early morning air. It almost looks like a pioneer scene from the 1700s. This is the state of things on campus after the Great Terrorist Attack of April. Fall comes all too quickly on the mountain of SWA. The cool breezes in the pines forecast even more cold to come.

The gang gathers in the common area to talk. Classes are starting up soon, and the rest of the graduates still haven't gotten to go home. Jamie has proven himself faithful and feels accepted.

"I, for one, am ready for classes; less work than tending the gardening," Gloria comments playing with Hope.

Hope will lunge at the string, and Gloria will jerk it away.

"At least letters from home are delivered on time," Devin says, thinking how his mom writes him long letters.

Yosef is always up on the latest news, "The news promises dates of the proposed restoration of gasoline supplies and the power grid, three months off. To add to the times of trouble are earthquakes and severe weather patterns. Some rivers have changed course, interrupting shipping channels. The supply of horses cannot meet the demand; bicycles also are in great demand. The nation, as always, emerges with hard-working, ingenious innovators, and many new ways of doing things are forthcoming."

Everyone stares at Yosef.

"Listening to the news has improved your English and your memory as well!" Eric tells Yosef.

Yosef smiles, feeling good about his newfound skills.

Ruby says, "I am so lucky to have my mom and brother staying on campus. I am so proud of my brother Arlo. He is a skilled woodworker, and he helped make hand tools that don't require electricity."

"So, classes will soon start in the mornings, with guilds and chores in the afternoons. Prayer times are open all hours of the day so we can pray for Israel, the war on terrorism, and justice for all the earth," Destiny tells everyone.

Milagros adds, "Ya know the great fog cloud from April has completely spread out all over the world now. The reports say the affected areas are the east coast, west coast, Texas — that's where I am from — and Louisiana. The fog caused the sterility of twenty percent of males in those states. I have only sisters, but I have some cousins who got tested. And good news! Travel restrictions lift. Trains and some buses are moving people around again as gasoline is now available."

"The government is trying to find where the terrorist cells are. It is scary — ya know?" Devin says, worrying about innocent families being put in camps like he read about in World War II history books.

"It's hard to think of going to classes. Everything is so different: lanterns and candles, fewer students, teachers doubling up on teaching. We will be in Tower West this year," Ruby says.

Milagros is right; buses will take the seniors to their homes and families. Change comes as suddenly as the crisis occurred a few months ago. The rest of the graduating class can now return home. Three charter buses will take them to Denver, where they get trains or adopt other means to return to their hometowns. There is no big graduation ceremony. The Great Terrorist Crisis of April had taken it from them. Their minds are on getting back to their loved ones and fashioning a new life amid all the chaos. One hundred out-of-state classmates say goodbye to SWA. Steven's mentor is packed up and getting on the bus. Steven hugs him; they have gotten close.

"Write me, man. Let me know if you get that job playing in that studio in Denver, okay?" Steven calls out as his mentor steps on the bus.

"He won't write much, trust me; me and Manuel barely write," Jesse says casually.

August will see the remaining students who are committed to the long haul at SWA. Two professors also resign and go back to their hometowns. They still have canned goods and candles to spare, but it is not over yet. The restoration of electricity remains uncompleted; it could be a long winter.

Ruby watches as the buses are being loaded, realizing how the older kids did not mingle much with the first-year kids. She doesn't know any second-year students, just their faces in the halls and at meals. However, the worship teams are well known, and they would have recorded worship albums if there was power. There is talk that one or more dorms might close.

If we get new students for fall, I will try to get to know them and be their friends.

Ruby decides to talk to the General about a mentor program for the newbies.

The buses load without ceremony and drive down the mountain. The SWA community sees them off with blessings and prayers. These graduated seniors as well as the juniors who chose to not continue their second year face an uncertain world out there.

The General's mother (Ira the prophetess) will come down off the mountain and soon join the SWA staff. SWA is changing and adjusting to the times. In this remote mountainside in the Rockies, SWA is together with a single purpose of following hard after the Lord. It turns out that she is indeed the General's mother. The cadets are surprised, even though the resemblance is there.

Jesse looks at all his friends standing next to him in the breezy fall air.

We are all friends, Destiny, Steven, Jacob, Gloria, Faith, Eric, Devin, Milagros, Audrey, Kristen, and Yosef, and Ruby. Ruby is a good friend; Destiny and I are getting to know each other better. Jamie is a dear friend, too; the crisis made us closer, no doubt. Yup, I am not the same scared guy that I was last year. I guess I have to admit I'm still scared a little. I need to stop pulling away from the girls, as my dream said last year. I guess I need to talk to Destiny and Ruby, let them know what has been going on in my head.

The General is father to over one hundred remaining cadets. Jesse is learning what a loving father is like, and he feels close to the General.

There is a "gathering of the eagles," as Ruby calls it every week. The General, Jamie, Aurora, Jesse, and soon the prophetess, among others, meet to see what Adonai is telling each other. Jesse is the only student to be included. Ruby is proud of him.

No new students are accepted till they know what the year has in store. Yarn and knitting are added to the sewing guild; the lemon trees are brought indoors for yearlong growth. A greenhouse takes over one classroom.

Lunch at SWA is deer stew. They are getting used to it, except for Kristen. She eats three rolls and cheese instead. Lettuce is rare, so is chocolate.

"I want chocolate! Give me chocolate!" Kristen's voice is still loud, but everyone is used to it.

"Overseas shipping is dedicated to the essentials. Chocolate might get through in a few months," interjects Yosef.

"Coffee, however, comes without any delay by governmental overseeing. The President is vigilant about it, saying, 'the nation can take a lot, but don't take our coffee,'" Jacob says with a sarcastic smirk.

That night Jesse still hasn't managed to tell the girls about the Fire King. He is through brooding and ready to talk to the girls.

Yosef prays for his family and then "cuddles" up with the radio:

"Israel is justified for bombing back on the Gaza strip. There is much damage to buildings. Sporadic fighting hinders rebuilding."

"On the U.S. front, two more offshore oil rigs are

up and running on the Gulf coast. Earthquakes in California and Missouri cause some damage; scientists also monitor Mt Saint Helens for potential activity."

"In China, a large earthquake caused many deaths and damage."

"A music tour called The Summer of Love is making headlines with record-breaking numbers of tickets sold. Several popular bands travel together, promoting positive thinking and encouraging all religions to join together for world peace. Their emblem is a yellow sun, with the words 'we are all under the same sun'."

"A group calling themselves the Followers travels from town to town, promoting a movement of anarchy. Churches tend to burn down in the towns they visit. An investigation has been started with no solid proof to indict them, as of yet. The only common thread to the church burnings is that they all had steeples on their buildings. Nathan Fox, their leader, has a history of violent behavior but a limited criminal record. The group constantly promotes the traveling music tour The Summer of Love. The tour organizers claim no affiliation with the radical Followers."

The newsman's voice has become very familiar.

In her bed, Ruby wonders if Jesse is cutting off their relationship. She has to find out why Jesse is so distant these days.

I might be overreacting to Destiny's not wanting to tackle Baal, but I don't think so. I feel Jesse still doesn't trust Destiny or me. He has his walls up again. Our callings hinge around us as a team; it might all crumble down! Father . . . I am afraid it will all slip through my fingers.

Jacob has gotten his hands on a box of chocolate bars, and he is deciding whether to sell them at the market or trade it for favors. It is a hard decision. Things such as this are on his mind in the night hours.

The next morning Faith is on her way to beg Devin for chocolate. As she walks towards the dining hall, she sees every building's little huts to keep the firewood dry. Ruben and Asher tribes are gathering firewood and stacking it in the new small wooden storage places. She helped sew the vinyl tarps that hang down the huts' front to keep the wood dry.

Devin ended up giving the bulk of his chocolate away. He couldn't tell the girls no, and then it was only fair to share with the guys. Levi dorm has all tasted the treasured chocolate. He gave Audrey two bars.

Before breakfast, Jesse grabs Ruby and Destiny and takes them to his prayer rock. Ruby is thrilled that Jesse is friendly all of a sudden.

As the girls step over the stone retaining wall and settle on the large boulder that overlooks the deep canyon, Jesse sits on the wall. He lowers his head and feels tears forming, and his chin quivers. Destiny and Ruby realize his struggle to tell them something must be important. He pulls out the old acceptance letter from his back pocket and holds it out for the girls. Ruby takes it, and both of the girls see where Jesse wrote Manuel's prophecy on it.

He manages to muster the courage to speak.

"Cling to the red ruby and the beautiful destiny . . . that's what Manuel said when I left New York. I am just now fully able to accept and yield to this. Sorry, I didn't capitalize the names on the paper, cuz I thought it wasn't people, but things. I hope you guys are ready to accept this and be a team together."

Jesse nervously kicks his feet on the wall.

"I know I have kept to myself recently. I . . . I just have a lot on my mind. Ruby, you are good to help me sort stuff out, but I wasn't ready to reveal some stuff. So, I'm gonna try to be more open with you guys from now on. I wrestled with pride and fear and stuff. I was afraid if you guys got to know me, you would look down on me and not want me as a friend, not to mention as a partner."

Jesse wipes tears from his face and looks down as he talks. The girls look down, so he feels comfortable to keep talking.

"I haven't been serving the Lord as long as you guys; you are way more mature in the faith than me. But I know . . . you deserve good friends, and I want to be a good friend to both of you. I am . . . truly sorry for being a jerk. . . you deserve better. Forgive me?"

"Of course, we do. You are a good person, Jesse. Look at us, Jesse," Ruby demands gently.

Jesse looks up at their serious faces; his eyes are red and teary. He pulls a bandana from his back pocket and wipes his face.

"You look down on yourself too much, you know?" Ruby says.

"Yeah, I am working on it," Jesse tells them, feeling very vulnerable.

Ruby is greatly relieved to hear Jesse's confession. Destiny had begun to be concerned that Jesse might pull away permanently from them both. She is fully aware of how he struggles and has a hard time connecting with people.

Destiny goes over and shakes his shoulders.

"Jess . . . lighten up . . . You are too intense. We are good. A threefold cord is not easily broken," Destiny declares (**Ecclesiastes 4:12** King James Version).

Jesse's expression changes from solemn to relief, and he smiles.

Jesse asks, "So, we are good?"

Both girls say, "We are good."

They all jump up and hug. Jesse can't remain too long in a hug, sits back down on the wall, and looks out across the rocks.

Ruby remains in front of him; she puts her hands on his shoulders and looks him in the eye.

"Next time you pull away, I won't let you off easy. I will get in your face and confront you. The Lord told me to give you space this time. But, if you pull away again, I won't let you off easy. Got it?" she rebukes gently.

Jesse blushes and looks away, "Got it."

After a moment of silence, with only the wind in

the pines, Jesse yells out, "I feel so much better!"

Ruby and Destiny grin; they are relieved and excited that the team is solid again. The enemy tried but failed to breach the prophecy.

Sitting down next to Jesse, Destiny reflects on the past year, as she grabs his hand and holds it.

Jesse blushes more and a slight smile forms on his face. Ruby turns to hide her full-on grin as she sits on a boulder outcropping. Destiny is feeling confident.

"We are a good team, you know? Remember the red storm? God used all of us; we all have to reach out to each other and not hold back. I know it is easy for me just to let things slide. I can be too casual about things," Destiny confides.

"Casual? I am the opposite, uptight and anxious," Ruby confides.

"You're like a racehorse Ruby. I wouldn't change that," Jesse says with a smile. "Anyway, we are all just learning. We're not officially a team until graduation, remember?" Jesse reminds them. "Right now, we have to worry about this Fire King called Abigor and this other dragon being I saw. The Lord said it is going to be a big battle; we have a lot to learn."

"When?" Ruby asks.

"Don't know," Jesse answers, looking out across the cliffs.

"So, this summer, when I recited that prayer about being safe through fire over you, it was about this fire king thingy?" Ruby leans forward to ask, her eyes getting intense with expression.

"Yeah, I heard your voice and everything," Jesse admits. "And then that other time, too."

"Cool," says Ruby. She is thrilled he acknowledged it.

Hearing this reinforces to Ruby how important her prayer time is.

"Well, there are three of us; let's bring it down!" Ruby is ready to go to battle, feeling zealous because Jesse is friendly again.

She stands up and declares before the others say anything, "Abigor Fire Spirit of Eastcliffe, we bind you and command you to go to the dry and desolate places where no man dwells and wait for judgment!" Ruby says with confidence.

The three stand up there waiting. Destiny keeps her grip on Jesse's hand.

"Nothing seems to have happened," Jesse observes. "I rebuked it too, and it didn't leave."

Then suddenly, the malevolent king manifests in front of them.

Ruby hears the laughing but doesn't see the fallen entity. Destiny and Jesse see him hovering over the canyon.

Once again, the apparition of a dragon manifests over the cliffs to cover the fiery fallen fire king. Destiny grabs on to Jesse's arm in fear. The Fire King's master, Baal, has come to protect his servant once more.

Ruby still doesn't see these supernatural beings.

She only senses his presence, along with hearing his voice. She now regrets taking on the entity without talking to Jesse and Destiny first.

Destiny discerns who the entity is.

"This is no demon guys . . . this is Baal. I am sure he is a strongman over the whole nation and many other places worldwide. I think he is from Babylon!" Destiny tells them.

"Depart from us, for we have no part with you!" Jesse yells out over the cliff to the powerful dark force.

The fire king gloats as his master materializes in the form of a dragon and presses up toward Jesse's face. It laughs, causing puffs of smoke to come from his mouth and nose.

"HO, HO, HO! But you *do* have a part with me . . . Jesse, look inside and see what monsters dwell in the dark!" the dragon cackles.

A spirit of Belial manifests from the smoke of the dragon. Ruby's eyes grow wide, seeing the image of smoke in the air.

"Idolaters, everyone!" It hisses out from its smoky form.

"We serve the Living God, be gone!" Ruby declares. She is shaking, and her voice is faltering.

"Oh, but you *all* have idols in your life. They came in unaware; these doors remain open for us, and we are not leaving. You can't find us right under your noses," the Belial spirit taunts with mocking laughter.

The remnant of smoke forms a sun, moon, and a

star in the sky that slowly drifts into the atmosphere. The evil entities are all out of sight but not gone from the region.

The girls look at Jesse, and Jesse looks at them.

"Demons are liars; we can't trust them to tell the truth. You saw the Belial demon in the smoke, right?" Jesse says, feeling exposed, but not sure of what.

"Jesse, I was told by the Lord that Baal is a stronghold in your life. Do you know anything about this?" Ruby asks in a soft serious voice. She doesn't want him to pull away again, but she has to deal with the stronghold and bring it to the light.

"I don't know any more about this Baal guy than you," Jesse says with a hint of defeat in his voice.

"Jesse, you will have to deal with the darkness you have shoved back. If you let us, we will help you," Destiny says, putting her hand on his cheek.

"When the time is right," Jesse says softly.

"Hey, that is my line!" Destiny laughs. "Remember Ruby; I told you we are not ready to fight Baal by ourselves." She drops her hand, and Jesse blushes slightly.

Ruby nods, understanding, a little more than before, that Destiny was right.

"So, what about idols from your family lines? Do you girls know anything?" Jesse manages to ask.

He knows they all have things to learn and deal with now. The girls shrug their shoulders.

"The Lord will bring to light anything we need to know; if we are willing to deal honestly with ourselves.

We will stay alert. If we keep talking like we did today, nothing will get past us," Destiny says with certainty. "We gotta stay close, all of us, Jesse. Promise to stay close, and don't pull away for days at a time like you used to . . . promise me."

She grabs his shoulders again and stares into his eyes.

"Okay, no more hiding," says Jesse, trying to keep her gaze.

"Now, Lord, we are ready to see the hidden things. Show us if there is any truth about the idols and darkness," Destiny prays out loud.

They all hug again and return to the dorms, knowing a strongman is out there somewhere, and he claims to have a connection with them. Therefore, some mysterious hidden darkness within must first be exposed and removed when the time is right. Jesse hopes he can let the girls in and deal with the secret things stuffed deep down inside him. He knows the darkness will overtake him if he doesn't look it in the face and deal with it. He is excited that Destiny held his hand and that their relationship is moving forward.

The fall semester will soon start for the remaining dedicated students. The SWA market will cut back to being just on Saturdays. Jesse has overcome many obstacles and grown in many ways, as have all the cadets at SWA. For now, just being part of the SWA community is essential. Yahweh will lead them one day at a time. They have Yahweh, and they have each other.

> "Therefore I tell you, do not be anxious about your life, what you will eat or what you will drink, nor about your body, what you will put on. Is not life more than food, and the body more than clothing? Look at the birds of the air: they neither sow nor reap nor gather into barns, and yet your heavenly Father feeds them. Are you not of more value than they? And which of you by being anxious can add a single hour to his span of life? And why are you anxious about clothing? Consider the lilies of the field, how they grow: they neither toil nor spin, yet I tell you, even Solomon in all his glory was not arrayed like one of these. But if God so clothes the grass of the field, which today is alive and tomorrow is thrown into the oven, will he not much more clothe you, O you of little faith? Therefore do not be anxious, saying, 'What shall we eat?' or 'What shall we drink?' or 'What shall we wear?' For the gentiles seek after all these things, and your heavenly Father knows that you need them all. But seek first the kingdom of God and his righteousness, and all these things will be added to you. "Therefore do not be anxious about tomorrow, for tomorrow will be anxious for itself. Sufficient for the day is its own trouble.
>
> **Matthew 6:25-34**

The General hikes up to see his mom. She is out in her courtyard, praying. The General can hear her as he walks up the trail, her voice strong and forceful as she prays.

"Mom!"

They embrace, and then he steps back from her and says, "I am hearing words about fire, mother. Pray that I will be strong." (See "Types and Shadows" 17)

"My son, I have prayed **Daniel 10:19** over you:

And he said, "O man greatly loved, fear not, peace be with you; be strong and of good courage." And as he spoke to me, I was strengthened and said, "Let my lord speak, for you have strengthened me."

"You will have the strength to receive what Adonai is revealing to you. I am ready to come down today to be with you and help with the academy."

Ira encourages her eldest son and immediately begins to bring out her things. The General helps her hike out with her bags. Everyone is excited to have the prophetess on campus.

Ruby, Jesse, and Destiny wrestle with the idea of hidden idols. They have no direction of where to look as of yet. Jesse knows his heart harbors some level of darkness; it will take strength to deal with it. The three will need each other more than ever; to deal with the mysterious idolatry issues.

Near Eastcliffe, Baal's fire king named Abigor rules from a cave. The king bides his time, looking for someone he can influence to do his bidding. Abigor is enraged that the gang knows he is there; it was his fault for manifesting to them. It is only a matter of time before they learn how to cause him much grief and threaten his realm of influence.

In his pride, he thinks: "It is worth it to make the pathetic little group think they have the upper hand," the king cackles in such a way that all of his armies cower in fear behind him.

Abigor, the fire king, lives in fear of two things on the earth — his boss, Baal, and SWA. In his misery, he spits fire out towards his minions and watches them cower and scream. It is little comfort, but it is all he can get for now.

The mayor watches the rain amounts for the summer; if an inch or two of rain doesn't come soon, they will be prime candidates for a forest fire. He hopes his covenant still holds with Abigor the Fire King. The mayor still lives with great fear, continually looking for wildfires that can flare up and destroy his beloved town of Eastcliffe. He uses occult objects and consults with new-age gurus.

The Followers arrive in Colorado, dancing in every little town they travel through. Delighting in violence, they dance to the Spirit of Anarchy — Thor and Odin. People come out to see their entertaining Irish style stomp dancing. They dress in neon-colored plaids, with tattoos of warlike symbols on their skin. The men have Mohawk hair while the women wear dreadlocks and beads. They skillfully play fiddles and Irish drums. They tag every town and church with neon spray paint with an image of a Native American legendary figure called Kokopelli. It looks like a man dancing while playing the flute. They tag buildings with the words "Anarchy" and "Lawlessness."

The fire king determines to draw them to SWA. If Abigor can just find someone angry enough, someone who hates Spirit Wings Academy as much as he does.

To be continued…

SPECIAL FEATURE

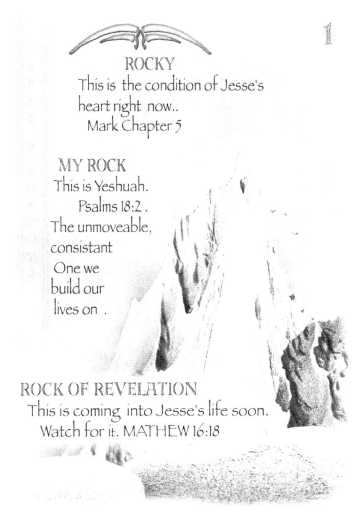

ROCKY
This is the condition of Jesse's heart right now..
Mark Chapter 5

MY ROCK
This is Yeshuah.
Psalms 18:2.
The unmoveable, consistant One we build our lives on .

ROCK OF REVELATION
This is coming into Jesse's life soon.
Watch for it. MATHEW 16:18

~FROM PAGE 12~

~ TYPES AND SHADOWS ~

JESSE'S QUILT

This humble blanket represents a
natural and spiritual covering.
Jesse now has people who pray for him and
he is part of a family.
There is covering in that.
Now that Jesse belongs to Yahweh,
 he has the Kingdom of God covering him.

THE BEAUTY OF THE CAMPUS

Ecclesiastes 7:12
The protection
of wisdom.
This academy is
also a natural
fortress
with stone
walls.

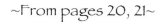

~From pages 20, 21~

b

SPECIAL FEATURE

LION, OX, EAGLE, MAN

These four creatures are found on four sides of Yahweh's throne.   Revelation 4:7
 It is my understanding
they may represent four kingdoms.
Lion - king of the beasts,
Ox - king of domestic animals.
Eagle - king of birds and the air,
Man - king of humans.

SNAKES, BUGS, DEMONIC FACES

Snakes can symbolize lies, bugs - Bealzibub the Lord of the flys. Demonic faces in dreams can be tormenting forces that need to be taken authority over.

~From page 95~

~ TYPES AND SHADOWS ~

GATES AT THE ENTRY OF SWA

There are gates to our hearts, gates to cities, and gates at fortified military encampments. Who sits to guard your gates?
Isaiah 45:2

THREE BALD EAGLES

These are a foreshadow of Jesse, Ruby and Destiny. It speaks of their prophetic callings and being in the high places. Eyesight that is keen, and ability to ride on the wind currents — all reflect the skills of prophets.
Isaiah 40:31

~From page 95 -chapter 3~

d

SPECIAL FEATURE

5

TRIBAL ASSIGNMENTS

It is good to belong, and be connected. When you have an indentity it is easier to recognize your tribe.

LEVI

I can't help but talk about Levi Strauss Jeans. In the 1870's this Jewish man from Germany began making the durable work pants we know as jeans. I think of the double seam that runs up the pant leg. Jeans represent to me a lifestyle, unpresuming and active. Clothed for action and ready to work!

JUDAH GOES FIRST

II Chronicles 20: 15-29. A wonderful spiritual concept, praise before the army. Guitars and swords, this army of young people do not wage war like the world.

~From Pages 118, 122~

e

~ TYPES AND SHADOWS ~

UNDER THE BANNER
Song of Solomon 6:10
Like the tribes, troups gather behind their banners. Elohim is raising an army . . .

SHEKINAH SANCTUARY
The mystical glory is the carrier of wonderful things. Healing, joy, wealth, encounters with Holy One.
Philipians 4:19

PSALM 63:2
So I have looked upon You in the sanctuary, beholding Your power and glory.

~From page 146~

SPECIAL FEATURE

THE GIANT
Most of our battles are in our minds. Jesse's hangups were allowed to grow to such a level that it appeared to be stronger than Jesse who created it in the first place. Once the issues (the giant) are confronted it looses power in his life.

THE GLASS AND THE BROKEN MIRROR
Often there can be found a natural manifestation of a spiritual thing. Whirlwinds are compared to the moving of Yahweh. Stars are referred to as angels in some Bible passages.

DREAMS
Psalms 33: 14-16
Joseph in the Old Testament was a dreamer. He told others that interpretation come from Yahweh. Genesis 40:8

~From page 156~

~ TYPES AND SHADOWS ~

SCEPTER

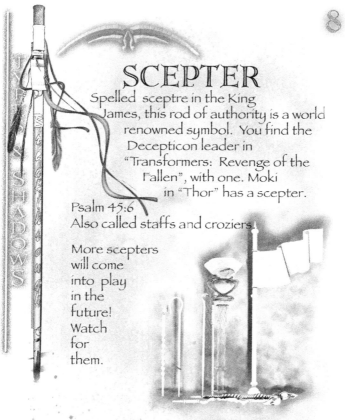

Spelled sceptre in the King James, this rod of authority is a world renowned symbol. You find the Decepticon leader in "Transformers: Revenge of the Fallen", with one. Moki in "Thor" has a scepter.

Psalm 45:6
Also called staffs and croziers.

More scepters will come into play in the future! Watch for them.

WOLVES AND SHEEP

Mathew 10:16 Behold, I am sending you out as sheep in the midst of wolves, so be wise as serpents and innocent as doves.

~From page 172~

SPECIAL FEATURE

THROUGH THE FIRE -

Psalms 12:6:
The words of the Lord are pure words, like silver refined in a furnace on the ground, purified seven times.

LIGHT OVER DARKNESS

John 1:5 The light shines in the darkness, and the darkness has not overcome it.

~From page 186~

i

~ TYPES AND SHADOWS ~

STORMS
Natural manifestations of the spiritual. This is often the case where things in the spirit realm cause things in the natural to be effected...

FEAR AND FAITH DON'T FIT IN THE SAME BOTTLE
Mark 5:36

~From pages 195, 210~

SPECIAL FEATURE

ALLEN'S VAN

Often in dreams, vehicles are a symbol of ministries or life callings. Jesse's parents van being full of trash can symbolize how they filled their life with things that are "junk food", no life giving power in them.

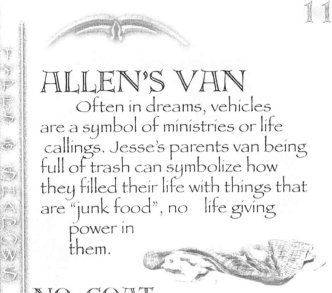

NO COAT FOR JESSE

This can be a type of covering in the spirit realm, specifically prayer. As Jesse leaves the campus some of his covering is lost for a short time.

~From page 207~

CANDLES

Mathew 5:14-16

You are the light of the world.
A city set on a hill cannot be
hidden. Nor do people light a lamp
and put it under a basket,
but on a stand, and it gives
light to all in the house.
In the same way, let your light shine
before others, so that they may see
your good works and give glory
to your Father who is
in heaven.

~See page 234~

SPECIAL FEATURE

PRAYER ROCK

Matthew 7:24
"Everyone then who hears these words of mine and does them will be like a wise man who built his house on the rock.

Psalm 144:2
Blessed be the Lord, my rock, who trains my hands for war, and my fingers for battle;

+As a positive symbol, a rock is a safe place and you can count on it. -In the negitive it is something that crushes...

~See Page 241~

LOOK TO THE SKY
Luke 21:28
Now when these things
 begin to take place,
 straighten up and
 raise your heads,
 because your
 redemption is
 drawing near."

SUMMIT
High places are spiritual
 symbols of power,
 both good and bad.
Mountain peaks, industial towers,
 sky scrapers...
   Psalm 78:58 (a negitive high place)
      Habakkuk 3:19
God, the Lord, is my strength;
he makes my feet like the deer's;
he makes me tread on my high places

~See page 251~

SPECIAL FEATURE

15

TYPES & SHADOWS

SANCTUARY
A place of safety, refuge.
Exodus 15:17,18
"You will bring them in and plant them on your own mountain, the place, O Lord, which you have made for your abode, the sanctuary, O Lord which your hands have established. The Lord will reign forever and ever."

END OF THE AGE - *Mathew 13*
Mathew 24

~See page 285~

~ TYPES AND SHADOWS ~

15 PART 2

WINDS OF CHANGE -

Ruach - Hebrew for breath or wind. A way to relate to the Holy Spirit is the idea of eagles on the wind. The majestic birds know how to catch the wind and coast effortlessly.

WIND BRINGS CHANGE-

Ezekiel 37:9
Then he said to me, "Prophesy to the breath; prophesy, son of man, and say to the breath, Thus says the Lord God: Come from the four winds, O breath, and breathe on these slain, that they may live."

~See page 284~

p

SPECIAL FEATURE

16

IRA'S CABIN

A secret quite place.
Psalm 91: 9,10
Because you have made the Lord
your dwelling place—
the Most High, who is my refuge—
no evil shall be allowed to befall you,
no plague come near your tent.

BAAL AND BELIAL
Judges 3:6, II Corinthians 6:15
False gods and lying spirits. . .
Baal is often shown as a
sun god, but he has many faces.

~See page 304~

9

FIRE

In the positive fire is a symbol of passion and energy.

Hebrews 1:7
Of the angels he says, "He makes his angels winds, and his ministers a flame of fire."

Revelation 4:5
From the throne came flashes of lightning, and rumblings and peals of thunder, and before the throne were burning seven torches of fire, which are the seven spirits of God,

In the negitive fire is a devourer and destroyer.

Revelation 20:10
and the devil who had deceived them was thrown into the lake of fire and sulfur where the beast and the false prophet were, and they will be tormented day and night forever and ever.

~See page 357~

Campus Map

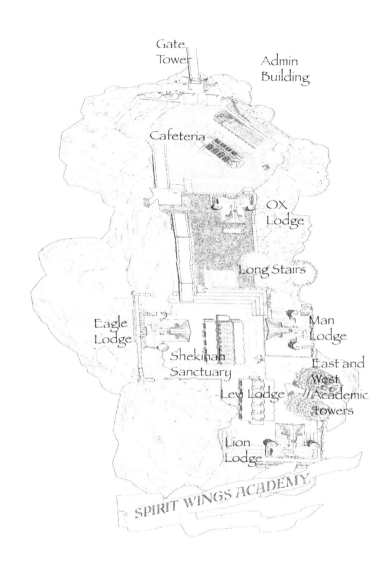

HIERARCHY

Hierarchy of Creatures

Seraphim, Cherubim, Thrones

Powers

Principalities
 Chief   Michael
   Princes   Gabriel

Angels

Recommended websites or books:

www.spiritwingsonline.com Authors website, artwork of characters and more.

www.ihopkc.org International House of Prayer, Kansas City, Mo

www.15minutewriter.com Get started writing for yourself.

*The Circle of H*ealing by Jeff Guidry. Read a true story of a man that raises an injured eaglet.

Meanings of a few names in the book:

Jesse- God is, Hebrew
Evan - Rock, Hebrew from Eben
Logan - low lying place
Ruby- Red stone, defending of the land
Alvarez-'Noble guardian'
Steven -crown, garland, Greek
Eric- brave ruler, Scandinavian
Destiny-fate, French
Devin-poet, Irish
Gloria-glory, Latin
Milagros-miracles, Spanish
Aurora-goddess of the dawn, Latin
Oliver-Olive tree
Eli (the General)-My God, Hebrew also, ascend
Ira-Watchful, Hebrew (male name)
Ruben - Behold a son, first of Israel's sons, Hebrew
Jamie-form of James, similar to Jacob supplanter- to get by deception or scheme
Gerard- apt, docile; one ready to do or learn, amiable
Dr. Luz-light, Spanish
Adora-Gifted, beloved, Greek
White-from the Anglo-Saxon "wiht" meaning valiant

Gerald-rule with a spear, German
Norman-from the north, German
Asher- one of 12 tribes, wealth and harvest, to be blessed
Allen-Little rock, harmony and peace

About the Author:

Sandy Solis currently lives in Oklahoma; she is a native of Colorado, born in Denver. She does 3D computer graphics in her spare time along with stained glass and home remodeling. She also loves playing guitar and keyboards.

Sandy began writing this series in 2006. Plans for graphic novels are still in the works.

Author's website is
www.spiritwingsonline.com

SPIRIT WINGS BOOK SERIES

Look for:

    Book One –
    Spirit Wings the Academy

    Book Two –
    The Cave of Abigor

    Book Three –
    The House of Asher

    Book Four –
    The Scepters of the Kings

    Book Five –
    The Landing Strip

    Book Six –
    The Jade Seal

    Book Seven –
    The Sound of Heaven

MORE BOOKS IN THE SERIES
COMING SOON

Made in the USA
Monee, IL
21 July 2023